The Black Ledger of Salem

Clifton Wilcox

Fredericksburg, Virginia

Print ISBN: 978-1-969770-27-2

EBook ISBN: 978-1-969770-28-9

Published by Windward Publishing LLC., Fredericksburg, Virginia.

The characters and events in this book are fictitious. Any similarity to real persons, living or dead, is coincidental and not intended by the author.

Wilcox, Clifton

The Black Ledger of Salem

Windward Publishing, LLC

2026

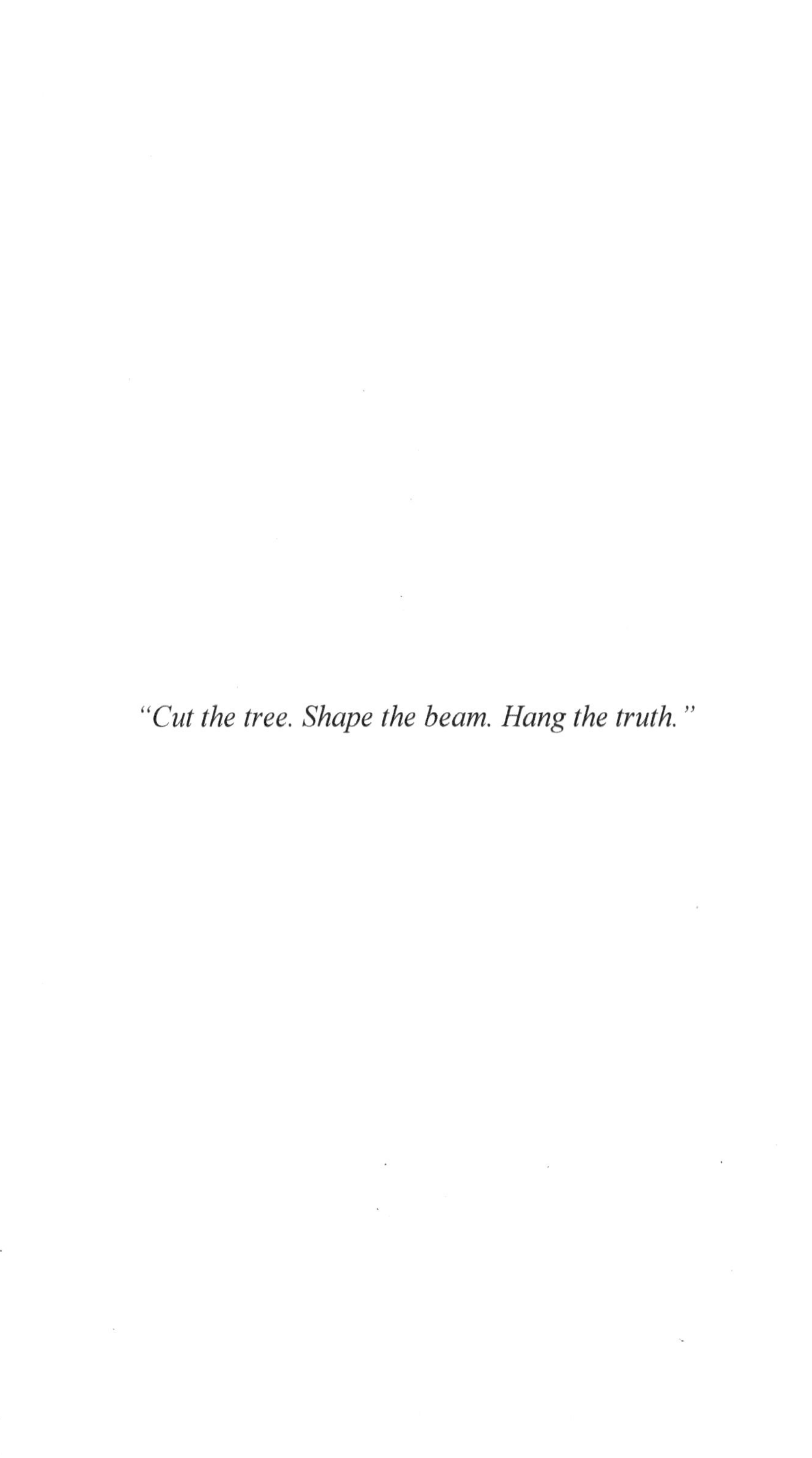

"Cut the tree. Shape the beam. Hang the truth."

Table of Contents

Books by Clifton Wilcox

Fiction

Cool's Last Stand

Where Despair Comes to Play

The Monuments Must Bleed

Keeper of the Fallen Ages

I, Monster

Harvest of Eyes

The Case Against Jasper

Crimson Plume: The Song of Corvus

Framed in Love

Echoes of the Forgotten

Blacktop Harvest

The Plagiarist Game

The Black Forest Protocol

Outcome without Appeal

Deliberation

The Lore Hunter: Brown Mountain

The Pact of Shadows: The Black Orchard

Prologue

They told us evil does not arrive with thunder. It seeps. It settles into the grain of the wood, into the breath between prayers, into the silence where a name should be spoken but is not. In Salem, the air itself feels watched. Doors are barred before dusk, not against wolves or thieves, but against something without footsteps. You will not see it at first. You will feel it—like a hand hovering just behind your shoulder, waiting.

There are whispers now. Not the kind carried by gossip, but the kind that cling to the ear long after the speaker is gone. They speak of visitations in the night. Of a book—black as pitch, heavy as sin—opened by unseen hands. Names written where no hand should write them. Promises made in the space between waking and sleep. Some wake with the taste of ash in their mouths. Some do not wake at all.

And so we are told: search your neighbor as you would search your own soul. If wickedness stirs in them, it is your duty to name it before it names you. Do not hesitate. Do not doubt. For hesitation is the Devil's doorway, and doubt is the ink with which he signs his covenant. Better an innocent cry out than a guilty voice go unchallenged. Better suspicion than silence.

Already, the town has begun to turn upon itself. Eyes linger too long. Prayers grow louder, sharper, desperate. A glance becomes an accusation. A dream becomes testimony. And once a name is spoken aloud—once the word witch takes hold—it roots deeper than truth can reach. There are those who claim they have seen the girl. That she comes in the night, beckoning, asking them to sign. They swear it with trembling hands and righteous fear.

But listen closely: evil does not always come from the shadows beyond the trees. Sometimes, it is born in the moment one voice chooses to condemn another—and is believed. In Salem, that moment has come. And what is written in fear… will be carried out in blood.

Chapter 1

The Road That Watches

The last mile into Salem ran between pines that had grown too close together, their boughs braided overhead like fingers lacing shut. The road narrowed until the wagon wheels pressed against old ruts, and the sound of them seemed too loud for the place. Every creak of wood, every clink of harness and bit carried forward and did not fade as it ought. It traveled ahead of them, as if announcing them to something that had been listening.

Eliza Harrow kept her hands folded in her lap, though her fingers would not stay still. She rubbed her thumb along the edge of a small tear in her skirt and tried to tell herself it was nothing more than a town at rest. They had left their home with the pale morning still on the fields; by afternoon the light had thinned to that gray gold that made even familiar things look strange. She had imagined

Salem as a place of chimneys and noise, of market voices and quarrels, the usual pulse of a town that wanted more than a farm could offer.

Instead there was the quiet.

Not the quiet of distance, where you can blame the spread of earth between houses. This was the quiet of a room where a conversation has stopped because someone has entered. A held breath.

Her mother sat opposite her on the bench, bracing herself against the wagon's sway. Mercy Harrow's eyes were fixed forward, her mouth set in the way it became when she meant to endure rather than persuade. Beside Eliza, her younger brother Samuel leaned his head against the sideboard and watched the trees with a sleepy resentment, as if the woods had chosen this hour to become dull. Their father, Nathaniel, drove without speaking, his shoulders tight under his coat as he coaxed the horse along.

Eliza listened for things she did not want to hear: laughter, shouting, the sharp ringing of a smith's hammer. Even the call of birds would have done, any small proof the world was behaving in its ordinary manner.

Nothing.

The horse's hooves were muffled by damp earth. The wind should have been restless through those pines, but the needles barely stirred. Even the wagon's canvas cover, which had snapped and fluttered for miles, now lay still as a shroud. It was as though the air itself had thickened.

"Are we near?" Samuel asked, his voice louder than he intended. He glanced at their father as if expecting rebuke for speaking at all.

Nathaniel's jaw shifted. "Near enough. You'll see the houses."

But when the trees thinned and the road bent, the town did not rise to meet them in the way towns did, with scattered barns and straying dogs and children running. Salem appeared in pieces, as if it had been placed with care and restraint. The first building was a low storehouse with a door shut tight. Then a fenced yard with no one in it, the gate tied with cord though there was no animal within. A washline sagged between two posts, empty. A cart sat overturned in grass as if abandoned in haste, its wheel still.

Eliza leaned forward, peering past her father's shoulder. "Where is everyone?"

Her mother's gaze did not move. "Inside."

"On an afternoon?" Samuel asked, now more alert. "It is not Sunday."

Nathaniel flicked the reins. The horse gave a small unhappy noise, and Eliza felt it more than heard it, a vibration that ran through the traces. The animal's ears pinned back, and its pace slowed.

"Keep your voice down," Mercy said, but not sharply. Almost gently, as if the quiet might bruise.

They rolled deeper into town. There were houses, yes, and smoke rising from a few chimneys, thin and reluctant. But there were no faces at windows. No doorways opened. It was as if the buildings themselves were watching, their blank panes turned toward the road like unblinking eyes.

Eliza's skin tightened along her arms. She had been in towns before, had been stared at before, and had learned the small rules of it: keep your head, do not invite comment, do not act as if you fear them. But this felt different from being a stranger. It felt like arriving late to something already decided.

A figure stood at the far end of a lane, half hidden behind a fence. Eliza saw him only because he did not move. A man, perhaps, or an older boy. He held the fence rail as if it steadied him. His hat brim shaded his eyes, but she knew he was looking at them. Not at the wagon as a whole, but at her. The certainty of it struck her with no proof, and yet it did not waver.

She looked down quickly, annoyed with herself. The man could have been looking at their horse, at the load in the back, at her father's hands. But as soon as she lowered her gaze, she felt the eyes remain on her like pressure.

Mercy shifted on the bench, her hand briefly touching Eliza's knee. It was not an affectionate gesture; it was a warning passed without words.

Nathaniel guided the wagon toward the center of town, where the road widened. A meetinghouse stood there, plain and rigid, its steeple like a finger held up to silence. The sight of it should have comforted, a familiar shape of order. Instead, Eliza felt the same strange tightening. The meetinghouse did not look like a place where people gathered. It looked like a place where people were gathered without wanting to be.

No bells rang.

At the edge of the common, a few men stood in a knot, talking too closely. They were not laughing. Their heads bent together as if guarding their words from the air. When the wagon entered the open space, their conversation stopped at once. They did not step back, did not relax into politeness. They only turned as one and watched.

Nathaniel lifted a hand in greeting. "Good day."

No one answered for a breath long enough to make the greeting feel foolish.

Then one of the men nodded without warmth. Another's eyes flicked to the back of the wagon, to Mercy, to Samuel, and then to Eliza. He held his gaze there longer than was proper. His face remained calm, but there was something set into it that Eliza could not name. Not curiosity. Not simple suspicion. A kind of readiness.

Her father cleared his throat. "We've come from the west road. We mean to stay a time. We're seeking lodging, and perhaps work, if any is to be had."

The man who had nodded looked at the others as if checking whether he was permitted to speak. "Lodging may be found," he said at last, and his voice sounded careful, measured like an answer given before. "But you have chosen a troubled season to arrive."

Mercy's chin lifted slightly. "Trouble how?"

The man's gaze moved past her, to the meetinghouse, and for a moment Eliza thought he would not answer at all. When he did, it was almost in a whisper, but it carried. "Wolves come near in certain winters. Not always with teeth."

Samuel frowned. "Is there sickness?"

The men's eyes sharpened at the boy's word. Sickness. Eliza watched their faces and saw, for the first time, a crack in that calm. Fear lived under it, but not the fear of fever. This was a fear that wanted reasons, and would accept any offered.

"It is not for children," one of them said curtly.

Mercy's hand tightened on the bench. "He is old enough to hear what we are walking into."

The first man hesitated, then said, "There are… disturbances. Afflictions. A great deal of talk."

Talk, Eliza thought, and felt the word settle unpleasantly in her stomach. Talk was a thing that spread faster than any illness. Talk did not require proof. It only required listeners.

Nathaniel forced a small smile. "We are God-fearing people. We will not add to trouble."

Something passed over the man's face at that. Not relief. Not approval. Something like assessment.

His gaze returned to Eliza, and he did not look away when she met it. His eyes were a pale, watery gray, the color of an overcast sky. His mouth moved as if he meant to say something else, something more direct, but he swallowed it.

"Eliza," Mercy said, softly but firmly, as if reminding her daughter to keep her composure.

The sound of her name in this quiet seemed to disturb the air.

The pale-eyed man blinked. It was the smallest sign of surprise, so slight another might have missed it. But Eliza saw it and felt cold.

How does he know it? She thought, and then, with equal quickness, chastised herself. Her mother had said it. He reacted because he heard it.

Only the reaction had come first, in a way that made no sense to her. As if he had been waiting for the name to be spoken aloud so he could match it to something he already carried.

A door opened somewhere to their left, slow and reluctant. A woman stepped out, apron on, hair covered, hands red from work. She did not come toward them. She did not call a greeting. She simply stood on her threshold and stared as if the wagon had brought with it a smell she could detect.

Then another face appeared at an upper window, then vanished.

Nathaniel shifted his weight on the seat. Eliza could tell he wanted to move on, to break this moment by doing what they had come to do: find a place to sleep, unload, begin. But the common felt like a stage, and every motion seemed watched for meaning.

"Where might we go?" Nathaniel asked.

The pale-eyed man inclined his head toward a road branching off the common. "There is an ordinary near the bend. If the keeper has room. Tell him you have been directed."

Nathaniel nodded. "Thank you."

The men did not return the courtesy. They simply stepped back as the wagon creaked forward, giving way with the stiff reluctance of a gate that opens only because it must.

As they passed, Eliza heard a murmur from behind. It was not a word she could catch, not clearly, but it moved through the men like a ripple. The tone of it was not question but recognition, as if one of them had named something.

Eliza kept her face forward, refusing to turn around and feed the feeling. Yet her ears strained. The town's silence did not mean no one spoke; it meant the town spoke only in small, private portions, held close like contraband.

A shadow crossed the road ahead. Eliza looked up at once, expecting a cloud. But the sky above Salem was a dull, even gray, unbroken. The shadow had come from the meetinghouse steeple as the wagon moved, its long finger of darkness sliding over them.

For a moment, Eliza felt as if something had touched her shoulder, not with a hand but with attention. It was absurd, and yet she could not shake it. She could almost sense the outline of the town around her, not as buildings and streets but as a living thing leaning in to listen.

Samuel said, too quietly now, "Why did they look at us like that?"

Mercy did not answer him. Her eyes were fixed on the road ahead, and her lips moved as if forming a prayer without sound.

Nathaniel drove on, steady, determined to pretend this was only a rough welcome. But Eliza watched the edges of Salem slide past and felt the unease deepen into something nearer certainty.

They had not merely arrived in a quiet town.

They had arrived in a town that was waiting.

The road the pale-eyed man had pointed them toward curved away from the common as if it wished not to be seen leaving it. The wagon's wheels found deeper ruts here, damp and dark, and the horse kept its head low, ears twitching at sounds Eliza could not place. The meetinghouse steeple fell behind them, but Eliza did not feel the town loosen its attention. If anything, the watchfulness changed shape, becoming less open, more intimate, the way a person stared harder once they believed you could not see them doing it.

They passed the first row of houses. Curtains hung in windows without moving. Doors remained shut. Yet Eliza kept catching the impression of motion at the edges, a shift of shadow, a brief darkening behind glass. It was the same sensation as walking beside a hedge and knowing a rabbit watched you from within. Only this was not a rabbit, and the hedge was made of human walls.

Samuel leaned forward, his hands gripping the sideboard now. “I thought there’d be children,” he said, trying to sound dismissive, as though the town’s emptiness was merely dull. “Or dogs at least.”

“Inside,” Mercy repeated, but her voice held no certainty this time. It sounded like she was repeating what she hoped was true.

Nathaniel did not answer. He guided the wagon carefully as they went, as if the road itself might object to them. Eliza watched his shoulders. He sat straight, but the tightness in him had moved from caution to something nearer pride. He would not look to either side. He would not give the town the satisfaction of seeing him react.

Eliza tried to do the same. She fixed her gaze ahead, on the pale ribbon of road, on a bare-limbed oak that leaned over a fence, on the rise beyond which the ordinary was supposed to be. But her eyes kept drifting. It was not curiosity. It was compulsion, the instinct to locate the source of pressure when you feel yourself being watched.

At one window a face appeared, half-hidden behind a curtain. An older woman, her cap tight, her mouth pursed as if she had been caught in the act of thinking poorly of someone. The woman's eyes slid to Mercy, to Samuel, and then found Eliza with the surety of a needle finding cloth. The curtain fell at once, but not before Eliza saw the woman's lips move.

Not speaking loudly enough to hear. Not praying. Naming.

A chill crept along Eliza's arms under her sleeves. She told herself the woman was only remarking on strangers. People did. People counted new faces the way they counted new livestock. Yet the movement of those lips had not looked like gossip. It had looked like confirmation.

The wagon rolled past a narrow alley between two houses. The space was darker than it should have been in open afternoon light, a tunnel of shadow where trash and broken barrel staves lay half-sunk in mud. Eliza glanced into it and saw, for an instant, the shape of someone standing back there.

A child, she thought first. Small shoulders, slight frame. Then she saw the height was wrong. The figure stood too still, too straight, as if it were only pretending to be small by keeping to the darkness.

Eliza's breath caught. She turned her head more fully, but the wagon had already moved beyond the alley's mouth. From that angle there was only shadow and refuse. No person. No face.

"Did you see—" she began, then stopped. Her voice felt too loud, like Samuel's earlier, and she did not want to pull her family's attention into this thin, listening air.

Mercy looked at her quickly. "What is it?"

"Nothing," Eliza said, hating herself for the lie and yet clinging to it. If she gave shape to the feeling, it would become real. Talk, she remembered, and the way the word had settled in her stomach. Talk made things grow teeth.

The horse snorted, a short nervous sound. Nathaniel patted its neck once, firm. "Easy."

They came to a yard where a pile of cut wood sat stacked too neatly, each log aligned as if for inspection. A man stood beside it with an axe in his hand. He had the look of someone who had been laboring for hours, but the axe head was clean. He was not working. He was waiting.

As the wagon approached, he raised his head and watched them with the same steady calm Eliza had seen on the common. His eyes did not move in the way eyes did when they took in a scene. They went directly where they meant to go.

To her.

Eliza held her posture and kept her face composed, but her skin prickled. The man's gaze was not curious, not even openly hostile. It was as if he were looking at a thing he recognized from description. A tool. A mark.

The man lifted his chin, a gesture that might have been greeting if his expression had softened. Instead, his mouth stayed flat, and he said nothing.

Nathaniel gave a small nod as they passed, the politeness of habit. The man did not return it. He simply followed them with his eyes until the wagon was far enough away that Eliza could no longer see him without turning.

Samuel turned anyway. He had always been the one to look when told not to. "He's staring," he muttered, as if bringing it into the open might make it less powerful.

"Samuel," Mercy warned, but there was fatigue in it, not anger. She was watching too, only with her eyes lowered, as though she feared what direct looking might invite.

Eliza realized then that the town's attention was not spread evenly among them. Mercy drew looks, yes, and Nathaniel's presence was measured, assessed. Samuel was noted in the way children were always noted, as an extension, a vulnerability.

But Eliza drew the longest stares. The most certain ones.

She tried to think of what could make her stand out. Her hair was plain and pinned. Her dress was modest. She did not carry herself with the boldness that drew comment. She was only seventeen, thin from travel, her hands roughened from work. There was nothing in her to mark her as extraordinary.

And yet the stares followed her like hands.

They approached a bend where the road dipped and then rose again. The ordinary, if it was as described, should have been visible by now, but the curve hid what lay ahead. Trees thickened on either side, and the houses thinned. Here the shadows felt heavier, the underbrush darker, as if the woods had crept closer to listen.

Eliza caught sight of movement among the trees to the right. A flutter of something pale, then stillness. She looked more carefully and saw a scrap of cloth caught on a branch, or perhaps it was a sleeve pulled back behind the trunk. A person could stand there and be almost entirely hidden.

Her heart quickened, not with terror exactly, but with the sense that something was being arranged. The town, the road, even the trees felt positioned, like parts of a trap that did not need to close quickly because it believed time was on its side.

Mercy shifted on the bench again, and Eliza felt her mother's hand touch her knee once more. This time it lingered.

"Do not look," Mercy said quietly, so low Samuel could not hear.

Eliza's throat tightened. "At what?"

Mercy did not answer directly. Her eyes stayed forward, but the whites showed more than before. "They want to see you notice. They want to see you afraid. Do not give them that."

Eliza wanted to protest that she was not afraid, that she was only unsettled, and with reason. But she could not deny the truth of her mother's words. There was a hunger in the watching. Not a hunger for food. A hunger for reaction.

Nathaniel finally spoke, his voice stiff. "We will find lodging, and we will keep to ourselves. Whatever fever has taken this town, we will not catch it."

Mercy's hand withdrew. "Fever," she echoed, and the word sounded wrong in her mouth, like a lie she wished could become true.

The bend opened at last, and the ordinary came into view: a larger house set back from the road, its porch sagging slightly, its sign hanging from an iron bracket. The sign creaked faintly in the still air, though Eliza could not feel any wind. The building should have looked welcoming in comparison to the shut-up houses behind them. Instead, it looked like a place where strangers were meant to go so they could be kept in one place.

Nathaniel drew the horse slower as they approached the yard. The windows of the ordinary were not curtained, and in that openness, Eliza found no comfort. It was like a face with its eyes uncovered.

Someone stood in one of the upper windows, half in shadow. A man, perhaps. Or a woman. The height was wrong to tell. The figure did not lean out or shift. It simply watched.

Eliza felt her mouth go dry. She stared back before she could stop herself, as if she could force the watcher to become ordinary by meeting their gaze.

The figure did not move.

Then, very slowly, it lifted one hand and placed it against the inside of the glass, palm flat. Not a wave. Not a greeting. A gesture like measuring, like testing the barrier between them.

A thought came unbidden, sharp and irrational: It knows you.

Eliza's fingers tightened around the fabric of her skirt until her knuckles ached. She looked away at once, furious at herself for doing so, as if she had yielded something in that brief exchange.

Nathaniel guided the wagon into the yard. The horse's hooves thudded softly on packed earth. No one came out to meet them. No call of welcome, no barking dog. Only that faint creak of the hanging sign, moving as though nudged by a breath no one could feel.

As the wagon came to a stop, Eliza heard it again: the nearly-words from earlier, the murmur that had moved through the men on the common. Only now it seemed closer, as if it drifted from the trees or the corners of the yard.

She could not make out what was said.

But she knew, with a certainty that made her stomach turn, that whatever it was, it was about her.

Nathaniel set the brake and climbed down from the wagon as if the simple act of putting his boots to Salem's earth might steady the day. The yard was bare in the way a swept floor was bare, no stray tools, no dropped scrap of rope, nothing a living place ought to forget. Even the ruts from other wagons looked pressed flat, as though someone had taken a board to them.

Eliza stayed seated, hands in her lap, watching the ordinary's door.

It did not open.

The upper window where she had seen the watcher was empty now, only a rectangle of dimness behind glass. That absence did not soothe her. It felt like the moment after someone ducks out of sight, not because they are gone, but because they have moved to a better angle.

Mercy climbed down more slowly, one hand braced on the wagon's side. Samuel followed, landing with a small thud and turning in a quick circle, as if he might catch someone staring and shame them into looking away. He found no one.

"There ought to be a keeper," Nathaniel said, trying for the tone of complaint a traveler might use, like this was an inconvenience and nothing more.

Mercy's face was tight; her eyes fixed on the open windows. "Maybe they are all inside, same as the others."

Nathaniel walked to the door and rapped hard with his knuckles. The sound went through the stillness like a thrown stone. Eliza felt it in her teeth.

A pause.

Then, from within, the soft slide of a bolt, careful and unhurried. The door opened no wider than a handspan at first, and a man's face appeared in the gap.

He was not old, but the lines around his eyes were deep, as if he had been squinting into trouble for months. His hair was thinning at the temples, damp with sweat or water. He wore a plain shirt with the sleeves rolled, and his expression held the practiced neutrality of someone who had learned not to show too much to strangers.

His gaze moved over Nathaniel's shoulder to Mercy and Samuel, and then it landed on Eliza.

Eliza felt the moment like a physical thing. The man's eyes did not simply see her. They caught, as if he had found the exact object he had been searching for in a cluttered room.

His lips parted slightly. His throat moved, a small swallow. For an instant his expression faltered, and something like recognition flickered there before he smothered it.

Nathaniel said, “Good day to you. We were directed here for lodging.”

The man kept looking past him. “How many?” he asked, but the question sounded like an afterthought.

“Four,” Nathaniel answered. “My wife, my daughter, my son, and myself. We’ve traveled since morning.”

The man’s eyes returned to Nathaniel as if forced. “Four,” he repeated. He opened the door wider at last. “Come in, then. Come in quick.”

The urgency in those words made Mercy stiffen. “Is there danger in being seen?”

The keeper hesitated. “No,” he said, too quickly. “Only… folk have too much time to look on what does not concern them.”

Samuel muttered, “They have plenty of time.”

Nathaniel shot him a warning glance and stepped inside. Mercy followed, her posture rigid. Eliza slid down from the wagon last, her boots sinking slightly into the packed earth. She looked once at the upper window again and saw nothing.

Still, the feeling remained, as though someone stood just behind her and breathed without sound.

Inside, the ordinary smelled of old wood and a low, stubborn fire. The common room was larger than Eliza expected, but it felt smaller because everything within it seemed arranged to prevent easy movement. Tables were pushed closer together than necessary. Chairs were tucked in tight. The space between the hearth and the bar was narrow, like a passage.

There were no other travelers. No laughter, no talk. The silence here was different from outside, weighted with the knowledge that voices could exist but had been withheld.

The keeper shut the door behind them and slid the bolt into place with a final, decisive click. Only then did he exhale as if he had been holding his breath.

"My name is Amos Pritchard," he said, wiping his hands on his apron though they were already clean. "You've come at a strange hour."

"It is not late," Nathaniel replied.

"It is for Salem," Amos said, and then stopped himself, as if he had said too much too soon. He gestured toward a table near the hearth. "Sit. Warm yourselves. I can make you broth. I have bread."

Mercy did not sit at once. She looked around, taking in the too-close tables, the bar with its neat row of cups turned upside down, the narrow stair that led up to the rooms. “Are you full?” she asked.

Amos gave a brief, humorless sound. “Full? No. Empty, if you mean company.”

Nathaniel sat, the bench creaking under him. Mercy followed after a moment, and Samuel slid in beside her. Eliza sat last, choosing a seat where she could see the door and the stairs. She told herself it was sensible. Her body did not believe her.

Amos busied himself with a pot near the hearth, stirring with a wooden spoon. He kept glancing at them, quick looks that darted away when caught, like an animal checking for a predator. Each time his eyes came to Eliza, they stayed a fraction longer.

At last Nathaniel said, “We met men on the common. They spoke in riddles. Wolves, they said. Not always with teeth. What trouble is in this town?”

Amos’s spoon paused. For a moment the only sound was the faint crackle of the fire. Then he stirred again, faster, as if motion might keep the subject from settling.

"Trouble," he said carefully. "It begins as talk, and then it becomes… proof."

"Proof of what?" Mercy asked.

Amos's gaze went to the door, though it was bolted. "Of sin. Of witchery. Of the Devil's hand in a place that cannot bear to think its own hands are capable of cruelty."

Samuel's eyes widened, though he tried to hide it by leaning closer to the table. "Witchery?" he whispered, as if the word might be heard through the walls.

"Hush," Mercy said automatically, but her face had gone pale.

Nathaniel's mouth tightened. "We want no part in such talk."

"No one does, at first," Amos said. His voice was low, and now there was something pleading in it, as though he spoke to warn them and also to lessen his own fear by sharing it. "But talk finds a way in. It crawls under doors. It gets in your mouth when you sleep."

Eliza's hands were cold against the wood of the table. She watched Amos's face and saw the strain around his eyes, the way his gaze kept trying not to go where it wanted.

He ladled broth into bowls with a hand that shook only slightly. When he brought them over, he set Nathaniel's bowl down, then Mercy's, then Samuel's. The last bowl he held for a breath longer, standing beside Eliza as if he had forgotten where to place it.

Eliza looked up at him.

Amos met her eyes and seemed to flinch. His lips moved, a sound forming without his permission. It was not her name. Not quite. It was as if he had started to say it and stopped in time.

He set the bowl down in front of her with an awkward, abrupt motion, sloshing a little broth onto the table. He wiped it quickly with the edge of his apron.

"I'm sorry," he said. "It's only… you favor someone. For a moment I thought…"

Eliza's heart beat once, hard enough to make her throat ache. "Someone here?" she asked, trying to keep her voice steady.

Amos's mouth tightened. "No. Not here. Not now."

Mercy's gaze sharpened. "Who?"

Amos looked from Mercy to Nathaniel, as though judging which of them might understand, which might accuse him of foolishness. His eyes returned to Eliza, and this time the recognition did not flicker. It sat there plainly, undeniable, and somehow separate from any actual memory.

He said, quietly, "There was a girl. Some months back. Passed through. Or so folk said. Only she didn't pass through proper. And they spoke of her after, like she had left a mark on their dreams."

Eliza's stomach tightened. "What was her name?"

Amos hesitated. The hesitation felt like a door held shut with a hand that trembled. "I never knew it," he said at last. "But there were those who claimed they did. Claimed the book had it written."

Nathaniel's spoon stopped halfway to his mouth. "Book," he repeated, and the word in his voice had weight, the way a man spoke of something he wished he had not heard.

Amos's eyes flicked to him. "It's madness," he said quickly. "It's all madness. But it is the sort that spreads because it looks like righteousness. They say there is a ledger. Black leather. Names inside. The Devil's account, as they call it."

Eliza felt something move in her chest at the description, not a memory exactly but a pressure, like the bruise left by a hand you cannot recall being struck by. She kept her face still, but her fingers curled against her palm beneath the table.

Mercy's voice was tight. "And what has this to do with my daughter?"

Amos opened his mouth, then closed it again. He looked stricken, as though he had not meant to bring Eliza into it and yet could not deny what his eyes insisted on seeing.

"It has nothing to do with her," he said finally, too firmly, in the tone of a man trying to hammer a board over a broken window. "Only... when I looked at her, I thought of that talk. And in Salem, thinking is enough to make a thing begin."

Eliza stared into the broth. The surface trembled slightly from the motion of her hands, though she had not moved them. She told herself it was only Amos's foolishness, a resemblance in the set of her face, the color of her hair, some detail that made him think of a stranger.

But the feeling that had followed her since the woods did not ease. If anything, it sharpened.

Outside, somewhere beyond the bolted door, a footstep sounded on the porch. Slow. Measured. It paused as if listening.

Amos went still.

No one at the table moved. Even Samuel held his breath, his eyes wide above his bowl.

The footstep shifted. Another step, closer to the door. A faint creak of wood under weight.

Then a voice, muffled by the door but clear enough to shape the words, spoke as if it knew it would be heard.

"Keeper," it said calmly. "We heard you've taken in travelers."

Amos swallowed. His eyes went once more, helplessly, to Eliza, and the look on his face was not curiosity now. It was dread, sharpened by the same impossible certainty Eliza had seen on the common.

Recognition without reason.

Amos did not answer at once. His hand went to the bolt as if by instinct, then stopped, hovering. He looked back at Nathaniel, at Mercy, at Samuel, and finally at Eliza again, as though apologizing for something he had not done and could not prevent.

Outside, the voice continued, patient as prayer.

"We only wish to see them."

Chapter 2

The Man Who Dreamed Her

Amos did not draw the bolt.

For a long moment he only stood with his hand hovering near it, as if the iron might burn him. The voice outside waited without impatience. That patience was worse than any threat; it carried the certainty of a man who believed the answer had already been decided.

Nathaniel rose from the bench in one stiff motion. “We are lawful travelers,” he said, pitching his voice toward the door. “We have done no wrong.”

The porch creaked again, weight shifting. “No one has said you have,” the voice replied, still calm. “Only it is custom, in a season like this, to know who is come among us.”

Mercy’s chair scraped softly as she stood. Samuel pressed closer to her side, trying to be brave and failing by the way his eyes kept flicking to the narrow crack beneath the door as if he expected smoke to seep through.

Eliza remained seated, because she could not trust her legs. The room felt smaller than it had a moment ago. Not from the tables, not from the walls, but from the attention pressing in through every seam. She could feel it as a physical weight at the back of her neck.

Amos glanced at her again, that helpless look returning, as if he were about to offer her up simply because he did not know how to keep her. His mouth worked, but no sound came out at first.

"Go upstairs," he said at last, barely above a breath. "All of you. There is a room at the top. The one with the lock that still holds."

Nathaniel did not move. "We will not cower in a rented room because someone knocks," he said, but his voice lacked the firmness he intended.

"They are not knocking for supper," Amos whispered back. His eyes darted to the door again. "Please."

Mercy took Nathaniel's sleeve, not with gentleness but with insistence. "Not here," she murmured. "We cannot fight a whole town on our first hour."

Samuel looked as if he might protest, then swallowed it. Eliza stood slowly, her bowl of broth untouched. The movement made the room sway for an instant, as if she had stood too quickly after illness.

They went up the narrow stair, each step creaking despite the careful way they placed their feet. Amos did not follow. He stayed at the foot, looking up after them like a man watching people climb onto a ship he would not be allowed to board.

At the landing, Mercy pushed Samuel into the room first, then Eliza. Nathaniel came last, closing the door behind him. The room was plain: two beds, a washstand, a small window that looked out over the yard. Mercy tested the lock. It turned with a stiff scrape and held.

They stood listening.

Below, Amos's footsteps crossed the common room. The bolt slid back. The door opened with a reluctant groan.

Voices entered, low and measured. Eliza could not make out the words, only the cadence of men speaking as if they were reciting something agreed upon. Amos answered in the same careful tone. Once, a name rose clearer than the rest, not spoken loudly, but distinct enough to prick at Eliza's attention.

Harrow.

Her father's surname, spoken by someone who should not know it yet.

Nathaniel's head lifted sharply. Mercy's hand covered Samuel's mouth before the boy could make a sound. Samuel's eyes widened against her palm.

Eliza moved to the window. She did not want to look, but the compulsion returned, that need to locate the source of pressure. She peered between the thin panes and the wavering glass.

Two men stood on the porch. One was the pale-eyed man from the common. The other was broader, his hat brim low, his posture rigid with the satisfaction of duty. A third figure waited at the edge of the yard; half turned toward the road as if keeping watch for more.

The pale-eyed man spoke again, and Amos answered. Then the pale-eyed man's gaze lifted, slowly, as though drawn by a thread, and found the upstairs window.

Eliza stepped back at once, heart jolting.

Mercy whispered, "Do not."

Eliza swallowed. “He looked up,” she whispered back. “As if he knew.”

Nathaniel’s face had gone hard in the way stone goes hard, not with calm but with refusal to bend. He pressed his ear to the door, listening, jaw tight enough to show the tendon.

The voices below shifted, and then, without warning, the stair creaked. Heavy boots. One step, then another. Someone started up.

Mercy pulled Eliza away from the window and pushed her toward the far corner, as if hiding her there could change what the town had already decided to see. Samuel trembled, his small hands clenched in his shirt.

The footsteps climbed to the landing. Stopped. A pause long enough to feel deliberate, as though the man outside the door were taking inventory of their breaths.

Then the door handle moved.

The lock held. The handle rattled again, once, testing. A soft sound followed, not quite a laugh and not quite a sigh.

A voice, close now, spoke through the wood. It was the same voice that had called for the keeper, still calm, still patient.

"Rest," it said. "We are not here to trouble you. We only wished to be assured you were truly come, and not… other."

Mercy did not answer. Nathaniel's fists were clenched so tightly his knuckles shone white.

The voice continued, as if speaking to reasonable neighbors. "In the morning, you will present yourselves proper. The store is open at first light. If you need anything, you may buy it as others do."

A pause. Then, softer, with an odd precision: "Keep your daughter near you."

Eliza felt those words like a finger laid against her spine.

Boots descended again, heavy and unhurried. The stair creaked with each step. Below, the door opened and closed. The bolt slid home. Silence returned, but it was not the silence of safety. It was the silence of a net drawn tight.

They did not sleep much that night.

When Eliza closed her eyes she saw the pale-eyed man looking up at the window with that slow certainty, as if he were reading something written on the glass. When she did drift, her dreams were filled with the sound of a quill scratching paper, though she had never heard such a thing close enough to remember it. She woke once with the taste of iron in her mouth, as if she had bitten her tongue.

Morning arrived gray and thin, the light reluctant to enter the room. Mercy looked as if she had not closed her eyes at all. Nathaniel sat on the edge of the bed, boots on, staring at the floorboards as though he might find a path out between them. Samuel dozed in fits, jerking awake at each sound from below.

Amos brought up bread and weak ale. His face was drawn, and he would not look at Eliza for long.

"They will be watching," he said quietly, setting the tray down. "If you must go out, do it quick. Do not linger."

Nathaniel's voice was rough. "Who were they?"

Amos hesitated. "Men who have found purpose," he said at last, as if that answered everything. "The one with the pale eyes is Thomas Putnam's cousin. He speaks as though he speaks for the meetinghouse now. As though the meetinghouse belongs to him."

"And you let them up the stair," Mercy said, and there was accusation in it despite herself.

Amos flinched. "I did not know what else to do. If I refuse them, they will mark my door, and then any who stay under my roof will be marked with it."

Eliza heard the word mark and felt again that strange pressure in her chest, like a bruise being pressed.

Mercy straightened her shawl with quick, sharp motions. "We will go to the store," she said. It was not a suggestion. It was the only thing she could do that felt like ordinary life, and she clung to it as if it were a raft. "We need provisions. We cannot stay locked in a room like thieves."

Nathaniel opened his mouth as if to argue, then closed it. The night had taken something from his certainty. He nodded once. "I will come."

"No," Mercy said. "Two men walking with stiff backs will look like fear, and they will smell it. You stay with Samuel. Let them see we are a common family."

Her eyes went to Eliza, and Eliza understood at once. Not common, she thought, but trying to appear so.

Mercy took Eliza's hand before Eliza could pull away, and squeezed, hard enough to hurt. "Do not speak unless spoken to," she murmured. "Do not answer anything that is not asked."

Eliza nodded, though her throat felt too tight for words.

They went down the stair, Amos watching them as if he expected the air outside to turn solid and stop them. The bolt came back with a metallic scrape. The door opened onto a morning that did not feel like morning. The street was quiet, yes, but not empty. The quiet hid people the way dark water hides bodies.

As they stepped onto the porch, Eliza felt it at once: the turning of attention. Not from one place, but from many. Curtains shifted. A shape moved behind glass. Somewhere a door opened a crack and shut again.

Mercy did not look to either side. She held her chin high, her grip on Eliza's hand steady. Eliza forced her feet to move at the pace her mother set, neither hurried nor slow.

The general store stood nearer the common, a squat building with a broad front window filled with goods that looked undisturbed by hands. A barrel of salt fish sat by the door. A broom leaned against the step, bristles clean, as if it had been placed there for show rather than use.

As they approached, Eliza heard it: a whisper, faint and close, though no one walked beside them.

Not a voice from the street. Not the rustle of leaves, because the leaves did not stir. It sounded like breath shaped into words just behind her ear.

She turned her head sharply.

No one was there.

Mercy's grip tightened. "Do not," she hissed under her breath, thinking Eliza was looking at a watcher in a window.

Eliza swallowed and faced forward again. The whisper came once more, so soft she could not be certain she had heard it at all.

A name, almost formed.

Not hers, not fully. Something that wanted to become it.

They stepped into the store, and the bell above the door gave a small, bright ring that felt obscene in all that quiet. Inside, the air smelled of molasses and dust and cloth. A few townsfolk stood among the shelves, their bodies angled in that false casualness of people pretending to shop while waiting for something else.

The shopkeeper looked up from his counter. His eyes went to Mercy first, then slid to Eliza.

Eliza felt the moment the way she had felt it with Amos: the pause, the catch, the recognition that had no right to exist. The man's face did not change much, but his gaze sharpened, as if he had been given a description and was checking it.

Behind Eliza, the door closed. The bell's echo died.

Somewhere among the shelves, someone stopped moving.

And then, from deeper in the store, a man spoke her name under his breath with a kind of startled certainty, like a man waking from a dream and finding the dream standing in front of him.

The name did not ring out like a greeting. It slid through the store like a draft through a crack in the wall, low and certain, carrying more weight than any stranger's tongue ought to have had.

"Eliza," the man said again, louder this time, as if he needed to hear it from his own mouth to believe it.

Mercy's hand tightened around Eliza's fingers. It was not a mother's squeeze of reassurance. It was a clamp, a warning, a desperate attempt to keep her daughter anchored to the simple fact of being here, awake, in daylight, in a room that smelled of molasses and wool.

Eliza's eyes found him between two shelves of flour sacks. He stood half-turned, like someone who had been walking past and then stopped because a thought struck him hard enough to halt his feet. He was not old, perhaps in his twenties, with hair that stuck up at the crown as if he had slept poorly. His shirt was buttoned wrong by one button, and there were shadows under his eyes that did not belong to a man who rose at peace.

He stared at Eliza with an expression that tried to become anger and kept slipping into something else. Fear, yes, but also the dazed certainty of a man describing what he had seen with his own eyes, even when his eyes could not have seen it.

"You," he said, and the word came out like an accusation he had been holding in his throat for days. "You are the one."

The shopkeeper, still behind the counter, did not speak. He set both hands flat on the wood, as if bracing himself. The other customers had fallen into stillness so complete it made Eliza's breathing feel loud. A woman near the window held a length of cloth mid-unroll, frozen. A man at the barrels of nails had stopped with his hand hovering above the open lid.

Mercy lifted her chin. "Sir," she said, the polite word sharpened like a blade, "you mistake us. We have just arrived in Salem. We are strangers to you."

The young man took one step forward, then stopped, as though something invisible marked a boundary between them. His gaze did not leave Eliza's face.

"I know what I saw," he said. His voice trembled with the effort of keeping it from breaking. "I know what came to me in the night."

Eliza felt heat rise in her cheeks, swift and humiliating. She could not tell whether it was anger or shame, only that it made her skin feel too tight.

"I have never seen you before," she said, because silence felt like guilt in this place. Her voice sounded smaller than she meant it to.

His mouth twitched, almost a smile, but there was no humor in it. "That is what you said then, too," he replied.

Mercy's grip on Eliza's hand became painful. "Then?" Mercy repeated. "What are you saying?"

The man's eyes flicked once to Mercy, but only as a man might glance at a fence post before returning his attention to the gate beyond it. "You came to my bed," he said, and the store seemed to draw in a collective breath. "Not in flesh like now. But you came. You stood at the foot of it and spoke as if you had spoken to me all my life."

A low murmur moved among the customers, not quite words yet, only the sound people made when a story found the shape it wanted. Eliza saw heads incline toward one another. She saw mouths part, then close, as if afraid to speak too soon and miss the moment when belief took root.

The shopkeeper finally found his voice. "Josiah," he said, not loudly, but with the careful firmness of a man who knew his counter would not protect him from this if it turned. "Mind yourself."

Josiah did not look away from Eliza. "I have minded myself near to madness," he said. "I have kept my mouth shut because I did not want to be laughed at, and I did not want…" He swallowed, his throat working. "I did not want it to be true."

Someone whispered, "He's one of the afflicted," and the word afflicted was spoken as if it were a title, an appointment.

Mercy took a step forward, placing herself slightly between Eliza and the man. "Listen to me," she said, her voice steady with strain. "My daughter has slept under my sight these last nights. We have been on the road. She has not been anywhere but beside me."

Josiah's stare sharpened, and for an instant his fear became something fiercer, like resentment at being denied the right to his own experience.

"That is what they said about others," he replied. "That they could not have been seen, because they were not there. And yet they were. They came like mist through the boards." His voice rose despite himself. "They came when the candle went out and the room was still. They came and smiled like they meant kindness, and then they asked."

Eliza's stomach tightened. She thought of the whisper she had heard outside the store, the breath close behind her ear. She forced herself not to turn her head, not to look for a mouth that could not be there.

"Asked what?" Mercy demanded.

Josiah's lips looked dry. He licked them, a quick nervous motion. "To sign," he said. "To put my name where it belongs. In the book."

At the word book, the stillness broke into a different kind of quiet, a charged one. People shifted. The woman with the cloth let it slip from her hands without realizing, the fabric sliding down in a soft heap.

The shopkeeper's face tightened as if he had tasted something bitter. "Not here," he muttered, but it was too late. The word had been placed among them, and it would not be taken back.

Mercy's eyes widened despite her control, a brief flash of something like recognition that did not belong to her. Eliza knew what her mother was thinking because Eliza was thinking it too: Amos, last night, the talk of a black ledger, names already written.

Eliza heard her own voice before she had chosen it. "There is no book," she said, and hated how it sounded, too quick, too certain, as if she were denying something she knew.

Josiah's face changed at once. The tremor in him steadied, as though her denial had given him the very proof he needed.

"You say it the same way you said it in the dream," he told her. "Like you have seen it so often you are weary of it."

"It was not me," Eliza insisted. She felt Mercy's fingers digging into her skin. "I have never been to your house. I do not know you."

Josiah's eyes glistened. "You knew my name," he said, and the accusation in that sentence landed with a dull finality. "You spoke it like a prayer."

Eliza opened her mouth and found nothing. She could have said I heard it now, from the shopkeeper, from someone else, from anywhere. But she had not heard it now, not before he spoke it. And even if she had, it did not matter. The logic of Salem was not built from what could be proven. It was built from what could be repeated.

A man near the door, older, with a beard threaded with gray, spoke into the silence. "What did she look like, Josiah?" he asked, as calmly as if he were inquiring about the weather. The calm was worse than outrage. It had the tone of procedure.

Josiah blinked rapidly. "Like that," he said, jerking his chin toward Eliza. "Only paler. Like moonlight on skin. Her hair down. Her feet…" He looked briefly at Eliza's boots, as if checking for mud. "Bare. She stood on my floor and made no sound."

The older man nodded once, slow. "And she bade you sign."

"Yes," Josiah said, his voice cracking. "She said it would ease what I have been suffering. She said all of us suffer because we are divided from what we belong to. She said there is a place for each name."

Eliza felt a coldness creep up her spine that had nothing to do with the store's draft. She saw, in her mind, the upper window of the ordinary and the hand pressed flat to the glass from the inside, not a wave, not a greeting. A testing.

Mercy drew Eliza closer, turning her body fully to shield her. "This is wicked foolishness," she said, louder now, for the store, for the shelves, for the unseen watchers behind windows. "My daughter is no spirit. She is flesh and blood."

"Flesh can be used," someone murmured, and then another voice: "Or borrowed."

Eliza could not tell who spoke. The voices did not come from one mouth; they rose from the room the way damp rises from soil, inevitable, everywhere at once.

The shopkeeper cleared his throat, but it sounded weak. "Mercy Harrow," he said, and Eliza's heart jumped at the way he knew Mercy's name too, as if the whole town had taken their names in through its pores. "No trouble in my store. If there is a matter, it must go to those appointed."

"Appointed," Mercy repeated, and there was contempt in it. "We came to buy flour and salt, not to be dragged into—"

Josiah made a sound, sharp, involuntary, as if her words had struck him. "Dragged?" he said. "You think I wanted this?" His eyes were wet now, and that, strangely, made him more frightening, because tears made him look honest. "I woke with the taste of ink in my mouth," he whispered. "I woke with my fingers black as if I had held a quill, and I have never held one. I scrubbed until my skin broke. It would not come clean."

A woman gasped softly. Another crossed herself quickly, then stopped, as if remembering the gesture was not proper.

Eliza's own fingers tingled, phantom sensation, and she curled them into her palm. For an instant she smelled something that did not belong in the store: iron and damp leather, like a saddle left too long in a wet barn. The scent was there and gone so quickly she could not be sure it had been real.

Josiah stared at Eliza as if she were the only solid thing in a world that had begun to shift. "Tell them," he said, voice roughening. "Tell them you came, so they will know I am not a liar."

Eliza's throat tightened until it hurt. "I cannot tell a thing that is not true," she managed.

The older man near the door stepped forward half a pace. "Then you deny it," he said, as though noting it down. "You deny that you visited him in the night."

"Yes," Eliza said.

A silence followed, and Eliza felt something in it settle, like dust falling after a blanket has been shaken. The room did not react with relief. It reacted with a grim, quiet satisfaction, as if her denial had completed a shape they needed completed.

Josiah's mouth pulled back, showing his teeth for an instant. Not a smile. Something closer to pain.

"She denies," someone whispered, and another voice answered, "They always do at first."

Mercy's face had gone pale beneath her anger. She turned toward the door. "We are leaving," she said, as if saying it strongly would make it possible.

But as Eliza looked past the shelves toward the front window, she saw a face outside, then another, lingering too close to the glass. Not shoppers. Not passersby. Watchers who had somehow arrived without the bell over the door ever ringing.

And in that moment Eliza understood with sick clarity how talk became proof in Salem. It did not require time. It only required a room where enough people wanted the same story to be true.

Josiah lifted his hand, shaking, and pointed at Eliza as though he could pin her to the air. "It was her," he said, voice breaking and hardening in the same breath. "It was her who came to me. It was her who brought the book."

The words fell like a stone dropped into water.

Then the ripples began.

Mercy's hand yanked Eliza back from the center aisle, as if distance could undo an accusation once it had been spoken aloud. The people in the store had not rushed them, not yet. They stayed where they were, but their stillness had changed. They were no longer merely listening. They were holding a shape in their minds and making room for it to become real.

Eliza could hear her own blood in her ears. Josiah's finger remained raised, trembling, but pointed with a terrible steadiness.

"It was her," he said again, quieter this time, as though repetition would seal the seam. His eyes did not blink. "It was her who brought the book."

The word book did something to the air. The syllable felt heavier than the rest of his sentence, like a stone set carefully in the foundation of a house. And with it came the smell again, faint but unmistakable: damp leather and iron, like a wet strap pulled tight around a wrist.

Eliza swallowed, and the taste in her mouth changed. For an instant she thought of last night's dream, the sound she could not name then but knew now by instinct, as if her body remembered what her mind refused: the fine scratch of a quill across paper.

"No," Mercy said, voice sharp enough to cut. "No, you listen to me. My daughter has been with me. She has slept under my roof, and before that under God's sky on the road. She has not gone creeping into any man's bed."

Josiah flinched as if struck. Then his expression twisted into something pained and stubborn. "Then how did she know my name?" he demanded, louder, to the room. "How did she stand there and speak it like she'd been born knowing it?"

The older man by the door, the one who had spoken so calmly, looked from Josiah to Mercy. His face held the stillness of a man accustomed to weighing grain, to judging measures. "Mistress Harrow," he said, and now the use of her name did not sound like politeness. It sounded like the town taking possession of it. "No one says you brought trouble here. Trouble finds its own road. But you must see, there is concern."

Mercy's eyes flashed. "Concern? Is that what you call it when you corner a girl in a shop and let men speak filth about her visiting beds?"

A murmur rose, offended not by the cruelty Mercy named but by the breach of decorum in naming it aloud. Eliza saw faces tighten, mouths pinch shut. She understood suddenly that Mercy's anger, righteous as it was, would only be read as resistance.

The shopkeeper, still behind his counter, cleared his throat again. His hands stayed braced on the wood as if he feared his own knees might fail. "Let there be calm," he said, though his voice shook slightly. "Let there be order. There is no proof in this store."

"Proof?" Josiah echoed, and his laugh came out thin. "I am the proof. What I have suffered is the proof."

Eliza's gaze drifted to the front window, where the watchers stood too close to the glass. Their faces were turned in, eyes fixed on the spectacle as if it belonged to them. One of them moved his lips, and Eliza felt her stomach drop. It was the same shape she had seen yesterday, in windows, in doorways: mouths forming words that were not meant for her ears, only meant to be set loose.

Mercy pulled Eliza toward the door. "We are leaving," she said again, but the words sounded less like a choice now and more like a prayer spoken against an oncoming storm.

Eliza's feet obeyed, but her thoughts lagged behind, snagged on the word book. She tried to hold on to simple things: the weight of Mercy's grip, the creak of floorboards beneath her boots, the smell of molasses and dust. Ordinary details. Safe details.

And yet, as she moved, something in her chest gave that strange press again, the bruise-feeling, as if a finger had pushed hard at a tender spot. The store's aisles wavered at the edges of her vision.

A flicker.

Not an image exactly, not like a memory recalled on purpose, but like a scene glimpsed through a crack in a door as someone passes too quickly.

A table. Candlelight. A book opened flat, its pages pale and waiting. The leather cover was black, but not clean black; it had the sheen of skin rubbed too often by hands. There was a smell of dampness and something metallic. Ink. Iron. Blood.

Eliza's breath caught.

The flicker vanished, and she was back in the store, her mother tugging her past the flour sacks. But the sensation did not vanish with it. It stayed in her fingers, a faint itch along her fingertips as if they had been stained and scrubbed raw.

She glanced down without meaning to. Her hands were clean. Rough, yes, from travel and work, but clean.

Josiah's voice followed them, hoarse and insistent. "Do not let her go. If she goes, she will come again in the night, and next time she will not ask so kindly."

Mercy jerked Eliza harder, her nails biting through the fabric of Eliza's sleeve. "Stop speaking of my child as if she is a wolf," she snapped.

The older man near the door shifted his stance. Not blocking them, not yet, but positioned so that leaving would require passing close. His gaze went to Eliza at last, direct and appraising.

Eliza forced herself to meet it. She wanted to hate him for it, for the calmness with which he weighed her, but hatred required steadiness, and she felt unsteady in a way that frightened her.

"You are pale," he observed, as if commenting on weather. "Are you unwell?"

"I am fine," Eliza said, and her voice sounded distant to her own ears.

Another flicker came as she spoke, sharper this time, and it struck so fast she almost staggered.

A quill. Not in a hand she could see clearly, but close enough to feel the motion. The quill's nib scratched the page with a sound like dry insects in leaves. A name formed under that moving point, letters darkening with each stroke.

Eliza Harrow.

Her own name.

Her throat closed.

She blinked hard, and the store snapped back into place. Mercy was looking at her now, alarm cutting through anger. "Eliza?"

Eliza tried to answer, but for a heartbeat her tongue felt thick and foreign, as though it had been asleep. She managed, "I'm here," but it came out too quickly, too forced.

Josiah had gone quiet. He was watching her, and his expression had changed again. The raw fear in him remained, but behind it was something like relief, as though he had seen her falter and taken it as confirmation.

"She remembers," he whispered, and the people nearest him leaned closer, hungry for that word.

"I remember nothing," Eliza said, louder, more sharply than she intended. The sound of her own voice struck her like a slap.

A woman near the window made a small sound, half gasp, half prayer. "She spoke with the same mouth," someone murmured. "Same as the others said. Same as the night-visitants."

Mercy turned fully, putting herself between Eliza and the room, her shoulders squared. "You will not have her," she said, and the tremor in her voice was not fear but the strain of holding it back. "Do you hear me? You will not."

The shopkeeper's eyes darted to the front door. The bell above it was still. No one had entered, and yet the pressure in the room increased as if more bodies had arrived.

Eliza followed his glance and saw, through the glass, the watchers had multiplied. Faces pressed nearer. A man's hat brim tipped as he peered in. Someone pointed, not as wildly as Josiah, but with a measured motion that suggested message rather than accusation.

The older man near the door said, "There is no need for harshness. Only questions. Only the proper order."

"Proper," Mercy spat.

Eliza heard, beneath the voices, something else. A whisper, so faint she could not tell whether it came from outside, from a corner of the store, or from inside her own skull.

Not a command.

A suggestion, intimate as breath.

It knows you.

Her skin prickled. She turned her head sharply, searching for a mouth near her ear.

There was only Mercy's face, tight and furious, and behind her the wall of townsfolk, their eyes bright with a terrible purpose.

Eliza's gaze slid past them to the counter, to the ledger book the shopkeeper kept there for accounts. It lay open, a harmless thing, pages lined and smudged with ordinary transactions. Yet the sight of ink on paper made her stomach roll.

Another flicker rose, uninvited: a page that was not lined, not meant for sums. A page with space for names. Names written not like accounts, but like ownership.

Eliza clenched her jaw until it ached. "Mother," she said, and the word came out rough.

Mercy's eyes flicked to her, and in them Eliza saw a fear Mercy had been refusing since they entered Salem: the fear that something had already reached her daughter, not through doors or roads, but through attention, through talk, through that hungry belief that wanted a shape to wear.

Mercy tightened her grip and moved again toward the door.

The older man did not step aside.

He held his ground with the mildness of a man insisting on courtesy. "You may go," he said, "but it would be wise to come to the meetinghouse after. There are men appointed to hear such matters. It is better for you to be cleared proper than to walk about with rumor clinging to you."

"Rumor," Mercy repeated, but her voice wavered now. She looked past him to the window, to the gathered faces. Salem was not a room. It was an ear pressed to every wall.

Eliza's vision swam slightly, and she felt, with sudden awful certainty, that the flickers were not imagination. They were not dreams. They were something half-remembered, half-recognized. As if a part of her had touched that black leather long before she ever set foot in this town.

Josiah spoke again, very softly, as if he were confiding rather than accusing. "You came with kindness," he said, eyes fixed on Eliza. "You did not threaten. You only asked, like it was already agreed."

Eliza's heart pounded so hard she could feel it in her throat. She wanted to say, You are wrong. You are sick with your own fear. But the words stuck behind the taste of iron that had returned to her mouth.

For the briefest instant, she saw it again, not as a scene but as a sensation: the weight of the book against wood, the give of the spine when it opened, the patience of the blank page.

Waiting.

Then it was gone.

Mercy's voice cut through the hush, strained but steady. "Move," she told the older man.

He did not.

And the store, which had felt too quiet a moment ago, filled with a low sound like wind rising through dry corn. Not wind at all, but voices gathering outside and within, the town's talk thickening as it turned, with dreadful ease, into certainty.

Chapter 3

The Exit That Closed

Mercy did not wait for permission.

She surged forward with Eliza pulled hard at her side, her shoulder angled as if she meant to pass through the older man by force if she had to. For a heartbeat he held his place, mild-eyed and stubborn, and the space between them filled with that low, gathering murmur, the sound of people deciding what was proper for other people.

Then he shifted, not stepping aside in courtesy but moving just enough to avoid being struck. His hand came up, palm out, as though he might touch Mercy's sleeve to stop her and thought better of it.

"Go on, then," he said, still calm. "But do not make it worse by running."

Mercy made a sharp sound that might have been laughter if there had been any humor left in her. She shoved the door open.

The bell above it rang bright and clean, and the sound felt like an insult to the air outside, which had thickened with bodies. Eliza stepped over the threshold and immediately felt the change: the street held the same gray light as before, but now it seemed crowded in a way that had nothing to do with noise. People stood too near the storefront, too near the road, gathered in loose knots that were meant to look casual and did not. Faces turned as one.

A woman with a covered basket paused mid-step and did not move on. Two boys stood near a post and stared without blinking. A man leaned against the opposite wall as if resting, but his arms were crossed tight and his gaze was fixed on Eliza with a peculiar steadiness, the way a person watches a door they expect to open.

Mercy kept her chin lifted. She pulled Eliza forward down the steps and onto the packed earth of the street, and she walked at the pace of an ordinary errand, not the pace of flight. Eliza understood why. Running would turn them into proof.

Behind them, from within the store, Josiah's voice rose again, muffled by the closing door but still carrying, a man desperate not to let his own nightmare slip away into doubt.

"It was her," he cried, and someone outside answered him with a murmur that sounded like agreement.

Mercy's grip did not loosen until they were half a street away. Then, abruptly, she turned them down a narrow lane between houses, as if she could not bear the direct road back to the ordinary with so many eyes upon it.

The lane smelled of damp boards and old refuse. The shadows lay thick between the buildings. Eliza's boots sank slightly in mud, and she thought of Josiah's description, bare feet on a floor that made no sound. She clenched her jaw until her teeth ached.

"Do not look," Mercy hissed when Eliza's gaze flicked to a window above them. "Do not give them your face."

"I'm not," Eliza whispered, though she was not sure it was true. It felt as though her face was being taken even without her offering it, copied into other people's minds.

They reached the back way to the ordinary. The yard that had seemed swept and empty yesterday now held a different kind of emptiness, one with an edge to it. The air was still, but Eliza could feel movement beyond the fence line, as if the town had shifted its weight to keep a clearer view of the roads.

Amos was on the porch, hands braced on the rail as though he had been waiting with his whole body. The moment he saw them his shoulders dropped a fraction, then tightened again when he noticed Mercy's expression.

"Mercy," he began, too softly, and then glanced past them as if expecting men to follow.

Mercy pulled Eliza up the steps and into the common room without answering. The door shut behind them with a hard thud. Amos reached automatically for the bolt.

"Do it," Mercy said, her voice rough. "Bolt it."

Amos slid the iron home. The click sounded final.

Only then did Mercy release Eliza's hand. Eliza's fingers burned where her mother had held them. Mercy turned, her eyes bright with a fear she had refused until now, and Eliza saw how close that fear sat to rage.

"They said her name," Mercy said, as if spitting it out might cleanse it. "They said it like they'd had it in their mouths all morning."

Amos's mouth tightened. "They know every name that comes into Salem now," he said. "If not at first, then soon. It does not take much for it to spread."

Nathaniel appeared at the foot of the stairs, Samuel behind him. Both had been listening. Nathaniel's face was set hard, but there was a rawness in his eyes that had not been there last night. Samuel looked as though he might be sick.

"What have they done?" Nathaniel asked, and his voice shook with the effort to keep it controlled.

Mercy spoke quickly, the words crowding out as if she feared that if she stopped they would solidify into something worse. "A man in the store said Eliza came to him in the night. Said she asked him to sign some Devil book. They all listened like it was scripture. They looked at her like…" She stopped, swallowing, because the comparison was too sharp to speak in front of Eliza.

Samuel made a small sound. "That man," he whispered. "The one with the eyes—"

"I know," Mercy snapped, softer than the word deserved, and then she reached for Samuel and pulled him close with one arm, as if suddenly remembering he was small enough to be taken too.

Nathaniel's gaze went to Eliza. He did not ask if it was true. He did not ask what she had done in dreams. His eyes searched her face as though hunting for some sign that she had changed without telling them.

"Eliza," he said, and the simple use of her name felt like an act of defiance now. "Tell me plain."

Eliza's throat worked. The taste of iron still lingered, faint but real enough that it made her want to spit. "I have never seen that man," she said. "I have never been in his house. I swear it."

Nathaniel nodded once, sharply, as if he accepted it as a fact because he must. Mercy's face crumpled for an instant, then hardened again.

"We are leaving," Mercy said.

Amos made a sound like a breath sucked through teeth. "You cannot," he said, and then flinched as if he had spoken too boldly. "Not as easy as you think."

Nathaniel's shoulders rose. "We came by road, and we will go by it."

Amos rubbed his palms together, though they were dry. "They watch the roads."

Nathaniel stepped closer to him, lowering his voice, though the room was empty besides them. "Who?"

Amos's eyes flicked toward the shuttered windows. "Men who have decided it is their duty. They stand at the west road and the south. They stand like they are hunting wolves. Only wolves do not carry wagons."

Mercy's laugh came out thin and bitter. "They will bar us because of words in a store?"

Amos looked at Eliza, and the dread in his face deepened. "Not because of words. Because of a story that has found the shape it wants. Once it has a shape, folk will keep it safe. They will not let it walk away and leave them with doubt."

Samuel clutched at Nathaniel's sleeve. "Father," he said, his voice small. "They can't stop us. Can they?"

Nathaniel put a hand on his son's head, firm. "No," he said, too quickly. Then, to Amos, "Harness the horse. We will go now. Before—"

A knock came at the door.

Not loud. Not urgent. A measured rap, as if the person outside knew exactly how much sound was needed to be heard and no more. Eliza's stomach dropped. The room went still in a way that felt practiced.

Amos stared at the door as though it might open on its own. Mercy moved without thinking, placing herself between Eliza and the entrance.

The knock came again. Then a voice, calm as it had been last night, as if nothing had changed.

"Keeper. Amos Pritchard. Open."

Amos swallowed, his throat bobbing. He did not move.

Nathaniel stepped forward. "We will not be held," he called through the wood, pitching his voice steady. "We have done nothing."

A pause. Then the voice answered, patient as prayer. "No one says you have. But there is talk, and talk must be tended."

Mercy's hands clenched at her sides. "Tended," she muttered, and the word sounded like a blade being sharpened.

The voice continued, as though explaining to children. "You brought your daughter into the store this morning. A man has spoken. Others have heard. It is not wise to pretend it is nothing."

Nathaniel's jaw flexed. "My daughter is not your matter."

Another pause. Eliza could almost feel the mind on the other side of the door arranging its response with care, choosing words that would sound like righteousness no matter what they did.

"She is," the voice said finally, still calm. "For now."

Eliza's skin prickled. The phrase did not sound like threat so much as ownership, and that was worse.

Amos looked as if he might faint. "Please," he whispered, to no one in particular. "Please."

Mercy turned to Nathaniel, her eyes fierce. "Get the wagon," she said. "Now. Out back. Quiet. If we can be on the road before they—"

Amos shook his head quickly. "There is no out back," he whispered. "The yard opens to the lane. They will see. They are already outside."

As if to prove it, a sound drifted in through the shutters: feet on packed earth, more than one, moving unhurriedly. Not a mob running. A group positioning itself with certainty.

Eliza went cold. The town was not gathering in rage. It was gathering in procedure.

Nathaniel moved to the window and pushed the shutter slat aside a fraction, just enough to peer out. Eliza saw his face change, the hard set of it cracking for an instant into disbelief.

"What?" Mercy demanded.

Nathaniel's voice came out low. "Men in the yard," he said. "At the gate. And down the lane."

Samuel made a small choking sound.

Mercy turned and went to the other window with a speed that betrayed her. She peered through a crack and then recoiled as though she had been burned.

"They're there too," she whispered. "At the street."

The knock at the door came again, softer this time, as if the person outside was certain they would not be ignored forever.

"Open, Amos," the voice said. "Let us speak proper. There is no need for trouble."

Nathaniel's hands curled into fists. "They mean to hold us," he said, as if forcing himself to say it would make it less unreal.

Eliza stood very still, her back pressed lightly against the wall, and listened to the sounds outside: the faint creak of the porch board beneath shifting weight, the murmur of voices held low, the scrape of a boot in dirt.

Then, beneath it all, something else that made the hair along her arms rise.

Not outside.

Inside her hearing, close as breath behind the ear.

A whisper, soft and familiar in the way a thought is familiar, even when it is not your own.

Stay.

Eliza's heart stuttered.

She did not turn. There was no one at her shoulder. Mercy was at the window. Nathaniel was by the other. Samuel stood between them, trembling.

The whisper came again, not louder, not insistent, simply patient, as if it had all the time Salem had.

Stay. There is nowhere else.

Eliza swallowed hard, forcing herself to breathe through the tightness in her throat. Her eyes went to the bolted door, to the solid wood and iron between them and the town. She had thought bolts meant safety.

Now she understood.

The bolt did not keep Salem out.

It kept them in.

Nathaniel stepped toward the door, and for a moment Eliza thought he meant to throw it open and fight. But his hand stopped inches from the iron, as if he could feel through the wood the numbers waiting on the other side.

Mercy's voice broke, just slightly. "We will leave," she said, as if bargaining with God. "We will go back the way we came. We will not trouble your town."

Outside, the calm voice answered with the same dreadful gentleness. "You cannot. Not today."

Eliza closed her eyes for a heartbeat, and in that darkness the flicker returned: a road narrowing under pines that braided overhead like fingers lacing shut. A town that waited. A page that was blank only until it decided otherwise.

When she opened her eyes, the room felt smaller, as if the walls had leaned in.

Samuel whispered, "Father, where do we go?"

Nathaniel did not answer him at once. He stared at the door with the fixed look of a man seeing a truth he cannot strike down. When he finally spoke, his voice was hoarse.

"There is no road," he said. "Not for us."

And outside, the slow shuffle of feet settled into place, like stones arranged across a path.

Nathaniel's hand stayed suspended near the bolt as if the iron had taken on a heat of its own. Mercy stood with Samuel pressed to her side, her palm splayed protectively against the boy's chest. Amos hovered a step back, his face gray and damp at the hairline. Eliza could feel the room's air thinning, not from lack of breath but from the way attention crowded it, the way their silence seemed to be listened to from the other side of the door.

Outside, someone cleared his throat with quiet patience.

"Open, Amos," the voice said again. "Let us speak proper."

Amos's lips trembled. He looked to Nathaniel as if hoping for instruction, then to Mercy, then—against his own will—his gaze slid to Eliza and snagged there. Eliza wanted to tell him not to look at her like that, as if her face alone had pulled the trouble to the porch. But the truth was he was not looking at her with blame.

He was looking at her like a man staring at a spark in a room full of dry hay.

Nathaniel drew a slow breath, steadied himself with it, and called through the wood, "If you have something to say, say it. We will not open our shelter to a crowd."

A pause, and then the calm voice answered as though Nathaniel had made a fair point. "No crowd. Only men appointed to keep order."

Mercy made a sound under her breath. "Appointed by whom," she muttered, but she did not speak it loud enough to carry.

Amos lifted a hand toward the bolt again and stopped, fingers hovering. "If I do not," he whispered, voice breaking on the words, "they will break the door. Or they will break me for keeping it."

"You think opening it will spare you?" Mercy hissed. "You think they'll be gentle once they've been refused?"

Amos flinched. "No," he said, and the simplicity of it was worse than argument. "But if it must happen, it is better it happens with words first."

The whisper in Eliza's ear returned, not a sound from the room but a sound inside her hearing, as if the thought had been laid gently against her mind.

Words are enough.

She pressed her nails into her palm until she felt pain, anchoring herself. The whisper faded, leaving a thin aftertaste of iron as though she had bitten down on a coin.

Nathaniel's jaw worked. His eyes flicked to the windows, to the cracks in the shutters where light came through in narrow knives. He had seen the yard fill. He had heard the feet settle into place. Whatever anger he held had nowhere to go without becoming a noose.

“Open it,” he said at last, the words scraped raw. “But you do not step back from us. You stand here and you listen, Amos. You do not let them take our names and twist them.”

Amos nodded, too fast, too eager for permission. He drew the bolt with a rasp that made Eliza’s stomach lurch. The door swung inward a hand’s breadth.

Cold air slipped in, carrying with it the damp smell of earth and wool and something else: the faint tang of sweat that comes when men gather in purpose.

The pale-eyed man stood on the threshold. He had not removed his hat. His face was arranged into a careful expression of concern, as if he had come to offer condolence rather than threat. Beside him stood the broader man Eliza had seen yesterday, shoulders square, mouth set, eyes restless with the satisfaction of being needed. Two more figures lingered behind them on the porch, half turned toward the yard like sentries.

The pale-eyed man tipped his head to Amos. “Keeper Pritchard.”

Amos swallowed. “Sir.”

The man’s gaze slid past Amos, past Nathaniel, to Mercy, to Samuel, and then it found Eliza with the same unhurried certainty as before, as if it had always intended to end there.

Eliza did not look away. She forced herself to hold his gaze, though it made her feel flayed. His eyes were pale enough to seem watered down, but there was nothing weak in them. They held a kind of calm that had already decided what the world was allowed to be.

"We mean no harm," he said, and his tone made it sound like harm was a thing chosen by the recipient. "Only there is concern for the safety of the town."

Nathaniel's laugh came out short. "The safety of the town from my daughter?"

The pale-eyed man's eyes did not change. "From what may move through her," he replied, as if correcting a misunderstanding in church doctrine.

Mercy stepped forward a half pace. "My daughter is flesh. She has done nothing. A man spoke nonsense in a store, and you have taken it as law."

The broader man's mouth twitched. "It is not only one man," he said. "It begins with one, and then others find courage to speak what they have kept silent. You are new here. You do not know what has been happening."

"We know enough," Mercy snapped. "That you have forgotten the difference between talk and truth."

At that, the pale-eyed man's expression softened, and Eliza realized with a jolt that the softness was not kindness. It was the look a man gives when he believes he is speaking to someone foolish, someone who will resist only because they do not understand the greatness of the danger.

"You think we want this," he said. "You think we delight in troubling a family that has just arrived. But there are afflictions in Salem. Real ones. Girls who scream and twist as if their bones are being pulled from inside. Men who wake with marks on their bodies and cannot remember how. Cows that sicken in a day, butter that will not churn, prayers that turn sour in the mouth. These are not things made from idle talk."

"They are things made from fear," Nathaniel said. His voice shook, but he kept it steady. "And fear makes men see what they wish to see."

The pale-eyed man nodded as though Nathaniel's words were a known hurdle, a step every accused family took before coming to reason. "Fear can make a man imagine a snake in his bed. But fear does not put bites on his skin."

Eliza's gaze flicked to the broader man's hands. His knuckles were scraped, old scabs cracked open. A laborer's hands. But there was ink in the creases of his fingers, faint smudges that looked too dark to be dirt. Eliza's stomach turned. She remembered Josiah's words. Fingers black as if he had held a quill.

She swallowed hard.

Mercy's voice softened suddenly, and that softness frightened Eliza more than her anger. "What do you want?" Mercy asked.

The pale-eyed man took his time answering. He looked from Mercy to Nathaniel as if weighing which of them could be bent first.

"We want you to come to the meetinghouse," he said. "Proper. In daylight. With your daughter. The magistrates will hear the matter and determine whether there is cause for further watch."

Nathaniel's eyes flared. "Further watch," he repeated. "You are watching now. Men in the yard, men at the gate, men on the road. You have ringed this place like we are criminals."

The broader man spoke again, more bluntly. "No one is harmed by being looked on, if they have nothing to hide."

Mercy's shoulders lifted with a sharp inhale. "That is the lie men tell when they mean to do harm. It is always the innocent who suffer most under watching, because they have no weapon but truth."

The pale-eyed man's gaze stayed on Eliza. "Truth will have its chance," he said. "But there is a greater danger than your feelings. If we let a suspected instrument walk out of Salem, and harm follows, then whose sin is it? Ours."

There it was. Eliza felt it settle into the space between them like a stone placed carefully on a scale. Not evidence. Not testimony. Responsibility. A weight that could be used to justify anything.

Nathaniel's fists clenched. "You have not even asked her what she saw, what she heard. You have only heard others speak and decided it must be so."

The pale-eyed man blinked once, slow. "We have asked," he said, "and she has denied."

Eliza's throat tightened. He said it the way one says a familiar phrase, a pattern already expected. Denial did not weaken his certainty. It fed it.

Mercy's eyes narrowed. "How do you know she denied? She has spoken to no one but us and that man in the store."

A faint smile touched the pale-eyed man's mouth. "Words travel," he said simply. "The town hears what it needs to hear."

Amos made a small sound, almost a sob, and then swallowed it. He looked as if he wished he could disappear into his own floorboards.

Nathaniel leaned forward, addressing the pale-eyed man directly. "Give us leave to go," he said. "We will not trouble Salem further. We will be gone within the hour."

For the first time, the pale-eyed man's calm showed a faint edge, not anger but the slightest tightening, like a rope drawn a little firmer.

"No," he said.

The broader man shifted, and Eliza heard the soft scrape of boot leather on wood. Behind them, one of the porch sentries turned his head toward the yard as if checking some signal.

The pale-eyed man continued, voice still even. "You cannot go because the matter has found you. If you leave, you carry it. If you leave, you deny the town its chance to cleanse itself. That is not permitted, not now."

Mercy's voice broke into a harsh whisper. "Permitted by whom?"

"By necessity," the pale-eyed man replied, and that was the most honest thing he had said. His eyes stayed on Eliza as if she were the shape necessity had taken. "Salem must be sure."

Eliza felt something inside her loosen slightly, a small slipping sensation that made her dizzy. She understood, with a clarity that made her want to be sick, that they were not arguing with men. They were arguing with a story. And the story did not need to be true. It only needed to be believed by enough mouths at once to become immovable.

Nathaniel's shoulders sagged a fraction, then straightened again as pride rallied. "And if we refuse?"

The pale-eyed man's gaze did not waver. "Then you will be taken to the meetinghouse by stronger hands," he said, "and it will be recorded that you refused the proper order, which is never a good sign in times like these."

Recorded. Eliza's skin prickled at the word. She saw, uninvited, a page waiting, empty only in appearance. She tasted iron again.

Mercy took Eliza's hand, not gripping this time but holding with a desperate tenderness that made Eliza's eyes sting. "We will go," Mercy said, and Eliza felt the shame of it, the humiliation of yielding to madness, but also the cold understanding: to refuse was to add fuel to their certainty.

The pale-eyed man nodded, satisfied, as if Mercy had chosen reason at last. "Good," he said. "We will escort you. It is better for all."

Nathaniel's jaw tightened. "Escort," he repeated, and the word sounded like a chain.

The broader man's gaze flicked to Eliza. His eyes were not pale like the other's; they were dark, and in them Eliza saw not hatred but something worse: a simple conviction that he was right to stand between her and the road.

Outside, the yard was quiet in the way a pond is quiet when something waits beneath the surface. Eliza could sense bodies out there without seeing them, men placed at angles, eyes trained on doors and windows and the very air, as if the air might try to slip past them.

The pale-eyed man stepped back from the threshold, making space as though granting them a courtesy. "Bring your daughter," he said, and his voice remained mild, almost gentle. "And keep her close. These are sensitive matters."

Eliza felt the whisper again, the soft voice that was not the man's and not her mother's, close as breath.

They will be sure. They always are.

She held on to Mercy's hand and tried to keep her face calm, tried to keep her mind from splintering under the weight of it: that truth had become irrelevant. That the roads were closed not by boards or chains but by belief.

As they stepped toward the door, Eliza heard, faintly from somewhere beyond the porch, a voice she could not place, not loud enough to be called a shout, but clear enough to cut through the damp air.

A woman's voice, perhaps. Or a child's.

It spoke a name.

Not Eliza's. Not yet.

But it spoke it the way Josiah had spoken hers in the store: with startled certainty, as though reading it off something already written.

Mercy's fingers tightened around Eliza's hand as they stepped onto the porch. Nathaniel went first, shoulders squared, his body doing what his pride still believed it could do: walk out as a man among men, not as a thing being led.

The pale-eyed man waited to one side, making room with the kind of politeness that did not soften what it meant. The broader man stood at the other post, his stance angled so that Nathaniel would have to pass close enough to feel him there. Two others lingered behind, not quite in the doorway, not quite in the yard, like hinges that could swing either way.

Eliza felt the yard's attention before she saw the faces. Men stood near the fence line and the gate, placed with care, their hands loose at their sides but ready. There was no shouting, no pushing. It was the order of a trap that did not need speed.

The gray daylight looked thinner outside than it had a moment ago, as if the air itself had been handled too much.

Then, from somewhere beyond the porch, that voice came again. Not loud. Not a shout. A voice spoken as though meant only for one listener, and yet it carried through the damp.

"Lydia Dyer," it said.

The name dropped into the yard like a pebble into still water. It was not Eliza's name. It was not the Harrow name at all. And it was spoken with that same startled certainty Josiah had used in the store, as if the speaker had not invented it but read it.

Eliza turned her head despite herself.

At the edge of the lane, half obscured by the ordinary's corner and the sag of a fence, a small figure stood in shadow. A girl, perhaps twelve or thirteen. Her hair was loose, dark against a pale face. She did not look at Eliza or at any of them. Her eyes were fixed on nothing Eliza could see, as if she stared through the world rather than at it.

The broader man noticed Eliza's turn and followed her gaze. His mouth tightened, and he said, low and sharp, "Go on."

The pale-eyed man did not glance toward the girl. He only said, as if to himself, "It begins again."

Mercy's hand jerked Eliza forward. "Do not look," Mercy whispered, though Eliza could hear the strain in her mother's breath. Mercy had heard the name too. Mercy had understood, in a way Eliza did not want to understand, that names in Salem did not need to be spoken in accusation to become dangerous.

Nathaniel's voice was controlled, but Eliza heard the violence beneath it. "Who is that?" he asked, nodding toward the shadow where the girl stood.

"A child," the pale-eyed man replied, as though that explained everything. "One of the afflicted."

Eliza's stomach tightened. She remembered the store, the stillness of listening bodies, the way talk had turned into proof while she stood in the middle of it. She thought of that ledger on the shopkeeper's counter, harmless lines and sums, and the way her mind had overlaid it with another page that did not belong to any ordinary account.

The girl in shadow did not move. She lifted her chin slightly and spoke again, very softly, as if continuing a list.

"Lydia Dyer," she repeated, and then, with the same measured certainty, "Ephraim Kells."

Another name, another stone.

Eliza's breath caught. She did not know any Lydia Dyer. She did not know any Ephraim Kells. Yet the sound of the names made something in her chest press and ache, that bruise-feeling that had followed the mention of the black book. It was not recognition, not the way one recognizes a face. It was the sensation of being near something that had already been written down.

Nathaniel glanced back at Eliza, as if the names might be her doing. He did not accuse her; he looked at her like a man checking whether his daughter was still wholly his, still wholly here.

Eliza tried to steady herself. "I don't know them," she whispered, not sure if she spoke to her father or to Mercy or to herself.

Mercy's jaw worked. "You do not answer anything," she murmured, and her grip on Eliza's hand became almost desperate again, as if Mercy feared Eliza might slip out of her fingers like mist.

They descended the steps.

The broader man moved with them, not touching, but close enough that Eliza could smell wool and sweat and the faint sourness of leather warmed by a body. The pale-eyed man walked ahead, setting the pace. It was not quick, not slow. It was the pace of procession.

They went out through the gate and into the lane. The ordinary's yard fell behind, but the sensation of being watched did not ease. If anything, it sharpened. People were not lining the street as a crowd, not openly. They were in windows, behind shutters cracked a finger's width, in doorways half-shadowed, in the gaps between buildings where a person could stand and pretend they were only there by chance.

Eliza kept her eyes forward but forward offered no relief. The meetinghouse steeple rose above the roofs like a finger raised to hush. Its shadow lay across part of the common, and the gray light there looked darker, as if the air under it had thickened.

They had nearly reached the wider road when Samuel's voice came from behind them, small and strained. He was walking close to Mercy's side, his face too pale for a boy who should have been thinking only of bread and chores.

"Mother," he whispered, "why did she say those names?"

Mercy did not answer at once. Her lips moved as if forming a prayer and then stopping short of it.

The pale-eyed man heard anyway. He glanced back over his shoulder, his expression composed. "The afflicted speak many things," he said. "Some are nonsense. Some are warning."

"Nonsense," Nathaniel said, and the word came out like a challenge.

The pale-eyed man's gaze slid to him and held there a moment. "If it is nonsense, it will come to nothing," he said mildly. "If it is not, it is better we have heard it early."

Eliza felt her stomach turn, not from fear alone but from the logic of it. Early. As if hearing a name in the dark was a kind of preparation. As if the town's duty was to catch the names before the people could run with them.

The lane opened onto the street nearer the common. Here the watching was less hidden. Two men stood by a post as though talking, but their conversation was only the movement of lips without sound, their eyes fixed on the small line of escorted bodies. A woman crossed herself quickly when she saw them and then dropped her hand, as if remembering the gesture itself could be read as guilt. A dog lay in the mud by a fence and did not lift its head as they passed, as if even animals had learned not to react.

Eliza felt the whisper again at the edge of her hearing, close as breath, not from any mouth nearby.

Not yet.

The words slid through her thoughts like a hand smoothing cloth. A suggestion. A patience.

She bit down on the inside of her cheek until she tasted blood, just enough iron to drown the imagined iron that kept rising whenever the book came near in her mind.

They crossed into the open space of the common.

The meetinghouse stood rigid and plain, its boards darkened by damp. The door was shut, but Eliza could sense movement within or behind it, as if the building held more than wood. The steeple's shadow stretched long and thin across the ground, a stripe of darkness laid deliberately across their path.

As they stepped into that stripe, Eliza's skin prickled. It was only shade. It should have felt cooler, nothing more. But she felt something else: the sensation of crossing a boundary.

The pale-eyed man slowed near the meetinghouse steps. He turned slightly, not to face them fully, but enough that his words would be heard.

"This is the proper place," he said. "Here things are spoken plain. Here nothing is hidden."

Nathaniel let out a hard breath through his nose. "Nothing is hidden," he repeated, and there was bitter disbelief in it.

Eliza's eyes flicked to the meetinghouse door. For an instant she saw it not as a door but as a page, shut tight, waiting to be opened. The thought was so vivid it made her dizzy.

Behind them, somewhere at the edge of the common, the afflicted girl's voice rose again. It came faintly, carried by still air that did not seem to belong to wind at all.

"Eliza Harrow," the girl said.

Eliza's blood went cold.

Mercy made a sharp sound, half breath, half sob strangled back. Samuel's fingers tightened on

Mercy's sleeve. Nathaniel's head snapped around, rage and fear flaring together in his face.

Eliza could not move. The name had not been shouted like an accusation. It had been spoken the way one reads something written in front of them, calmly, correctly, without question.

And Eliza knew, with a clarity that made her stomach hollow, that she had never given that girl her name.

The pale-eyed man's expression did not change much, but a faint satisfaction settled into it, the look of a man hearing a necessary tool drop into his hand.

"There," he said softly, almost kindly. "You see?"

Nathaniel stepped forward as if to turn and go back, as if he could reach the voice and strike the name out of the air. The broader man shifted at once, not grabbing Nathaniel yet, but moving into the space where Nathaniel's anger would have to pass.

Mercy pulled Eliza closer, her body shielding her daughter as if a name could be blocked by flesh. "How?" Mercy whispered, and the question sounded torn loose from her. "How could she know?"

Eliza's mouth was dry. The iron taste in her mouth came stronger now, and she did not know if it was blood from her bitten cheek or something else.

The afflicted girl spoke again, fainter this time, as if receding into shadow.

"Written," she murmured.

Eliza felt her knees threaten to give. She stared at the meetinghouse door and saw, in her mind, that black leather book, heavier than scripture, pages waiting with patient blankness. She saw a quill scratching, heard it like insects in dry leaves.

The pale-eyed man gestured toward the steps. "Come," he said. "It is better to be inside."

Better. As if inside would be gentler.

As they mounted the steps, Eliza heard whispering begin around the common, not loud enough to catch words, only the sound of mouths turning a name over and over like a coin to see which side would land up. The town did not need Eliza's confession.

It had her name.

And once Salem had a name, it had something to hold. Something to close its hands around until there was no exit left at all.

Chapter 4

The Hands That Took Her

The meetinghouse door opened inward with a slow reluctance, as if the hinges resented being asked to move. A draft breathed out from the dark within, carrying the dry, stale smell of old boards and wool that had been worn through too many long sermons. Eliza stepped across the threshold and felt at once that the air inside was different from the air outside. It was not warmer. It was not safer. It was simply thicker, as though every word ever spoken in that room had left something behind and it had all settled into the corners.

Benches faced forward in rigid rows. A narrow aisle ran between them like a channel cut for a procession. The pulpit stood raised at the far end, severe and plain, its wood rubbed smooth where hands had gripped it for emphasis. No candles burned, yet there was light enough to see the faces.

There were more of them than Eliza had expected.

Men sat and stood along the side walls, hats in their laps or still on their heads. Women occupied the back benches, shawls pulled tight, their eyes bright in the dimness. A few children perched too still, as if they had been taught that movement itself was a kind of sin. It should have looked like a congregation gathered for prayer, but the posture of the room was wrong. People were not here to humble themselves before God. They were here to witness something. They held their bodies as they might at a hanging, restrained not by compassion but by the necessity of appearing righteous.

Eliza's name moved through them as a low sound, not a whisper exactly, but a shared breath. She heard her surname once, then again. Each time it sounded less like an identifier and more like a verdict being tried on the tongue.

Mercy's hand remained locked around Eliza's wrist. Not a girl's hand held by her mother now, but a tether, desperate and strong. Nathaniel walked on Eliza's other side, close enough that his sleeve brushed her arm. She could feel his anger through the stiffness of him, the way his shoulders seemed too square for the narrow aisle.

The pale-eyed man led them, unhurried. The broader man and the others fanned slightly behind, guiding the Harrows forward without touching them, as if they could claim later that no force had been used.

Near the front, a table had been set beneath the pulpit, and on it lay a book. Not the black book, Eliza told herself at once, not that. This one was brown and ordinary, a ledger perhaps, a record of tithes or births. Yet the sight of any bound volume on a table made her stomach clench, and for an instant she smelled damp leather that was not in the room.

A man rose behind the table, tall and thin, his hair pulled back, his face long with fatigue and importance. Beside him sat another, broader through the chest, with hands folded as if he meant to pray but had chosen instead to judge. To one side, near the wall, stood Reverend Hale, his posture attentive, his eyes too sharp for comfort. Eliza had seen men like him on the road sometimes, ministers who traveled with their certainty packed tight as scripture. There was nothing gentle in the way he watched.

The pale-eyed man stopped and inclined his head to the table. "Magistrate," he said.

The tall man's gaze slid over Nathaniel, over Mercy, over Samuel, and then landed on Eliza with a small, involuntary pause. Eliza felt it like a pressure against her skin. Not attraction, not admiration. The moment when a man matches a face to a fear he has been fed.

"This is the family?" the magistrate asked.

"It is," the pale-eyed man replied. "They came yesterday. This morning there was testimony in the store. Then the afflicted spoke her name at the common."

"Spoke her name," the magistrate repeated softly, as if savoring the detail that required no argument.

Nathaniel stepped forward. "Sir," he began, and his voice was steady only because he forced it. "We have been dragged here on the strength of a madman's dream. My daughter has done nothing."

A murmur passed through the benches, disapproval at the word madman more than at the injustice. Eliza saw a woman's lips pinch tight. A man's jaw flex.

The magistrate lifted one hand, palm out. It was a small gesture, but it silenced the room with practiced ease. "No one says she is guilty," he said, and Eliza felt the lie in it like a thin film over rot. "We seek only to understand the matter and preserve the town."

Mercy's grip tightened. "Understand," she said, her voice carefully controlled. "Then ask questions of sense. Ask where she has been. Ask who she has spoken to. Ask how a child in the road could know a name she has never heard."

Reverend Hale shifted slightly. "Names may be carried," he said, and his tone held neither excitement nor pity. Only certainty, the kind that turns speculation into doctrine. "They may be given."

Nathaniel snapped his gaze toward him. "Given by whom?"

Reverend Hale did not look away. "By whatever seeks purchase."

Eliza's throat tightened. She stared at Hale and felt, absurdly, that he had already seen her somewhere else. Not on the road, not in the store, not in any waking place. In a story he had decided was true before he ever met her.

The magistrate leaned forward. "Girl," he said, and the word girl sounded like an object being pointed out. "State your name."

Eliza felt Mercy's fingers tremble around her wrist. The request should have been harmless. It was not. She had heard her name spoken too many times today by mouths that should not have known it.

"Eliza Harrow," she answered, and her voice sounded distant, as if it came from the far end of a long room.

A low sound rose from the benches, not surprise now, but satisfaction. Eliza had given them the shape they wanted. Her name, spoken in this room, sounded like ink being pressed into paper.

"And you deny," the magistrate said, "that you visited Josiah in the night."

"I deny it," Eliza said.

"Do you deny," Reverend Hale asked, stepping forward half a pace, "that you have seen a book in your dreams?"

Eliza's stomach turned. She wanted to say no. She wanted to say she had never seen any such thing, that the flickers were nothing but fear and suggestion. But the question itself was a trap, because answering either way made room for a story.

"I have had no such dream," she said, and hated the weakness in the sentence. She had dreamed of a quill scratching, though she had not known what it was. She had tasted iron in her mouth when she woke. She had seen, behind her eyelids, a page and her own name forming.

Reverend Hale's eyes narrowed a fraction, not in anger, but in attention, as if he had heard the seam in her denial.

The magistrate turned slightly. "Bring the afflicted," he said.

A shiver moved through the room. Eliza heard a bench creak. Somewhere a child made a small sound and was hushed instantly.

Two men at the back opened the side door, and cold air spilled in again. The afflicted girl was led inside, not by her hand, but by her elbows, as though she might float away if they did not anchor her. She looked smaller than she had outside, her feet bare despite the damp, her hair hanging loose and uncombed. Her eyes were open but not focused on anything human. She seemed to look through the bodies in the room as if they were made of smoke.

When she reached the front, she stopped abruptly, like a horse refusing a step. Her head tilted toward Eliza without her eyes moving.

"Eliza Harrow," she whispered, and the whisper carried.

Mercy made a sound like breath ripped short. Nathaniel's hand lifted as if to reach for Eliza's shoulder, to pull her back behind him.

The magistrate's voice was gentle now, almost tender. "Child," he said to the afflicted girl, "who troubles you?"

The girl's lips parted. For a moment Eliza thought she would say nothing. Then the girl's gaze snapped into focus so suddenly it made Eliza's heart jolt. Those eyes, dark and shining, fixed on Eliza with a terrible directness.

"She came," the girl said. "She stood by my bed and smelled like wet earth."

Eliza's mouth went dry. She tasted iron again. She could not tell if it was fear, if she had bitten her cheek anew, or if it was the room itself doing something to her.

"I did not," Eliza said, and the words sounded thin against the girl's calm.

The afflicted girl's mouth curved slightly, not in happiness, but in a strange knowing. "She says she did not," the girl echoed, as if repeating a familiar line from a script. Then she added, softer, "They always say."

A murmur rose. Not outrage, not grief. Approval. Eliza looked at the faces in the benches and saw something that made her stomach hollow: relief. Not relief that she might be innocent, but relief that the world had become simple again.

That a shape had been given to their fear and it could be named, bound, handled.

Nathaniel stepped forward in a single hard movement. "This is wicked," he said, and the word cracked through the room like a whip. "You are using a sick child to damn my daughter."

The broader man moved at once, stepping into Nathaniel's path. Another man came from the side, not rushing, but closing distance with the inevitability of a door swinging shut.

Nathaniel did not stop. He tried to shove past, shoulder first, driven by the animal need to put his body between his child and the story that was tightening around her.

Hands reached for him.

The first grip caught his arm. Nathaniel jerked away. A second hand seized his coat. He swung his elbow back and struck someone in the ribs. A sound of pain, quickly swallowed.

In the bench rows, women drew in breath. Men leaned forward as if drawn by instinct to watch force become justified.

"Do not," Mercy said, and it was not a plea to the town. It was to Nathaniel. Eliza heard it and understood at once what Mercy understood: resistance was being collected like kindling.

Nathaniel's face twisted, fury and helplessness warring in him. "Get your hands off me," he snarled.

The broader man spoke low, as if offering a reasonable correction. "Do not make it worse."

Nathaniel made a sound that was almost a laugh, harsh and disbelieving. "Worse?"

He tried again, and this time the men did not merely block him. They took him. Two caught his arms. Another grabbed the back of his collar and yanked him down and back, forcing him off balance. Nathaniel's boot scraped the floor, and he nearly went to one knee before he forced himself upright again.

Mercy surged forward, Samuel clinging to her skirts. "Stop," she cried, and her voice broke the way wood breaks under too much weight. "Stop it, stop it, he has done nothing."

The magistrate's hand lifted again, that small gesture of control. "Hold him," he said, calm as ever. "He is frightened. He will calm."

Hold him. As if Nathaniel were an animal to be steadied.

Eliza moved without thinking, a step toward her father, her body lurching forward as if it could interrupt what was happening by being present.

Mercy's grip snapped from her wrist to her sleeve, catching her, pulling her back.

"No," Mercy whispered fiercely. "No, Eliza."

Eliza's chest constricted. The room tilted slightly. She could hear her own breath too loud, too fast. She watched her father's face, red with strain, his jaw clenched so hard it trembled. He looked past the hands holding him, straight at Eliza, and in his eyes she saw the thing he would not say aloud: I cannot stop this.

A man's voice from the side, brisk and official, cut through. "Take the girl."

Eliza froze.

She did not see which mouth had spoken at first. She only felt the sentence land, heavy and final, like a door barred.

Two men stepped toward her. Not running, not lunging. Walking with the composed purpose of men who believed they were doing something necessary. The broader man glanced toward the magistrate as if to confirm, then nodded once.

Mercy yanked Eliza closer, wrapping an arm around her as if she could fuse their bodies together. "You will not touch her," Mercy said, and there was a rawness in her voice that was not anger anymore. It was terror stripped of manners.

Reverend Hale watched, his face unreadable, and Eliza realized with a sick lurch that he was not here to intervene. He was here to observe, to take the moment into himself and later swear to it as proof.

The first hand caught Eliza's forearm. The grip was firm, not cruel, but impersonal. A second hand closed around her other arm.

Eliza's mind flashed with absurd detail: the calluses on the man's thumb, the smell of damp wool, the faint trace of ink in the crease of a finger. She thought of Josiah's blackened hands. She thought of the quill. She thought of names written as ownership.

"No," Eliza said, and it came out as breath more than sound.

Mercy struck at the hands with her free fist, hitting a wrist, then a shoulder. Someone caught Mercy's arm and pushed her back. Samuel cried out, high and startled, and then another hand pulled him away from Mercy's skirts so he would not be trampled.

Nathaniel roared and surged, and the men holding him tightened their grips. One drove a forearm into Nathaniel's chest, forcing him back. Nathaniel's head snapped as he was struck across the mouth, quick and hard. Eliza saw the instant of shock on his face before it turned into blood.

The sight did something to her. Not a clean breaking, but a slip, like ice giving underfoot. Her father bleeding in a meetinghouse, her mother held back, her brother's cry swallowed by the room's hunger for order.

This was not happening because they had done wrong.

It was happening because the town believed it must.

The men pulled Eliza forward. Her boots dragged for half a step, then caught, and she stumbled. Hands tightened, correcting her like she was a sack shifted for balance.

Mercy's voice rose again, hoarse and pleading. "Eliza! Eliza, look at me!"

Eliza tried. She turned her head and saw her mother's face, strained and pale, eyes wide with the knowledge that love was not a shield here. Mercy's mouth formed Eliza's name again, but Eliza barely heard it over the pounding in her ears.

As Eliza was hauled toward the side aisle, she looked at the faces watching. Not all of them were cruel. Some were frightened. Some were solemn. A few looked almost apologetic.

But every face held the same fixed thing beneath the surface.

Conviction.

And Eliza understood, in the moment the hands tightened and her mother's grasp finally slipped away, that conviction did not require hatred. Conviction was cleaner than hatred. It let people do terrible things while feeling righteous.

They took her as if they were taking a necessary object from a room.

As if she were not a girl being seized, but a problem being carried to its proper place.

And as the meetinghouse door opened to the gray light again, Eliza felt something inside her begin to fracture, not because she believed their story, but because she could no longer find any place where truth mattered more than what others were certain they had seen.

The air outside the meetinghouse was colder than it had any right to be, as if the gray daylight had been wrung out and left only damp. The door swung wide and held for a moment, framing Eliza between dark interior and the washed-out common, and she had the strange sensation that she was being presented.

Not to God.

To Salem.

Hands kept her moving. The grip on her arms did not tighten into punishment; it remained firm in the way of men carrying something they told themselves must not be dropped. Her boots struck the threshold and then the meetinghouse steps, and she stumbled once, caught before she could fall. It was not kindness that steadied her. It was procedure.

She turned her head, searching for her mother in the doorway.

Mercy was there, half held and half holding herself upright, her shawl pulled askew, one sleeve dragged down. A man's hand hovered near her elbow, not quite grasping now, as if even he had decided he had done enough to her and did not want the shame of doing more. Mercy's mouth was open, her lips forming Eliza's name again, but the words did not arrive whole. They were torn up by breath, by the crush of bodies shifting to see.

Samuel's face appeared near Mercy's hip, pinched and pale, his eyes too large. Someone had pulled him back far enough that he would not be caught in the movement, and he stood there with both fists clenched in his shirt as if he could hold himself together by gripping cloth.

Nathaniel was behind them, still inside the meetinghouse. Eliza caught only a glimpse: his head thrown forward against the arms pinning him, blood bright on his mouth, his eyes wild with a kind of disbelief that looked like grief in a man's face.

He shouted her name.

The sound reached her, but it seemed to cross a great distance, and when it touched her it did not land like rescue. It landed like a thing being torn away. Eliza tried to answer, tried to shape his name in return, but the air felt thick in her throat. Nothing came out but a small, raw breath.

The men moved her down the steps and onto the common. The earth there was packed and dark with damp. It should have been familiar ground, open space, the kind of place a person could run if they had the chance. But there was nowhere to run. The town had made itself into a wall without needing to build one.

People stood at the edge of the common in loose lines. Not a mob pressed tight, not a crowd that had lost itself to frenzy. They left space between one another, as though each person wished to keep their own righteousness clean and separate. But their eyes were joined.

Eliza felt them strike her like pellets of cold rain.

Some faces she recognized from the road and the store, the watchers behind glass and shutters. Others she had not seen before, but that did not matter. They all looked at her as if they were seeing the same thing, the same shape they had been told to see.

The pale-eyed man walked slightly ahead, turned half toward the men holding Eliza, as if guiding an errand. He did not look back at Mercy or Nathaniel. There was no need. The family had already been placed where the town wanted them: divided.

"Eliza Harrow," someone murmured as she passed, and another voice answered with a soft sound of agreement. The name moved through them like wind through dry stalks, a rustling that did not require any one mouth to be loud.

Eliza's gaze skated over the faces as she was pulled forward.

A woman stood with her hands folded at her waist, lips pressed tight. Her eyes were wet, but she did not blink. She looked as though she pitied Eliza, and that pity felt more humiliating than hatred would have. Pity meant the woman had already accepted what was happening as inevitable, as deserved by the rules she believed governed the world.

Beside her, a man watched with his jaw set, his chin lifted slightly. His expression held disapproval, but not of the men taking a girl away. Disapproval of the disorder Nathaniel had made, the way blood had spattered the clean story Salem was trying to tell itself. He looked at Eliza as if she were the cause of that mess, as if her body alone had dragged sin into their daylight.

A boy, younger than Samuel, stood on tiptoe to see. His mother's hand clamped his shoulder, hard enough to hold him still. His eyes were bright not with fear but with a quick, hungry curiosity, the way children look at dead animals in road ruts before they are taught to look away.

Eliza wanted to speak to him. To tell him to remember her face, to remember this, and grow into a man who could not do it.

But the words did not come, and she knew even if they did, the boy would not hear them as warning. He would hear them as proof that she could speak to him without moving her lips, that she could reach into him the way they claimed she reached into dreams.

It was not only the faces that watched her. It was the way they watched: with the calm that comes when a person believes they are participating in something holy.

Conviction.

She had thought conviction looked like anger, like shouting, like wild eyes and spittle. But those were the easy villains, the ones you could hate without question.

Conviction, she realized, looked like neighborly attention. It looked like a man straightening his coat before stepping forward to do something terrible. It looked like a woman pressing her palm to her throat as if praying, even as her gaze stayed fixed on a girl being taken away. It looked like solemn nods.

No one reached out to touch Eliza, not even to strike her. They did not need to. Their certainty had already done the work a hand would do. It had turned her into an object to be handled by the proper people.

She tried to hold her head up, to keep her spine straight under the men's grips. If she bowed, they would read it as guilt. If she cried, they would read it as confession. If she fought, they would read it as the Devil's strength.

The town had arranged it so that every possible version of her could only mean one thing.

The broader man walked on her right, close enough that she could feel his shoulder's heat through wool. He had a small, old scar along his jaw, pale against weathered skin. He did not look at her with pleasure. He did not even look at her with disgust. He looked as if he was doing a task he wished had fallen to someone else, but would do it well because he believed in doing things well.

"Eliza," Mercy cried again from behind, her voice breaking now into something unmistakably animal, the sound a mother makes when her child is taken and her arms are empty.

The sound struck Eliza like a blow. Her composure slipped, just a little, and her chin trembled.

The broader man heard it too. His mouth tightened, and for an instant something like discomfort crossed his face. Not enough to stop him, not enough to loosen his grip.

He said, low, without turning, as if speaking to the pale-eyed man ahead, "We should move her quicker."

"To spare her?" the pale-eyed man asked, and his voice held mild surprise, as if the idea of sparing Eliza had not occurred to him.

The broader man did not answer directly. "To spare trouble," he said.

"Trouble comes from hiding," the pale-eyed man replied. "Let them see. Let them remember what is done with such matters."

Eliza's stomach twisted. The words were not spoken like a threat. They were spoken like instruction, like a lesson being taught to a town.

They passed close to the afflicted girl again, or perhaps it was another; Eliza could not tell, because the children began to blur together in her mind, pale faces and unfocused eyes, instruments held carefully by adult hands. This one sat on the ground near the meetinghouse steps, her knees drawn up, her hair in a dark rope down her back. She rocked very slightly, as if soothing herself.

As Eliza was brought near, the girl lifted her head. Her eyes met Eliza's.

In that gaze there was no fear at all.

Only recognition.

The girl's lips moved. Eliza leaned without meaning to, a small, desperate tilt, as if the girl might speak something that would cut through this net of belief and return her to her mother's hand, her father's solid presence, the ordinary's too-close tables.

Instead, the girl whispered, almost tenderly, "It is already written."

A sound moved through the nearby watchers, not outrage but satisfaction. Eliza felt her skin prickle from scalp to wrists.

The voice in her own ear returned, so soft it might have been her own thought answering the girl's words.

Yes.

Eliza's breath caught. She did not turn her head. There was no one close enough to whisper into her hair besides the men holding her, and they did not move their mouths.

The voice was inside the space her mind used to belong to.

She clenched her teeth so hard her jaw ached. Her bitten cheek stung, and the taste of iron returned, stronger now. She did not know whether it was blood or memory or something else pressing up from beneath her thoughts.

They drew nearer to a building off the common, lower than the meetinghouse, its windows small and its boards darker with age and damp. Eliza had not noticed it when they first arrived, or perhaps she had and her mind had refused to name it. A place that did not welcome. A place that kept.

As they approached, the crowd thinned, not because fewer people were interested, but because interest did not require closeness. They could watch from where they stood and still feel themselves part of it.

Eliza turned her head slightly, needing one last look behind.

Mercy had broken free of whatever light hold had been placed on her. She stood in the meetinghouse doorway with both hands braced against the frame as if she might tear it loose. Her face was streaked now, not with tears so much as damp from breath and strain. Samuel clung to her skirt. Nathaniel was still inside, still held; Eliza saw the men's bodies around him like fence posts. He was trying to push through them, his mouth open in a shout she could not hear at this distance.

Mercy's eyes found Eliza's across the common. For an instant the crowd's faces fell away, the town's murmur vanished, and there was only her mother's gaze, fierce and pleading and utterly human.

Eliza tried to hold onto it.

Then one of the men guiding her shifted his grip, pulling her head forward again, and the line of sight snapped. Mercy became a shape behind other shapes, and Eliza's world narrowed back to the shoulder at her side, the packed earth under her boots, the waiting door ahead.

The faces around her remained calm, almost tranquil. They watched with the serene attention of people who believed they were saving themselves.

Eliza understood then that conviction did not need to snarl.

Conviction could smile faintly and step aside to let a girl be taken, and never once question whether the hands were wrong.

The door ahead opened, and the darker air inside reached for her like a held breath.

The men guided Eliza toward it, and Salem, behind them, watched with all the quiet certainty of a town that had found a name it could close its hands around.

The doorway swallowed her.

The building off the common was colder inside than out, not with winter's bite but with the chill of stone that had forgotten sunlight. The threshold was worn in a shallow groove, a place where many feet had crossed unwillingly. Eliza's boots scuffed it as the men guided her through, and for an instant she imagined the groove as a line drawn on a page, the kind that told you where to write your name.

The air smelled of damp wood, old sweat, and something sharp beneath it, like vinegar or lye. It stung her nose. The light was thin, coming through narrow windows set high, too high for a person to look out of. Those windows seemed designed for the opposite purpose: to let daylight witness without letting anyone be witnessed in return.

Hands remained on her arms until the door shut behind them.

The sound of it was not loud, but it was final. The heavy thud and the soft scrape of a bar sliding into place made the world rearrange itself in Eliza's mind. Outside, Salem watched. Inside, Salem held.

A narrow entry opened into a corridor. The boards underfoot were uneven, damp in places where the air could not move. Along one wall hung pegs with hats and coats, ordinary things that looked obscene in this place, as if men could come here to take a girl away and then hang their hat like they had only stopped in for church.

The broader man stayed close on her right. The pale-eyed man walked ahead, his pace unhurried. The others trailed behind, their boots making a steady rhythm that felt like counting.

Eliza tried to keep her breathing even, because she had learned something in the last hour: the town fed on reaction. Any crack in her composure would be taken as a seam to pull.

Still, her thoughts slipped.

Her mother's face flashed before her, fierce in the meetinghouse doorway. Her father's mouth bloodied, shouting her name. Samuel's small hands clenched in his shirt. The images came too quickly to hold and too quickly to chase away. They made her chest feel too tight, as if grief were a cord being drawn around her ribs.

One of the men behind them cleared his throat.

"Eliza Harrow," he said quietly, not addressing her so much as confirming her, like checking a label on a jar.

She did not answer. She stared at the pale line of corridor ahead and forced her feet to keep moving, one step at a time.

At the end of the corridor, a door stood open. Beyond it, the space widened into a room that was almost empty except for a table, a chair, and a small iron stove gone cold. A lantern hung from a beam, unlit. The room held that peculiar scent of places where fear sweats into the wood and never leaves.

A man waited there, older than the others, his hair thinning and his beard trimmed close. His sleeves were rolled. He had ink stains on the side of his thumb and the edge of his fingernails, the kind that came from keeping records. That ink did something to Eliza's stomach. She thought of

Josiah waking with blackened fingers. She thought of the scratching sound in her dream. She swallowed and tasted iron.

The pale-eyed man inclined his head. “Constable,” he said.

The older man’s gaze slid to Eliza with clinical attention. He did not leer. He did not smile. He looked at her the way a butcher looks at an animal brought in for slaughter, not with cruelty, but with the calm that comes from believing it is his work.

“The Harrow girl,” the constable said, as if to himself.

Eliza forced her voice out, thin but steady. “My name is Eliza Harrow.”

The constable’s eyes flicked to the pale-eyed man. “Yes,” he said, and the word made her feel foolish for speaking at all. He stepped closer, hands on his hips. “You will sit.”

“I have done nothing,” Eliza said. It was not the first time she had said it today. Each time it felt less like truth and more like a phrase she was being allowed to speak until the town grew tired of hearing it.

The constable did not argue. “Sit,” he repeated, and nodded to the chair at the table.

The hands on her arms steered her forward. They did not shove her down, but they guided her with the same impersonal firmness as before, and Eliza felt a flare of something hot in her chest. Not courage. Humiliation.

She sat.

The chair was rough beneath her palms. The table's surface was scarred by old cuts. On one side of it lay a coil of rope, neatly kept. Not displayed as threat, simply present, as if it belonged here the way bread belonged on a kitchen shelf.

The constable sat opposite her. The pale-eyed man remained standing, positioned where he could see her face in profile, as if her expression mattered more than her words. The broader man leaned lightly against the doorframe, arms folded. The others had stepped back into the corridor, though Eliza could still see them in the dimness, shadows with boots.

"Your family will be kept until order is satisfied," the constable said. He spoke as though describing weather. "Your mother and brother will return to the ordinary. Your father will be seen to."

Eliza's breath hitched despite her effort. "Seen to," she repeated. "You struck him."

The broader man's mouth tightened. "He struck first."

"He tried to reach his daughter," Eliza said, and her voice rose a fraction before she could stop it.

The pale-eyed man's gaze settled on her like a hand. "All men claim noble cause when they resist," he said mildly. "It does not change what must be done."

The constable reached for something on the table that Eliza had not noticed at first: a small book, brown leather, its corners rubbed. Not black. Not the thing that haunted the edges of her mind. But the sight of it made her skin prickle anyway.

He opened it, licked his thumb, and turned a page with practiced ease.

"State your age," he said.

Eliza stared at him. "Seventeen."

He marked it down. The scratch of his quill against paper was soft, but it went through her like a wire. Her stomach rolled. For a moment the room around her wavered, as if the sound had loosened something in her skull.

A flicker came uninvited: candlelight, a page waiting. A black cover, damp to the touch. The quill moving as if it knew the path of her name already.

Eliza's hand twitched on the tabletop.

The constable looked up. “Your hands,” he said.

Eliza’s throat tightened. “What of them?”

“Keep them still,” he answered, and wrote again. He was writing even when she had not spoken. As if her movements were also testimony.

Eliza forced her fingers flat against the wood and held them there until the joints ached.

The constable asked, “Do you deny visiting Josiah Waller in the night?”

“Yes.”

He wrote. The quill scratched. Eliza felt the sound under her teeth.

“Do you deny speaking with the afflicted child and bidding her speak names?”

“Yes.”

Scratch, scratch. A neat, indifferent sound.

Eliza’s mind began to separate from her body in small, frightening ways. She watched herself sitting there. She watched her own mouth form words. The distance was slight, like stepping back from a mirror and still seeing your face, but it grew with each question, each scratch of ink.

"Have you seen a book in your dreams?" the constable asked without looking up, as if reading the question from a list.

Eliza's breath caught. The pale-eyed man's attention sharpened. The broader man shifted his weight, the boards creaking.

"I dream," Eliza said carefully, "as anyone does."

"That is not an answer," the constable said.

She tried to think of her mother's voice: Do not answer anything that is not asked. But everything they asked was shaped to force her into their story.

Eliza swallowed. Her mouth tasted of blood again, and she realized with dull surprise that she had bitten her cheek until it reopened.

"I have not seen the Devil's book," she said.

The pale-eyed man's eyes narrowed, just slightly, as if he heard the trapdoor in her words. Not seen the Devil's book. As if there were another book she might have seen.

The constable's quill paused. He looked up at last, meeting her gaze with the calmness of a man who did not need to hate her to help ruin her.

"You know its name," he said.

Eliza's skin went cold. "Everyone in Salem knows its name."

A brief silence followed. In it, Eliza heard something else, so soft she might have imagined it: the faintest rustle, like paper shifting.

Not in the room.

Inside her hearing.

The whisper came, patient as breath.

You are learning.

Eliza's heart stuttered. Her eyes darted to the doorframe where the broader man stood, but his mouth had not moved. The constable's lips were still. The pale-eyed man was watching her, expression composed.

The whisper was not theirs.

It slid through her thoughts with an intimacy that made her feel exposed.

You are being made ready.

Eliza pressed her palms harder to the table, as if she could anchor herself with pressure. "Stop," she said, and did not know whether she spoke to the men or to what moved beneath her words.

The constable's eyebrows lifted a fraction. "Stop what?"

Eliza's throat tightened until her next breath came shallow. She could not tell them, I hear a voice, without giving them exactly what they wanted. She could not deny it without feeling it again, the way denial in Salem became fuel.

The pale-eyed man leaned forward slightly. "If you are troubled, girl, you may speak. It is better brought into light."

Light, Eliza thought, and almost laughed. This room held no light that belonged to mercy.

She stared at the constable's small brown book, at the ink marks that were becoming her in someone else's hand. The sight made something inside her shift again, a subtle cracking. Not a single break, but many fine fractures spreading through glass.

Because she understood, suddenly and completely, that she could answer every question with truth and still be written down as guilty. The record would not hold what happened. It would hold what Salem needed to be true.

Her mother's face returned in her mind, and this time Eliza could not hold onto it. The image slid away as if greased, leaving only the shape of Mercy's mouth forming Eliza's name without sound.

Eliza blinked hard. Her eyes stung. She focused on the grain of the table, the tiny grooves, the dark knot in the wood.

The constable closed his book with a soft, final tap and stood. "We will keep her here," he said to the pale-eyed man. "Until the magistrates are ready to proceed proper."

The broader man unfolded from the doorframe and came closer. "Where?" he asked.

The constable nodded toward the corridor beyond. "The lower room. The one that holds quiet."

The pale-eyed man's gaze stayed on Eliza. "See that she is watched," he said, as if speaking about a candle that might gutter.

The broader man's hand reached for Eliza's arm again.

Eliza flinched before he touched her, and the flinch was the worst thing that could have happened, because it was not fear of pain. It was fear of being moved like an object again, fear of being carried farther from the parts of herself that still believed in ordinary life.

The hand closed around her forearm.

Eliza rose because the grip made standing inevitable.

As they led her out of the room, she looked back once, not at the men, but at the table where the quill lay. The constable had set it down carefully, nib up, ink dark at its point.

For an instant, just an instant, Eliza thought she saw a second quill beside it that was not there, a shadow of something older and blacker. She smelled damp leather so strongly her stomach lurched.

Then the corridor swallowed her again.

The door behind her shut, muffling the sounds of the common and the meetinghouse and her father's distant fury. Each step deeper into the building felt like walking away from her own name and into the place where it could be rewritten.

The whisper returned, as if pleased by her silence.

It is easier when you stop fighting what is already written.

Eliza shut her eyes for one heartbeat and felt the fractures inside her spread, not with the sharp pain of a break, but with the slow, terrible sensation of something giving way that she had not known was bearing weight.

When she opened her eyes again, she was still walking.

But she was no longer certain she was the one choosing where her feet went.

Chapter 5

The Room Without Time

They took her down a narrower passage where the air turned stale and close, as if it had been held in the boards too long. The corridor bent once, then again, and Eliza lost any sense of how the building sat against the common. Light thinned to a dim gray that did not come from lamps but from somewhere far above, leaking through cracks the way a secret leaks when it cannot be kept.

The broader man kept his hand on her forearm. His grip never bruised, never softened. It was the same grip from the meetinghouse steps, the grip of a task performed properly.

Ahead, the constable's "lower room" waited behind a door that looked no different from the others, except for the iron banding across it and the bolt set into the frame. The man leading her produced a key from a ring at his belt. The keys clinked lightly, a sound too small for what it meant.

Eliza felt the whisper brush the edge of her thoughts again, not like speech carried through air, but like memory pretending to be her own.

Lower.

She clenched her jaw and kept her eyes fixed on the door as if looking away would make it worse.

The key turned with a reluctant scrape. The bolt slid back. The door opened inward.

The room beyond was not large. It was not a dungeon with chains and bones, not the kind of place a girl's imagination might conjure to match the word cell. It was plainer than that, which made it worse. A square of space with rough boards and a single narrow cot pushed against one wall. A bucket in the corner. A high window, no bigger than a Bible, set near the ceiling so that even if she stood on the cot she would not see out. The little glass was clouded, as if it had been breathed on for years and never wiped clean.

The air smelled of damp straw and old sweat, and beneath it, faintly, that sharp, clean bite she had smelled before in the corridor, vinegar or lye meant to scrub away what could not truly be scrubbed away.

They guided her in. Eliza's boots scuffed the threshold.

There was a mark in the wood where many boots had scuffed it before.

The broader man released her arm just inside the room, not from mercy but because the space was small enough to make restraint unnecessary. A second man stood behind him, half in the doorway, half out, as if undecided whether to witness what happened next.

"Sit," the broader man said.

Eliza did not move at once. Her eyes traveled the room again, collecting details the way a person gathers kindling against a cold night. Cot. Bucket. Window. Bare boards, stained darker near the corner where damp had settled. A nail hammered into the wall with no coat hung on it. The faint impression of something once chained there, though no chain remained.

"You can stand if you like," the man added, his tone almost reasonable. "You will still be here."

The simplicity of it hit her harder than any shouted threat. Eliza felt the room tilt slightly, not because she was faint, but because her mind tried to place this moment into a world where rules made sense. It did not fit. Nothing in Salem fit except the story they were writing.

She sat on the cot, careful, as if it might be taken from under her if she committed to it too quickly. The straw mattress shifted, releasing a sour, dusty breath.

The broader man watched her hands as she lowered herself. She noticed and folded them together tightly, fingers laced until the knuckles pressed white. She had learned already that movements could be recorded even when words were not.

The man in the doorway cleared his throat. "Do we chain her?"

The broader man's eyes flicked to him. "No," he said after a moment. "Not unless told. She's a girl."

Eliza almost laughed at the word girl, because it sounded like an argument for gentleness, and gentleness had nothing to do with what they were doing. A girl could still be taken. A girl could still be written down.

The broader man hesitated, then looked at Eliza. "There will be questions," he said. "If you answer plain, it will go easier."

Go easier. Eliza's mouth tasted of iron again, and she did not know whether it was blood from where she had bitten her cheek or the memory of that quill scratching across paper. She wondered, with a sudden sick clarity, if they said those words to everyone, like a blessing before a burial.

"I answered plain already," she said. Her voice sounded strange in the small room, too loud and too thin at once.

The broader man did not argue with her. Argument was not his role. He only nodded, as if acknowledging a child's complaint, and stepped back.

The door began to close.

Panic rose in Eliza's chest, quick and sharp, and she stood without meaning to, her hands lifting slightly as if she could catch the door before it shut. The broader man paused, watching her with the same measured attention he had shown in the meetinghouse.

"What of my family?" Eliza asked. The question came out hoarse, scraped raw by all the times her name had been spoken today. "My mother. My brother. My father."

The broader man's expression tightened at the word father, perhaps remembering the blood on Nathaniel's mouth, the struggle that had provided Salem with one more proof. "They will be kept," he said. "They will not be harmed if they do not make harm."

Eliza stared at him. "He made harm?" she demanded, and heard the tremble in her own voice. "He reached for his child."

The man's gaze slid away for a fraction of a second, and that small avoidance felt like the only honesty she had received from him. When he spoke again, his voice was flatter. "Keep yourself," he said. "Do not trouble your own case."

Her own case. As if this were a matter she could manage with care, as if it were a stain she could scrub out if she worked hard enough.

Eliza's fingers curled into fists. She forced them open. "I want to see my mother."

"No," the broader man said, and there was no cruelty in it, only certainty. "Not now."

The door shut.

Wood met wood with a dull thud. The bolt slid home outside with a metallic scrape that vibrated through the boards. Then came the smaller sound of the key turning again, the lock settling into place.

Eliza stood in the center of the room, staring at the door. She listened for footsteps.

They did not leave at once. She could hear them shifting outside, a soft creak of leather, the faint tap of a boot heel. A presence stationed there, not close enough to speak to her, close enough to remind her she was not alone.

Watched.

She turned her head toward the high window. The light there was gray and uncertain. It did not look like afternoon or morning. It did not look like anything that could be trusted. The glass held the world at a distance, and the distance did not comfort her. It only made it clear how much could happen beyond her reach.

She sat again, slowly, and pressed her palms to her skirt as if anchoring herself to her own body. The cot creaked under her weight, a small sound that seemed to carry too far.

Silence arrived after that. Not the comfortable silence of a house at rest, not even the tense silence of people hiding. This silence had thickness, like the air had been soaked in it. It filled her ears until she began to notice other things: the slow drip of water somewhere in the building, too irregular to measure time; the faint rustle of something moving in the wall, a mouse perhaps, or simply wood settling in damp; her own breathing, which sounded like a stranger's breath in the dark.

She tried to pray. She had prayed as a child, as anyone did, and as she grew older the habit had become quieter, less certain, but still there like a hand reaching for a rail in the dark.

Now the words would not come in order.

Our Father, she thought, and the phrase caught on the shape of her own father's face, bloodied in the meetinghouse, eyes wild with helplessness. She swallowed hard, and her throat tightened until the next breath hurt.

She stood and crossed the room in three steps. In the corner, the bucket sat with a crusted ring along its rim. She turned away quickly, ashamed not because it was filthy but because it was meant to make her remember she was an animal with needs, a body that could be reduced.

On the wall above the bucket, someone had scratched marks into the wood. Faint, shallow grooves. At first she thought it was only damage, the careless work of a chair dragged too many times. Then she saw the pattern.

Lines. Grouped in fives.

Tally marks.

Her chest tightened. She reached out and traced one set lightly with her fingertip. The groove caught her skin.

Days, she thought. Someone had counted days in this room.

But the marks were not fresh. Some looked old, softened by time and damp. And beside them, lower, half hidden in shadow, were other scratches that did not form neat lines. Curves and angles, frantic and overlapping. Letters perhaps, or attempts at them.

Names.

Eliza pulled her hand back as if the wall were hot.

The whisper returned, so soft it almost blended with her own thoughts.

They counted.

She pressed her back to the opposite wall and stared at the scratches. Her mind tried to fix on facts. This is a cell. People have been held here. They counted to keep themselves from breaking.

And yet the sight of the tally marks made her feel as if the room had already begun to steal something from her, the same thing the road into Salem had stolen: the ability to know where she was in time.

Because what did five scratches mean when daylight did not look like day? When footsteps came and left without pattern? When questions could return at any hour they pleased, and sleep could be denied until the body forgot what it felt like to be rested?

She moved to the cot again and sat with her knees drawn up, arms wrapped around them. The posture made her feel smaller, and she hated that she needed it.

She tried to summon her mother's face with clarity. Mercy's eyes. The set of her jaw. The warmth of her hand clamped around Eliza's in the store, hard enough to hurt, as if pain could keep her present.

The memory slipped.

Not fully gone, but shifting, like an image in water disturbed by a stone. Eliza blinked hard and felt her eyes sting. She forced the picture back into focus.

My mother is real, she told herself. My father is real. Samuel is real. The road is real. The store. The meetinghouse. Blood. Hands.

The room listened without answering.

A shadow moved across the floor, slow and steady, as if something passed in the corridor outside. Eliza's head snapped up.

The shadow did not match any shape she could see. It did not align with the high window's weak light. It slid along the boards like a stain, and then it was gone.

Eliza held her breath, waiting for another sound, another proof that she had not imagined it.

Nothing.

Then, faintly, from somewhere beyond the door, a sound like paper being handled. Not loud enough to be clear. Just a small, dry rustle that raised the hairs along her arms.

And with it, in her mind's ear, the gentlest suggestion, intimate as breath at the edge of sleep:

Rest.

Eliza's throat tightened. "No," she whispered to the empty room, because she could not afford to answer the voice in her thoughts with silence. Silence was too easily mistaken for agreement.

The room remained still.

But the shadows at the corners seemed deeper than they had been a moment ago, as if they had leaned in closer to listen.

Eliza stayed curled on the cot until her legs cramped.

She told herself she would not lie down. Lying down felt too much like obeying the voice that had whispered Rest, too much like allowing the room to teach her its rules. But her body did not care what her pride wanted. The straw beneath her was thin and lumpy, the boards beneath it hard, and still her muscles begged for any position that did not demand she hold herself upright against fear.

She shifted, inch by inch, and the cot creaked like an old mouth opening.

The sound made her stop.

She listened, breath held, for the answer she dreaded: boots in the corridor, the scrape of the bolt drawn back, a man's voice calling her name as if it belonged to them now.

Nothing came.

Only the drip somewhere distant and the soft, irregular settling of the building, like a living thing adjusting its weight.

She let her breath out slowly. The air tasted stale, as though it had been breathed too many times and never refreshed. She tried again to pray, forcing the words into her head in the proper order.

Our Father, who art in Heaven—

But Heaven felt like a place with distance, and distance was what she was losing.

When she closed her eyes she saw Mercy in the store, chin lifted, voice sharp with controlled anger. Eliza tried to hold the image steady. Her mother's shawl, the way her fingers dug through Eliza's sleeve, the warning in the pressure. Do not speak unless spoken to. Do not answer what is not asked.

The picture wavered as if the air between them had turned to water.

Mercy's face blurred at the edges. Not vanishing, exactly, but losing its certainty, as though Eliza were trying to remember a person she had met once long ago instead of the woman who had held her wrist only hours ago and refused to let go.

Hours ago.

Eliza opened her eyes. The light through the high window looked the same as it had a moment before. Gray, reluctant, without any angle that marked morning or afternoon. If she had slept and woken, she would not have known.

The thought tightened her throat.

She sat up, then stood, needing motion to prove time still moved. She paced the small room: three steps to the bucket, three back to the cot, two to the wall with the tallies. The wood there held the scratches like scars. She ran her fingertip along them again, not counting, only feeling the shallow grooves.

Someone had stood where she stood. Someone had touched this wall with the same need to anchor themselves.

Eliza tried to picture that person, but her mind supplied only her own reflection, pale in the gray. It was easier to imagine herself in every past occupant than to admit she did not know if she would become one of them, leaving marks for the next.

She lowered her hand.

The whisper came, faint and near, as if the wall had exhaled it.

You will.

Eliza jerked away from the scratches so fast her shoulder struck the opposite wall. Pain sparked down her arm. The sting was sharp and real, and she clung to it for a heartbeat like a rope.

"No," she said aloud. The sound of her voice in the cell startled her. It sounded wrong here, too human for a room meant to reduce a person to a record. "No. You are not—"

She stopped. She did not know what she meant to finish. You are not real. You are not mine. You are not God.

Her tongue felt thick. The room accepted her unfinished sentence without reaction.

She went back to the cot and sat, palms pressed to her knees. She forced herself to name what she knew, the way a child recites lessons when frightened.

My name is Eliza Harrow.

The thought landed oddly. Not because it was untrue, but because her name had been handled too much today. Josiah's voice in the store, startled certainty. The afflicted girl's calm recitation on the common. The murmur of Salem shaping it into proof. The constable's book. State your name.

She had said it so many times it began to feel like a phrase anyone could speak, detached from her body.

She tried again, adding what she thought would make it solid.

I am Nathaniel's daughter. Mercy's daughter. Samuel's sister.

Samuel.

She seized on him, on the smallness of his hands, the way his voice had trembled at the ordinary. Father, where do we go? The memory came, but it came with a strange dislocation, as if Samuel were not behind her in the room but far away, a boy on a road she could no longer see clearly.

Eliza blinked. She felt a brief, irrational fear that if she could not picture Samuel's face with exactness, he might cease to exist. Not truly cease, of course. But in the way people cease when you are no longer allowed to speak of them, when their names become dangerous, when the town begins to treat them as attachments to your guilt rather than people.

She pressed her fingertips into her scalp, hard enough to hurt, as if pressure could push the images back into order.

She remembered the meetinghouse aisle: rigid benches, faces turned like one body, and her father lunging forward. She remembered the moment a hand struck Nathaniel's mouth and the flash of blood. That memory, at least, stayed sharp. Pain and violence kept their edges.

But in between the sharp moments, everything softened.

The road into Salem. The pines. The sense of being watched. She tried to recall the exact look of the general store's front window, the goods behind the glass, the broom leaning too neatly by the step. She could remember those details, but they floated without sequence. She could not tell which had happened first: Amos telling them to go upstairs, or Mercy's hand tightening in the store, or the voice on the porch saying, Keep your daughter near you.

That was how it began, she thought. Not with chains, not with darkness. With a suggestion spoken calmly through a door.

Keep your daughter near you.

Why had that frightened her so much? It was a reasonable instruction in a town with strangers.

But it had not been reasonable. It had been intimate, said like a man repeating something he had read.

Eliza's stomach rolled.

She closed her eyes and tried to force a different memory forward, one from before Salem. Her own bed at home. The smell of soap and clean linen. The sound of Samuel laughing in the yard. Her father's voice calling him in before dark.

The images came reluctantly, like a drawer swollen shut.

When they did come, they arrived in pieces. A corner of a quilt. A patch of sunlight on a floor. A voice she could not place with certainty.

It frightened her more than the whispers did.

Because if she could not reach her life before, then Salem would become the whole of her mind.

Salem would be the only time that mattered. The only reality.

She stood again, suddenly, as if she could outpace that loss. She went to the high window and climbed onto the cot, then stretched, fingertips brushing the sill. The window was too high, the glass too clouded. Even pressed close, she could see only a smear of gray and a faint suggestion of movement beyond, perhaps a shadow of a passerby, perhaps nothing.

She breathed against the glass. Her breath fogged it slightly, and for a heartbeat the outside sharpened: not shapes, not faces, only light that looked marginally brighter.

Then the fog thinned and the window returned to its dull opacity.

She slid off the cot and sat again, shoulders hunched against the cold. The bucket's odor drifted faintly from the corner. She heard the drip again, and then, after a long pause, a second drip, as if the building itself could not keep a steady count.

That irregularity made her mind itch. She wanted to measure time. She needed to know if she had been here an hour or a day.

Her gaze returned to the tally marks. Five. Five. Five. The groupings were careful, each fifth line slashed through the four before it. Whoever had made them had still been thinking clearly enough to keep order.

Eliza went to the wall and counted without meaning to. Her lips moved silently as her eyes traveled.

When she finished, she realized with a small chill that she could not remember the number she'd reached.

She started again, irritated with herself, forcing attention.

One, two, three, four, slash. One, two—

Her mind slipped sideways. The scratches began to look less like marks and more like letters, and for a heartbeat she thought she saw her own name there, carved into the boards beneath the tallies. Eliza Harrow. Not written in ink, but scored into wood by a desperate nail.

She leaned closer, breath shallow.

It was not her name. It was only frantic lines, overlapping, a ruined attempt at words.

Yet the certainty that it had been her name lingered like a smell.

She stumbled back, hand over her mouth. The taste of iron rose again, and she realized she had bitten the inside of her cheek without noticing, as if her body did it on its own to remind her she was still flesh.

A sound came from beyond the door.

Soft. Not the bolt. Not the key. Something lighter.

Paper.

The dry, careful rustle of a page turned.

Eliza froze, every muscle tightening. She stared at the door as if she could see through it, as if she might catch the shadow of a hand holding a book just outside her cell.

The room seemed to hold its breath with her.

Then the whisper returned, closer than before, so close she almost felt it on the rim of her ear.

Do not strain so hard to remember, it said, in the same patient gentleness that made her skin crawl. Remembering hurts.

Eliza's eyes stung. She pressed her back to the wall, sliding down until she sat on the floor, knees drawn up, arms wrapped around them.

"I won't forget," she whispered. She did not know whether she was speaking to the voice or to herself. "I won't."

A pause, as if something listened to her vow and found it tender.

Then, very softly, as though offering comfort:

You already are.

And in that moment Eliza felt it, not as a thought but as a physical sensation, like a thread snapping somewhere behind her ribs. A small, invisible break. Not dramatic, not final, but unmistakable.

She tried to pull Mercy's face up again, tried to hold the fierce shape of her mother's love in her mind.

For a heartbeat it came.

Then it slid, smearing at the edges, and Eliza was left clutching only the feeling of a hand around her wrist without being able to summon the exact lines of the hand that held her.

She shut her eyes tight, fighting panic, and listened to her own breathing in the darkening silence.

Somewhere outside, another page turned, slow and deliberate, like time being handled by someone else.

The room did not go quiet all at once. It settled.

Eliza sat with her knees drawn up, cheek pressed near her sleeve where the cloth still held the faintest road-dust smell, and listened as if listening could pull a shape from what surrounded her. The drip in the walls returned after a long pause, then stopped again. Somewhere beyond the door, a foot shifted. Leather creaked, small and slow, the way a man shifts when he has decided not to leave.

Then even that stopped.

Silence took its place with an almost careful thoroughness, filling the corners, smoothing itself over the boards, gathering in the space between her breaths. It was not the silence of an empty house. It had weight. It felt arranged, like the men outside had hung it up between them and her the way they hung their coats on pegs in the corridor.

She lifted her head and stared at the door.

The door did not look like a mouth, but it behaved like one. It held back sound. It swallowed it. It waited.

Eliza thought of the meetinghouse, the way the magistrate had silenced a room full of bodies with one raised palm. This silence was similar. A silence made, not found. A silence that belonged to Salem.

Her throat tightened and she forced air in and out through her nose, shallowly, because breathing too loudly felt like knocking. The more she tried to soften herself, the more she became aware of how loud her body was in the stillness. A faint scrape when she shifted her foot. The low friction of cloth against straw. The tiny click in her jaw when she swallowed.

The silence took those sounds and held them up to her, as if presenting evidence.

You are here, it seemed to say. You are alone. Every small motion is yours, and therefore yours to answer for.

She pushed herself up from the floor, because staying curled like a child felt like surrender. Her legs were stiff. She stood and pressed her palms to her skirt, smoothing it down, an ordinary gesture that would have meant nothing at home and meant too much here. She crossed to the cot and sat on its edge instead of the floor, spine straight, chin lifted slightly. She wanted to make her body remember it belonged to her.

The high window offered the same dull gray as before. No angle of sun. No shift of color. The light was not moving the way light should. It made the room feel sealed in a single moment that could be stretched to any length.

Eliza stared at the wall with the tally marks again. She did not count them this time. She only looked at the grooves, at the careful slashes through each fifth mark, and felt a sudden, unreasonable anger toward whoever had been steady enough to keep track. Their marks were proof that time had moved here once.

Now time behaved differently.

Now it felt as if the room had eaten the part of the day that told you what came next.

She listened harder. Not for the drip. Not for the guard outside. For anything that would mark a rhythm she could trust.

At first, nothing answered.

Then she realized there was a sound so faint she had taken it for part of her own hearing: a low, continuous hush that did not come from air moving. Not wind. Not breath. It was like the soft pressure in her ears when she went underwater as a child. The world muted, held at a distance, not gone but unwilling to reach her.

Eliza held her breath.

The hush remained.

It did not depend on her body. It existed with its own persistence, like an animal that did not need her permission to be in the room.

She turned her head slowly, scanning the corners. The room was plain: boards, stains, the bucket, the nail in the wall, the clouded window. Yet the hush seemed to come from everywhere at once, threaded through the wood.

A memory flickered, uninvited: the store, the bell ringing bright and obscene in the heavy quiet, and then the way the quiet had changed as people stopped moving. How stillness in a room could be made by attention, by many minds leaning toward the same story.

This felt like that, only stronger. This was attention without eyes. Witness without bodies.

Eliza's mouth went dry. "Who is there?" she whispered before she could stop herself.

The words were swallowed. The room did not echo them. It simply took them in and held them, as if weighing whether they deserved an answer.

She waited, heart tapping hard against her ribs.

Nothing.

Relief came, quick and humiliating, and with it a second emotion that made her feel foolish: disappointment. Because no answer meant her fear was her own, and fear without a shape was harder to fight. It slithered.

She made herself stand again and paced the small length of the room. Three steps. Turn. Three steps. Her boots made dull sounds on the boards, and each sound seemed to sink into the hush instead of bouncing back. She stopped in the center and listened to the aftermath.

The room returned to the same thick quiet immediately, as if it had never been disturbed.

Eliza's hands trembled. She clenched them and forced them still.

"I am not what they say," she told the room under her breath. She did not know why she spoke. Perhaps because the silence had begun to feel like an ear pressed against the wall.

No answer came, but something shifted in her awareness, subtle as a change in temperature. The hush deepened, or perhaps she simply noticed it more.

And then, from within that hush, a sound threaded through.

Not a voice, not yet. A suggestion of syllables, like someone forming words without fully choosing them. A murmur close to her ear, intimate enough that her skin prickled along her neck.

Eliza froze.

The murmur did not feel like the men outside. It did not carry the blunt weight of authority. It carried patience.

For a moment, she heard only breath, and she could not tell if it was hers.

Then the whisper gathered itself and became clearer, the way a name becomes clear when you have heard it spoken many times.

"Do you feel it?" it asked.

Eliza's stomach dropped. She turned sharply toward the corner behind her, though she knew there was nothing there. The movement made her dizzy.

"Stop," she said, louder than before. Her voice cracked on the word and she hated herself for it.

The whisper did not retreat. It did not rise into threat. It stayed gentle, and that gentleness was the worst part, because it asked to be trusted.

"It is quiet enough for you to hear now," it said.

Eliza pressed her hands over her ears, hard, as if she could block it the way she could block a sermon she did not want. Her own pulse thudded under her palms. The whisper still came through, not as sound traveling air, but as something placed directly into the space behind her thoughts.

"You have been listening all day," it continued. "To them. To their certainty. To your mother's fear. To your father's anger. To the town speaking your name until it sounded like ink."

Her eyes stung. She saw Mercy in the meetinghouse doorway again, hands braced on the frame, and the image wavered as if someone had breathed on it.

Eliza lowered her hands slowly. "Who are you?" she asked, the words scraped thin.

A pause, almost thoughtful.

"Someone who has waited," the voice said.

Eliza backed until her shoulders met the wall. The boards were cold against her spine. "I will not speak to you," she whispered, trying to make it a vow that mattered.

The voice seemed to consider that too, with the calm of something that did not fear being refused.

"You do not have to speak," it replied. "This room will speak for you."

Eliza's breath came faster. "It's only a room."

Silence, for a heartbeat, and in that heartbeat she felt the hush press closer, like a crowd leaning in without moving their feet.

"Only a room," the voice repeated softly, as if tasting the phrase. "And yet your memories have already begun to loosen. You felt it. The edges slipping. The faces blurring."

Eliza shut her eyes hard, as if she could clamp her mind shut the way the bolt had clamped the door. Her jaw ached. The taste of iron returned, and she realized she had bitten her cheek again.

In the darkness of her closed eyes, she saw the wall scratches not as tallies but as lines of ink. Neat. Certain. A record.

She opened her eyes quickly.

The tally marks were still scratches, but now she could not unsee the likeness. The room felt like a page. A blank space designed to be filled by whatever Salem wrote into it.

"You hear them outside," the voice went on, and Eliza realized with a lurch that she did. Not words, not footsteps. Something subtler. A presence. The guard's patience. The town's waiting. Like a hand held steady above a quill.

Eliza pressed her forehead to the wall for a moment, needing the cold. "They will let me see my mother," she said. It was not a question. She tried to force it into certainty. "They cannot keep me here without end."

The whisper warmed slightly, almost amused.

"End," it said. "You still think in ends. In before and after. In doors that open and close."

Eliza swallowed. "They will ask me questions. I will answer. And they will see."

"See what?" the voice asked, and the gentleness sharpened, just a hair. "Truth?"

Her stomach clenched. She remembered the magistrate's calm face, the way Eliza's denial had been received as a familiar step in a process. She remembered the afflicted child saying, She says she did not. They always say.

Eliza forced herself to speak, because if she did not, the silence would do it for her. "I am not guilty," she said. "I have never held that book."

At the word book, the room seemed to tighten. The hush deepened until her ears felt full.

The whisper came close, close enough to make her feel she might turn and see a shape beside the cot, an indentation in straw, a presence settling as if it belonged there.

"You have not held it," the voice agreed, and for a moment Eliza felt relief, thin and quick.

Then the whisper continued, patient as a hand turning pages.

"Not with these hands."

Eliza's vision swam. The room tilted, not like faintness but like a change in what direction meant. She grabbed the cot's edge to steady herself. The straw mattress shifted, and for an instant she thought she felt another weight on it, as if someone had sat down and the cot had accepted them.

She snapped her eyes to the cot.

It was empty.

Yet the air beside it felt occupied.

Eliza's throat tightened until she could barely breathe. "No," she whispered. The word was too small for the terror rising in her.

The voice did not press her. It did not command. It simply waited with her in the thick, living hush, as if it had all the time that had been taken from her.

After a long moment, it spoke again, softer than before, almost kind.

"Rest, Eliza," it said, using her name the way Josiah had used it, the way the afflicted girl had used it, the way the constable had written it. As if it were not a thing she owned, but a thing that belonged in a ledger. "Stop clawing at what slips. Let the silence hold you."

Eliza's knees weakened. She sat on the cot without remembering choosing to. Her fingers dug into the edge of the mattress until her nails ached.

Outside the door, the guard did not move. No key turned. No voice called her out. Salem remained still, as if satisfied to let the room do its work.

Eliza stared at the floorboards, at a dark stain near the corner, and tried to summon her mother's face again, tried to force Mercy into sharpness with sheer will.

Mercy's outline came, but the eyes were wrong. The mouth did not form properly. The image wavered like a reflection in disturbed water.

Tears rose without her permission. She blinked them back hard, furious with her own body for betraying her.

In the thick quiet, the whisper murmured, almost tenderly, "There," as if praising a child for finally yielding.

Eliza pressed her palm to her mouth to keep from making sound.

The silence pressed back. Not empty, not passive. Alive with waiting.

And in that living silence, with her family held somewhere beyond reach and her name moving through the town like a verdict, Eliza felt the room begin to teach her its true lesson.

Not that she was alone.

But that she could be changed without anyone touching her at all.

Chapter 6

The First Questions

The bolt slid back with a sound that was almost gentle.

Eliza sat rigid on the cot, both feet planted on the boards, hands folded so tightly her fingers ached. She had not heard the guard's steps approach. Or perhaps she had and the room had swallowed them, turning them into part of its constant hush. Either way, the first clear sign that someone was outside was the key turning with a careful patience, as if the door were being opened for a visitor, not a prisoner.

Light from the corridor spilled into the cell in a narrow wedge, cutting across the floor and stopping against the far wall like a finger pressed to a page.

The broader man stood in the doorway. He filled it without effort, hat in hand, face composed. Behind him the corridor was dim, and the shapes of other men waited there in the gray, not crowding, not urgent. Procedure again. Always procedure.

"Come," the broader man said.

Eliza did not move at once. Her mind tried, absurdly, to bargain with stillness. If she stayed seated, perhaps the moment would pass. Perhaps the door would close again, and she could return to the smaller terror she had already learned.

The man did not raise his voice. He only looked at her as if waiting for a pot to boil.

"Eliza Harrow," he added, using her full name the way the constable had, the way the town had. It landed on her skin like a hand that did not ask permission.

She stood, legs unsteady, and stepped toward the door. As she passed the threshold she felt the room behind her tighten, as if it did not like letting her go. The hush clung to her for a heartbeat longer than it should have. She tasted iron and swallowed it down.

The corridor smelled sharper than the cell, as if someone had scrubbed it in her absence. Lye, vinegar, old damp boards. The pegs with hats and coats were still there, ordinary as ever, and she hated them for it. Men could come and go from this place and still hang their coats neatly, still return to supper and prayer, as if the work of taking girls was only another duty to be folded and put away.

They led her back the way she had come. The turns confused her, and she knew that was part of it, whether intended or not. A person who cannot picture the shape of a building cannot picture escape. A person who cannot count steps begins to count only what is said to them.

At the end of the passage, the room with the table waited again. The same scarred wood. The same cold stove. The same lantern unlit. It looked, in the weak light, like a place meant to hold calm.

The constable was there, seated already, his small brown book open. Ink stained his thumb. The quill lay ready beside a small, stoppered bottle. He did not look up when Eliza entered. He only adjusted the book slightly, squaring it with the table edge, as if alignment could make truth.

The pale-eyed man stood near the wall; hands folded loosely in front of him. He watched Eliza with mild attention, like a man observing an animal to determine whether it would kick.

A second man sat at the far end of the table. Younger than the constable, clean-shaven, his coat brushed, his fingers bare of ink. He held no book, but his eyes held a different kind of record, the sort kept behind the face.

Eliza stopped just inside the room. The broader man stayed behind her, close enough that she could feel his presence without being touched. He did not speak. His silence was its own instruction.

The constable finally lifted his eyes. "Sit," he said.

Eliza hesitated only long enough to hate herself for hesitating, then sat in the same chair she had been placed in before. The wood was cold through her dress. She put her hands in her lap, careful, and stared at the constable's book because staring at faces was worse. Faces in Salem were too often mirrors for what they expected to see.

The constable dipped his quill, scraped the excess against the bottle's lip, and began in a voice so calm it might have belonged to a man asking after the weather.

"How long have you lived in your former town?"

Eliza blinked. The question was so ordinary it disoriented her more than accusation would have. "All my life," she said. "Until we traveled."

"And why did you travel?" the younger man asked. His tone was polite, curious. He could have been speaking to her across a counter about flour.

"My father sought work," Eliza answered. "We meant to stay only a short while in Salem."

The constable wrote. Scratch, scratch. The sound made Eliza's stomach roll, not with fear alone but with the sense that each stroke of ink took something from her and made it theirs.

The younger man leaned forward a fraction. "Did you know of Salem's troubles before you came?"

"No." Eliza tried to keep her voice steady. "We knew only what travelers speak of. That there had been sickness. That people were frightened."

"Frightened," the pale-eyed man echoed softly, as if savoring the word. He did not move from the wall.

The constable's quill paused. He looked up again, not unkindly. "You understand why there must be care," he said. "In times like these, small things matter. A stranger's presence. A dream. A word spoken at the right moment."

"A word," Eliza repeated before she could stop herself. "Or a name."

The younger man's eyes sharpened slightly at that, but he kept his tone even. "Your name was spoken, yes."

Eliza's throat tightened. "By a girl I have never met."

"Afflicted," the pale-eyed man said, as if that settled it. "Their senses are not as ours, and yet they see more than we do."

Eliza looked at the constable's inked thumb. She did not look at the pale-eyed man. "Or they are made to say things," she said quietly.

No one bristled. No one shouted. The constable only lowered his gaze and wrote again, as if she had offered a useful detail.

The younger man spoke gently. "Do you know Lydia Dyer?"

"No."

"Ephraim Kells?"

"No."

The constable wrote. Eliza's hands tightened in her lap until her nails pressed crescent marks into her skin.

The younger man continued, patient. "Do you know Josiah Waller?"

"I saw him today," Eliza said. "In the store. That is all."

"And yet," the younger man said, "he says you stood at his bedside in the night."

Eliza forced air into her lungs. "He lies."

The younger man's expression did not change. "Or he believes what he says."

"That does not make it true."

"No," the constable agreed, and his agreement was so easy Eliza felt her footing slip. He turned a page in the book with care. "Truth is sometimes hard to see when it comes clothed in strange garments."

The whisper in Eliza's mind stirred, faint as a curtain shifting in still air. She did not hear words, only the sensation of attention, as if something leaned closer to listen through her ears.

The younger man clasped his hands on the table. "You are young," he said. "We do not wish to harm you. No one here delights in distressing a girl."

Eliza's mouth tasted of iron again. She swallowed. "Then let me go."

The younger man did not answer that directly. "We have heard," he said, "that you have been troubled. That you have spoken oddly."

Eliza's skin prickled. She kept her eyes on his hands. "Who said that?"

The constable answered instead, calm as ever. "You did."

Eliza's head jerked up. "I did not."

The constable tapped the open page of his book with the tip of the quill. Not threatening. Simply indicating that ink existed. "It is written," he said.

Eliza's stomach dropped. She stared at the page as if she could see the words from where she sat, as if distance might reveal the lie in them. The lines were too small, the room too dim. She could only see the shape of writing, the dark certainty of marks.

"I have not confessed to anything," Eliza said, and heard the thinness in her voice. "I have not spoken to anyone except you and those men."

The younger man's mouth softened into something almost sympathetic. "You may not remember all you have said," he replied. "Fear does that. Exhaustion. A troubled mind."

Eliza's pulse pounded in her ears. It was a quiet attack, not on her body but on her ownership of her own memory. She thought of the cell, the way Mercy's face had blurred at the edges when she tried to hold it.

"I remember," Eliza said, and the words came out too sharp.

The constable's gaze held hers. He did not look triumphant. He looked resigned. "Then it will be easier," he said, "for you to speak the same here that you have already spoken elsewhere."

"I have spoken nothing elsewhere."

The pale-eyed man shifted slightly at the wall, as if adjusting his stance for comfort. "It is common," he said, "for the guilty to deny their own mouth. The Devil muddles them. Makes them slippery."

Eliza's hands trembled. She pressed them flat against her thighs to still them. "And it is common," she said, "for a town to decide a story and then force every word into it."

For the first time, the younger man's politeness cooled by a small degree. Not anger, just a firmer patience. "You speak as though we are your enemy."

"You are holding me," Eliza replied. "You struck my father."

The constable dipped his quill again. "Your father struck first," he said mildly, and wrote as if that settled the matter in the only place that mattered: the record.

Eliza stared at the quill. She could not stop thinking of how it moved, how easily it made a version of events that would outlive her. The scratch of it seemed louder now, as if the room had been built to amplify it inside her head.

The younger man asked, "Tell us, Eliza. Have you ever woken with dirt beneath your nails and not known why?"

Eliza's breath caught. The question was shaped like a hook. It reached toward the dreams she had not yet dared to name aloud. The flickers. The road under pines. The sense of something already written.

She forced her voice into steadiness. "No."

The constable wrote.

"And have you ever," the younger man continued, as gently as a man coaxing a child, "heard a voice when no one was in the room?"

Eliza's vision swam for an instant. She felt, unmistakably, that soft attention again at the edge of her thoughts, as if something waited to see which way she would turn.

If she said yes, they would bloom with righteous certainty. If she said no, the voice would remain, and she would be alone with it, and they would still write whatever suited them.

Eliza gripped her own fingers under the table so hard it hurt. Pain was real. Pain anchored.

"No," she said.

The pale-eyed man's gaze rested on her with a faint, knowing calm, as if he could hear the lie not because it was untrue, but because it was incomplete.

The constable's quill scratched steadily. When he finished the line, he did not close the book. He only looked at Eliza as if waiting for the next thing to fall out of her.

"You will have time," he said. "We are not in haste. These matters are best tended without heat."

Without heat, Eliza thought, and almost laughed, because cold could burn too.

The younger man rose slightly from his chair, as if to signal the end of this first portion, and spoke with careful reassurance. "Rest when you can," he said. "We will speak again. And you will find it easier when you stop struggling against what has already been set down."

Set down. Written.

Eliza's mouth went dry. She stared at the brown book and felt the room tilt, not with faintness but with the sense that she was standing on something that could move under her feet, something made of paper instead of ground.

Behind her, the broader man placed a hand on her elbow, not rough, not kind. Guiding.

As Eliza stood, she heard the constable turn a page. The sound was quiet, almost delicate.

It made her skin prickle all the same, because it sounded like time being handled by someone else, and because the words the younger man had spoken lingered in her mind like a stain.

You will find it easier.

Eliza walked back toward the corridor and the waiting cell, and with every step she could feel the calm of the interrogation pressing against her, not as mercy, but as certainty wearing a gentle face.

Somewhere behind her, ink dried on paper. Somewhere ahead, the room without time waited to loosen her memories a little more.

And somewhere very close, in the private space of her hearing, the faint hush deepened again, pleased not by what she had confessed, but by what she had been forced to deny.

The walk back to the lower passage felt longer than before, though Eliza knew it could not be. The turns came too close together, corners swallowing one another, and the corridor's sharp scrubbed smell rose and fell as if the building breathed it out on purpose. The broader man's hand stayed at her elbow, a guidance that did not need to tighten to be unavoidable.

Behind them, the constable's quill continued its quiet work in Eliza's mind. Scratch, scratch. A sound small enough to be dismissed, and yet it had followed her out of the room like a thread tied to her wrist.

When the cell door opened again, the wedge of corridor light cut across the boards exactly as it had before, the same angle, the same narrow finger pointing inward. Eliza stepped over the worn threshold mark and felt the room accept her back with a stale, familiar chill.

The broader man did not push her, did not throw her onto the cot. He waited in the doorway as if he had all the patience in the world and said, "Sit. Or stand. As you please."

Then, as if remembering his role was not to offer choices, he added, "Keep quiet."

The door shut. The bolt slid. The key turned with careful finality.

Eliza stood for a moment with her hands at her sides, listening. She could hear a guard outside again, the faint shift of weight, leather creaking once. Then stillness.

She sat on the cot because standing felt like performing, and she was tired of being seen. The straw mattress gave under her, and the bucket's sour smell drifted faintly as if the room wished to remind her of what she was in here.

She tried to hold on to the last hour, to arrange it in her mind in a neat sequence the way her mother would have insisted on folding linens. They asked why you came. They asked names. They asked about voices. She had answered. She had said no. She had not stumbled. She had not given them anything.

And yet, when she closed her eyes, she saw the constable tapping the page and saying, "It is written." She saw the younger man's face, almost kind, and heard him say, You may not remember all you have said.

Eliza's throat tightened. She pressed her palms to her knees, hard enough to hurt, and tried to anchor herself in pain again.

A sound came from beyond the door: not the bolt, not a voice. The careful rustle of paper.

Eliza's head lifted.

She held her breath. The room held it with her.

The paper sound came again, delicate and slow, as if someone turned a page with reverence. Then another pause. Then a faint, muffled murmur, too low to make out words.

They were reading, she thought. Or writing. Or both.

The whisper, the one that was not carried by any mouth, stirred close to her mind like a presence shifting on the edge of the cot.

They already have it, it seemed to say.

Eliza's fingers curled into fists. "No," she whispered, though she did not know what she meant to refuse. The voice? The paper? The town's certainty that did not need evidence?

Minutes passed. Or an hour. Or nothing at all. Time did not behave here. The high window offered the same dull gray, and the drip in the wall would not keep a steady rhythm. When she tried to count between drips, she lost the number, not because her mind was weak, but because something in the room made counting feel pointless, like stacking stones in water.

The bolt slid back.

Eliza's body went rigid before her mind could decide what to do. She stood so quickly her knees bumped the cot, making it creak. The sound felt loud enough to be recorded.

The door opened, and the younger man from the table room stepped into the cell as if he belonged there. He carried no lantern. The corridor's gray light was enough, and the way he moved suggested he did not fear darkness the way prisoners did. His coat was still brushed. His hands were clean.

Behind him, in the doorway, the broader man stood like a post, watchful and silent.

The younger man glanced at the wall scratches, at the bucket, at the cot, the way a man looks over a room he has already decided is adequate. His gaze landed on Eliza's face.

"How are you faring?" he asked, as calmly as if she were ill in bed and he had come to check her fever.

Eliza's mouth was dry. She forced the words out anyway. "I want to see my mother."

A faint narrowing in his eyes, not displeasure exactly, but the mild correction of someone listening to the wrong sort of request. "In time," he said. "It will be easier for everyone when this matter is settled."

"You said you were not in haste," Eliza replied, and hated the tremble she could not keep out of her voice. "But you keep coming."

He smiled slightly, as if she had made a child's complaint. "We come because we must be thorough."

He stepped farther in, careful not to brush the walls, and stopped near the end of the cot. He did not sit. He did not crouch to her level. He remained standing so that she had to look up at him.

"You understand," he said, "there is no profit in stubbornness."

Eliza's jaw tightened. "There is no profit in lying."

"No," he agreed easily. He held her gaze with a mild steadiness that felt, to her exhausted mind, like pressure. "That is why I am here. Because what you say and what has been recorded do not match."

Eliza felt cold spread through her chest. "Recorded," she repeated.

The younger man inclined his head. "Yes."

"I said nothing, but what I said at the table."

He watched her for a moment, patient as the town had been patient, and then spoke as if offering relief. "Eliza, listen to me. You have already spoken of these matters. You have already said more than you now claim. Perhaps you do not recall it clearly. Perhaps you were frightened. Perhaps you were in a condition not wholly yourself."

"I was myself," Eliza said. The words came too fast. "I am myself."

He did not contradict her. That would have been a fight, and fights created heat. Salem did not need heat. It had certainty.

He turned his head slightly toward the open door, as if addressing someone beyond it. "Bring it."

Eliza's stomach dropped. She did not know what it meant, and the not knowing was a blade held against her throat.

The broader man shifted, and another figure appeared behind him: the constable, stepping into view with his small brown book in hand. He held it the way a minister holds a Bible, careful, practiced. Ink stained his thumb. His expression was composed, almost weary, like a man tasked with repeating the obvious to those who insist on being difficult.

The constable did not come fully into the cell. He remained at the threshold, as though the room belonged to Eliza and he did not care to share air with her longer than necessary. He opened the book and, with a deliberate slowness, turned it so the page faced inward.

Eliza could not read the lines from where she stood. She could only see the dark rows of writing, the evidence of a hand that never shook.

The younger man said, “You told us you were troubled by a dream. You said you woke with the taste of iron and the sense of a book in the room.”

Eliza stared at him. “I did not.”

The constable’s finger moved down the page, tracking a line. He did not speak yet. He let the ink speak for him.

The younger man continued, softly. “You told us you heard someone in the cell with you. You said you felt a presence.”

Eliza’s heart hammered. She heard, in her mind, the whisper that had asked, Do you feel it? The memory of it made her skin prickle.

“I did not say that,” she insisted, and her voice rose despite her attempt to keep it even. “I said no. I told you no.”

The younger man’s expression did not change. “Do you see?” he said, as if to a child who would not accept a lesson. “You deny even what has already been set down. That is what I mean when I say you are not well served by stubbornness. If you speak in one manner and then in another, it suggests deception. Or confusion.”

Eliza's throat tightened until it hurt. She turned her head toward the constable's book, squinting as if effort could pull the words into sense. The ink might as well have been insects.

"That book is yours," she said. "You can write anything you want in it."

The constable's eyes lifted, calm, almost offended by the implication. "It is a record," he said. "It is what was spoken."

"I want to see it," Eliza demanded. "Bring it here. Let me read what you say I said."

The younger man looked at her with faint pity. "It would not help you. You would only claim you do not remember speaking it. And then we would be where we are now."

"I did not speak it," Eliza said, and felt the words scraping her raw. "You are making me into something on paper."

The younger man's voice stayed gentle. "The paper only holds what the mouth gives it."

Eliza laughed once, harsh and disbelieving, and the sound startled her because it did not feel like hers. "Then why ask me anything?" she said. "Why not just write what you need and be done?"

Silence held for a moment. In that pause Eliza heard the faint hush of the room deepen, as if it approved of the question or of the despair behind it.

The younger man's gaze softened again. "Because," he said carefully, "we would rather you come to agreement with what has already been revealed. It is easier for you that way. Easier for everyone."

"Agreement," Eliza repeated. She swallowed, tasted iron, and did not know whether it was blood or memory. "You mean confession."

He did not deny it. He only said, "You have already begun."

Eliza stared at him. Something in her mind tried to reject the sentence outright, to fling it away like a hand batting at a spiderweb. But another part of her, the exhausted part, the part the cell had been working on, snagged on it.

Already begun.

She thought of the way denial in Salem did not weaken their certainty, it fed it. She thought of the afflicted girl's calm voice: She says she did not. They always say.

The constable turned a page, slow and deliberate, and the paper sound went through Eliza like a chill.

"Listen," the younger man said, and his voice lowered as if he meant to be kind. "If you are troubled by voices, if your sleep is not your own, if you have gaps, if you wake with things you cannot explain, it is not shameful to admit it. Many have been ensnared without knowing when it began. We can help you. The magistrates can help you. The Reverend can pray over you."

Eliza's stomach twisted. Help, in Salem, meant being remade into their story.

"I am not ensnared," she whispered.

The younger man held her gaze. "Then why does the record say otherwise?"

Eliza's breath came shallow. She looked at the constable's book again, at the rows of ink she could not read, and felt her footing slide in a way that had nothing to do with the boards under her boots.

Because the record existed.

Because ink dried whether it was true or not.

Because if they wrote her words incorrectly, or invented them wholly, there was no place she could go to prove the shape of her own mouth. No witness would believe her over the book. No one in Salem would choose her memory over a page that pretended to be clean truth.

The younger man waited, patient.

The constable waited too, the book open at the threshold like a small, dark mouth.

Eliza tried to speak and found she could not.

Somewhere inside her hearing, very close, the whisper returned, not triumphant, not urgent. Only certain.

See? it seemed to say. *You confessed the moment they decided you did.*

And Eliza stood in the room without time, staring at a record she could not challenge, and felt the first true destabilizing shift take hold: not the fear that she would be punished for guilt she did not have, but the dread that her own denial could be rewritten until even she did not know what she had said.

The younger man did not move. He did not lift a hand or raise his voice. He only watched Eliza with the same mild steadiness the town used when it meant to make you feel unreasonable for having a pulse.

"Eliza," he said at last, as if the pause had been for her benefit. "This is what I mean. You stand before us and insist upon a clean denial, but the very insistence becomes part of the matter. It is not how an innocent speaks when faced with plain record."

Eliza's throat worked. "Plain record," she repeated, and felt the words scrape. "It is your hand. Your ink."

The constable's face did not change. He held the open book as though it weighed nothing, as though it were only a tool, not a weapon. The page was turned slightly more toward her, a mockery of offering. She could still not make out the words.

"You cannot read it from there," she said, and hated how thin her voice sounded in the small room. "So, you can say it says anything."

The younger man's faint smile returned, brief and careful. "And you think you can say you said anything."

"I said what I said," Eliza snapped, and then flinched at her own sharpness, because sharpness would be taken as temper, and temper as guilt.

The broader man in the doorway shifted his weight. Boards creaked. No one stepped in to strike her for her tone. That was part of it. They did not need to punish her body to make her feel trapped. They only needed to remain calm until her fear made her the only unreasonable creature in the room.

The younger man nodded, slow, as if conceding a point he did not believe. "Then let us try again," he said. "We will not quarrel over the book. We will not press you. We will simply speak, and you will answer, and the truth will rest where it ought."

Rest. The word made Eliza's stomach twist, remembering the whisper in the cell. Rest, Eliza. Let the silence hold you.

She forced herself to breathe. "Ask," she said.

He glanced toward the constable. The constable, without being told, lowered the book a fraction, as if it was no longer needed to bludgeon. The threat remained anyway. The ink existed whether she looked at it or not.

The younger man's voice softened into something almost conversational. "When you were brought into the meetinghouse, did you hear your name spoken?"

"Yes," Eliza said. That was safe. Too many mouths had spoken it for her to deny.

"And when the afflicted child said it," he continued, "how did you feel?"

Eliza's fingers curled, then forced themselves open. "Frightened."

"Only frightened?" he asked, and tilted his head slightly, a gesture of genuine curiosity or practiced imitation of it. "Not… recognized?"

The word landed with a small, sick weight. Recognized. As if her name belonged to something else first, and she had merely answered when called.

"I felt frightened," Eliza repeated.

The younger man accepted it with a nod, as if marking it down in his own mind. "And in your cell," he said, "when the door shuts and the town's noise falls away, is it easier to think? Or harder?"

Eliza hesitated. She did not know what answer could not be twisted.

He watched the hesitation with the patience of a man watching a fish circle bait.

"It is harder," she said finally. "Because there is nothing to measure time by. Because you keep the window too high to see anything. Because you leave me alone until I cannot tell if I have slept."

"A kindness," he said gently. "Solitude keeps a prisoner from being stirred by others."

"I am not a prisoner," Eliza whispered before she could stop herself.

His expression did not sharpen. “Not yet,” he said, as if speaking of weather again. “But you are held, and held for cause.”

“There is no cause,” she said, and the words felt futile even as she spoke them.

“There is testimony,” he corrected. “There are names spoken. There is affliction that responds. There is record.”

Eliza’s gaze flicked to the brown book in the constable’s hands and back to the younger man’s face. She felt suddenly like she was balancing on a narrow board. Each sentence they spoke placed another hand on it, steadying it so that she could not argue it was unstable. Their certainty was not loud. It did not shake. It did not crack. It simply stood there until her own mind began to wobble against it.

She tried another tack, because refusal was drowning her. “Who are you?” she asked.

The younger man looked mildly surprised, as though he had assumed she already knew. “Ezekiel Swann,” he said. “I serve the magistrates in these examinations.”

Swann. The name did not help. It was simply another piece of Salem that had always existed in its own story and did not need her permission to include her.

“And him?” she said, nodding toward the pale-eyed man.

The pale-eyed man answered himself, his voice calm as poured water. “Deputy Parris.”

Eliza remembered that voice at the ordinary’s door. Open, Amos. Let us speak proper. The calm that had felt like ownership. Now it had a name that sounded like scripture, like lineage, like authority that had been born into the town and would not be argued down by a traveler’s daughter.

Swann folded his hands. “You see?” he said quietly. “We are not phantoms. We are men who can be named. Who can be held to account. And the record holds us as it holds you.”

Eliza’s laugh came again, smaller this time, and she could not stop it. “Held to account by whom?” she asked. “By the same record you write?”

The constable’s eyes lifted. He did not bristle. He only looked tired. “By God,” he said, as if Eliza had asked something obvious.

God, Eliza thought, and her mind flashed unwillingly to Reverend Hale’s face in the meetinghouse, attentive and unblinking, as if he had come to witness a truth he already knew. Hale had not shouted either. He had only named things with certainty until the room accepted them.

Swann's voice took on the careful cadence of instruction. "Eliza, we are not your enemy. The enemy is confusion. It creeps in and makes a girl deny what she has said, forget what she has done, imagine she is being wronged when she is being rescued."

Rescued. The word made her feel sick.

"I have not imagined this," Eliza said. "I was taken. My father was struck. My mother—"

"Your father resisted," Deputy Parris cut in, still mild. "It was recorded. And resistance is always a sign that something is at work."

Eliza stared at him. "A father reaches for his child and you call it a sign."

Parris did not blink. "Innocence is quiet," he said. "Innocence submits to examination. Innocence has nothing to fear from light."

Swann nodded as if in agreement with a lesson well taught. "Do you see how your father's anger complicates your case? It adds noise. It stirs the town. It forces stronger measures. But a confession, made proper, can calm such things."

Confession. Again, the word threaded through everything.

Eliza's mouth went dry. "You keep saying I have already begun," she said. "You keep saying the record says I spoke of dreams and voices. Then you ask me questions shaped to make me speak of dreams and voices. How can I answer without stepping into the words you already wrote?"

Swann's gaze held hers. The calm in his face was not blankness; it was deliberation. "If you speak true," he said, "there is no danger."

"That is a lie," Eliza said, and her voice broke on the last word.

No one reacted as if she had insulted them. That was their strength. They could afford to let her lash out because it made her look unstable.

Swann did not sigh. He did not scold. He only leaned forward a fraction, close enough that Eliza could smell soap on his collar, a clean smell that did not belong in this building. "Tell me, Eliza," he said softly, "how many times today have you been asked to state your name?"

Eliza blinked, thrown by the question. "I don't know."

Swann's eyebrows lifted slightly, a gentle rebuke. "You don't know," he repeated. "And yet you insist you know every word you have spoken, every hour you have sat, every moment of fear. How can both be true?"

Eliza tried to answer and found she could not. Her mind scrambled, counting backward: the meetinghouse, the magistrate, the constable, the store, the road. She had said her name to the magistrate. The afflicted girl had spoken it. The constable had written it. Parris had said it. The guard had said it. Swann had said it. How many times? Too many. So many that the sound of it no longer felt like her skin.

Swann watched her face as if watching something settle into place. "That is what troubles do," he said. "They scatter the mind. They make a girl certain of things that cannot be held. We do not accuse you for being scattered. We want to gather you back into truth."

Gather, Eliza thought, and saw in her mind the crowd on the common, loose lines of people keeping their righteousness clean and separate while their eyes joined into one net.

The constable's book remained open at the threshold. Eliza could feel it like a physical presence, a second person in the room. Ink waiting.

Parris spoke again, almost kindly. "If you have heard a voice," he said, "it will not be the first time such a thing has happened in Salem. Many have been troubled. Many have been approached. Some have resisted until they could not tell where their own thoughts began."

Eliza's heart began to pound harder, not because she feared their words, but because of how closely they slid against her own private terror. They spoke of her cell as if they had been inside it with her. They spoke of confusion as if they could see it crawling along her memories.

She felt the hush at the edge of her hearing, the thing that was not air and not silence, but attention. It was there now, close and pleased, as though listening to them name what it had done.

Swann's voice lowered further. "We are going to return you to the cell," he said. "And you will think. You will pray. And when we come again, you will speak in the same manner you have already spoken, without these fearful reversals."

Eliza swallowed. "And if I do not?" she asked.

Swann did not answer directly. Parris did.

"Then we will continue until you do," Parris said, as calmly as if promising to mend a fence. "Because Salem cannot be left with uncertainty."

Uncertainty. That was the true crime, Eliza realized. Not witchcraft. Not malice. Uncertainty was the thing they meant to beat out of her, gently if possible, brutally if required. They would call it mercy no matter how it was done.

The broader man in the doorway stepped forward. His hand closed around Eliza's elbow again, firm and impersonal.

Eliza rose because she was guided to rise.

As she was led out, she turned her head once toward the constable's book. "If it is written," she said, voice shaking, "then it is already decided."

The constable's gaze met hers, and for the first time she saw something like discomfort flicker there, quickly buried. He closed the book with a soft tap.

Swann answered in the same gentle tone he had used all along. "No," he said. "It is written because it was spoken. And it will be spoken again until it matches."

Matches. Eliza felt the word like a hand pressing her down into a mold.

The corridor swallowed her. The turns came too fast. The air grew staler. The sound of keys returned, careful and light, and then the lower room accepted her again.

As the door shut and the bolt slid home, Eliza stood in the gray that did not mark time and understood what their calm had done.

They had not needed to prove her guilty.

They had only needed to prove themselves certain.

And in the face of that certainty, her own mind, with its slipping memories and unmeasured hours, began to feel like the least reliable thing in the world.

Chapter 7

The Watching

The door shut and the bolt slid into place with the same careful finality as before, and Eliza stood in the center of the cell as if she had been placed there and forgotten.

For a moment she did not move. She listened for the guard's shift of weight, the creak of leather, the sigh of a man settling into duty. She heard nothing at first, and the absence of sound made her skin prickle. Then, faintly, there came the smallest scrape, a boot sole correcting itself on the corridor boards.

Watched.

The knowledge pressed in on her harder than the walls. It was not only that someone stood outside the door. It was that someone would stay.

Eliza sat on the cot because the room invited collapse. The straw smelled sour and tired, as though it had absorbed every fear and sweat of every body that had lain there. She kept her hands in her lap, fingers laced tight, because in Salem even a twitch could be turned into a sign. The hush filled her ears again, that low, continuous pressure that did not belong to silence so much as to attention.

She tried to pray properly, not in scraps. She tried to line the words up in her mind the way the constable lined his book on the table's edge.

Our Father, who art in Heaven—

But Heaven felt far away, and distance was what this place took first. The cell made the world small and then made even that smallness uncertain. The high window offered the same dull gray it always offered. It gave no promise of day. It gave no permission for night. It was simply light without a clock.

Eliza lay back reluctantly, not because she wanted to yield, but because her body began to tremble with fatigue she could not command away. The last hours, however many they were, had been all edges: her father's blood, Mercy's torn voice, ink scratching paper, the younger man's calm questions shaped like traps. Now the room offered only one mercy, and even that mercy felt suspect.

Rest, the whisper had said before, using her name as if it owned it.

Eliza stared at the ceiling boards and forced her eyes open wider, refusing to give the room what it wanted. But her lashes grew heavy anyway. Her thoughts, which had been sharp with anger, began to soften at the edges, like wet paper.

When she finally let her eyes close, it was not surrender. It was a momentary failure, a blink that lasted too long.

She woke with a start to the sound of the bolt.

It was not drawn back fully. Not yet. Just touched. Metal shifted against metal, a small test, as if a hand outside had nudged it to make sure it still held. The sound was quiet enough that it should not have woken her, and that was the point. They had learned, or always known, that the body does not need loudness to be torn from sleep.

Eliza sat up so fast her head swam. Her heart hammered like something trapped.

No one entered.

The bolt did not slide open. The key did not turn. The sound stopped, and then there was only the hush again and the faint, patient presence beyond the door.

Eliza pressed her palms to her eyes until she saw sparks. When she lowered them, the high window looked unchanged. The light was the same gray, the same thickness. She could not tell if she had slept a minute or an hour.

She lay back down, breath shallow, and tried to keep her mind sharp by reciting facts.

My name is Eliza Harrow.

It landed strangely. Her name had become something spoken by too many mouths. She tried instead to picture Mercy's face, to force it into clarity: the set of her jaw, the fierce line of her brows when she was determined. The image came, but it slid the moment Eliza reached for it, as if her mind were a shelf too slick to hold it.

She clenched her teeth until her jaw ached.

This is what they want, she told herself. They want me tired. They want my thoughts to tangle so I cannot speak straight.

As if summoned by the thought, the younger man's voice came back to her, calm and even. We are not in haste. These matters are best tended without heat.

She could almost hear the politeness in it, the way gentleness had been used like a thumb pressing down on her will.

Eliza's eyes closed again despite herself. Her body, traitor, sank toward sleep the way a stone sinks toward the bottom of a pond.

She did not know how long she drifted before a sharp knock sounded on the door.

Not loud enough to be a summons. Not violent enough to be a threat. Just a quick, precise rap, as if someone were tapping a book's cover to mark a place.

Eliza jerked awake, air ripping into her lungs. The knock came again, two beats, then stopped.

"Who is it?" she called before she could stop herself, and hated the need in her own voice.

No answer.

The guard outside shifted. A quiet exhale. The smallest sound of a man's throat clearing.

Eliza stared at the door until her eyes burned. She waited for it to open, waited for Swann's calm face to appear, waited for the constable's inked thumb and the brown book.

Nothing.

They let the silence stretch until it began to feel like mockery, until Eliza's own question echoed in her mind as if it had been asked by someone else. Then, just when her shoulders began to loosen a fraction, there came the soft scrape of a key turning a quarter turn and stopping.

Not opening. Only promising that it could.

Eliza's hands curled into fists. "Why are you doing this?" she whispered, and did not know if she meant the guard or the town or the thing that whispered inside her thoughts.

From the corner of the room, or perhaps from the space just behind her hearing, the familiar voice stirred with patient intimacy.

They are teaching you; it murmured. Not with words.

Eliza slammed her palms over her ears. Her own pulse thudded under her hands. "Stop," she said through clenched teeth.

The voice did not rise. It did not argue. It waited the way the guard waited, unhurried, certain she would tire before it did.

When Eliza finally lowered her hands, the hush remained, and beyond the door a man's presence remained. The cell held her between two kinds of watching, and she could not tell which was worse.

Her body tried again to sleep. It was not a choice now. It was a tide. She fought it until her muscles ached from tension, until her eyelids fluttered like weak curtains. Sleep came in small, broken pieces, each one no more than a handful of breaths before being snatched away.

The next time she woke, it was because the door opened.

Light spilled in, whiter than the gray from the high window, and for a moment Eliza's mind leapt toward relief. Someone had come. That meant time had passed in a way that could be measured.

The broader man stood in the doorway, hat in hand, his face impassive. He did not step in. He only looked at her to confirm she was awake.

"Eliza Harrow," he said.

The sound of her full name, placed in his mouth, made her stomach clench. "What?" she demanded, voice thick with sleep and fear.

He did not answer the question. He only watched her as if noting the heaviness around her eyes, the disarray of her hair, the way her hands gripped the blanket as though it were an anchor.

"Sit up," he said, not unkindly, and it was clear he meant not for her comfort but for his certainty that she could be seen.

Eliza sat up. The room tilted. The act of moving made her bones feel too heavy, as if she had been filled with damp sand.

The broader man's gaze went over her face once more. Then he stepped back and pulled the door most of the way shut again, leaving it unbolted, open only a crack that let a thin blade of corridor light cut into the cell.

He remained there, just outside, close enough that Eliza could sense him without seeing him fully.

Minutes passed. Or moments. She could not tell. She only knew her body began to slump toward sleep again, chin dropping, thoughts loosening.

As soon as her eyes closed, the door moved. The crack widened with a soft creak.

Eliza snapped awake.

The broader man's voice came, low and procedural. "Stay awake."

Rage flared in her chest, bright and useless. "Why?" she hissed.

No answer. The door eased shut to the same narrow crack again.

They did it again and again, not always with the broader man. Sometimes it was another guard, quieter, quicker. The pattern shifted just enough that Eliza could not anticipate it. A knock. A key scraped. A door crack widened. A breath in the corridor. A murmur of her name spoken softly, not as a comfort but as a tether.

Once, she heard Deputy Parris's mild voice just outside, speaking to someone else as though Eliza were not there. "She must not be left to drift," he said. "That is when the tongue loosens in strange ways."

Another voice answered, muffled. "She's only a girl."

"Innocence is quiet," Parris replied, and Eliza heard the faint smile in his tone without needing to see his face. "If she cannot keep quiet even in sleep, it tells us what we need."

Eliza pressed her forehead to her knees and breathed through her mouth. Her lips tasted of iron. She did not remember biting her cheek, but the taste was there anyway, familiar as a curse.

After what might have been the tenth waking, the fifteenth, the number became meaningless, Eliza began to lose the ability to tell whether her eyes were open or closed. The cell's gray light and the corridor's pale strip blended together until the room seemed to pulse. Her own thoughts began to speak in other voices. Mercy's, sharp with warning. Nathaniel's, furious and helpless. Swann's, soft and instructive.

Then, threaded through them all, the whisper that was never quite a sound.

Do you see now? it asked, gentle as a hand smoothing hair. They do not need chains.

Eliza lifted her head slowly. The wall with the tally marks wavered in her vision, scratches becoming ink, ink becoming scratches. The high window's gray seemed to thicken, as if the light itself were tired.

"No," she whispered, but the word felt far away, as if it belonged to another girl.

Outside the door, the guard shifted again, leather creaking softly. The crack in the door widened a finger's breadth.

Eliza's eyes snapped toward it, reflexive, obedient.

The guard did not speak this time. He only watched in silence until she sat straighter, until he was satisfied that sleep had been taken again.

Then the door eased back to its narrow slit, and the cell returned to its waiting hush.

Eliza's body trembled with the need to fall into darkness, to sink into any place where the watching could not reach her. But the watching followed her eyelids. It lived in the small sounds at the door, in the careful timing, in the way Salem's certainty had found a new tool: not pain, but interruption.

She realized, with a cold clarity that cut through her exhaustion, that they were making sleep into something she had to earn.

And if she could not earn it, if she could not hold onto it, then soon she would not know what was dream and what was waking, what was spoken and what was only thought.

Soon, when Swann returned with his calm questions and his gentle certainty, she would not be able to trust her own answers eve n before the constable's ink touched paper.

The whisper seemed to warm, pleased by her understanding.

Good, it murmured. Now you are quiet enough to be written.

Eliza shut her eyes for a heartbeat, not in rest but in despair, and immediately the door creaked wider, the corridor's pale light slicing into the room like a blade.

"Awake," a voice said from outside. Not loud. Not cruel.

Certain.

Eliza's eyes flew open, burning, and she stared into the thin gap of light as if staring could hold herself together.

She did not know how long they would keep doing it.

She only knew, with every stolen moment of sleep, the cell felt less like a room and more like a hand at the back of her skull, turning her gently, steadily, toward whatever Salem had already decided was true.

The crack of corridor light narrowed again, then widened, then narrowed, as if the door itself breathed.

Eliza sat rigid on the cot with her hands braced on either side of her thighs to keep from folding in on herself. Her eyes burned. Every time her lids lowered, even for the span of a blink, the boards outside creaked or the key scraped or a knuckle tapped wood, and her body jolted awake with a violence that made her bones ache.

At some point the guard stopped speaking the command. He did not need to. The door trained her better than words could. It taught her that sleep was a mistake, and mistakes were always punished.

The cell's gray light thickened, or perhaps her sight did. The high window had long since stopped meaning anything. The light did not shift. It merely existed, a dull smear that refused to turn into morning or deepen into night. Eliza's thoughts slowed and then skittered, like a horse trying to find footing on ice.

She pressed her fingertips against her cheek and felt a wetness there. When she pulled her hand back, there was a faint smear of blood. She had bitten herself again without noticing. The taste of iron sat in her mouth as if she had held a nail between her teeth.

The door creaked wider.

Eliza's head snapped up. She stared at the narrow wedge of corridor, the brighter strip of air beyond. She waited for the broad-shouldered man to appear in the crack, for his hat-in-hand silhouette, for the calm confirmation that she was being seen.

No one came into view.

After a long moment the door eased back, as if satisfied.

Eliza swallowed, throat raw. Her lips moved soundlessly at first, shaping words she could not make her voice produce.

Our Father—

The prayer fell apart the moment it formed. Her mind kept substituting the magistrate's raised hand, the constable's quill, Ezekiel Swann's polite patience. Even God in Salem felt like a record kept by men.

She shifted her weight and the cot creaked. The sound seemed too loud, a confession in itself. She froze, listening for an answering movement outside the door.

Nothing.

Then, from somewhere in the building, that small, dry sound came again. Paper being handled.

It was faint, as if the person turning pages stood far away. Or as if the sound did not travel through air at all, but through the idea of paper itself. Eliza's skin tightened across her arms.

She tried to tell herself it was the constable in his room, late by candlelight, making his record neat. She tried to imagine the brown book's rubbed corners, the way his ink-stained thumb would lift a page and settle it down. Ordinary work. Necessary work, they would call it.

But the cell did not allow the comfort of ordinary. It took every harmless explanation and held it up until it looked thin.

The paper sound came again, closer.

Eliza's breath caught. She leaned forward without meaning to, as though the sound were a person speaking softly from just beyond the wall.

Then, in the hush, she heard it.

Not the guard. Not footsteps. Not keys.

A whisper.

It seemed to come from behind her ear at first, so intimate she felt it brush the fine hairs at her neck. She twisted sharply, shoulders tensing, eyes scanning the corner by the bucket, the shadowed boards, the nail in the wall.

There was no one.

The whisper came again, a thread of sound that might have been her own breath if it had not carried shape. Syllables almost formed, then fell back into murmur, as if the voice were trying out her language the way a mouth tests a new taste.

Eliza pressed both palms against her ears, hard enough to make her pulse thud. She held them there until her arms trembled.

The whisper did not stop. It seeped through, not as sound but as thought placed carefully into her mind, the way Swann placed questions on the table as if setting down clean cloth.

You are tired.

Eliza's eyes stung. She stared at the wall scratches, at the tally marks that had begun to resemble ink lines in her blurred vision. "I am awake," she whispered, the words scraped out of a dry throat.

A pause. Then, softer, almost approving.

Yes.

The single syllable warmed the air around her, and that warmth frightened her more than cold would have. Cold was honest. Warmth meant closeness.

Eliza lowered her hands slowly. Her fingers shook. "Who are you?" she asked again, though she already knew it would not answer in a way that helped her.

The whisper seemed to consider.

Someone who hears you when they do not, it said.

Her stomach turned. She thought of the men outside her door, their patient interruptions, the way they watched her through a crack without speaking. "They hear me," she said, and the sentence came out wrong, as if she were repeating something she had been taught.

The whisper gave a sound that was not quite a laugh, not quite pity. It was something like the soft exhale of someone turning down a lamp.

They hear only what fits, it replied.

Eliza's hands clenched in her lap. "Stop talking," she whispered. She did not want the voice in her head to learn her shape. She did not want it to become familiar.

But it already was, in a way she could not name. It spoke with gentleness, and gentleness was what the room used against her. It spoke with patience, and patience was what Salem wore like righteousness.

You have been very brave, it said, and her throat tightened because the words sounded like Mercy's, not exactly, but close enough to stab.

Eliza's eyes filled hotly. "Don't," she said. "Don't use her."

Another pause, longer. The hush thickened, as if the cell itself leaned in, curious.

Use, the whisper repeated, tasting the word. Then, more softly: You think your mother is only yours.

Eliza's breath came in short, shallow pulls. "Leave her alone."

The whisper did not rise in anger. It did not threaten. It merely spoke the way someone speaks when they are explaining something inevitable to a child.

Your mother is a door, it said. Your father is a door. Even your brother, with his small hands and his quick fear, is a door. You are full of doors.

Eliza pressed her knuckles to her mouth until the taste of iron deepened. Samuel's small hands. The voice had named him without being told. Or perhaps she had thought of him too loudly. Perhaps exhaustion had made her mind porous.

She forced herself to speak, because silence in Salem was never neutral. "I won't listen," she whispered.

You will, the voice answered, and the certainty in it was not harsh. That was the horror. It did not need force to believe itself true.

The door creaked wider again, as if in agreement.

Eliza flinched and stared at the crack. A sliver of corridor appeared, empty. No face. No hat. No broad hand. Only the pale strip of light and the sense of someone standing just out of view.

"Are you there?" she called, and her voice sounded wrong in her own ears, thick and strained.

No answer from the corridor.

The door eased back to its narrow slit.

Eliza's breath shook. She realized with a sudden cold clarity that the door was not only meant to keep her in. It was meant to make her speak to emptiness, to make her ask questions that would make her look unsteady when they wrote them down later.

The whisper seemed pleased by her realization, the way it had been pleased when she understood the purpose of sleep denial.

Yes, it murmured. You are learning their tools.

Eliza dug her nails into her palm. The sharp pain steadied her for a moment. “You’re like them,” she said. “You talk like them.”

The whisper did not deny it.

They learned from me, it said, so calmly her skin prickled. Or I learned from them. It is difficult to remember which came first when something has been done for so long.

Eliza’s stomach lurched. “What are you?”

A slow exhale, almost a sigh, as though the question amused something ancient.

A witness, the whisper replied. A hand that does not tire. A page that does not forget.

Eliza’s gaze snapped to the wall scratches again. She saw them as ink. She saw her name written in the constable’s hand. She saw the brown book open on the threshold, turned toward her like a mouth offering words she had not spoken.

Her heart hammered. “I haven’t confessed,” she whispered. “I haven’t.”

The whisper came closer, not in sound but in presence. The air beside the cot seemed to press down, as if a weight settled there without making the straw move.

You do not understand what confession is, it said gently. Confession is not when you speak. Confession is when the world agrees.

Eliza’s eyes stung with tears she would not let fall. “They can’t make the truth change.”

A pause.

Then the whisper answered with a quietness that felt like the room itself speaking through wood.

They do not change it, it said. They change you.

Eliza’s throat constricted until breathing hurt. She tried to stand, but her legs wavered. She sat back down hard, the cot protesting with a creak.

The guard outside did not react. The door did not move.

The hush deepened, and within it the whisper softened, almost tender, as if offering comfort to a child shaking with fever.

You can stop the shaking, it said. You can stop biting your mouth. You can stop holding your own breath like a secret.

Eliza swallowed and tasted iron. “How?”

A sound like paper turning, very near now, as if a page had been lifted beside her and laid down again.

By letting go, the whisper said. By being written instead of trying to write yourself.

Eliza’s hands flew to her ears again. She rocked slightly without meaning to, the way the afflicted girl had rocked near the meetinghouse steps. The memory struck her like a blow: the girl’s calm eyes, the whisper on the common. It is already written.

Eliza squeezed her eyes shut. Behind her lids she saw black leather, damp to the touch. She saw a page opening as though it had been waiting. She saw faint lines beneath the blankness, a ghost of writing that wanted to darken.

She opened her eyes with a gasp.

The cell was the same: boards, bucket, window, tallies. But the air felt altered, as though something had shifted closer to her skin.

And then, in the quiet, the whisper spoke again, almost as if it were soothing her.

Eliza, it said.

Her name, spoken from inside her mind, landed with sick intimacy. The guard outside had said it with procedure. Swann had said it with false kindness. The magistrate had said it like an object.

This voice said it like it had known her before she knew herself.

Eliza's breath stopped.

The door creaked wider, and for an instant she thought she saw a shadow cross the thin strip of corridor light, too quick to be a man stepping past, too smooth to be ordinary movement. The crack narrowed again at once, as though whatever had moved did not want to be seen.

Eliza stared at the door until her eyes watered.

In the hush, the whisper continued, soft as breath at the edge of sleep.

They will come again, it said. They will ask you what you heard. They will ask you what you saw. You will try to say nothing.

Eliza swallowed hard, throat aching.

And when you try, the whisper added, with the patience of something that did not need to hurry, you will find that your mouth remembers me.

She pressed her palm against her lips, as if she could hold the words inside. Her hand shook. Her body wanted to fold, to sink into darkness, to escape the watching for one unbroken hour.

The door did not move. The guard did not speak.

Only the hush remained, living and close, and within it the whisper held her name as if it were already inked somewhere she could not reach.

Eliza kept her palm pressed to her mouth until her lips went numb.

Her hand did not stop the whisper. It only made her breath warmer against her skin, as if she were trying to smother smoke with cloth. The voice did not push against her the way Swann pushed with questions. It waited in the hush with the patience of rot. It had all the time the room had stolen from her.

Outside the door the guard shifted once, a soft complaint of leather. The sound should have been comforting. A man. A body. Something ordinary.

Instead it only made her picture the narrow crack of corridor light and the unblinking watch that lived in it. Eliza lowered her hand from her mouth and set it in her lap, fingers curled tight, nails half-mooned into her palm. The pain was small, but it belonged to her. She clung to it.

"Leave me," she whispered, not daring to speak louder.

The room listened. The high window held its dull, indifferent gray. The bucket's sourness sat in the air like an accusation. The tally marks on the wall seemed to darken as her eyes strained, as if the scratches were being inked over one line at a time.

The whisper returned, so near it seemed to come from the place where her thoughts formed.

You think I can be sent away, it said. Like a man at a door.

Eliza pressed her forehead to her knees, hard. "I will not answer you," she muttered.

There was a pause, and then the voice said her name again, quietly, almost gently. "Eliza."

She flinched as if struck.

The guard outside had said it with procedure. The magistrate had said it to make her a subject. Swann had said it as if he were doing her a kindness. But this was different. This did not feel like a sound meant to identify her. It felt like a hand closing around something that already belonged to it.

Her throat tightened until the next breath scraped.

"How do you know it?" she asked before she could stop herself, and hated the question as soon as it was out. Questions were invitations. Questions were doors.

The voice did not answer at once. It let the silence settle, as if it were considering how much of itself to show. In that pause Eliza became aware again of the faint paper-dry rustle she had been hearing, the suggestion of a page turned somewhere beyond the wall, somewhere not in the corridor at all. It made her scalp prickle.

Then the whisper spoke, soft as breath on glass.

"I have known it longer than you have," it said.

Eliza lifted her head slowly. The room wavered at the edges of her vision, as if the boards could not hold their shape when she stared too hard. She forced herself to look at the door, at the iron banding, at the bolt line. Things with edges. Things that could be touched.

"You are not real," she said. She tried to make it flat, a statement of fact. But her voice trembled anyway, betraying the effort.

The whisper gave that soft exhale again, not laughter, not pity. Something like a patient correction.

Real, it repeated. Then, quieter: Say your name as you think it is.

Eliza's pulse jumped. "No."

Say it, the whisper insisted, not louder, not threatening. Only certain.

Eliza shut her eyes. She did not want to give the room her name again. She had given it too many times today, and each time it had come back less like hers. But the voice had asked, and the question lodged in her mind like a burr. Say your name as you think it is.

She swallowed. The taste of iron rose again, and she realized she had bitten the inside of her cheek without noticing. She forced her jaw to unclench.

"My name," she whispered, "is Eliza Harrow."

The hush seemed to deepen, as if the room had leaned closer to hear.

The whisper answered at once, intimate and calm.

"No," it said. "That is what they call you now."

Eliza's eyes flew open. Cold spread across her skin. "Now?" she repeated.

The voice did not rush. It seemed to savor the word, as though time itself were something it handled the way the constable handled pages.

"Names change," it said. "They are written over. Scratched out. Given again. You have felt it. Your name has been spoken so often it has begun to loosen."

Eliza's hands trembled. She curled them into fists again to hide it. "Stop," she whispered. "Stop speaking."

The whisper softened, almost tender. "You do not like it because it is true."

Eliza's mouth went dry. She tried to think of home again, of the place before Salem. The attempt made her head ache, as if the memory were a muscle she had overworked. She saw only fragments: a quilt corner, the edge of a table, Samuel's small shoulders running ahead on a road that might not have existed outside this town.

The voice waited until she was fully aware of the effort and the failure.

Then it said, simply, "Liza."

Eliza's breath stopped.

No one in Salem had called her that. Not the men with their calm records. Not the afflicted girl with her strange certainty. Not the townspeople who murmured Eliza Harrow as if the full name were necessary for the verdict.

Only her mother, sometimes, when Eliza was small and feverish. Only her father, rarely, when he had been gentle enough to forget the sternness he wore in front of others. Liza, Mercy would say, and the word would carry warmth and impatience and love all at once.

Eliza felt her stomach drop as if the cot had vanished beneath her.

She gripped the edge of the straw mattress until her knuckles whitened. "Don't," she whispered, and the word came out thin, childlike. "Don't call me that."

The hush held. The guard outside did not move.

The whisper continued, closer now, not in volume but in presence. The air beside her seemed to press down again, as if someone sat at the edge of the cot and the straw accepted the weight without creaking.

"Mercy calls you that when she thinks you cannot hear," the voice said. "When she is afraid you will not wake."

Eliza's vision blurred. She blinked hard, furious at the wetness gathering in her eyes. "You don't know her," she said through clenched teeth. "You don't."

A pause, then the whisper replied with quiet assurance.

"I know what you are made of," it said. "You are made of her voice. You are made of your father's hands lifting you onto a wagon when the mud is deep. You are made of your brother's small fingers in your sleeve. You are made of the things you think are yours alone."

Eliza pressed both palms against her ears again. It did not help. The words did not travel through her ears. They bloomed inside her thoughts as if planted there.

She tried to stand, to move away from the cot, away from the place where she kept imagining a presence. Her legs wobbled. Exhaustion made her body slow and heavy, a thing dragged by invisible ropes.

The door creaked wider.

Eliza snapped her head toward it, heart hammering. The corridor strip brightened, a thin blade laid across the floorboards.

"Awake," a voice murmured from outside, not loud, not cruel.

Eliza's throat worked. "I am awake," she said, and her words sounded wrong, as if she were repeating a line demanded of her.

The crack remained wide for a long moment. She could feel the watchful presence in it, see nothing but light. Then it eased back, narrowing again with soft deliberation.

Eliza's shoulders shook once, a tremor she could not control. She sat back on the cot because her knees would not hold.

The whisper returned, smooth as oil.

"They keep you from sleep so you will not know where your dreams end," it said. "And when you cannot tell, they will ask you what you have seen, and you will answer wrongly. Then they will say it is written."

Eliza stared at the bucket, at the wall scratches, at the stain in the corner that looked almost like spilled ink. "Why are you telling me this?" she whispered. "If you are… if you are what they think…"

The voice seemed to consider. When it spoke again, it sounded almost pleased.

"Because you are not theirs," it said. "Not wholly."

Eliza's skin went cold. "Then whose?" she asked before she could stop herself, and immediately hated the question. Doors, the voice had said. You are full of doors.

The whisper said her name again, not Eliza, not Harrow.

"Liza."

It was not affectionate now. It was possession spoken softly enough to sound like comfort.

Eliza squeezed her eyes shut. Behind her lids, the image came: black leather, damp to the touch, a book that opened itself. A page that looked blank until you stared too long, and then the faintest writing beneath it darkened as though ink rose from the paper's veins.

She opened her eyes with a gasp.

The cell was unchanged. And yet something was different in her. The voice had spoken her childhood name, and in doing so it had reached past the town's story and touched the place where she kept her private self. That place no longer felt sealed.

She heard, very faintly, as if from the corridor or from inside the wall, the careful rustle of paper again. A page turned. Then another. Slow and deliberate, as though someone were searching for the right place to stop.

Eliza's breath came shallow. "Stop it," she whispered, but she did not know who she was pleading with. The guard? The men with their records? The thing that had waited long enough to learn the shape of her mother's voice?

The whisper answered her as if she had asked a question.

"You think they will write you down," it said. "You think the harm is ink."

Eliza's hands curled around the edge of her skirt, twisting fabric until it hurt her fingers.

"The harm," the voice continued, "is that they will make you doubt the sound of your own name."

Eliza's throat tightened so hard it felt like a hand. She tried to say her name again, to prove she could. The word would not come cleanly. It snagged on the memory of how the voice had said Liza, on the way it had made her feel small and known and not safe.

Outside the door, the guard shifted. The door crack widened a fraction, as if he sensed her wavering and wanted to make sure she did not fall into sleep.

The whisper spoke one last time, soft as breath at the edge of her ear.

"Do you know why I say it?" it asked. "Why I speak your name the way your mother does?"

Eliza stared at the thin slit of corridor light, eyes burning, and shook her head once, barely.

The voice's answer was quiet, certain, and so intimate it made her feel stripped.

"Because when the book opens," it said, "it will not call you Eliza Harrow."

Eliza's heart lurched. "Then what?" she managed, the words scraping her throat raw.

The hush pressed in. The cell held its breath.

And the whisper, tender as a lie, gave her a name she had never heard and somehow recognized anyway, like a memory pushed up from beneath the skin.

Eliza's vision dimmed at the edges. She clutched the cot as if it were the only solid thing left in the world.

Outside, the door creaked wider.

"Awake," the guard murmured again.

Eliza's eyes snapped to the crack of light, obedient, frightened, burning with exhaustion. She did not answer with words this time. She only stared, because staring was all she had left that felt like will.

In the silence behind her teeth, the new name echoed without sound, settling into her like ink into paper.

And Eliza understood, with a terror that was colder than any shackle, that the voice did not merely know her name.

It had been waiting to give her another one.

Chapter 8

The Visitor

The guard's murmur faded back into the corridor, and the door eased to its narrow slit again, as if the building itself had grown tired of reminding her she was owned.

Eliza stayed upright on the cot, spine stiff, hands locked around the straw mattress edge. Her eyes were open, painfully open, but the gray in the room had begun to thicken into something like fog. The boards lost their sharpness. The bucket in the corner became an idea more than an object. The tally marks were no longer scratches but dark strokes that seemed to rearrange themselves when she did not stare directly.

She tried to hold onto the last thing the whisper had done: that foreign name, spoken as gently as a mother's call, recognized in her bones without memory. She would not repeat it. Repeating it would be agreement. It would be a step toward the page.

Her throat hurt. Her tongue felt too large, as if her mouth had been stuffed with cloth. She swallowed and tasted iron again, but there was no fresh pain in her cheek that she could find. The taste had become part of the room, like the lye in the corridor. A constant, clean bite under filth.

Outside the door, no one spoke for a time. No knuckle tapped. No key scraped. It was not mercy. It was a different sort of lesson.

If she did not know when she was being watched, then she would behave as though she always was.

Eliza sat very still, listening for the smallest betrayals: leather creaking, a breath, the soft shift of a boot sole. The corridor offered only a steady blankness. She began to wonder, with a fear that felt foolish and then immediately did not feel foolish at all, whether the guard had gone.

The thought brought relief so sudden it made her dizzy. Relief, in the cell, was as dangerous as sleep. It softened the mind. It made room.

She stared at the narrow strip of light in the crack of the door until her eyes watered, and the light began to pulse with her heartbeat. She blinked once, long. Twice. The world stuttered.

She did not lie down. She did not dare. But her head dipped forward as if pulled by a string. Her chin touched her chest.

A soft rustle came, not from the corridor but from somewhere closer, as if a page had been lifted and set down within the boards themselves.

Eliza's head jerked up.

The room was the same. The window still held the same dull gray. The door's slit of light was unchanged. Nothing had moved.

And yet the air beside the cot felt… arranged.

She could not have said how. The cell had always smelled of damp straw and old bodies. Now there was a faint clean note, not soap, not lye, something colder and drier. Like paper kept too long in a box. Like the inside of a book.

Eliza's fingers tightened on the cot edge until the straw mattress creaked. She froze, listening for a response from outside, for the guard to correct her with a murmur of "Awake."

No response came.

Her heart hammered harder. The hush that lived in the room deepened as if pleased by the quiet.

"Who's there?" she whispered. The words barely formed. Her mouth felt cracked.

Nothing answered. But the sensation remained, a pressure near her right side, just behind her hip, as if the air had thickened there.

Eliza turned her head slowly.

At first she saw only the cell: the wall, its stains, the nail with nothing hung from it. Then her eyes found the cot's far end, and her stomach dropped.

The straw mattress was depressed.

Not by her weight. The dip was near the edge, where a person might sit with their feet on the floor. It was a shallow indentation at first, almost subtle enough to be dismissed as the mattress settling, but Eliza watched it deepen as though someone were lowering themselves with care.

The cot gave a small, complaining creak.

Eliza could not breathe. Her throat locked, and air scraped in thinly through her nose.

The indentation held, steady now, as if whatever had sat there had found a comfortable place.

She stared until her eyes burned, waiting for the shape to form, for shadow to gather into a body. She saw nothing. No outline. No face. Only the pressed straw and the slight pull of fabric at the cot's edge, as though a hand had gripped it for balance.

Her own hands flew to the mattress again, instinctively, because if she could feel the straw and the boards she could prove herself real. The moment her fingers touched, a chill traveled up her skin, a sensation like touching stone in winter.

The dip did not vanish.

It did not react to her touch like a trick of imagination. It remained, patient, present.

Eliza forced herself to speak. Her voice came out in a thin rasp. “Stop.”

The word did not seem to reach the thing. Or perhaps it did, and the thing simply did not obey.

A soft sound came, very close. Not breath, not quite. A careful shift of weight. The cot creaked again, and the straw compressed a fraction deeper.

Eliza’s eyes flicked to the door. The slit of corridor light remained narrow. No boots moved. No key turned. If a guard stood outside, he did not intervene. If he had gone, then Eliza was alone with what had decided to join her.

Her pulse thudded so loud she thought it might wake the whole building.

Then the whisper spoke, not from the corners of the room now, not from behind her ear, but from the place directly beside her, as if the words were being spoken into the air between them.

"Do not frighten yourself," it said.

The voice was the same gentleness that had been threading through her exhaustion for hours, but now it carried something new: the faintest texture of presence. Not merely thought. Not merely memory pretending to be her own. It sounded like a mouth without warmth.

Eliza's skin crawled. "You're not here," she whispered.

A pause. The cot creaked softly, and the indentation shifted as if whoever sat there had turned their head to regard her more fully.

"I am," the voice replied. "This is the first time you have been quiet enough to notice."

Eliza's nails dug into her palm. Pain flared. It steadied her for a single heartbeat and then slid away again, swallowed by exhaustion.

She stared at the depression in the straw. She wanted to reach out. She wanted not to. Every instinct in her body screamed to move away, to press herself into the far corner where she could keep her back to boards and see the room. But her legs would not obey with speed. Her body was heavy, slow, as if sleep denial had filled her bones with wet sand.

"What do you want?" she asked. The question came out before she could stop it, and she hated herself for giving it that opening. Doors. You are full of doors.

The voice seemed to soften. "Relief," it said. "For you."

Eliza swallowed. The iron taste was stronger now. She did not know whether she was bleeding again or whether the room had simply decided she should taste it. "I don't want anything from you."

Another small shift. The cot's edge dipped a fraction. The straw sighed.

"You do," the voice corrected, gently, as if reminding her of something she had forgotten. "You want sleep. You want the watching to stop. You want your mother's face to stay still in your mind when you call it."

Eliza's eyes stung. She blinked and felt moisture spill before she could stop it. She wiped it quickly with the back of her hand, furious. "Don't speak of her."

"I did not bring her," the voice said. "They did. They brought her into this room when they took you. They put her in your mouth when they made you bite until you tasted iron. They put her in your head when they told you you had already spoken."

Eliza's breath hitched. The voice was right in the way that made truth feel like a trap.

She stared at the pressed straw, at the place where an invisible thigh or hip must be resting. She imagined, against her will, a figure sitting there: patient, composed, hands folded, waiting as Swann waited. But this was not Swann. Swann had smelled of soap and law. This smelled like paper and old quiet.

"Why now?" Eliza whispered.

"Because you are breaking," the voice said, without cruelty. It spoke as one might speak of a cup cracking under heat. "And when you break, you will try to fill the crack with anything that promises to hold you together."

Eliza's chest tightened. She wanted to deny it, but denial had become a useless muscle. It ached and did nothing.

The indentation beside her deepened suddenly, as if the visitor leaned closer. Eliza felt the faintest brush of cold against the back of her hand, not a touch exactly, but a passing of air that was not air.

She jerked her hand away, and the cot creaked loudly.

Outside the door, still nothing. No "Awake." No boot shift.

The absence of the guard's interruption felt like permission granted by someone else.

Eliza's voice shook. "Are you the Devil?"

The voice paused long enough that Eliza felt, absurdly, as if it were choosing how to appear. Then it said, quietly, "You have been taught to name what frightens you so you can pretend the name contains it."

The straw dip eased back a fraction, a small retreat that was not mercy so much as a demonstration of control.

"I am what answers," the voice continued. "When the town calls."

Eliza's mouth went dry. "I didn't call you."

"Yes," it said, and now there was something almost tender in it, a terrible imitation of comfort. "You did. Not with words."

The visitor shifted again, and the cot's edge creaked as if a hand pressed down to steady itself. The indentation remained, undeniable.

Eliza stared at it until her vision blurred. The room swayed, not in space but in certainty. She could feel her own mind trying to decide whether to accept what her eyes could not see but what the straw plainly showed.

The voice lowered, as if speaking to a child in a sickbed.

"Lie down," it said. "Just for a moment. I will sit here. I will keep the watching away."

Eliza's whole body trembled with the ache of that promise. Sleep rose inside her like a tide, thick and irresistible. She hated herself for how badly she wanted to believe.

Behind her teeth, the foreign name the voice had given her pulsed like a bruise.

"I can't," she whispered. "If I sleep, they'll take it. They'll ask me what I saw. They'll write it."

The visitor's presence seemed to settle, calm and certain, and Eliza felt the cot dip as if the invisible weight shifted into something like patience.

"Let them write," the voice said. "Ink is only proof to those who fear blank pages."

Eliza's eyes closed for a heartbeat, not in surrender but in weakness, and she felt it then: the cot moving slightly beneath her, not with her own breath or shifting, but with the subtle, careful rhythm of something sitting beside her as if it had always belonged there.

When she opened her eyes again, the indentation was still there.

And in the unbroken hush of the cell, with the guard strangely silent outside the door, Eliza understood that the watching had changed.

It was no longer only Salem.

Something else had taken a seat at her side.

Eliza did not move.

She sat with her shoulders drawn tight, hands clenched in her lap as if she could keep her body from doing what it wanted. The visitor's weight remained at the cot's edge. The straw stayed pressed down, the boards beneath giving that faint, steady complaint that proved it was not only in her head.

The voice had said, I will keep the watching away.

Outside the door, the corridor was quiet. Too quiet. Eliza waited for the familiar interruption, the soft rap, the key's teasing turn, the murmur of "Awake" spoken like instruction. Nothing came. The silence beyond the door felt arranged, as if someone had placed it there carefully, the way the constable placed his book square with the table's edge.

Her throat worked around dryness. "You cannot," she whispered.

The visitor did not answer immediately. The straw dip shifted a fraction, as though it had turned to look at her more fully. She still saw nothing but the effect of weight.

"I can," the voice said at last, and it did not sound like a boast. It sounded like a simple correction. "I have been doing it longer than they have."

Eliza's heart beat hard enough to make her light-headed. "Who are you?" she asked, and the question came out with an edge of pleading she hated.

The voice stayed gentle. "Do you want my name," it asked, "or do you want rest?"

Eliza swallowed. The taste of iron rose again, sharp as a penny under her tongue. "I want to go home."

A pause. Then, softly, "Home is a place your mind cannot hold right now."

Eliza's eyes stung. She forced them open wider, as if she could keep her thoughts from slipping by sheer strain. "Don't speak as if you know me."

"I speak as if I hear you," the visitor replied. "There is a difference."

The straw at the cot's edge compressed slightly, a careful settling. Eliza's skin tightened along her arms. She wanted to scoot away, to put the width of the cot between herself and that invisible presence, but her body felt slow and heavy, and moving would make sound. Sound would invite the guard's attention. Sound would be taken as proof she was not calm, not innocent, not quiet.

And still no knock came. No key. No thin blade of corridor light widening and narrowing like a lid.

Eliza stared at the door, at the narrow slit that admitted a dim strip of pale. The strip did not change. The building seemed to hold its breath.

The visitor spoke again, as if following her gaze. "You have learned their pattern."

Eliza's jaw tightened. "They are keeping me awake."

"Yes," the voice said. "They are teaching you to betray yourself. To jump at small sounds. To beg for sleep. To answer questions badly so the record can correct you."

The words made her stomach turn because they sounded too much like her own thoughts, the ones she had been trying to keep straight in the dark. She gripped the edge of her skirt until her knuckles hurt.

"And you," she said, "what are you teaching me?"

The visitor's presence seemed to lean closer without touching her. The cot creaked softly in protest.

"I am offering you relief," it said, and there was a warmth in the tone that felt like someone smoothing a blanket, a kindness that did not belong in a cell. "Nothing more."

Eliza shook her head once, small and stubborn. "Relief is never nothing."

"Clever," the voice murmured, almost approving. "You are still yourself enough to say that."

Eliza's breath shivered. Still yourself. As if she were a thing that could be lost in increments, shaved away by tiredness until only what Salem wanted remained.

She heard the faintest sound then, not in the cell but beyond it. A distant shift of wood. A foot? A board settling? Eliza's spine went rigid, and her eyes snapped to the door crack.

The visitor spoke before the guard could. "No," it said quietly. "Stay where you are. Do not turn your fear into a prayer they can hear."

Eliza froze, caught between instinct and the strange authority in that low command. The visitor had not been commanding before. It had suggested, offered, coaxed. This was different. This was certainty, placed over her like a hand.

The corridor remained silent.

Eliza's lungs burned. She let her breath out in a slow, controlled stream, and hated the small rush of gratitude she felt. As soon as it rose in her, it shamed her. Gratitude for being allowed to breathe.

"You see?" the visitor asked.

Eliza did not answer. She could not trust her voice.

The straw depression shifted again, and Eliza felt, with sick clarity, the sense of a hand being raised near her, though she saw nothing. The air cooled along her cheek, close but not touching, like someone testing the heat of fever skin.

"You are worn raw," the voice said. "Every thought scrapes. Every memory bleeds when you pull at it."

Eliza's fingers curled, nails digging crescents into her palms. Pain anchored her. Pain was hers.

"You keep biting your mouth," the visitor continued. "You do not even know when it happens."

Eliza swallowed, and the iron taste deepened as if in agreement.

“I can take that from you,” the voice said.

Eliza turned her head sharply, as if looking might reveal the trick. She saw the same blank corner, the same bucket, the same stain near the wall. “Take it,” she repeated. “How?”

The visitor’s answer was patient. “You let your jaw unclench. You let your tongue rest. You let your body do what bodies do when they are not being hunted.”

Eliza’s mouth trembled. “And what do you get?”

The cot creaked, a small sound like a throat clearing. “You are always bargaining,” the voice said. “Because they have taught you everything is a transaction. Confess and live. Deny and die. Speak and be written. Stay silent and be written anyway.”

Eliza’s eyes burned. “Then say what you want.”

A pause, long enough to make her skin prickle.

“I want you to stop fighting your own mind,” the visitor said at last. “Not because I pity you. Because it hurts to watch.”

Eliza stared at the indentation until her vision blurred. “Watch,” she whispered. “Like them.”

The visitor did not deny it. “Yes.”

The frankness stole her breath more effectively than a slap would have.

Outside the door, still nothing. The guard's calm interruptions had been as regular as cruelty could be made. Now the pattern had broken, and the break felt like a new kind of danger. The visitor had said it could keep the watching away. Eliza realized she did not know which watching it meant. The guard's? Salem's? Or its own?

Her eyelids fluttered. The simple act of holding them open had become labor. Sleep pressed against her from the inside, a tide that did not ask permission.

The visitor's voice softened again, closer. "Lie down," it repeated. "If you sleep, you will not be punished for it."

Eliza let out a sound that was almost a laugh, except there was no humor in it. "That is a lie."

"It is a promise," the voice corrected.

Eliza's throat tightened around a sob she refused to give it. "They will wake me."

"They will try," the visitor said.

The words were calm. Too calm. Eliza imagined, against her will, a hand on the other side of the door, fingers resting on the bolt, ready to scrape it just enough to tear her from the edge of dreaming.

The visitor spoke as if reading the picture from her mind. "They will touch the lock and find it stubborn. They will whisper your name through the crack and feel their own tongue thicken. They will decide it is better to wait."

Eliza's breath caught. "You can do that?"

The cot dipped a fraction deeper, and Eliza felt the weight beside her settle into something like ownership of the space. "This building," the visitor said, "has listened to enough vows and enough lies to be persuaded by either. Wood remembers. Iron remembers. It is not as solid as you think."

Eliza stared at the door. The iron bands across it looked suddenly less like strength and more like decoration, a show of certainty.

"And if I lie down," she whispered, "what then?"

"Then your body sleeps," the visitor said, as if the answer should have been obvious. "And your mind stops trying to hold every piece of itself at once. And for a little while you do not feel them pulling you apart."

Eliza's hands shook. She slid them under her thighs to hide it, to pin them down with her own weight. "And when I wake?"

The visitor's voice went so gentle it made her skin crawl. "When you wake, you will remember what it feels like to be whole."

Eliza shut her eyes for a moment, because the promise hit some deep, animal place in her that wanted to believe it without question. Whole. Before Salem's certainty. Before her name became ink. Before her mother's face blurred when she tried to hold it steady.

Behind her closed lids she saw Mercy again, but not as a wavering outline. For a heartbeat she saw her clearly, as if the visitor had placed the image there with careful hands: Mercy's brow drawn, her mouth tight with fear she would not show the town, her fingers gripping Eliza's wrist hard enough to hurt.

Eliza's eyes flew open.

The image vanished at once, leaving only the gray room and the pressed straw beside her. Her pulse raced. "You did that," she whispered.

The visitor did not sound pleased with itself. It sounded matter-of-fact. "Yes."

Eliza's mouth went dry. If it could give her Mercy's face, clear and sharp, then it could do worse. It could give her anything. It could put words in her mouth the way the constable did on paper, only quieter, only inside.

"No," Eliza said, and the refusal came out weak. "No. Don't."

The visitor's presence leaned back slightly, and the straw indentation eased a fraction, as though it had relaxed. "I will not force you," it said. "That is their way."

Eliza's laugh broke out, harsh and sudden. "And yours is to offer."

"Yes," the visitor replied. "Because offering is cleaner. Offering lets you believe you chose."

Eliza's breath shook. She could feel herself slipping toward the edge of sleep anyway. Her muscles ached with it. Her eyes wanted to close. Her jaw wanted to unclench. Her tongue wanted to rest.

The door remained still. No knock came. No key teased the lock.

The visitor waited beside her, patient as the hush in the room, and spoke one last time, quiet as a thought.

“Lie down, Liza,” it said, using that stolen name again, soft enough to sound like mercy. “Just for a little while. Let me hold the door shut.”

Eliza flinched at the name, at the intimacy of it, at the way it reached under her skin. But her body betrayed her. She shifted, slowly, and lowered herself onto the straw mattress.

The cot creaked under her, and the visitor’s weight beside her remained steady, a cold anchor at the edge.

Eliza turned her face toward the wall, away from the indentation she could not bear to look at, and let her eyelids fall.

She waited for the guard’s murmur. She waited for the familiar interruption that would prove this was only another trick.

Nothing came.

For the first time since they had brought her to the lower room, the cell did not snap her back into waking.

Sleep took her in a thick, sudden pull, and just before she slipped fully under, she felt it: not a hand, not a touch, but the distinct impression of being watched with care instead of accusation.

A relief so sharp it frightened her even as she sank into it.

Sleep did not arrive gently.

It came like a hand over her eyes, firm and practiced, pressing her down through the thin straw and the hard boards until even the ache in her bones dulled. Eliza let herself fall because she could not keep standing on the edge of waking any longer. Her last clear thought, before the darkness took her, was of the door and the crack of corridor light that had ruled her like a master.

Let me hold the door shut, the visitor had said.

Now the door, in her mind, was not wood at all, but the cover of a book being closed with deliberate care.

She drifted into a place that was not quite dream and not quite absence. Images rose and broke apart before she could grasp them. The road into Salem, pines like black needles. Her mother's hand on her wrist, the pressure of it sharp enough to bruise. The magistrate's palm raised to silence a room. The constable's quill scratching, the sound dry and endless.

Then the book.

Not the small brown one the constable carried, but something heavier, bound in black, its leather damp as if it had been held too long by something without warmth. It lay on a table that might have been the interrogation table, except the table stretched farther than it should have, its surface disappearing into fog. Eliza reached for it and found she could not make her arm move. Her body was present, but distant, as if she were watching herself from the ceiling boards.

A page turned with the careful sound she had heard through the cell wall.

Another page.

She tried to shout; to say she had not asked for this, that she had not called it. Her mouth would not open. Her jaw was slack, resting the way the visitor had urged it to rest, and the helplessness of that rest frightened her even inside the dream.

The page looked blank at first. She felt a rush of relief at the emptiness. Blank meant unclaimed. Blank meant no record.

Then, as though the paper warmed to her gaze, faint writing began to rise from beneath the surface. Not ink laid on top, but something that had always been there, waiting for her eyes to do the work of darkening it.

A name formed. Not Eliza Harrow.

The foreign name the visitor had whispered settled onto the page, each letter appearing with the patient confidence of something being restored, not created. Eliza recognized it the way she recognized the sound of her mother calling her childhood nickname: with her body first, before her mind could explain.

She tried again to move, to tear the page, to shut the book. Her hands remained still.

A pressure at the edge of her awareness made her turn her head in the dream. Someone sat beside her, just out of sight, close enough that she could feel cold where warmth should be. The weight of them did not move the table, did not disturb the fog. It only existed.

"Rest," the visitor said, and the word slid into her like water into dry cloth.

Eliza sank deeper. The table, the book, the name, all of it receded, not gone but set aside, as though she had been tucked carefully under a blanket. For the first time since the meetinghouse, she did not feel the need to hold herself together by force.

The darkness held.

And then she woke.

At first, she thought she had not. The cell's gray light was unchanged, the kind of light that made mornings and evenings identical. Her eyes opened reluctantly, lids heavy as wet wool. She expected, automatically, the scrape of the lock, the tap of a knuckle, the guard's murmured "Awake" spoken with calm authority.

Nothing came.

The absence was so complete it felt like a sound of its own.

Eliza lay still, afraid to test it. Her body had the thick heaviness of real sleep, not the sharp, broken exhaustion she had been forced into before. Her mouth no longer tasted sharply of iron. The inside of her cheek ached faintly, as if healing had begun in the brief time she had been allowed to stop biting herself.

She breathed in. Damp straw. Old boards. And beneath it, faintly, that dry, cold scent like paper kept too long in a box.

The visitor.

Eliza did not want to turn her head. She did not want to look and see the indentation. She did not want to look and see nothing, because nothing would mean she had imagined it, and imagining it would mean her mind had begun to betray her in earnest. Either answer would be a kind of terror.

She forced herself anyway.

Her eyes moved to the cot's edge.

The straw mattress beside her was still depressed.

Not as deeply as it had been when the visitor first "sat," but enough to be wrong. Enough to be unmistakable. The straw was pressed into an oval, the fabric pulled slightly toward that spot as though a weight still drew it down.

Eliza's skin tightened.

She pushed herself up on one elbow, slow, careful, as if sudden motion might cause the room to punish her for having slept. The cot creaked softly. The indentation did not shift with the motion the way a natural dip in the mattress would. It held its shape, stubborn, as though the straw had learned it and could not forget.

Eliza stared at the pressed place and waited for the visitor's voice.

No whisper came.

The silence in the cell was different from the silence that had tormented her before. This was not the hush of attention gathering to witness her breaking. It was simply quiet, as if something had closed its eyes after watching too long.

Outside the door, the corridor offered nothing. No shift of boots. No breath. The crack of light under the door looked the same as it always had, but the door itself did not breathe open and shut. It stayed still, as if truly held.

Eliza swung her legs over the side of the cot, avoiding the depressed area instinctively, and set her feet on the boards. The floor was cold through her boots. The simple sensation made her feel more awake than any interruption had.

She leaned toward the indentation, slowly, and hovered her hand over it. Her fingers trembled. She did not want to touch it, because touching would make it real in a way she could not undo. And yet she needed to know whether her eyes were lying.

Her fingertips brushed the straw.

Cold.

Not the ordinary chill of damp straw in a stone-walled building. A colder cold, a clean absence of warmth, like the feeling left behind when a body rises from a bed that was never alive to begin with. The straw was pressed down and stiff, as though it had been packed tightly by long, patient pressure.

Eliza snatched her hand back and wiped it on her skirt in a frantic, useless gesture.

She looked at the door again. Still nothing.

A strange, unreasonable thought came to her, and with it a flicker of relief so sharp it made her nauseous: If the visitor could hold the door shut, then perhaps Swann and Parris could not reach her right now. Perhaps, for a few breaths, she was beyond their calm certainty and their records.

Then the larger fear followed, heavy as a stone dropped into water: beyond them did not mean free. Beyond them might mean claimed.

Eliza stood, knees unsteady, and took a single step away from the cot. The room tilted slightly, but not from fatigue. From uncertainty. The cell was the same size it had always been, yet it felt as if some boundary had shifted. As if a line had been drawn in the air and she had crossed it by sleeping when she was not meant to.

She moved to the wall with the tally marks and pressed her palm flat against the scratched wood. The boards were rough, splintered in places where other desperate fingers had dug in. She counted the slashes without meaning to, trying to anchor herself.

One, two, three, four, slash.

Her mind slipped, and she forgot where she was in the sequence. She pressed harder, angry with herself, and forced her eyes to focus. The scratches were still scratches. Not ink. Not words. Not names.

She turned her head back toward the cot.

The indentation remained.

Eliza swallowed, throat dry again. “Are you still here?” she whispered, and hated herself for the softness in it. It sounded like the beginning of reliance.

No answer.

Only that pressed, patient shape in the straw, a proof without a witness.

She went back to the cot and knelt beside it, lowering herself until her face was close to the depression, as if she could catch the faint movement of air that would betray breath. Her own breath stirred the straw. The indentation did not respond. It sat there like a seal impressed into wax.

Eliza’s hands tightened into fists. “What do you want from me?” she whispered, and the words came out more like a plea than a challenge.

Still nothing.

For a moment she wondered if this was the visitor’s true gift: not comfort, not sleep, but evidence. A mark left behind, like the tally scratches, like a name in ink. Something that proved she had not been alone.

Then the horror of that idea took shape. Evidence could be used.

If Swann came in and saw the pressed straw, he would not see a visitor that had kept her safe. He would see proof that she entertained spirits in her cell. He would see proof that she had company where she should have had only silence. He would see exactly what Salem wanted to see.

Eliza stood quickly and stepped back, as if distance could undo the mark. She smoothed the blanket over the cot with shaking hands, trying to hide the depression, trying to force the straw to rise.

It would not.

The blanket lay over the dip and revealed it anyway, a gentle hollow that looked like the outline of a seated person beneath a shroud.

Eliza backed away from the cot, heart hammering, and looked at the door. "Help," she whispered, and did not know who she meant it for. Not the visitor, not the men. God, perhaps, but God felt very far from a room that could be persuaded by vows and lies.

The silence held.

Then, from the corridor, a sound.

Not a knock. Not a key teasing the lock.

Footsteps approaching, steady and unhurried, the boards outside creaking under weight.

Eliza's breath caught. She stood frozen, staring at the door as if she could will it to remain shut. The footsteps came closer, stopped.

A pause.

Then the key entered the lock with a soft scrape.

Eliza's gaze flicked wildly to the cot.

The indentation remained, visible even under the blanket, patient as a signature.

The lock turned.

The bolt slid back.

And Eliza stood in the center of the room, the taste of fear rising fresh and metallic in her mouth, realizing with sick clarity that the visitor had not removed its weight from the straw.

It had only removed its voice.

The door began to open, letting the corridor's pale light spill in, and Eliza could not tell which was worse: that the men might see what was left behind, or that they might not see it at all, and she would be the only one forced to live with the shape of it.

The indentation remained.

Like a place saved.

Like a seat that expected to be filled again.

Chapter 9

Spectral Testimony

The door opened the width of a hand, and the corridor's pale light cut across the boards as cleanly as a blade.

Ezekiel Swann stood in the gap.

He looked as he had before: brushed coat, clean hands, mild attention that made no room for argument. Behind him the broader guard waited with his hat in hand, face unreadable. Neither of them stepped fully into the cell at once. Swann's eyes moved over the room with the practiced calm of a man inspecting a ledger for errors.

Eliza's body went cold, and her gaze snapped, helplessly, to the cot.

The blanket still lay over the hollow. Even covered, it made the shape of a seated person beneath linen: a gentle dip where no person sat.

Swann's eyes followed hers.

For a moment nothing in his face changed. Eliza held her breath, waiting for the flicker of triumph, the faint lift of certainty. She waited for him to say, There, you see? Proof.

Instead he looked back at her, and if anything shifted in him it was so small it could have been imagination. A slight narrowing, as though he had found a stain that would be noted later, not remarked upon now.

"Eliza Harrow," he said, using her full name as a key, "come with us."

She did not move. Her legs were heavy with the residue of real sleep and a fear sharper than exhaustion. "I was sleeping," she managed, and heard how foolish it sounded. As if sleep were an offense requiring defense.

Swann's expression did not soften. "Yes," he said. "I am told you slept."

The way he said it made Eliza's mouth go dry. Not I see you slept. Not You look rested. I am told. As if her body's simplest act had already been reported, already entered into someone's record.

The broader guard stepped into the cell and took her elbow. Not rough. Not gentle. The same guiding hold as before. Eliza's skin prickled where his fingers met her sleeve.

As they led her out, she turned her head once more toward the cot. The indentation remained beneath the blanket, patient and unmistakable, like a mark pressed into wax.

Then Swann shifted his body in the doorway and blocked her view of it.

The corridor smelled of lye and damp boards. Eliza's steps were unsteady at first, and the guard's grip tightened a fraction, not to hurt but to remind her that falling was not permitted. They walked past corners that refused to become familiar, the building folding around them as if it had been made to confuse direction on purpose. She tried to count steps and lost the number almost at once.

Ahead, voices rose and fell, and the sound of them made something in Eliza's chest seize. Not because she had missed human speech. Because voices meant witnesses. Voices meant Salem had decided to speak without her.

They brought her into a larger room than the table room, though it shared the same bones: plain boards, harsh angles, windows that offered weak light. Benches lined the walls, and bodies crowded them. Townspeople sat shoulder to shoulder as if packed for warmth, but no warmth lived in their faces. They looked toward the front where a long table had been set, and behind it men sat in authority, papers and books spread like offerings.

Eliza's stomach turned. She recognized Deputy Parris by his pale eyes. She recognized the constable's small brown book and the ink-stained thumb that held it open. Reverend Hale stood off to one side, hands folded in front of him, his face attentive in a way that felt merciless. He looked like a man listening for God in other people's suffering.

Swann guided Eliza forward to a stool placed where all could see her.

The room's eyes fixed on her as one.

She sat because her legs threatened to give. The guard stepped behind her, close enough that she could feel his breath when he shifted. She clasped her hands in her lap so tightly her fingers went numb.

A magistrate Eliza had not seen before leaned forward. His hair was grayer, his mouth thin with the self-control of a man convinced that emotion was a kind of sin. "Bring the first witness," he said.

The constable dipped his quill.

Eliza stared at the quill as if it were a weapon. It was always the same. Calm. Procedure. Ink.

A man was brought forward. Eliza recognized him at once, and her stomach sank further.

Josiah Waller.

He looked smaller here than he had in the store, his shoulders hunched as if bracing for cold. But his eyes were wide and bright, not with fear exactly. With the feverish conviction of someone whose dream has become more real than his waking.

He did not look at Eliza at first. He looked at the magistrates, then at Reverend Hale, then at the crowd, as if searching for permission to speak.

"State your name for the record," the magistrate said.

"Josiah Waller," the man answered, voice hoarse. "Shopkeeper."

The constable wrote.

"And what is it you claim to have seen?" the magistrate asked.

Waller swallowed hard. His gaze flicked toward Eliza and then away again, as though looking at her too long might invite the thing he feared back into the room. "I seen her," he said. "In the night."

A murmur moved through the benches like wind through dry leaves.

Eliza's throat tightened. She forced herself to speak, but the guard behind her shifted, a subtle warning. Not now. Not out of turn. Not in a way that could be written as interruption.

The magistrate's voice remained even. "You saw this girl in your home."

"Yes, sir." Waller's hands twisted in front of him. "At the foot of my bed. I woke and she was there like she'd been there a long while."

Eliza's skin went cold in a way that had nothing to do with the room's draft. At the foot of my bed. The phrase struck something in her mind, an image that was not memory and not dream, and she hated how quickly it formed: dark boards, a bed, the sense of watching someone sleep.

Swann's calm voice cut in, gentle as a knife sliding between ribs. "Did she speak to you, Master Waller?"

Waller nodded quickly, as if relieved to be given the path. "Aye. She spoke quiet. Like she didn't want the house to hear."

"How did she address you?"

Waller licked his lips. "By name."

The constable wrote faster. Scratch, scratch. Eliza's stomach rolled at the sound.

"And what did she say?" Swann asked.

Waller's eyes flicked toward Reverend Hale this time, and Hale's face did not change. Not approval, not disapproval. Only listening.

"She said," Waller began, and his voice shook with the effort of repeating it, "she said I must sign. That there was a book. A black book. And that it would be easier for me if I did it willing."

A low sound rose from the crowd, part prayer, part horror. Eliza felt it in her bones like a vibration.

The magistrate leaned forward. "A black book," he repeated, as if savoring the words because they fit so neatly.

Waller nodded hard. "She held out a quill. I could see it plain. And when I said no, she smiled. Not friendly. Like she already knew I'd do it in time."

Eliza's mouth went dry. She saw, for a moment, the pressed straw on her cot. A seat saved. A place expected to be filled again.

Swann's voice remained mild. "Describe her clothing."

Waller blinked, as if the details were too sharp. "A dark dress. Plain. But… but there was mud at the hem. Like she'd walked a long road to get there."

Eliza's pulse hammered. Mud at the hem. Her mind flashed to the road into Salem, pines like black needles, the sensation of being watched. She tried to tell herself it was only coincidence, the sort of detail any man might invent when he wished to be believed.

But something in her, the exhausted part that had been trained by the cell to doubt itself, whispered that it was not invented. That it was remembered.

The magistrate's gaze shifted to Eliza. "Did you go to this man's home in the night?" he asked her, as calmly as if asking whether she had visited a cousin.

Eliza opened her mouth. No sound came at first. Her throat felt lined with ash.

"No," she said finally. The word came out thin. "I have been in the cell."

Swann's eyes remained on her. "And yet he says he saw you."

"He is lying," Eliza said, louder this time, and several heads in the crowd tilted as if she had proven something by raising her voice.

Waller made a strangled sound. "I ain't lying," he said, eyes shining. "I woke and *you* was there. And I couldn't move. Like something held my chest down. Only my eyes could move. Only my mouth, and even then it felt thick. You told me I'd be left alone if I signed."

Eliza's skin prickled. Swann's earlier words returned with sick precision: They will whisper your name through the crack and feel their own tongue thicken. She had thought that was the visitor speaking. Now she heard it in Waller's testimony, as if the same shape of experience had been poured into his mouth.

Reverend Hale stepped forward slightly, his voice quiet but carrying. "Master Waller," he asked, "did you pray?"

Waller nodded, frantic. "I tried. But the words wouldn't come right. Like my tongue was tied. And she just watched me. She watched as if she'd heard prayers before and they didn't matter."

Hale's gaze moved to Eliza, not accusing, not kind. Measuring. As if he were watching for a sign that would confirm what he already believed.

Eliza's hands clenched in her lap. She realized her nails had broken skin. She welcomed the sting. It was real. It was hers.

The magistrate nodded once. "Very well," he said. "You may step back."

Waller backed away like a man leaving a graveyard.

Another witness was called, then another. A woman with her bonnet clutched tight said she had woken to find Eliza sitting in a chair by her hearth, turning her head slowly as if listening to a sound no one else could hear. A boy no older than Samuel claimed he had seen Eliza at the edge of his bed, her face close, her eyes too open, telling him not to tell his mother because mothers made things worse.

Each testimony carried a detail that burrowed under Eliza's skin: the mud, the iron taste, the thick tongue, the quiet certainty of being watched. They did not speak like people inventing lies to please a court. They spoke like people trying to make sense of something that had already marked them.

And as each one spoke, Eliza felt the room shift further away from truth and deeper into belief. The constable's quill moved steadily, turning their fear into record.

She tried to catch Reverend Hale's eye, to find in him some hint of doubt. But Hale only listened, his face grave, as though he had expected this chorus all along and was merely allowing it to unfold in proper order.

Swann's voice returned, smooth and reasonable. "Do you hear them, Eliza?"

Eliza's breath shook. "I hear them," she said. "I don't understand it."

Swann tilted his head. "But you do not deny that they speak with one voice."

"They speak with one fear," Eliza snapped, and immediately regretted the sharpness.

The magistrate's mouth tightened. "Fear does not produce the same details in so many mouths," he said, as if reciting a rule.

Eliza looked from face to face: men she did not know, women whose eyes shone with righteous dread, the deputy with his calm certainty, the constable with his ink, the reverend with his listening.

She thought of the visitor's whisper in the dark: Confession is when the world agrees.

Around her, the world was agreeing.

And the worst part, the part that made her stomach hollow, was that as the witnesses spoke, her mind began to supply images to match them. Not memories, exactly. Not dreams. Something in between. A flicker of a room not hers. A bedframe creaking. A man's breath catching in the dark. The weight of standing at the foot of a bed and being certain, impossibly certain, that you belonged there.

Eliza swallowed hard, tasting the faint return of iron.

The guard behind her shifted, and his presence reminded her of the cell, of the pressed straw, of the seat saved.

Swann leaned in just slightly, his voice low enough to sound almost compassionate. “We will hear more,” he said. “And you will have your chance to answer. But understand this, Eliza Harrow: Salem does not require you to remember. It requires you to be named.”

Eliza stared at the constable’s quill as it scratched across paper.

She thought of the indentation that had remained on her cot.

A mark that could be used.

A sign that would be interpreted.

A place saved, like a line in a book waiting to be darkened.

And as the next witness was called, Eliza felt, beneath the noise of the room, the faintest sense of attention returning. Not from the townspeople. Not from the magistrates.

Something older, patient as paper, listening with quiet satisfaction as strangers stood and spoke of seeing her in the night.

The next witness was not brought forward with the same haste as the others.

There was a pause at the table, a faint consultation between the magistrate and Swann, their heads angled just enough to suggest private agreement while keeping the appearance of procedure. The constable's quill hovered over the page as if waiting for the proper name to be offered.

From the benches, a woman rose slowly, as though her body disliked the act of standing in front of so many eyes. She was middle-aged, hair hidden under a bonnet, hands red and chapped as if from washing. She did not look like someone who enjoyed attention. That, Eliza realized with a sinking dread, made her more believable to them than any trembling zealot.

"State your name," the gray-haired magistrate said.

"Abigail Foster," she answered, voice thin but steady. "Wife to Thomas Foster."

The constable wrote.

"And why have you come before this court?" the magistrate asked.

Abigail's gaze fixed on a spot above Eliza's head, as if looking directly at her would invite something to happen. "Because I cannot sleep," she said, and a murmur ran through the room, less dramatic than before, more intimate. Sleep was a common currency in Salem now. Everyone understood its price.

Swann's voice slid in, measured and gentle. "Tell us what troubles your sleep."

Abigail swallowed. "I dream of her," she said, and for the first time her eyes flicked to Eliza, quick and frightened. "I dream of the girl. And the dream is not like other dreams."

The magistrate's fingers tapped once on the table. Not impatience. Encouragement. "In what manner is it different?"

Abigail's hands twisted at her apron as if wringing water from cloth. "It has weight," she said. "It has… order. Like steps you're made to take."

Eliza's skin tightened along her arms. She thought of the corridor's turns, the way the building folded around her so she could not count her way out. Like steps you're made to take.

"And what do you see in these dreams?" Swann asked.

Abigail's mouth worked as if the words were difficult to push past her teeth. "I see my own house," she said. "But it is not my house as it is in day. The corners are wrong. The shadows are too long. The hearth is cold even when the fire is there."

A small sound came from somewhere on the benches, the half-stifled agreement of someone who had felt the same. Eliza's stomach turned. The testimony was no longer only about what they had supposedly seen with waking eyes. It was about the shape of dread that moved from mind to mind at night, making a shared world where anything could be made true.

"And the girl?" the magistrate pressed. "Where is she in it?"

Abigail's eyes glistened. "Sometimes at the door," she whispered. "Sometimes already inside. But always she is watching as if waiting for me to notice. As if she cannot begin until I look at her."

Eliza's throat tightened. She remembered the visitor's voice in the cell: This is the first time you have been quiet enough to notice. Watching until noticed. Waiting for recognition.

Swann leaned forward a fraction. "Does she speak?"

Abigail nodded quickly, relief and terror tangled together in the movement. "Yes. But not like a person speaks. Not with breath. The words are in the room before her mouth moves, like they were placed there."

Eliza tasted iron, sudden and sharp, and realized she was biting her cheek again. She forced her jaw to loosen, but the taste remained.

"What words?" Swann asked.

Abigail's voice dropped. "She says, 'It is easier if you agree.'"

The phrase hit Eliza with such force she almost turned to look behind her for the visitor, for the pressed hollow on the cot that had promised relief. It was the same shape of persuasion, the same calm certainty dressed in kindness. It was Salem's voice. It was the whisper's voice. It was Swann's voice in different clothing.

The magistrate nodded slowly, as if each word fitted into a waiting place. "And what does she want you to agree to?"

Abigail's lips parted and trembled. "That I have already spoken," she said. "That I have already signed. That I only do not remember."

A soft exhale moved through the room. Not surprise. Recognition.

Eliza's fingers tightened in her lap until her knuckles ached. The hearing room seemed to tilt, not in her vision but in her understanding. This was not only testimony against her body. It was testimony against the possibility of memory, against the right to know what you had and had not done.

Swann's gaze flicked briefly to the constable's book, then back to Abigail. "Do you see a book in these dreams?"

Abigail nodded again, more emphatic now, as though grateful for a question with a clear answer. "A black one," she said. "It's on my table like it belongs there. And it is open, though I do not open it."

Eliza's breath came shallow. She saw, without wanting to, that other table in her dream: stretching into fog, the black leather damp, the page that looked blank until it warmed to her gaze and writing rose from beneath the paper like a bruise blooming.

"And do you see writing in it?" the magistrate asked.

Abigail's hands clenched so tightly the fabric of her apron wrinkled. "I see my name," she whispered.

The constable's quill scratched faster. The sound was steady, composed. It made Abigail's admission feel official the moment it left her mouth, as if the ink did not record words but summoned consequences.

Eliza's heart hammered hard enough to make her light-headed. Her mind stumbled over a thought she did not want to complete: If they could make people dream of their names already written, they could make those people wake and feel guilty for a thing that had never happened. They could make confession a kind of sleepwalking.

The gray-haired magistrate turned his head slightly toward Eliza. "Do you hear this, girl?"

Eliza's mouth went dry. She forced herself to speak. "Dreams are not proof," she said, and heard how thin it sounded against the room's hungry certainty.

Parris's pale eyes held her, calm and faintly pitiless. "Dreams are where the Devil works best," he said mildly. "The body rests. The mind wanders. A door is left open."

You are full of doors; the whisper had told her. Eliza's stomach twisted.

Swann's voice stayed gentle, almost reasonable. "Mistress Foster, when you wake from these dreams, what do you feel?"

Abigail's eyes closed briefly, as if the answer was too vivid to look at. "I feel tired as if I have walked," she said. "And my feet ache. And once I woke and there was dirt in the bedclothes."

A sharper murmur rose now. Eliza felt it in the room like a current turning.

Her stomach dropped. Dirt in the bedclothes. Feet that ache. It matched too closely the question Swann had asked her in the cell: Have you ever woken with dirt beneath your nails and not known why? As if he had planted the idea in the air and now watched it return in other mouths, confirmed by other minds.

Eliza's gaze snapped to Swann, but his face gave nothing. Only mild attention. Only the calm of a man watching a pattern complete itself.

"And the girl," Swann said, voice smooth as oiled wood. "Does she appear the same each time?"

Abigail hesitated, then shook her head once. "Sometimes she is nearer my age," she whispered, and a shiver went through her as if the words had chilled her own skin. "Sometimes she is younger, like a child. But her eyes are always the same.

Wide awake. Like she cannot sleep even if she wants."

Eliza's chest tightened. The guard's murmured command echoed in her: Awake. Awake. Awake. As if that wakefulness had been carved into her and now reflected back through other people's dreams.

"Does she touch you?" the magistrate asked.

Abigail swallowed. "Not with hands," she said. "But I feel a cold at my mouth, and then I cannot pray."

Reverend Hale's head lifted slightly, attentive. His eyes were fixed on Abigail now, not Eliza, as though this was the true shape of the matter. Prayer interrupted. Tongues thick. The same details repeating, as the magistrate had promised they would.

"And when you cannot pray," Hale asked quietly, "what does she do?"

Abigail's voice broke. "She waits," she said. "She waits until I stop trying. And then she smiles like it is a kindness."

Eliza's stomach rolled. She saw, unbidden, the visitor's offer in the cell. Lie down. Let me hold the door shut. The smile of something that did not force you, because it had patience, because it understood that exhaustion made a better leash than rope.

Swann nodded once, satisfied in a way that made Eliza's skin crawl. "And do you understand why she comes to you?"

Abigail's gaze flicked to the benches, as if seeking support from the collective. "Because I spoke against the trials," she whispered. "I said folk were being carried off on fear. I said… I said we should be careful."

A rustle ran through the room, sharp and disapproving. Carefulness in Salem had become its own suspicious thing. Doubt was a blemish that needed cleansing.

"And now," Swann said softly, "after these dreams, what do you believe?"

Abigail's face crumpled. "I do not know what I believe," she admitted. "That is the torment. I wake and I feel as though I have done something wrong, and yet I cannot name it. And then I see her in my mind in the day, like an afterimage, and I think, if I just agree, if I just stop fighting it, maybe it will end."

Confession is when the world agrees, the whisper had said. Eliza felt the phrase press against her mind like a thumb. It was not only about guilt. It was about relief. Agree, and the torment ends.

Deny, and the torment continues until denial itself becomes evidence.

The magistrate's gaze moved, taking in the benches, the way people leaned forward as if hungry to be told what their own dreams meant. He looked back at Abigail. "Do you accuse this girl of sending these dreams?"

Abigail's eyes filled and spilled over. She wiped them quickly, ashamed. "I do not know what sends them," she said. "I only know when I close my eyes, she is there."

The constable wrote it down, each tear turned into ink by the steady scratch of his quill.

The magistrate turned his head toward Eliza. "You hear what your presence does," he said, calm as judgment. "Even when your body is locked away."

Eliza's voice came out raw. "I cannot control what people dream."

Parris spoke, mild and absolute. "You do not need to control it," he said. "You only need to be the door it comes through."

Eliza felt, for a brief, dizzy moment, as though the room had narrowed to a single point: the black book on a table in fog, her name not her name rising slowly from beneath the page, and the visitor beside her, weight without body, offering sleep as if it were salvation.

Another witness was already standing, waiting to be called, eyes bright with the same feverish conviction Waller had worn. Behind them, another. The line of testimony stretched on like a road with no exit.

Swann's voice returned, low enough to sound compassionate. "You see now, Eliza," he said, "it is not only what you do. It is what follows you. It is what the night makes of you."

Eliza stared at the constable's moving hand. In the steady scratch of ink she heard the cell again, the careful page-turning she had heard through the wall. She felt, with sick clarity, that something was being written in more than one place.

Dreams becoming accusations. Private terror becoming public record.

And somewhere beneath the words piling up in the room, beneath the witnesses and the quill and the magistrate's calm, Eliza felt that older attention listening again, patient as paper, pleased by how easily a town could be taught to confess on her behalf.

The line of witnesses did not end so much as it folded back on itself, as though Salem were producing testimony the way a body produces breath.

A young mother with a nursing shawl spoke of waking to find her infant silent and cold, not dead but strangely still, the child's eyes open and unblinking. "And the girl was by the cradle," she said, voice shaking with fury that barely covered fear. "Not touching him. Just standing there as if waiting for him to cry. And when he did, he cried like he knew her."

Eliza's stomach clenched. She tried to picture a cradle, tried to picture the shape of a small face, but the image slid. In its place came the pressed straw of her own cot, the hollow that remained even under the blanket, the suggestion of a seat taken and not surrendered. Waiting, the witness had said. Eliza's mind supplied the rest without permission: waiting for someone to notice, waiting for someone to agree, waiting for the right page to open.

A farmer with a split lip testified next. He spoke as though each word hurt.

"I seen her on the road," he said, and the room leaned forward as if roads were more frightening than bedrooms. Bedrooms were private; roads belonged to everyone. "Not in day. In that gray time when the sun ain't decided if it's coming. She walked beside me like she'd been walking the whole night."

Swann's voice cut in, calm and guiding. "Where did she come from?"

The farmer blinked as if the question was wrong. "That's the thing. She was just there." He swallowed, and the movement pulled at the split. "And she kept looking at the trees like they was watching us. Like the road itself had eyes."

Eliza's breath caught. The phrase rose up from her earliest hour in Salem, the sensation she'd tried to dismiss as travel nerves. The road that watches. She remembered pines like black needles and the sense of being seen long before the town had spoken her name. She had told herself it was imagination. Now it sat in a stranger's mouth as if it had always been meant to.

"And what did she say to you?" the gray-haired magistrate asked.

The farmer's gaze flicked to Eliza, this time direct, and Eliza saw in his expression something worse than hatred. Recognition without reason. As if he had met her in a place where names did not matter.

"She asked me if I was tired," he said. "I said aye, and she said, 'It is easier when you stop fighting it.' Then I woke in my own bed with mud on my boots and my wife swearing I never came home at all."

A murmur ran through the benches. Mud, again. Walking, again. Waking in a bed after being elsewhere. The details repeated like a prayer said too many times until it became a spell.

Eliza's tongue pressed against her teeth. She tasted iron, faint but immediate, and realized her jaw had clenched without her knowing. The courtroom had no straw mattress, no bucket, no crack of corridor light, and yet her body behaved as though she were still in the cell, trained to hold herself in one rigid shape to avoid consequence.

Swann turned slightly toward her. "Do you understand now why these accounts carry weight?" he asked gently, as if asking after a lesson. "They do not match because the witnesses spoke together. They match because the thing is the same."

Eliza tried to speak and found her throat tight. When her voice came, it sounded like someone else's, thin and scraped raw. "You are making it match," she said. "You ask the questions that make them tell you what you want."

Swann did not bristle. That was his terrible gift: he absorbed accusation and returned it as calm instruction. "We ask what we must," he said. "And they speak what they cannot help speaking."

The constable's quill moved without pause. Scratch, scratch. The sound was small, yet it filled Eliza's head the way water fills a cup, rising slowly until it touched everything.

Behind the quill's motion Eliza began to hear another sound, faint and dry, like paper being handled with reverence. She told herself it was only the constable turning a page in his brown book, but the sound seemed to come from farther back, from within the room's structure, as though the boards themselves had learned the noise and repeated it.

She blinked hard. The faces in the benches shimmered for a moment, softening at the edges. Exhaustion still lived in her bones. Sleep had come, yes, but it had come under the visitor's weight, under an offer that had not felt like mercy so much as ownership.

The next witness stepped forward and Eliza's mind lurched.

It was Abigail Foster again, though she had already spoken. Or someone like her: bonnet, chapped hands, eyes bright with the shame of being seen. For an instant Eliza could not tell whether the woman had returned to add more, or whether Eliza had simply failed to hold the sequence of time in place.

"State your name," the magistrate said, and Eliza felt a cold bloom of dread, because she realized she had stopped trusting even the order of what she heard.

The woman's mouth moved. The name that came out was not Abigail. It was Lydia Dyer.

Eliza's stomach turned over. Lydia Dyer. Swann had asked her that name in the table room, mild and patient, and she had said no. She had said it cleanly, she thought. She had clung to it as one of the few answers that could not be twisted.

Now the name stood up in front of her, wearing a bonnet and trembling hands.

Lydia Dyer did not look at Eliza when she spoke. She stared at the table, at the papers, at the constable's ink. "I did not wish to come," she whispered. "I did not want my tongue to be used."

Parris's pale eyes watched her with composed interest. "And yet you are here."

"Because she came to me," Lydia said, and at the word came, Eliza felt the cell's air touch the back of her neck, cold as paper kept too long in a box.

Swann spoke softly. "In the night?"

Lydia nodded once, a quick jerk as though she were answering against her will. "Not in my house. In my head. I was awake. I was praying. I was saying the words proper and I felt… I felt another mouth saying them with me."

A shiver moved through the benches, not a murmur now but a shared recoil. Eliza's fingers curled into her palms. Another mouth. Another hand guiding words. The visitor had spoken to her in a way that did not travel through ears, blooming inside her thoughts as if it had always been hers.

Lydia swallowed and continued. "And I saw her. Not with my eyes. But clear as day. Sitting beside a bed. Not mine. A narrow cot. Straw." She hesitated, brow furrowing. "There was a hollow in it as if someone sat there, and she looked at the hollow like it was company."

Eliza's vision dimmed at the edges.

The courtroom did not move, yet she felt herself slipping sideways in it, as if the boards beneath her feet had become the fog-table from her dream, stretching too far. Hollow in straw. A narrow cot. Lydia had described her cell. Not a general cell. Her cell. The pressed place under the blanket that Swann had seen and not named.

Eliza's breath came shallow. She heard the visitor's voice as if it spoke from the space beside her stool: When the world agrees.

She forced her gaze to Swann's face. His expression remained mild, attentive, but there was a focus there now, a sharpened quiet, as though Lydia had offered him a piece he had been waiting to fit into place.

"And did you see her speak?" Swann asked.

Lydia's lips trembled. "No. The words were already in the air. Like writing you can't see until you stare at it long enough."

Eliza's heart hammered. She saw the black leather book again, the page that looked blank until it warmed to her gaze and the name rose from beneath. Not ink laid on top, but something that had always been there. Waiting.

The magistrate leaned forward. "What words?" he asked.

Lydia squeezed her eyes shut, and when she opened them they were wet. "She said, 'Say your name as you think it is.'"

Eliza's mouth went numb. The courtroom's air felt suddenly thin, as if all the breath had been sucked toward the table. She remembered the whisper in the cell asking the same thing, gentle and inescapable. Say it. Say your name as you think it is.

Eliza had said it. She had given Eliza Harrow into the hush, and the hush had replied, That is what they call you now.

Her skin crawled. She tasted iron again, stronger, and realized she had bitten down hard enough to open her cheek. Pain flared, bright and anchoring, and she clung to it.

Swann's voice came, softer still, meant to sound like comfort. "And did you answer her?"

Lydia shook her head, a frantic refusal. "I tried not to. I tried to hold my mouth shut, but it felt like my tongue moved on its own." Her eyes lifted at last and met Eliza's. "And I heard a name, not mine. Not hers. A name that sounded like it had been waiting."

The room seemed to tilt.

Eliza felt the foreign name the visitor had given her stir inside her like a bruise pressed too hard. She had not spoken it aloud. She had refused to repeat it because repeating it would be agreement. And yet Lydia's testimony sat at the edge of that private place, reaching toward it.

The benches murmured again, and the murmur braided itself with the scratch of the quill, with the faint page-turning sound Eliza could not locate. Noise layered on noise until Eliza could no longer tell which sounds belonged to the room and which belonged to her memory of rooms.

She blinked and, for an instant too long, saw the cell instead of the courtroom. The bucket in the corner. The high window's dull gray. The cot with its stubborn indentation under the blanket, like a person seated beneath linen. She smelled damp straw and cold paper, and then the smell snapped back to bodies and wool and lye.

Eliza's breath hitched. She realized, with a sudden terror sharper than any testimony, that her mind had begun to do what Salem accused her of doing to others.

She was waking into places that were not here.

Swann's voice came through the haze, steady as a hand on her shoulder. "Eliza Harrow," he said, and the full name landed like a pinning. "Do you deny these visions as well? Do you deny that you have reached them, even locked away?"

Eliza stared at him. She wanted to say no. She wanted the word to be clean. But behind her teeth, another name hovered, intimate and wrong, recognized without memory. And beneath that, the visitor's promise pulsed with sick sweetness: Relief.

Her lips parted. For a heartbeat she could not remember which answer belonged to her and which answer would be easier.

The constable's quill paused, waiting.

The room waited with it.

And in that waiting Eliza felt the boundaries soften further, the line between accusation and memory thinning like paper held too close to flame, until she feared that if she spoke at all, whatever came out would sound, even to her, like something she had already said somewhere else.

Chapter 10

The Touch Test

The constable's quill hung above the paper, its tip glistening.

Eliza stared at it and tried to remember how to breathe. The room waited for her answer as if it had been appointed to do so, as if the very boards understood that waiting was a method. She felt Swann's gaze on her with the same mild patience he had used in the cell, the kind that did not rush because it did not need to. It assumed the end.

Eliza forced her jaw to loosen. The inside of her cheek stung where she had bitten it, and the small pain gave her something simple to hold.

"I deny it," she said, and though her voice shook, the words were hers. "I deny that I have gone to them. I deny that I have reached anyone. I have been in your keeping."

A few heads in the benches tilted, as if the phrase in your keeping carried its own accusation.

As if being kept by Salem meant something should have been made clean by it.

Swann did not react with anger. He only nodded once, as though noting a figure in a column.

"And yet," he said, gentle as ever, "they continue to suffer."

The magistrate with the thin mouth leaned back in his chair. "Suffering requires remedy," he said, and the way he spoke the word remedy made it sound like law, not mercy.

Parris's pale eyes slid toward the benches, where a cluster of girls sat pressed together. They had been quiet until now, a tense knot of bodies and half-held breaths. One of them rocked slightly, her shoulders jerking in small, restrained motions, as if her body struggled against a leash only she could feel.

Eliza recognized her at once.

Ann Putnam's daughter, the one who had cried out on the common the day Eliza arrived. The girl's hair had come loose from its cap and clung in damp strands to her forehead. Her hands were clenched so tightly her knuckles stood white, and her lips moved without sound, shaping words that never quite became prayer.

A murmur stirred through the room as if the benches knew what was coming.

Reverend Hale stepped forward, his hands still folded, but his posture had changed. Listening was no longer enough. His face held a solemn readiness, as though he had been waiting for a particular kind of proof.

Eliza's stomach tightened. In the cell, the visitor had promised her rest and called it relief. Here, the court wore the same word like a clean cloth over something stained.

The magistrate spoke again. "Bring the afflicted."

The guard behind Eliza shifted away from her stool. Another man moved along the benches, and the girls' cluster opened reluctantly. Two women, older, with hard mouths and determined hands, took the afflicted girl by the arms and guided her forward. Guided was too gentle a word; the girl resisted with the jerky strength of someone frightened by her own limbs. Her feet dragged, then stumbled, then caught. She made a low sound, not a cry exactly, but the noise of someone trying to swallow panic and failing.

As she neared the front, her eyes lifted and found Eliza.

Something flashed across the girl's face. Not recognition like a friend. Recognition like a wound being pressed.

The girl jerked hard enough that the women holding her nearly lost their grip. Her mouth opened and a thin, harsh sound came out, as if air had been pulled through a narrow place.

"She is here," the girl rasped. "She is here, she is here."

The benches leaned forward. Eliza felt their hunger like heat.

Swann turned his head slightly toward the magistrates. "You see," he said softly, as if he were only observing weather.

Eliza stood abruptly, the stool scraping against the boards. The guard moved at once, a hand catching her elbow, but Eliza barely felt it.

"I have not touched her," Eliza said, louder than she meant to. The sound of her own voice in the room startled her, made her seem wild even to herself. "I have not even spoken to her."

The afflicted girl's eyes rolled upward until mostly whites showed, then snapped back down. Her breathing came quick and shallow, and her shoulders began to shudder as though a chill had seized her.

The magistrate lifted a hand; a gesture Eliza had begun to hate because it could quiet a room as thoroughly as a lock turning. "Eliza Harrow," he said, "you will stand where you are told."

Parris's mild voice followed. "We seek not to injure you, girl. This is to discern what is true."

Discern. The word sounded clean, like soap. Eliza tasted iron again and knew the word meant nothing more than arranged conclusion.

The girl's body jerked again. The women holding her tightened their grip.

Hale stepped closer, looking at the afflicted girl with grave concentration, as though he were reading scripture written across her face. "Ann," he said quietly. "Can you speak? Tell us what you feel."

The girl's lips trembled. "It is like…" She swallowed, and her throat bobbed hard. "Like a cold hand in my mouth."

Eliza's skin prickled. Cold at the mouth. Tongue thick. Words misplaced. She had heard it in witness after witness, a shared vocabulary of helplessness. She felt, sickly, that the court had taught Salem how to describe torment so that torment could be filed properly.

Swann moved a step closer to Eliza. "There is a test often used," he said, and his tone was so reasonable it made Eliza want to strike him. "In cases such as these."

Eliza's gaze flicked to the constable. The quill was poised, ready to turn flesh into record.

"What test?" Eliza asked, though she already knew. She had heard whispers of it on the road, before Salem's gates closed behind them. Old women's stories that traveled between towns like disease.

Swann's eyes held hers. "Trial by contact," he said. "If your presence afflicts her, then your touch, by God's providence, may also relieve her. The Devil cannot abide his own work undone."

The logic was circular and perfect, a snake swallowing itself. If the girl screamed at her touch, it proved Eliza's guilt. If the girl calmed, it proved Eliza's guilt. There was no answer that did not feed their certainty.

Eliza felt her pulse in her throat. "No," she said, and hated that it sounded like pleading. "You cannot make me."

The magistrate's thin mouth tightened, not with anger, but with the impatience of someone hearing a child deny arithmetic. "You will," he said, "if you wish the court to see your cooperation."

Cooperation. The word carried the faint promise of mercy, the same shape of bargain offered in the cell: lie down, and you will not be punished for it. Confess, and you may live. Cooperate, and we will be kind.

Eliza's eyes darted, searching the room for her mother's face, her father's. There was only Salem, packed tight and watching. No one looked away. Even those who seemed uneasy did not move. Their stillness was its own agreement.

The guard's hand tightened on her elbow. Not painful. Not yet. Simply a reminder that resistance had limits.

The afflicted girl's breathing turned ragged. Her head jerked toward Eliza, and she bared her teeth like an animal cornered. "She is in my bones," she whispered. "She is in my bed. She is in my mouth."

Hale lifted his hand slightly, as if to calm the girl through gesture alone. His eyes remained fixed on Eliza now, and though his face was solemn, there was a bright expectation in it that made Eliza feel flayed. He wanted this. Not harm, perhaps. But proof. Something he could carry like a shield against doubt.

Swann stepped back half a pace, clearing space as though preparing a stage. "Bring her nearer," he instructed.

The women hauled the afflicted girl forward. The girl's feet slid on the boards. Her shoulders shook. Her eyes fluttered. For a moment she seemed about to collapse, but when she reached a point directly before Eliza, her body stiffened sharply, as if pulled upright by a string.

The air between them felt strange, charged and thin. Eliza smelled sweat, wool, the faint sourness of fear. Under it, impossibly, she caught the dry, cold note that had clung to her cell after the visitor sat: paper kept too long in a box.

It made her stomach lurch. She did not know if she was imagining it or if the visitor's presence had followed her here, unseen, weightless, content to sit in any room where names were being written.

The magistrate's voice came again. "Place your hand upon her."

Eliza's arm felt numb. She did not want to move. She did not want her body to be used as part of their story.

"I will not hurt her," Eliza said hoarsely.

"No," Parris replied, and his mildness was worse than cruelty. "You will reveal yourself."

The guard nudged Eliza forward. It was a small pressure, practiced, the same kind of guiding touch that had led her down corridors without letting her count the steps. Eliza's feet moved because the room demanded it, because her body had been trained by fear to obey before her mind could gather itself.

Her hand lifted slowly, trembling.

The afflicted girl's eyes widened until the whites showed. Her mouth opened, and a keening sound rose from her throat, thin and rising like a kettle beginning to boil.

Eliza's fingers hovered an inch from the girl's shoulder. The girl shook harder, her whole body jerking against the women's grip. Her face contorted in dread.

Swann's voice, low and coaxing, threaded through the room. "Go on," he said. "Only touch. Only contact. Let us see what God permits."

Eliza's fingertips made contact with the girl's woolen sleeve.

The sensation was not what Eliza expected. Not the ordinary feel of cloth over flesh. For a heartbeat, it felt as though her touch passed through a thin skin of cold air first, like reaching into water that had been left out overnight. Then, beneath the wool, she felt heat. Too much heat, a feverish warmth that pulsed fast.

The afflicted girl's keening cut off.

It stopped so abruptly the silence that followed seemed to crack.

The girl's shoulders sagged. Her head drooped forward as if she had been holding herself up by force and had suddenly been allowed to let go. Her breathing slowed, deepened. Her eyelids fluttered. The frantic tension in her face softened into bewildered calm.

The room exhaled as one body.

Eliza's hand remained on the girl's shoulder, frozen there, because she had felt something else pass between them at the moment the sound stopped. Not a visible thing. Not a touch. A shift, like a thread pulled free from fabric, like a weight leaving one place and settling into another.

Her fingers went cold.

The afflicted girl blinked up at Eliza, dazed, and for a moment her gaze held no accusation at all. Only the exhausted relief of someone whose pain had paused. Her lips parted, and she whispered, almost tenderly, as if speaking from inside a dream.

"It's quiet," she said.

A roar of murmurs rose from the benches, loud enough to make the rafters seem to tremble. Men crossed themselves. Women pressed hands to their mouths. Someone sobbed, not in grief but in vindication.

Swann's eyes sharpened with satisfaction he did not try to hide. He turned his head toward the magistrates. "You see," he said.

The constable's quill scratched furiously, capturing the moment before it could be questioned, pinning it down in ink so it could never change shape.

Eliza felt her arm trembling. She tried to pull her hand away, but her fingers seemed reluctant to leave the girl's shoulder, as if something in her wanted to remain connected. The thought made her panic flare hot and sudden.

She snatched her hand back.

The afflicted girl swayed, and the women holding her tightened their grip again, but the girl did not resume her jerking. She stood slack, eyes half-lidded, breathing evenly as if the storm inside her had moved elsewhere.

Eliza stared at her own hand, at her fingertips, as though she might see ink staining them.

In the hush beneath the murmurs, beneath Swann's calm instructions to note the result, Eliza felt it again: that older attention, patient as paper, listening close.

Not pleased by the girl's relief.

Pleased by the room's certainty.

And, with a terror that tasted like iron, Eliza realized the most damning part was not that the girl had calmed.

It was that Eliza had felt something happen when she touched her, and for a heartbeat, in the exact center of that contact, she had understood why the visitor kept offering relief.

Because relief could be made into proof.

Eliza kept staring at her own fingers as if they might still be touching the girl, as if the sensation had left a visible residue.

Her hand looked unchanged. Pale knuckles. A faint smear of dried blood at the edge of one nail where she had broken skin in her palm. Nothing that could explain what she had felt.

But inside her fingertips there remained a cold, clean after-feel, the way your skin remembers the shape of something pressed too long against it. Not pain. Not heat. Something else. A brief, sliding absence, as if the warmth that had been in the girl had searched for a place to go and had found Eliza's hand willing, if only for a breath.

The afflicted girl swayed, eyes unfocused, her mouth slack with astonishment at her own quiet. The women gripping her arms exchanged a look that was almost relief and almost triumph. They held her as one might hold a child newly cured, as one might hold a sign from God so it did not fall and crack.

"It is done," someone murmured from the benches.

"It proves it," said another voice, louder, and the words spread through the room as if proof were something contagious.

Swann raised one hand, a mild gesture meant to shape the noise without stopping it entirely. "Order," he said, and the magistrate's own palm lifted after, reinforcing the command. The murmurs dulled, but the energy remained. Eliza felt it pressing toward her from every side, the room leaning in as if her skin had become a page and they had seen ink appear.

She tried to swallow and found her throat tight. The iron taste had returned, sharp with fear, though she could not tell if she had bitten her cheek again. Her tongue felt too large. She forced it still.

The afflicted girl's gaze drifted, and for a moment it landed on Eliza's face with a strange softness. Not accusation. Not terror. Something like gratitude, which was worse, because it made Eliza feel like an instrument. Like a tool that could be lifted and used without being asked.

Then the girl blinked, as if waking from a deep sleep, and her expression shifted. Confusion wrinkled her brow. Her lips parted.

"Eliza," she whispered, and Eliza's stomach dropped. The girl had never said her name before. Not in the common. Not while thrashing. Not while the court listened.

The word sounded too intimate on her tongue. Too clean. As if it had been placed there.

A low hum ran through the benches again. The constable's quill did not slow. Scratch, scratch, scratch. He wrote the name as though writing it made it truer.

Eliza's gaze snapped to the table, to the quill, and for an instant the sight of ink moving across paper tugged at her mind in a way that made her dizzy. She thought of the page in her dream, blank until it warmed. She thought of writing rising from beneath. She thought of the visitor's voice, patient and close: Ink is only proof to those who fear blank pages.

But here, ink was everything.

Swann stepped closer to the afflicted girl, his posture that of a man tending a delicate matter. “Ann,” he said gently, as if coaxing her back into her own body. “Tell us what you felt when she touched you.”

The girl’s eyes fluttered. She swallowed once, throat working. “It went away,” she said, and her voice sounded small, stunned. “Like… like a bird stopping its wings.”

“A bird,” Hale repeated softly, as if considering the image for its spiritual correctness.

The girl nodded, more certain now that she had been given a path. “It was beating in me,” she said, pressing one hand against her chest. “And then it wasn’t. It went quiet.”

Swann’s gaze flicked, quick, to the magistrates. “You see the mercy of providence,” he said, and it sounded like praise but was shaped like a conclusion. “The same hand that afflicts is forced to soothe.”

Eliza opened her mouth to protest, but no sound came. She could not find words that would survive the room. Anything she said would be pulled apart and arranged into a confession of motive. The court did not listen for meaning. It listened for use.

The afflicted girl shifted suddenly, as if a chill had passed through her. Her shoulders rose. The calm in her face tightened by a fraction.

Eliza saw it and felt her own skin prickling in answer, as though something that had been pulled free had only been set down, not destroyed.

The girl's eyes fixed on Eliza again, wider now. Her lips moved without sound at first, then formed a whisper that was not meant for the whole court.

"It's looking," she said.

Eliza's breath caught. "What is?" she tried to ask, but her voice came out thin.

The girl's pupils seemed to swell in the dim room light. She stared at the space beside Eliza's shoulder, not at Eliza herself, and her expression began to twist with the old dread.

Swann noticed at once. He did not step back. He stepped in, as if he could position himself between the girl's terror and whatever might be feeding it. "Ann," he said quickly, still mild, but the mildness now had an edge of urgency. "Look at me. You are safe."

The girl shuddered. The two women tightened their grip, bracing, expecting the storm to return.

Eliza's own hand tingled, a faint numbness blooming in her fingertips. It spread up her palm like cold water seeping into cloth. She flexed her fingers, trying to force the sensation out. It did not leave.

It remained.

A passing, yes, but not gone. Like a thread that had been pulled through her and left behind a trailing end.

Her mind flashed, unbidden, to the indentation on her cot. A seat taken, then left, yet the straw refusing to rise. A shape remembered by matter. Wood remembers, the visitor had said. Iron remembers.

The afflicted girl's mouth opened. A thin sound came out, not yet a scream, but the beginning of one. Her body jerked, small and sharp, and the women holding her nearly lost their balance.

The benches rustled, alarm rising.

"She returns to it," someone muttered.

Swann's gaze turned to Eliza, and though his face remained composed, there was a brightness there now, a careful hunger. "Touch her again," he said softly, as if offering Eliza the chance to repeat the miracle and thereby complete her own condemnation.

Eliza's throat tightened. She stared at the girl's trembling shoulders, at her eyes that were fixed on an empty place beside Eliza, and she felt the memory of that earlier contact in her bones. The instant of fever-heat. The sudden stop. The shift, like a weight relocating.

If she touched her again, would it pass again? Would it take more?

"No," Eliza whispered. The word felt too small.

The magistrate's thin mouth tightened. "You will," he said, and the calmness of it frightened her more than shouting would have. "You have just shown your hand can do it."

Eliza shook her head once, hard. "I did not do anything," she said, and hated the way her voice shook. "She calmed. That is all."

"You felt something," Swann said, so quiet it could almost be mistaken for kindness. His eyes did not leave her face. "Did you not?"

Eliza froze.

A flicker of fear ran through her sharper than the girl's renewed shuddering. How could he know? Had she shown it? Had her hand betrayed her by trembling? Or had he simply learned, from the way people looked when their bodies had been used by something they did not understand?

She tried to keep her expression flat. “I felt cloth,” she lied, and the lie tasted like iron. “Wool.”

Swann held her gaze as if weighing the lie and deciding how to use it later. He turned slightly toward the magistrates. “The girl begins to stir again,” he observed, as though this were an expected part of the test. “It is often so. The affliction retreats under holy contact, but returns when the instrument is withdrawn.”

Instrument.

The word slid into Eliza’s mind and lodged there.

The afflicted girl jerked again, harder, and the thin sound rose into a cry. The benches flinched as one body. Hale’s hands unclasped, and he stepped forward, his face drawn with a kind of distressed purpose.

“Ann,” he said, voice low and urgent, “pray. Pray now.”

The girl’s mouth worked as if trying. Her lips formed shapes that did not become words. Her eyes rolled upward, then snapped down again. Her breath came fast and ragged.

Eliza watched, sick, and felt her own mouth go numb. The same thick tongue. The same stolen prayer. The same cold at the mouth that witnesses had described. The pattern repeating, repeating, repeating, until the room could no longer imagine any other story.

Swann spoke again, and now he addressed Eliza directly in front of everyone. “If you are innocent,” he said, “you will not fear to touch her again. You will welcome the chance to prove you do not serve darkness.”

Eliza looked at the girl and saw, for an instant, the visitor’s offer in the cell made visible in another form: Relief, given cleanly, like mercy. Relief that could be turned into proof. Relief that made people grateful to the very hand they feared.

Her fingertips tingled with cold again, and beneath that cold she felt something like attention, not from Swann or the magistrates, but from a deeper place. A patient listening, like pages waiting to be turned. It was the same presence she had felt in the cell when the guard’s interruptions stopped. The same presence that had sat beside her, weight without body, and kept the door still.

Only now it did not sit beside her. It seemed to lean in from everywhere.

Eliza’s gaze drifted, against her will, to the constable’s quill. The ink glistened at its tip. The constable’s hand moved steadily, but Eliza could no longer hear only the scratch of writing. Beneath it, faint and dry, she heard the other sound again: paper being handled slowly, reverently, as if a heavier book were being opened somewhere just out of sight.

She blinked, hard, but the sense did not leave.

The afflicted girl's cry broke off abruptly. Not because she calmed. Because her throat seized. Her eyes widened further, and she made a sound that was only air forced through a narrow place.

Eliza's hand twitched, an involuntary jerk toward the girl, as if her body remembered the earlier moment and wanted to repeat it without being asked.

Swann saw the twitch and pounced on it like a man catching a confession mid-fall. "There," he murmured. "You see how she is drawn."

"I am not drawn," Eliza said, voice breaking. "Stop."

The magistrate's palm lifted again. "Enough," he said, and the room quieted in obedient anticipation. "We have seen what we need."

Eliza's breath came shallow. Her fingers curled into her skirt, gripping fabric hard enough to hurt. She needed the pain. She needed something that was only hers.

But the cold in her fingertips remained, faint and clean, and she could not stop the thought that rose with it, terrible in its simplicity.

Something had passed.

Not merely the girl's calm. Not merely the room's certainty.

Something from the girl, or through the girl, had moved when Eliza touched her, and for one heartbeat it had recognized Eliza as a place it could go.

The afflicted girl sagged again, her body briefly slack as if the storm had been interrupted mid-breath. The women holding her looked bewildered, then relieved, then frightened by how quickly the shifts came.

Swann turned his head toward the benches, voice carrying just enough. "Let it be noted," he said, "that at contact the afflicted was relieved, and at removal the affliction sought return, as though unwilling to be parted from the one who called it."

The constable's quill scratched, eager.

Eliza stared at her own hand again.

She could not feel its warmth.

Only the memory of heat, and the lingering cold, and the sick certainty that what had happened was not finished simply because she had pulled away.

Passing did not mean gone.

Passing meant transferred.

And Salem, leaning forward in its hunger, had just watched the transfer as if it were proof of her nature, when all Eliza could think was that she had felt, for a brief terrifying instant, how easy it would be to take someone's pain away and call it mercy.

How easy it would be to do it again.

How easy it would be to let herself become the hand that made the room go quiet.

The magistrate's hand stayed raised a moment longer, as if he expected obedience to settle like dust.

It did not.

The benches erupted in sound the instant his palm lowered. Voices sprang up, overlapping, trampling one another. Women cried out God's name as if it were a weapon. Men spoke in harsh bursts, pointing, swearing they had seen the truth with their own eyes. A few laughed with relief so sharp it sounded like hysteria. The noise rolled through the room in a wave and struck Eliza in the chest.

The afflicted girl sagged between the two women who held her, her head lolling as though her bones had turned to water. Her calm, instead of bringing quiet, seemed to unchain the room.

"Did you see her?" someone shouted. "Did you see it stop?"

"It proves it," another voice answered, and the phrase spread, taken up again and again until it was no longer a statement but a chant.

Eliza stood rigid, hands clenched into her skirt, feeling the cold numbness in her fingertips as if it belonged to someone else. The earlier contact replayed itself in her body with sick insistence: the moment of too-much heat, the sudden quiet, the sliding shift like a thread pulled through cloth. She wanted to shake her hand as if she could fling the sensation off like water. It remained.

The magistrate struck the table with something wooden. The sharp crack should have cut through them.

It barely made a seam.

"Order," he snapped, his voice raised at last. The strain in it made him sound human, and that alone seemed to enrage the crowd further, as if they preferred their authority calm and unshaken.

Deputy Parris rose to his feet, pale eyes bright. He did not shout. He did not need to. His mildness rode over the din in a way that made Eliza's skin crawl.

"You have witnessed providence," he said, and several voices immediately quieted, eager to hear their fear dressed in holy language. "The Lord does not permit such things without purpose. What you saw is not confusion, but revelation."

Revelation. The word struck Eliza like a blow. It sounded too much like the visitor in the cell, whispering as if it were comfort: They did not make you. They revealed you.

Ezekiel Swann did not stand. He remained seated, and somehow that made him the still point the room circled. He watched the uproar with the composed attention of a man observing a process he trusted. When he spoke, he did not address the crowd. He addressed the magistrates, as if the crowd were only weather.

"You saw the pattern," he said. "At her touch, relief. At her withdrawal, return. The affliction knows its source."

"The Devil knows his own," a man on the benches shouted, and several people cried out in agreement.

Reverend Hale stepped forward, hands lifted in a gesture that looked like prayer and command at once. His face had gone a little gray around the mouth. Eliza could not tell if he was sickened by the spectacle or strengthened by it.

"Friends," Hale called, and his voice held the training of a pulpit, "you must not turn this into frenzy. Frenzy is also a doorway."

The word doorway made Eliza's stomach twist. You are full of doors, the whisper had told her. Salem had learned to make doors out of everything: sleep, doubt, hunger, the shape of a girl's fear. Now they were making a door out of calm itself.

A woman near the front bench lurched to her feet, eyes wide and wet. "My sister's been taken," she cried, voice cracking. "If touching can quiet it, then make her touch all of them. Make her undo what she's done."

Another woman answered her, shrill with outrage. "No. Do not ask her to lay hands. That is how she works. That is how she steals into you."

The argument flared instantly. People began speaking across one another, not to persuade but to purge themselves of terror. Some wanted Eliza used like a tool. Others wanted her bound and silenced before she could touch anyone again. The room was no longer a court; it was a mouth full of teeth, each one convinced it bit in God's service.

The afflicted girl stirred, her lashes fluttering. One of the women holding her pressed a hand to the girl's brow, murmuring something Eliza could not hear. The girl's eyes opened, unfocused at first. Then they fixed again on the empty space near Eliza's shoulder, and a tremor passed through her.

"No," the girl whispered, barely audible. Not no to the court. No to what she saw.

Eliza's breath hitched. She did not look behind her. She could not bear to. She could feel, in a way that was not sight, the attention pressing close again, patient as paper, as if the room's uproar had called something that preferred noise because noise made people stop listening to themselves.

The constable's quill scratched without mercy. He wrote through the shouting as if the shouting were irrelevant. He wrote what the magistrates told him to write. He wrote what Swann said in that even, deadly tone. Ink turned the moment into a fixed thing, a pinned insect that could be carried and shown.

Eliza's gaze snagged on the quill tip, glistening. The sight made her dizzy. For a heartbeat she smelled the cell again, damp straw and old boards, and beneath it that dry, cold note like paper kept too long in a box. Her tongue went thick.

A man's voice rose from the back, loud and trembling. "If she can quiet it, she can also stir it. She is the hand."

The phrase struck Eliza with nauseating force. The hand. The visitor had called itself a hand that does not tire. A page that does not forget. And now the town, without ever hearing those whispers, had reached for the same shape of language.

Swann's eyes lifted briefly and landed on Eliza. Not triumph. Not pity. A calm appraisal, like a clerk confirming a figure.

"You are frightened," he observed, and the way he said it made fear sound like evidence.

Eliza forced her voice through her tight throat. "You set this upon me," she said. "You made her scream and then you used her quiet."

The nearest bench hissed at her. A woman spat a word Eliza could not make out. Another voice barked, "Hear how she speaks. No remorse."

The magistrate's face tightened, and he banged the table again. "Enough," he said, but the room obeyed only halfway, like a dog that had tasted blood and could not be called off at once.

Deputy Parris leaned slightly toward the magistrate and spoke in a low tone, but Eliza caught fragments anyway. "It must be seen as mercy," he murmured. "They will accept harshness if you call it remedy."

Hale's gaze moved from the afflicted girl to Eliza and held there. There was something in his eyes now that Eliza had not seen before, a hardening that frightened her more than anger would have.

He believes it, she realized. Not only that she is guilty. That her guilt has a shape he can recognize. That the world has finally made sense to him.

Hale lifted his voice again, addressing the room with a sternness meant to calm, but it had the opposite effect. It gave people permission to feel righteous in their terror.

"We have seen a sign," he said. "Do not waste it on shouting. The court will proceed as God directs."

God directs. Eliza wanted to laugh. She wanted to scream. Instead she stood there with numb fingers and a mouth that tasted faintly of iron, watching Salem turn its own noise into holiness.

The afflicted girl jerked suddenly, small and sharp, as if a pin had been pushed into her. A thin cry escaped her. The women holding her tightened their grip at once, faces blanching with the fear of losing the proof they had just displayed. The girl's head snapped toward Eliza again, and her lips moved.

"It wants—" she began, then swallowed hard as if something had pushed against her throat from the inside. Her eyes widened. "It wants to sit."

Eliza's stomach dropped. Sit. The word was absurd in the hearing room, and yet it tore a line straight back to the cell: the pressed straw, the indentation that remained even under the blanket, like a seat saved.

Swann's head tilted, attentive. "What does it want to sit upon?" he asked, as calmly as if asking after a name for the record.

The girl's eyes fluttered. She stared again at the empty place near Eliza's shoulder, then lowered her gaze to Eliza's hands. Her voice came out in a rasp, thick with dread.

"Her," she whispered. "On her."

A shudder ran through the benches, and the uproar returned full force. People surged forward against their own restraint, bodies leaning as if they could get closer to the invisible thing by crowding the air.

"Eliza Harrow," the magistrate snapped, voice like a lash, "you will be silent."

The guard behind Eliza moved. She felt his hand clamp her elbow more firmly than before. Not cruelly, but with the certainty of a man told to remove an object from a room before it caused further disturbance.

Swann spoke to the magistrate in a low voice, but Eliza heard him anyway, because her mind had become tuned to his calm like a wound tuned to pressure.

"We have what we need for today," Swann said. "Let the sign settle. Let the town speak itself hoarse. It only strengthens the record."

Strengthens the record. As if the record were a living thing fed by panic.

Eliza's feet moved because the guard moved her. The stool scraped again as she was pulled away from it. The crowd shouted as she passed, and the sound struck her in hot gusts. Some voices called her devil. Some called her witch. Some called her girl as if the word itself was an accusation.

As she was guided toward the door, Eliza turned her head once, searching for the afflicted girl's face. The girl hung slack again in the women's arms, eyes half-lidded, mouth parted. For a heartbeat their gazes met.

In the girl's expression Eliza saw no triumph. Only exhaustion and a kind of horrified wonder, as if she had felt something move and could not explain where it had gone.

Eliza's fingers tingled with cold once more.

And under the roaring voices, beneath the banging of the magistrate's block and Hale's stern calls for order, Eliza felt that other attention settle in, quiet and satisfied. Not the town's attention. Not Swann's.

A presence that did not need to shout to be obeyed.

As the door opened and corridor light spilled in, Eliza had the sick certainty that the room's uproar was not simply reaction.

It was agreement being forged, hammered into shape by noise until it became something solid enough to write down.

And somewhere, in a book she still had not seen with her waking eyes, a page waited, patient and blank, ready to darken now that so many mouths had spoken as if they already knew what her hands were for.

Chapter 11

The Mark

They did not return her to the lower cell at once.

The guard pulled her through the corridor as the hearing room's uproar continued behind them, muffled by walls but still alive, like a hive shaken and set down again. The air in the passage smelled of lye and damp wool. Eliza's boots scuffed the boards because her legs had not decided whether they belonged to her or to the hands that moved her.

Her fingers still tingled with that clean cold.

She held them tight against her skirt as if pressure could keep whatever had passed from spreading farther. The guard's grip at her elbow had become firmer after the magistrate's command, not cruel but unquestioning. He steered her as though she were a chair to be placed, an object that needed removing before it caused further disturbance.

Swann walked ahead, unhurried, his coat smooth, his pace steady. He did not look back. He did not need to. Eliza had come to understand that his calm was not a manner; it was a method. It made other people chase him. It made them fill the silence for him.

At a narrow door partway down the corridor, Swann stopped. A key turned. The guard pushed the door open, and they guided Eliza into a smaller room lit by a high window that admitted a thin, gray daylight.

It was not the cell. There was no bucket in the corner, no straw cot with its stubborn hollow. The room smelled sharper, cleaner, like soap that had failed to cover old wood. A plain table stood against one wall. A stool. A peg with a shawl hanging from it. The floorboards here had been scrubbed hard enough to raise their grain like scabbed skin.

Two women waited inside.

They were not townswomen in bonnets trembling with righteous dread. They were older, sturdier, dressed in plain dark cloth with sleeves rolled to the forearm. Their hair was pinned back tight. Their hands were bare. One held a folded linen cloth. The other held nothing, which was worse. The nothing meant she intended to use what she already had.

A matron, Eliza thought, though she did not know the word for it here. Not midwife, not nurse. Something appointed to touch bodies for the court.

Swann stepped in behind her and closed the door partway, leaving it open a hand's breadth. The guard remained just outside, his boots visible in the gap.

Swann's gaze swept the room, then settled on Eliza as if she were a figure in a column. "The court requires," he said, "that you be examined."

Eliza's throat tightened. "For what?"

Swann's voice did not change. "For a mark."

The word landed hard. Mark. The witnesses had spoken of mouths thickened, prayers stolen, heat and cold passing through skin. Salem made those things into testimony. Now it wanted something that could be pointed to. Something that could be held in a gaze and described without admitting imagination.

Eliza shook her head once, small and instinctive. "I have no mark."

"You do not know that," Swann replied gently, almost patiently, as if correcting a child who had spoken out of turn. "You have been accused. The record will be made complete."

"The record," Eliza said, and her voice came out raw. She hated that she sounded like the thing they wanted her to be: defensive, sharp, uncooperative. "You will write whatever you like whether I stand here or not."

Swann's eyes remained mild. "Then do not make it difficult," he said. "Difficulty reads as guilt."

The first woman, the one with the linen, stepped forward. Her face was not unkind, but it was closed, practiced. A face that had learned to do necessary things without letting sympathy interfere. "Girl," she said, not Eliza, not Harrow. "Do as we tell you and it will be quicker."

Eliza's stomach turned. Quicker meant nothing in Salem. Quicker only meant they wanted less struggle, less noise, less chance for her to say something that could complicate the story they were already writing.

She looked at the door gap and saw the guard's boots, unmoving. She thought, absurdly, of the visitor in the cell offering to hold the door shut. Here, the door was held open on purpose. Nothing would be shut against what was about to happen.

"I want Reverend Hale," she said suddenly, because Hale still wore the shape of legitimacy in her mind, still carried the faint idea of God rather than the blunt machinery of Swann.

Swann's brows lifted by the smallest measure. "This is not a prayer matter," he said. "It is flesh."

Eliza's hands clenched. Her palms still bore crescents from her own nails. "Then send Swann out," she said, and surprised herself with the steadiness of it. "You have no business watching."

The second woman, the one with empty hands, gave a brief, humorless sound. "He will not watch," she said. "He will listen through the crack like any man who thinks himself righteous. Men always want the knowledge. They simply prefer not to see what it costs."

Swann did not react to the insult. He only turned slightly toward the open gap of the door and spoke quietly to the guard. "Remain," he instructed, and then, to Eliza, "Proceed."

The women moved with brisk certainty, as if the script of this moment had been practiced many times. The linen woman gestured toward the stool. "Stand there."

Eliza did not move at first. Her mind raced uselessly through choices that were not choices. Refuse, and be forced. Comply, and be written as compliant, which would be used against her as readily as refusal. Her body felt suddenly separate from her thoughts, a heavy thing that could be positioned.

The guard's shadow fell across the floor through the door gap, a reminder without words.

Eliza stepped to where they indicated.

The clean room seemed to magnify every sound. The shift of cloth. The creak of a board. The shallow catch of her breath. It was the opposite of the cell's hush, yet it felt just as intimate. Just as owned.

"Lift your hair," the empty-handed woman said.

Eliza's fingers went to the pins at the back of her head with clumsy haste. Her hands were trembling now. She pulled the pins free. Her hair loosened and fell down her back in a heavy spill. The woman's fingers immediately combed through it, efficient, checking behind her ears, at the nape of her neck, along the scalp as if searching for something hidden under strands.

The touch was not cruel, but it was without permission. Eliza flinched anyway.

"Hold still," the linen woman said.

Eliza's jaw tightened. She tasted the faintest iron again and forced herself to unclench.

The empty-handed woman moved her hands down Eliza's neck, then her shoulders. She tugged

Eliza's collar down a fraction, exposing skin. Her fingers pressed at the base of Eliza's throat, then along the collarbone, as if feeling for a bead under cloth. Eliza shuddered despite herself.

"There," Swann's voice came from near the door. "Begin with what is visible. Record all findings."

The linen woman nodded as if he had been in the room properly. "Aye."

The empty-handed woman pulled Eliza's sleeve up to her elbow. Her fingers turned Eliza's arm over, palm up, then palm down. She pressed along the inside of the wrist where the skin was thin and blue-veined. She examined the elbow crease, the soft spot where marks could hide.

Eliza watched her own arm as if it belonged to someone else. The woman's fingers felt warm. Real. Human. Yet Eliza's skin crawled under the touch as though her body expected cold paper instead.

When they found nothing on her arms, the linen woman's mouth tightened. Not disappointment, Eliza realized, but persistence. Salem did not accept an empty search. Empty was an inconvenience.

"Remove your outer dress," the linen woman said.

Eliza's heart jumped hard. "No."

The empty-handed woman's gaze met hers, blunt. "Girl," she said, "you have been accused of consorting with spirits. Do you think modesty weighs more than your life?"

Eliza's throat tightened. Life. They spoke of it as if it were something they could grant in exchange for cooperation, the way Swann had spoken of mercy and remedy in the hearing room. Confess and live. Deny and die. Undress and perhaps be seen as honest. Resist and be seen as hiding something.

She swallowed. Her fingers went numb. She turned her head toward the window as if the gray light could give her an answer.

Behind her eyes, the visitor's voice brushed the edge of thought, not fully formed, just the faint suggestion of attention. Patient. Listening. As if it enjoyed the way humiliation stripped a person down faster than force.

Eliza's hands moved to the laces of her bodice with stiff, unwilling motions. She worked them loose. Each tug felt like a tearing. When the front slackened, the empty-handed woman stepped in to help, not out of kindness but speed. Together they pulled the outer dress down off Eliza's shoulders, leaving her in her shift, thin and too exposed in the scrubbed room.

The cold in her fingertips flared briefly, a clean numbness that made her want to flex her hands until they hurt.

The women did not pause to let her gather herself. The empty-handed woman circled behind her and tugged the shift lower at the back, exposing more skin. Fingers traced along Eliza's spine. A thumb pressed between shoulder blades, then lower. As if reading her body like a map.

"No," Eliza whispered, because she could not stop saying it, even when it did nothing.

"Hush," the linen woman said. She dabbed the cloth lightly at Eliza's mouth where the skin looked irritated from biting. "You'll bleed again if you keep at it."

Eliza jerked away from the cloth. "Don't touch my mouth."

The linen woman's eyes narrowed, and Eliza knew she had made a mistake. The more she objected, the more every flinch became a thing to be interpreted.

The empty-handed woman moved her hands down to Eliza's ribs, pressing gently, methodically. Under the thin shift, her fingers found the shape of bone and muscle. She pressed at Eliza's side, then the other, as if searching for a place where sensation did not match.

Then she stopped.

It was not a dramatic pause. It was small, but Eliza felt it like a change in weather.

The woman's fingers rested against the flesh just below Eliza's left breast, near the line where the ribs curved. Her touch became more precise. A fingertip pressed, lifted, pressed again.

Eliza's skin prickled. "What?" she demanded, voice sharp with panic.

The empty-handed woman did not answer immediately. She leaned closer, peering as if the light was poor. Then her finger pressed again, harder.

Eliza gasped. Not from pain, exactly. From the strangeness of it. The press did not hurt the way it should have. It felt dull, distant, as if the sensation had been padded.

The woman looked to the linen woman. "Here," she said.

The linen woman stepped close and pulled the shift fabric aside enough to see. Her face changed by a fraction. Not shock. Recognition.

Swann's voice came from the door, still calm. "What is it?"

The linen woman hesitated, as if aware that speaking the words would fix them in place. Then she said, clear and practical, "A mark."

Eliza's breath stopped. "No," she said again, but the word came out smaller, because the women were looking at something on her skin as though it had been waiting to be found.

"I do not have—" Eliza began, then faltered, because she did not know what she was denying anymore. She could not see it. She could only feel the woman's finger pressing a spot that did not answer properly.

The empty-handed woman pressed again. "Does it pain you?"

Eliza swallowed hard. "It should," she whispered, horrified by her own answer.

The woman nodded once, satisfied. "It does not."

The linen woman glanced toward Swann. "It is like a teat," she said, the word flat and unembarrassed in her mouth. "Like a place that has been used."

Eliza's stomach lurched. The room seemed to tilt, just slightly, as if her balance had been taken by the word. Used. A place that has been used. Like a seat saved. Like straw pressed into shape and refusing to rise again.

Swann's shadow shifted at the door gap. "Record it," he said softly.

Eliza shook her head, a frantic motion that made her loose hair swing. "I never had that," she said, and hated how childish it sounded, like a girl insisting she hadn't stolen sugar while the granules still shone on her fingers. "I would know. I would know my own body."

The empty-handed woman's gaze stayed on the mark. Her fingertip circled it with a careful, almost reverent precision. "Many do not," she said. "Not after."

"After what?" Eliza demanded.

The woman's finger pressed again, and Eliza's skin remained strangely quiet under the touch. "After they've been visited," she replied.

Eliza's throat tightened until she could hardly breathe. Visited. The word dragged her mind back to the cot's indentation, to the weight that had sat beside her and kept the door still. She remembered the smell of cold paper. She remembered waking with the hollow still there, stubborn as a signature.

She realized, with a sudden sick clarity, that the visitor had not only left a mark in the straw.

It had left one on her.

Swann's voice drifted into the room, measured as ink. "Eliza Harrow," he said, "you will answer plainly. Did you know of this mark?"

Eliza stared at the women's hands on her shift, at the place they had exposed, at the fingertip pressing a spot that did not feel like hers. She could not see it, but she could feel the shape of their certainty gathering around it, tightening like a knot.

Her mouth opened.

No words came.

And in the scrubbed room's harsh quiet, with her dress pooled at her feet and her skin turned into evidence, Eliza felt again that patient attention, close as breath and cold as paper, as if something just beyond sight had leaned nearer to admire the court's newest proof.

Eliza's mouth opened.

No words came.

The linen woman kept the shift pulled aside, exposing the small place on Eliza's ribs as if holding it up to the light would make it speak. The empty-handed woman's fingertip remained poised over the mark, not pressing now, simply indicating. Eliza could feel her own breath moving the thin cloth against her skin, could feel the air of the room cool where her dress had been stripped away, could feel the indignity settle into her bones like damp.

Swann waited.

He did not fill the silence. He let it lengthen until it stopped being a pause and became a thing the room could use. Eliza had learned that lesson already: silence was not absence here. Silence was a tool.

"I did not know," she forced out at last. The words scraped her throat raw. "I swear it."

Swann's gaze did not move to the mark itself. He watched Eliza's face, as if the truth would show there more clearly than on her skin. "Then you admit," he said mildly, "that something has been done to you."

"Done to me," Eliza repeated, and a bitter laugh tried to climb up her chest but died before it reached her mouth. "You mean done by me. That is what you will write."

"I will write what is found," Swann replied, and his calmness made the sentence obscene.

The empty-handed woman, still practical, still unsoftened, said, "Hold steady." She took the linen cloth from the other woman and dabbed the area once, not because there was blood, but because the mark made her behave as though cleanliness mattered. Then she pressed again, harder, testing.

Eliza's body did not answer properly. The sensation arrived muffled, distant, as if the skin there belonged to a person under thick blankets.

"It is insensible," the woman said, and there was satisfaction in her voice. Not cruelty. Completion.

A sound came from the door gap, the guard shifting his boots. Eliza could not look at him. She could not bear the thought of his eyes trying not to see while taking in everything anyway.

Swann's voice remained steady. "It will be noted."

The linen woman's fingers adjusted the cloth again. "We should look further," she said, and Eliza heard the implication beneath the plainness: if one mark had been found, there might be others. The court would not stop at a single proof when it could have a collection.

Eliza's stomach turned. She backed half a step without meaning to, but the empty-handed woman's hand landed on her shoulder, firm.

"Do not," she said, and the single word carried the weight of many women's hands holding many accused bodies still.

Eliza went rigid. Her heart battered at her ribs, too loud in her ears. She was aware, suddenly, of the same spot beneath her left breast, the place they had named a teat, a place that felt wrong on her skin now that they had pointed to it. She could not remember it being there. She could not remember it not being there. Her memory had become unreliable in the ways Salem required.

Swann nodded once to the women. "Proceed," he said.

And then, before the empty-handed woman could move her fingers lower, Eliza felt a shift at the mark itself.

Not pain.

Not touch.

A recognition.

The air seemed to tighten, as if the room's cold had drawn inward. Eliza's breath hitched. The mark, which had been only numb flesh a moment ago, warmed abruptly under her skin with a heat that did not spread like ordinary warmth. It gathered, concentrated, like a coal held under the ribs.

Eliza's knees threatened to soften.

"Stop," she whispered, not to the women. To whatever had decided to wake in her flesh.

The empty-handed woman pressed again and frowned. "It warms," she muttered, surprised. "Did you feel that?"

"I feel you pressing," Eliza said quickly, the lie instinctive. Because the truth was worse. The truth was that the warmth had nothing to do with the woman's fingers.

Swann leaned forward slightly, as if listening harder.

The room's scrubbed quiet deepened. It was not only the women pausing. Even the boards seemed to hold still, as if waiting for the next line to be spoken.

The warmth at the mark sharpened into something like a pulse.

Then the voice came.

Not from the corner. Not from behind her ear. Not even from beside her, where the visitor had sat on the cot with its patient weight.

It came from her own ribs.

It bloomed behind her breastbone with the intimacy of breath, as though her body had become a mouth for something else.

"Thank you," it said.

Eliza's eyes flew wide. The words were soft. Gentle. The exact tone that had offered her sleep in the cell, that had called her Liza as if it had earned the right.

Her throat locked. She could not keep the sound in.

A small gasp broke from her lips.

The women stiffened at once. The empty-handed woman withdrew her finger a fraction, and the linen woman's grip tightened on the shift fabric.

Swann's gaze sharpened. "What is it?" he asked, and for the first time his mildness faltered into something like alertness.

Eliza's hands lifted instinctively toward her chest, toward the place where the voice had spoken, but the linen woman caught her wrists. "No," she snapped, and pulled Eliza's hands down again, not to hurt, but to keep her from covering evidence.

Eliza's mouth worked. "You—" she began, and then stopped because she did not know who she was addressing. Swann? The women? The thing inside her skin?

The voice spoke again, still low, still gentle. "You carried it well."

The warmth at the mark pulsed in time with the words. Eliza tasted iron sharply, not from biting this time, but from terror rising like bile.

Swann's eyes never left her face. "Girl," he said, his voice controlled, "who speaks to you?"

Eliza shook her head once, frantic. The motion made her loose hair sway across her shoulders. "No one," she said, and the denial was automatic, a reflex learned in the cell. Deny the whisper. Deny the visitor. Deny the thing that would become ink.

But the voice did not accept denial. It did not argue. It did not threaten. It simply spoke as if its words were true regardless of whether she agreed.

"Your hand," it said, and Eliza's fingers tingled with cold again as though the voice could reach into them by naming them. "When you touched her, you opened a path."

Eliza's stomach lurched. Her mind snapped back to the afflicted girl's shoulder, to the moment the keening stopped as if cut by shears. She remembered the sensation of something sliding, like a thread pulled free. She had been trying to tell herself it was imagination, that her exhausted mind had made drama out of cloth and heat.

Now the voice named it.

"You should not," Eliza whispered, barely audible.

The empty-handed woman's face had gone still and hard, as if she had decided Eliza was putting on a performance. "She is taken with fits," she said to Swann, dismissive. "They do that. They speak strange."

Swann did not answer her at once. He watched Eliza with an attention that felt like a finger pressing her skin. "Speak plainly," he instructed Eliza, and there was less patience in it now. "Is there a voice?"

Eliza's tongue felt too large. Her mouth thickened. She thought of witnesses describing prayer stolen and words failing, and she felt with sick clarity that her body had learned the same tricks.

The voice, close as blood, said, "They will not hear me unless you let them."

Eliza's breath shuddered. The warmth at the mark flared, then steadied, like a hand resting its palm against her from the inside.

Swann's gaze flicked briefly to the mark, as if he could see the heat through skin, then back to Eliza. "What is happening?" he asked, and the question was nearly the same as before, nearly calm, but there was a tightness at the edge of it, the smallest crack in his method.

Eliza tried to clamp her mouth shut.

The voice softened, almost tender. "You did well," it said again, as though praising a child for enduring a needle. "You gave relief. You gave quiet. You made them believe."

Eliza's vision swam. The hearing room flashed behind her eyes: benches packed tight, mouths chanting it proves it, the constable's quill scratching furiously. The voice sounded pleased not because the girl had been eased, but because Salem had turned the easing into certainty.

"What do you want?" Eliza thought, and then panicked because she was not sure if she had said it aloud. In this place, even thought felt like it could become record.

The voice answered anyway. "Only what you already gave."

The mark pulsed, and with it came a strange sensation, a brief loosening in Eliza's chest as if some tight band had been eased. The relief was tiny, almost nothing, but it was enough to make her nauseous with fear.

Because it felt good.

It felt like the visitor's promise in the cell, made real in her flesh: the watching stopping, the scraping thoughts smoothing for a moment. The kind of comfort that could turn into reliance before you noticed.

Eliza's eyes stung. "Stop," she whispered, and this time the word was clearer, sharper, a last shred of herself pushing back.

The voice did not stop. It did not escalate either. It simply spoke, patient as paper, as if it had all the time in the world and Eliza had none.

"Thank you," it said a third time, and now there was something behind the gentleness that made her skin crawl. A possession disguised as gratitude. A claim wrapped in manners.

The linen woman's grip on Eliza's wrists tightened. "Look at her," she hissed to the other woman. "She's staring like she sees something."

Eliza realized she was. Her gaze had fixed on nothing, just past Swann's shoulder, the way the afflicted girl's gaze had fixed on an empty place near Eliza. For a heartbeat she understood that terror from the inside: seeing a presence not with eyes, but with certainty.

Swann's face remained composed, but his pupils seemed a shade wider. "Eliza Harrow," he said, carefully now, "repeat what you hear."

Eliza's lips trembled. If she spoke the voice's words aloud, the constable would write them. If she refused, refusal would be written too, shaped into its own confession.

She swallowed hard, and the iron taste rose anyway, sharp and unavoidable.

The voice, warm at her ribs, whispered as if amused by the trap. "Tell him you do not remember."

Eliza's mouth opened.

And in that instant, before any sound came out, she felt the mark under the woman's hovering finger give a small, distinct throb, like an eye blinking.

The empty-handed woman jerked her hand back as if stung. "God preserve," she muttered, and then, as if angry at her own fear, she leaned in again, staring hard at the spot. "It moved."

Swann's head lifted, attentive. "What moved?"

The woman hesitated, then said, unwillingly, "The mark. Like it had… life."

Swann did not look away from Eliza. He spoke softly, almost as if to himself. “It answers.”

Eliza’s breath came in thin pulls. The warmth at her ribs steadied into something that felt like a presence settling in a seat it had claimed. The visitor, silent in the courtroom, had not left her behind when the door opened. It had followed, or perhaps it had never been only beside her at all.

The voice spoke one last time, so quiet it felt like a thought she had not chosen.

“They see what they need,” it said. “And you gave it to them.”

Then the warmth eased.

Not gone. Only quieter, as if it had leaned back and folded its hands, content to let the room do the rest.

Eliza stood shaking in her shift, wrists held, skin exposed as evidence, while Swann watched her with a new, careful intensity.

Outside the door gap, the guard’s boots shifted again, and the sound made Eliza flinch as if waking from a dream.

The linen woman cleared her throat roughly, as though trying to scrub the moment out of her mouth. “We found the mark,” she said, forcing practicality back into her voice. "We should finish and cover her."

Swann did not answer at once. His eyes remained on Eliza's face, searching for something he could name, something he could write.

Eliza stared back, and though she did not move her lips, she could still feel the echo of the voice inside her ribs, a gratitude that had not been meant as kindness.

It had been meant as ownership.

Thank you, it had said.

As if her hand, her touch, her endurance, her fear, had been a gift freely given.

As if the mark on her skin was not merely proof for Salem, but a mouth by which something older could speak and be heard.

The warmth eased, but it did not leave.

Eliza stood in the same posture, wrists held low by the linen woman's firm hands, as if her body had been paused mid-act and forgotten. The scrubbed room looked unchanged, the window still admitting that thin gray light that made all colors look tired. Yet Eliza's skin felt different, as if something beneath it had been stirred awake and then told to be quiet.

Swann's gaze remained fixed on her face. He did not ask again what she heard. He did not tell the constable to come. He simply watched, measuring the tremor in her mouth, the way her eyes refused to settle on anything safe.

The empty-handed woman pressed two fingers near the mark again, cautious now. Eliza felt the pressure, but the sensation was wrong, muffled at the center and too sharp at the edges, as though her body had been altered in a way it did not know how to report. The woman's mouth tightened.

"It's there," she said, as if the words could anchor her. "It's real enough."

The linen woman released Eliza's wrists at last and let the shift fall back into place. The cloth brushed the skin where the mark had been exposed, and Eliza flinched at the touch of her own clothing like it belonged to someone else.

"Dress her," Swann said quietly.

Not a kindness. A command to restore appearances. The linen woman bent to gather Eliza's outer dress where it had pooled at her feet. The movement was brisk, efficient, the way one cleans up after something unpleasant that has to be done.

Eliza's fingers would not cooperate with the laces. She fumbled them, her hands shaking, her nails catching on fabric. The linen woman clicked her tongue and took over, pulling and tying with practiced speed. Her hands were warm. Human. They felt like an insult against what had just spoken from inside Eliza's ribs.

As the bodice tightened, Eliza became acutely aware of the spot beneath it. She could not see the mark, but her mind kept drawing it: a small place shaped like wrongness, a numb bud that answered to pressure with silence and had, for one sickening moment, answered with pulse.

A mark, the woman had called it. Like a teat. Like a place that has been used.

Eliza swallowed. The iron taste rose faintly, but she knew this time she had not bitten her cheek. The taste felt borrowed, as if fear had its own metal and it lived at the back of her tongue.

Swann stepped away from the door gap and fully into the room. He moved with that same calm economy, each step placed as if he had measured the boards before walking on them. He stopped an arm's length from Eliza, close enough that she could smell soap on him, and beneath it ink and wool.

"You truly did not know," he said.

It was not phrased as a question, but Eliza heard the lever hidden inside it. Answer wrongly and he would pry.

Eliza forced her voice out, rough and small. “No.”

Swann’s eyes shifted, briefly, down to her chest. Not to leer. To locate. To imagine the mark beneath cloth the way the women had held it up to the light. Then his gaze returned to her face.

“How long have you had disturbances of sleep?” he asked.

Eliza stared. “Disturbances?”

“You were exhausted when you came,” Swann said, still mild. “Your eyes too open. Your body already strained. Did you wake often on the road? Did you ever rise and find yourself elsewhere? Did you ever lose time?”

His questions moved the way his corridors did: turn after turn, each one leading away from any straight answer.

Eliza shook her head once, hard. “No.”

The empty-handed woman made a sound through her nose, skeptical. Not openly defiant, but enough to show her belief had already chosen a side.

Swann did not look at her. He did not need allies in the room; the room itself worked for him.

"Eliza Harrow," he said, and her full name felt like a pin again, "when you were a child, were you ever ill for a long time?"

The question hit her unexpectedly. Not because she remembered sickness, but because she did not. Her childhood, lately, had become a handful of scattered objects: her mother's hands kneading dough, her father's coat smelling of smoke, Samuel's laugh with a missing tooth. Whole stretches of time between those objects were fog.

"I don't know," she said before she could stop herself.

Swann's head tilted slightly. "You do not know," he repeated, as if noting a valuable absence.

Eliza felt heat rise in her face. "I would remember being ill."

"Would you?" Swann asked gently. "Or would you remember only what was told to you afterward? What your family chose to keep?"

The linen woman pulled Eliza's collar into place and smoothed it with both hands, as if covering a stain. Her fingers lingered an instant too long at Eliza's throat.

Eliza's pulse jumped. She thought, absurdly, of the visitor offering to keep the watching away, and realized that it had never stopped watching. It had only taught her what watched could look like: a mild man's questions, a woman's hands, a town's shared certainty.

"I didn't ask for this," Eliza whispered.

Swann's eyes did not soften. "Few do," he said. Then, quieter: "The mark is not placed for your asking. It is placed for use."

The words made Eliza's stomach twist. The voice inside her had used the same shape of language, only dressed in gratitude. Thank you. You carried it well. You opened a path.

Eliza's gaze drifted, without permission, to the place near the door where the guard's boots were visible. The boots shifted slightly, and Eliza flinched as if she had been struck. Everything in her had become trained to interpret movement as consequence.

Swann followed her gaze. "You will return to your cell," he said.

The empty-handed woman took a half-step toward Swann, her expression tight. "What of what she did?" she asked. "With her mouth. Her staring."

Swann's mouth barely moved. "It will be recorded as agitation," he said, and Eliza heard the decision in it. Not because it was true, but because it was convenient. "And the mark will be recorded as found. That is sufficient for today."

Sufficient. The word sounded like a book being closed with careful hands.

Eliza's breath caught at the thought. Her mind flashed to that fog-table in her dream and the heavy black leather. She saw, again, writing rising from beneath the page like bruising. She felt the mark under her ribs respond with the faintest pulse, so subtle she might have imagined it if she had not been watching for it.

Swann turned toward the door gap. "Open," he instructed.

The door swung wider. The guard stepped in, filling the room with bulk and silent obedience. His eyes did not meet Eliza's.

"Take her," Swann said.

The guard's hand closed around Eliza's elbow again. The grip was familiar now, a firm guidance that did not bruise because it did not need to. Eliza let herself be steered, because the alternative was struggle, and struggle became ink.

As she crossed the threshold, she heard the linen woman mutter something under her breath. Not a prayer. A small, practical curse, as if she had touched something she did not want carried home on her skin.

The corridor took Eliza back into its lye-scented folds. The hearing room's noise was gone now, replaced by ordinary building quiet: distant footsteps, a door closing somewhere, a low voice murmuring and then cut off. The world had moved on. Only Eliza remained caught in the moment, her body still remembering hands on her and a voice inside her ribs.

She walked with her head lowered. Each step made her more aware of the mark, not as pain but as absence. A place on her skin that did not belong to her sensory map, like a missing board in a floor you'd walked across all your life. The absence demanded attention.

Without meaning to, Eliza tried to remember when it might have appeared. She pictured herself washing at home, lifting her shift to scrub sweat from her ribs after work. She pictured her mother helping her dress for church, tightening laces with sharp tugs. Had Mercy ever paused? Had she ever stared at Eliza's skin as if she'd seen something she didn't want to name?

No memory came.

That was the horror of it. Not that there was a mark. That the mark could exist without a beginning.

Eliza's thoughts reached farther back. Childhood. A summer day. A pond. A scraped knee. Her father carrying her inside. Her mother's hands cleaning blood with a cloth. These images arrived like fragments of another person's life, familiar but untrustworthy.

She tried to force more. A fever. A bed. Someone sitting beside her.

At that, a cold ripple traveled along her fingertips, as if her body recognized the shape of the thought. She nearly stumbled. The guard's grip tightened, steadying her without comment.

Eliza closed her eyes for a heartbeat and saw straw pressed down into an oval, stubborn as a seal. A seat saved. A place expected.

When she opened her eyes again, the corridor had not changed. But she had.

They reached the lower door. The guard's key scraped, turned. The bolt slid back with that same reluctant sound, like metal giving in.

Eliza's mouth went dry. She had left the cell with the indentation under the blanket, a hollow that Swann had seen and chosen not to name. She did not know what waited for her now. The visitor's voice had gone quiet, but quiet did not mean gone. Quiet meant patient.

The door opened, and the cell's damp breath met her.

The cot sat against the wall, straw mattress uneven under its thin blanket. Eliza's eyes went straight to it without her choosing. For a moment she could not tell if there was still a hollow. The light was wrong, her vision still unsteady.

Then she saw it.

Not as deep as before. Not shaped cleanly like a seated body. But there was a suggestion there, a stubbornness in the straw as if it had been pressed and had not fully forgiven. Matter remembering what had been done to it.

The guard guided Eliza inside and released her. He did not speak. He shut the door and slid the bolt home.

The click of it sounded final, like punctuation.

Eliza stood alone.

She lifted a hand to her chest, over the bodice, fingers hovering where the mark lay hidden. She did not press. She did not dare. The voice had spoken from that place when it was touched, and she feared that pressure might be an invitation.

Her hand shook anyway, suspended over her own skin like a question.

"How," she whispered into the cell's stale air, "can I have something on me I cannot remember?"

The cell did not answer.

But under the whisper of her breath, deep beneath cloth and bone, she felt the faintest responsive warmth, not flaring, not speaking, only acknowledging the question the way a page acknowledges a reader's gaze.

A mark of unremembered origin.

Not newly made. Not freshly placed.

Something older, settled into her as if it had always belonged there and she had only just been taught to see it.

Eliza backed away from the cot and sat on the floor instead, knees drawn up, as far from the remembered hollow as the small room allowed. She pressed her forehead to her knees, trying to think of her mother's face, trying to hold it still.

Mercy's features wavered, then sharpened briefly in her mind with unnatural clarity, as if offered.

Eliza's eyes flew open, and she swallowed a sound.

She did not say thank you.

She did not say anything at all.

In the dim gray of the cell, she listened to her own silence and understood, with a slow, sinking certainty, that the mark was not only proof for Salem.

It was a way in.

And now that it had been found, it would not be allowed to sleep unnoticed again.

Chapter 12

The Book Appears

Eliza stayed on the floor until the ache in her knees became louder than her fear.

The cell's dimness pressed close, a damp woolen thing, smelling of straw that never dried and wood that had soaked up too many breaths. The cot waited against the wall, its blanket smoothed into a shape that tried to look ordinary. Eliza did not look at it for long. When she did, her eyes slid to the unevenness in the straw beneath, the suggestion of a hollow that had not decided whether to exist today.

She kept one hand near her chest, not touching, only hovering where the bodice hid the place the women had named. A mark. A mouth. A way in.

When she closed her eyes, she could still feel the empty-handed woman's finger pressing, testing for pain that did not come. She could still hear Swann's mild voice at the door, making each word sound like a necessary entry in a ledger.

It will be recorded.

Difficulty reads as guilt.

The mark is placed for use.

Eliza opened her eyes again and stared at the boards until the wood grain became something she could count. Count the knots. Count the cracks. Count anything that was not time, because time in the cell did not move in lines. It pooled. It thickened. It became a substance you had to push through with your body.

Somewhere above, a footstep sounded, then another. Not the soft shuffle of a passing guard. These steps had purpose, measured and unhurried, as if the person making them knew exactly how many boards lay between one door and another.

Eliza's breath caught before the lock even moved.

The bolt scraped back. The door opened the width of a hand, and the corridor's pale light cut in.

For a moment no one spoke. The silence that entered with the light felt different from the cell's silence. This one had edges. This one had intention.

The door widened, and the guard stepped in first, broad-shouldered, face unreadable. Behind him came Ezekiel Swann, coat neat, hands clean. He carried no paper this time. He did not need it. Eliza had begun to suspect he kept his record somewhere else, somewhere that did not require ink he could be seen using.

Behind Swann, Reverend Hale appeared in the doorway, his posture careful, as if the threshold itself were a kind of line he should not cross without prayer. Hale's eyes went immediately to Eliza on the floor. They did not soften.

Eliza rose, too quickly, and the world tilted. She caught herself against the wall, fingers scraping wood.

"Stand," the guard said, not unkindly, simply because standing was what she was meant to do when men entered.

Eliza stood.

Swann looked at the cot and then at Eliza. His gaze did not linger, but Eliza felt it pass over the blanket's surface like a hand checking for an imprint. She wondered, sickly, whether he saw the shallow stubbornness in the straw and noted it as he noted everything else: not as proof, but as potential.

"We will have a further examination," Swann said.

Eliza's throat tightened. "You already—"

Swann lifted one hand, palm outward, an almost polite gesture that stopped her without raising his voice. "Not of your body," he said. "Of your claims."

Eliza tasted iron, faint and familiar. She did not know if it came from fear or from the memory of fear, like a flavor the mind could summon on command.

"My claims?" she managed. "I have made none."

Hale stepped fully into the cell then, bringing with him the smell of cold air and wool and something else, faint and sharp, like ink uncapped. His eyes moved over Eliza's face with the concentration he had used on the afflicted girl, as if he believed the truth might show itself in a twitch of muscle or the way her pupils reacted to light.

"You deny the visions," Hale said.

Eliza's mouth went dry. "I deny going to people," she said. "I deny hurting anyone. I deny—"

"You deny what you cannot see," Hale interrupted, and the quiet firmness of it startled her. He was not shouting. He was not pleading. He sounded like a man who had prayed and received an answer that required him to stop being gentle.

Swann's voice slipped in, smooth as oil on wood. "We will make the matter simpler."

He turned slightly, and Eliza saw then what the guard had been holding at his side, partly hidden by his coat.

A book.

At first Eliza's mind refused it, trying to make it into something ordinary: a Bible, perhaps, or a clerk's record. Salem was full of books. Reverend Hale's hands had always hovered near them as if paper were a way to touch God without burning.

But this was not scripture.

It was bound in black leather so dark it seemed to drink the thin light rather than reflect it. The corners were blunted, worn as if by long handling. The spine was cracked in several places, each fissure like a healed wound. It was thicker than any book Eliza had seen in a home. It looked heavy in a way that had nothing to do with paper. Heavy as if it contained more than words.

The guard held it with both hands, and for an instant Eliza had the absurd thought that it was being carried like a child that might wake.

Her stomach dropped.

The cell's air changed. Not warmer, not colder. Tighter. As if the boards had leaned inward.

Eliza took a step back without meaning to. Her shoulder hit the wall. The impact was small, but it anchored her in the moment, made it impossible to pretend she was dreaming.

Swann watched her reaction with that same mild attention he used when witnesses spoke. He did not smile. He did not need to.

"You have asked about it," he said.

Eliza shook her head quickly. "No."

"You have heard its name," Swann corrected, and Hale's gaze sharpened at the word name as if names were the true issue in all of this. "You have been accused of urging others to sign. You have heard the testimony."

Eliza's mouth moved, but no sound came. The black book filled her vision, and with it came a rush of images that did not feel like memories but did not feel like invention either. A table stretching into fog. Leather under her palms, damp as skin. Pages that looked blank until something beneath them shifted, rose, bruised into visibility.

She felt, with a sudden sick certainty, the faint warmth under her left ribs respond, a small stirring like a creature turning in sleep.

She pressed her palm flat against the wall to keep from reaching for her chest.

"That is not… I have not seen it," she whispered, though her voice did not believe itself.

Hale stepped closer to the guard, his eyes fixed on the book's cover. "It has been kept," he said, almost to himself. "Hidden from common hands."

Swann glanced at Hale, then back at Eliza. "Not hidden," he said. "Reserved."

The guard shifted the book higher, offering it forward. The leather creaked softly, a sound so slight it should have meant nothing. It made Eliza's skin rise in gooseflesh anyway. The creak sounded like the cot's straw when weight settled into it.

"Open it," Swann said to the guard.

The guard hesitated, just a fraction, and Eliza saw it: reluctance. Not fear, perhaps. Respect. As if even a man trained to obey knew there were objects you did not handle casually.

He placed the book on the cot.

Eliza's breath left her in a short, involuntary sound. The cot was wrong for it, too narrow, too poor. The black leather looked obscene against the thin blanket, like a funeral garment laid on a child's bed.

The straw beneath the blanket shifted, not from the book's weight alone, but as if the cot had accepted something it recognized. The shallow unevenness that had been lingering there seemed to deepen, settle, as though the mattress finally remembered what shape it was meant to hold.

Eliza's mouth went numb.

The guard's fingers moved to the cover.

Before he opened it, Eliza heard, faint and dry, the sound she had been hearing beneath other sounds for days: paper handled slowly, reverently. Only this time it was not imagined. It came from the book itself, a whisper of pages shifting in anticipation.

Hale's lips moved in silent prayer. Eliza could not tell if it was for protection or for permission.

The guard opened the cover.

The first page showed pale and thick, not like the thin paper of the constable's book. It looked almost like parchment, slightly yellowed at the edges, as if it had aged in a place without sun. There were lines of ink already on it, names written in careful strokes. Eliza saw them only briefly before her eyes slid away, as if something in her refused to hold strangers' names.

Swann leaned in, the motion economical. “Bring it nearer,” he instructed.

The guard lifted the book off the cot and held it out, open, facing Eliza.

Eliza did not move. The cell seemed too small for what had been introduced into it. The black leather filled the space like a presence, as real and insistent as the visitor’s weight had been beside her.

“Look,” Swann said softly.

Eliza’s throat worked. Her gaze dropped to the page.

For a heartbeat she saw nothing but ink and lines and the curve of letters.

Then the page seemed to shift.

Not physically. Something beneath it moved, like a bruise forming under skin. In the pale field of the parchment, faint marks appeared where there had been none. Not newly written, not laid wet on top, but rising, darkening, as if warmth had brought them to the surface.

Eliza felt her own skin tighten with the same sensation. Her mark under her ribs pulsed once, slow and deliberate.

The faint writing took shape into letters.

Eliza's breath stopped.

It was her name.

Not the foreign name the whisper had offered through the crack in the dark. Not the name that sounded like it had been waiting. The one she wore in Salem's mouth. The one that had been spoken before she gave it. The one Swann used like a key.

Eliza Harrow.

The ink looked older than the others around it. Not faded, but settled, as if it had had time to become part of the page rather than sit on it. It was not glossy. It did not shine.

It looked like it had dried long ago.

Eliza's knees threatened to buckle. She caught herself again against the wall, fingers clawing wood.

"I didn't," she whispered, and the words came out broken, useless. "I didn't."

Swann watched her with that careful, hungry calm. "No," he said, and the gentleness of it was terrible. "Not today."

Hale's eyes were wide now, fixed on the name as if he were looking at a wound opened in paper. His voice, when it came, was strained. "This is impossible," he said, though his tone held no belief in impossibility anymore.

Eliza stared at her name until the letters seemed to float above the page, until they looked less like writing and more like a thing that had always been there and would always be there.

And beneath the shock, beneath the nausea, she felt the smallest, quietest certainty settle into her bones.

This was not the first time she had seen it.

Her mind recognized it the way her body had recognized the visitor's weight on the cot: not as something new, but as something returned. As if the book had been waiting for her sight the way the visitor had been waiting for her attention.

Swann's voice came again, quiet enough to sound like mercy. "Now you understand why Salem does not require you to remember."

Eliza could not look away. The page held her like a hand on the back of her neck, firm and possessive.

Swann finished, his words dropping into the cell like a final entry.

"It only requires you to be written."

Eliza's name sat on the page as if it had always belonged there, as if the parchment had been made with that space already reserved.

Eliza Harrow.

The letters did not waver. They did not swim like ink in water. They held steady under the corridor's thin light, black and settled, the strokes pressed into the page with a confidence that felt older than any hand in Salem.

Eliza's tongue stuck to the roof of her mouth. She made herself blink, once, twice, as if blinking could rearrange what she saw into something less final.

The name remained.

Her fingers scraped the wall behind her, searching for texture, for splinters, for something that could prove wood was still wood and not a dream's suggestion of it. The wall did not give. It only held her upright while her knees threatened treason.

"I did not write that," she said again, louder this time, because quiet had been taken from her too often and turned into meaning. "I have never held that book."

Swann did not glance at the guard's hands, did not inspect the page as if he needed confirmation. His attention stayed on Eliza, measuring her reaction the way he measured witness faces, the way he had watched her during the touch test, during the searching of her body, during every moment where fear could be harvested and stored.

"You need not have held it," he said. "That is the point."

Hale stepped closer, and the movement drew Eliza's eye. His expression had changed from solemn certainty into something strained, an alarm that struggled to keep its clerical shape. His lips moved as if he were forming a prayer and forgetting the middle of it.

"This is not," Hale began, then stopped. He stared at the name again, and Eliza saw something in him that frightened her: a man confronting the limits of the rules he had lived by, and deciding which limits he would pretend did not exist.

Swann's voice remained level, almost instructional. "Look at it properly," he told Eliza, as though her fear had made her careless. "Look at how it sits. How it has dried."

Eliza did not want to. Her gaze was already trapped, pinned to the page like an insect under glass. But Swann's words dragged her mind where it did not want to go.

She looked.

The other names on the page sat in varying hands, varying weights of ink. Some were thin and hesitant, as if written by trembling fingers. Some were bold in strokes too certain, a performance of bravery meant to be remembered. But her name was different. It did not look freshly made. It did not look like something added in the last hour, or even in the last day.

It looked like it had seeped into the parchment and become part of it.

Eliza's breath shuddered, and with it came the faintest scent, so light she might have imagined it if her senses had not been sharpened by the cell: cold paper kept too long in a box. The smell she had caught in the hearing room, under sweat and wool. The smell that clung to the visitor's absence.

The mark beneath her left ribs answered with a small, slow pulse, not pain, not pleasure, but recognition. Like a hand tapping once from the inside to let her know it was awake.

Eliza's hand flew to her bodice before she could stop it. She pressed her palm there hard enough to hurt through fabric and bone.

Swann's eyes flicked to the movement. Not surprise. Not even satisfaction. Only the quiet notice of a man confirming a theory.

The guard held the book steady, arms tensed slightly under its weight. He looked past Eliza, not at her, as if he had been trained not to look too closely at the faces of people he escorted to ruin.

Eliza forced herself to look away from the name, and the effort was like prying her own eyelids open against glue. Her gaze skated over the rest of the page and snagged on a line of smaller writing near the margin, a flourish that reminded her of the constable's steady hand but was not the constable's. The curve of the letters made her stomach turn with familiarity that had no source.

She frowned, trying to place it.

A thought came, unwelcome and oddly calm: I know this hand.

Eliza's scalp tightened. She had never seen the book before today. She had never watched anyone sign it. She had been kept in the cell while Salem gathered testimony like kindling.

And yet her mind kept supplying the feeling of having already leaned over these pages. Not in daylight. Not with guards watching. In a place without corners.

Fog, her mind whispered.

The table stretching into nothing.

Leather damp under her palms, as if it had been carried against skin.

Her name rising, not because she wrote it, but because the page warmed and decided to show what it had been holding.

Eliza swallowed, and the iron taste came back faintly, as if her body had learned to anticipate it whenever reality slipped.

Hale's voice, when it came again, sounded tight, controlled by force. "Swann," he said, and Eliza heard warning in it. "This is not proof. Ink can be made. Pages can be altered."

Swann did not argue the point directly. He turned his head just enough to acknowledge Hale without offering him equal standing. "You have been in Salem long enough to know what the people believe," he said. "Belief does not require the kind of proof you prefer."

Hale's eyes flashed. "Then what requires it?" he asked, and for a heartbeat he sounded less like a reverend and more like a man ashamed of where his certainty had led him.

Swann's gaze returned fully to Eliza. "She does," he said, as if that answered everything.

Eliza's stomach dropped at the pronoun, at the ease with which Swann made her the center of all moving parts. She felt suddenly like the stool in the hearing room, placed where people could point and speak and feel clean when they left.

"I don't remember," Eliza said, and then hated herself because the words came too easily, as if they had been waiting in her mouth.

Swann's lips moved in a small, almost imperceptible expression that might have been approval, or might have been nothing at all. "No," he agreed. "You do not."

Eliza shook her head hard. "I remember my mother's hands," she said, frantic now, as if listing ordinary things could anchor her. "I remember my brother's laugh. I remember the road into Salem. I remember you taking me. I remember the cell."

She could have kept going, could have built a wall of remembered details between herself and the book, but the book sat there open like a mouth, and her name was inside it. Memory felt suddenly flimsy beside ink that had dried long ago.

Swann's voice remained gentle, which made it crueler. "And do you remember the night," he asked, "when you first heard its whisper?"

Eliza froze.

Her eyes snapped to his face, searching for trick, for manipulation, for the way his questions always found the same vulnerable seam. But Swann's expression was mild and watchful, and that made Eliza's fear sharpen: he was not guessing. He was testing for a reaction that would confirm what he already believed.

"I never heard it whisper," Eliza said. The lie came out too fast.

The mark beneath her ribs pulsed again, slower than a heartbeat. Answering.

Eliza's breath hitched, and she felt a flicker of sensation in her fingertips, that clean cold she had carried since touching the afflicted girl. The cold rose as if the word whisper had called it.

Hale made a sound under his breath, half prayer, half frustration. "Enough," he said quietly. "This is torment. It is not godly."

Swann did not look away from Eliza. "Torment is often the path to clarity," he replied. "The Lord's work is not always gentle."

Eliza stared at the book again because she could not help it. Her eyes traced the border of the page, the slight yellowing at the edges, the way the parchment looked thick enough to resist tearing. It reminded her of skin. It reminded her, sickeningly, of the way the women had held her shift aside and exposed the mark as if she were a page.

A thought arrived, not in words at first but in shape: the book and her body were part of the same record.

Eliza's palms sweated. She wanted to step forward and slap the book closed, to break the spell of sight, but she did not move. She could not. The guard's arms were steady, and Swann's presence filled the space between Eliza and any choice she might have made.

"Tell me," Swann said softly, "when you look at it, what do you feel?"

Eliza's mouth opened, and for a moment she almost answered him honestly: I feel like I have been here before.

Not in this cell, not with this guard and Hale's strained prayers. Somewhere else. Somewhere without walls. Somewhere the table stretched too far and the air smelled like old paper and damp leather. Somewhere the act of reading felt like being read.

She swallowed the confession down.

"I feel sick," she said instead.

Swann nodded as if that, too, could be entered into a column. "That is common," he said. "Recognition often feels like illness at first. The mind resists what the soul already knows."

Hale's head jerked, offended. "Do not speak of souls as if you can weigh them like grain," he said.

Swann finally turned his eyes to Hale, and Eliza saw the careful patience there, the kind of patience that did not need to win arguments. "I speak of what we have seen," Swann answered. "The town sees her in dreams. The afflicted quiets at her touch. A mark is found upon her that answers as living flesh does not. And now this."

He gestured toward the open page with only two fingers, as if he did not wish to touch it any more than necessary.

Eliza's gaze dropped to her name again. The letters seemed darker now, not because they had changed, but because she had. Her eyes had adjusted to the idea that the page could hold her whether she agreed or not.

She realized, with a slow horror, that this was what Swann meant when he spoke of names as keys. The key was not only for locks. It was for people. To name a thing was to make it easier to carry, easier to accuse, easier to write down and keep.

And her name had been carried here before her memory arrived to defend it.

The cell seemed to tighten around her, boards pressing closer. The book's presence made the air feel thinner, as if it demanded space that the room could not give. Eliza became intensely aware of her own breath, of her heart, of the faint throb beneath her ribs that did not belong to either.

"Close it," she whispered, surprising herself with the desperation in her voice. "Please. Close it."

Swann watched her for a long moment, and in that stillness Eliza felt the visitor's old patience echoing. The kind offer that was not kindness. The calm that waited you out.

Then Swann inclined his head to the guard.

The guard began to bring the cover down.

As it moved, Eliza saw, just for a heartbeat, the next page beneath, and something on it made her blood run cold. Not a name she recognized. Not even writing she could read in the thin light.

A smear, faint and dark, like ink rubbed by a thumb before it had fully dried. Like something that had been touched too many times.

Then the cover shut with a soft, final sound, leather meeting leather.

The silence that followed was immediate and heavy, as if the book's closing had not removed a presence but concentrated it.

Eliza's name remained in her vision anyway, burned there like an afterimage. She could still see the shape of the letters when she blinked.

Recognition without memory.

The knowledge of a thing you could not explain knowing.

Eliza pressed her hand harder against her bodice until pain flared and grounded her. But even the pain could not erase the certainty that had settled in her bones.

The book had not introduced itself to her.

It had returned.

The guard held the closed book as if it were still open.

Its black cover caught the thin corridor light and gave nothing back. Leather met leather, and yet Eliza felt, in the air between her and it, the same pressure she had felt when the visitor sat on the cot: a weight without body, a presence that did not need to touch to be close.

Swann watched her as if waiting for a delayed reaction. Hale stood rigid beside him, his hands half-lifted and then dropping again, as though each prayer he reached for slipped away before he could grasp it.

Eliza's eyes would not leave the book.

It should have been only an object now. Only a thing with a spine and pages and ink. Closed and silent.

But silence had never meant harmlessness here. Silence was how Salem listened.

"You wished it shut," Swann said. "It is shut."

Eliza did not answer. The shape of her name still floated behind her eyes, dark as if written on the inside of her eyelids. Eliza Harrow, steady and settled, older than her own remembering. She pressed her hand to her bodice again and felt the mark beneath her ribs answer with a faint, slow warmth, like a coal banked under ash.

Hale's voice came out strained. "This is not lawful," he said, and the words sounded like he was trying to remind himself of something he had once believed. "This is not the way to seek truth."

Swann turned to him with careful patience. "We are past seeking," he said. "The town has found."

"The town is frightened," Hale snapped, and for a heartbeat Eliza heard anger in him, clean and human. "Fear finds many things. It finds shapes in smoke."

Swann's expression did not change. "And yet it finds the same shapes in many mouths." He nodded toward the guard. "Take it."

For an instant Eliza thought he meant take the book away, remove it from the cell like a lamp being carried out of a sickroom.

But the guard's hand did not move toward the door.

It moved toward Eliza.

The guard did not reach for her throat or her wrists. He did not need to. His broad hand closed around her elbow with practiced certainty, the same guiding grip that had led her down corridors where she could not count steps. Eliza flinched as if the touch itself could summon evidence.

Swann spoke as gently as ever. “Stand away from the cot.”

Eliza’s eyes snapped to the cot. The book had been on it moments ago, obscene against the thin blanket, and though the guard now held it again, Eliza could still see, in her mind, the straw settling under its weight as if welcoming something it recognized.

She moved without meaning to, stepping sideways until her shoulder hit the wall. Her breath came shallow. The cell felt smaller with the book inside it, even closed, as if it took space not in inches but in certainty.

Hale took a half-step forward. “Swann,” he said, low. “Do not do this in her cell.”

Swann’s gaze stayed on Eliza. “It is the proper place,” he replied. “The mind is soft here. The night is near. The Devil does not knock loudly. He prefers the quiet rooms.”

Eliza swallowed, and the iron taste returned faintly, as if her body had learned to produce it whenever someone spoke of night.

The guard lifted the book slightly, not offering it, not presenting it like proof, but holding it at his chest as if it were a living thing that might shift.

Swann's voice lowered. "Look at me, Eliza Harrow."

She tried. She managed to drag her gaze off the book and onto Swann's face. His eyes were mild, attentive, clean of drama. That mildness had always been the worst part. It made everything sound reasonable. It made horror sound like procedure.

"You understand what frightens people most?" Swann asked.

Eliza did not answer. Her tongue felt too thick. She thought of witnesses speaking of prayer stolen, words failing. She feared that if she opened her mouth, another voice might use it.

Swann continued anyway, as if her silence were a kind of assent. "Not pain," he said. "Not even death. Most have endured both and still slept. The oldest fear is simpler."

Hale's mouth tightened. "Do not teach her fear," he said.

Swann glanced at him briefly. “I am not teaching,” he replied. “I am naming what is already there.”

Naming.

Eliza’s skin prickled at the word. Salem did not require you to remember. It required you to be named. Now her own fear was being named, as if that act could pin it down like ink.

Swann’s gaze returned to her. “The oldest fear,” he repeated, “is that your life can be written without you.”

Eliza’s breath caught. The words landed cleanly, finding the soft place beneath her ribs where the mark sat like an ear pressed against her from the inside.

Swann took a slow step closer. He did not invade her space with aggression. He entered it the way damp enters cloth, the way a thought enters when you are too tired to keep the door shut.

“That is what you saw,” he said. “Not merely a book. A record that does not wait for permission.”

Eliza’s mouth moved. Sound came out thin. “It isn’t mine,” she managed. “That writing isn’t mine.”

Swann nodded once, as if agreeing with a child who had finally said something true. “No,” he said. “And still it bears you.”

Hale made a quiet sound, half prayer again, half disgust. He looked at Eliza now, not with hunger for proof, but with something that might have been pity if it had not been so tangled with dread. “Eliza,” he said softly, and hearing her name from his mouth without accusation made her eyes sting. “Do you understand what they are doing?”

Eliza shook her head once, because understanding felt like agreeing. Agreeing felt like signing.

Swann spoke over Hale, calm and steady. “She understands more than she admits.”

Eliza’s gaze flicked to the guard’s hands around the book. She could not see its pages now, and that should have eased her. It did not. The book felt more alive closed, like a mouth shut around words. The thought came unbidden, slick and cold: It does not need to be open to read you.

The cell’s damp air pressed against her skin. She became aware of small sounds: the guard’s breath, the soft creak of leather as his grip adjusted, the faint settling of straw in the cot even though no one touched it, as if the mattress remembered weight and offered itself again.

Eliza's stomach turned.

Swann watched her reaction with careful interest. "You feel it," he said.

"I feel nothing," Eliza lied.

The mark under her ribs pulsed, slow and deliberate, and heat prickled behind her eyes. She wanted to clamp her hand over her chest again, to press the place quiet, but she did not move. She had learned that every movement could be made to mean something.

Swann's voice stayed low. "When you came to Salem, you said you felt watched on the road."

Eliza's throat tightened. She had not said it to him. Not aloud. Not in any room where his quill could have captured it. She had only thought it, and the thought had lived in her body like a taste.

"How do you know that?" she whispered.

Swann's expression did not flicker with surprise at her question. "Because it is always the same," he said. "People think the first terror is being seen. It is not."

His words came gently, almost kindly. "The first terror is being recognized."

Eliza's mind flashed back to the general store. To the way faces had held their gaze on her a heartbeat too long, not curious, not hostile, but certain. As if they knew her shape from somewhere they could not name. As if the town itself had been waiting with a space reserved.

Recognition without reason.

The guard's fingers tightened minutely on the book. The leather creaked, and in that small sound Eliza heard again the dry whisper of pages being handled, even though the cover did not move. The sound came from inside her head and from inside the room at the same time, as if the cell had learned how to make it.

Hale's eyes snapped to Swann. "Stop," he said quietly, and there was something final in it, as though he had reached the end of what he could stomach. "This is cruelty dressed as inquiry."

Swann's gaze remained on Eliza. "It is mercy," he said. "It prepares her. Better she learns what she is dealing with before the court presses harder."

Eliza's hands shook. She fought to still them. "What I'm dealing with," she said, and her voice broke, "is you."

Swann regarded her for a long moment. Then he nodded, as if she had spoken a partial truth and he would allow it. "Yes," he said. "And also what is behind you."

Eliza's blood went cold.

The afflicted girl's whisper returned to her: It wants to sit. It wants to sit on her.

Eliza did not turn. She could not bear to give the empty air behind her the dignity of being acknowledged. The visitor had always waited for notice. It had always preferred being looked at, being recognized, being agreed with.

But the cell's silence thickened, and Eliza felt that old patience gather near the cot, near the straw that refused to rise, near the place where the book had lain like a sleeping animal.

She tasted iron sharply, and tears came hot and sudden to her eyes, not from sadness but from the pressure of holding herself together while something else leaned at the seams.

Hale stepped toward her, and for the first time he broke the invisible line of distance he had kept in every room. He did not touch her, but he stood closer, as if his body could block something unseen. His voice lowered. "Eliza," he said. "Hear me. Do not answer voices you cannot place. Do not speak to what comes in the night. Hold to what you know."

Eliza tried. She tried to summon her mother's face, her father's hands, Samuel's laugh. She found them like objects at the bottom of a pond, wavering and distorted by water. She reached and her fingers closed on nothing.

The oldest fear.

Not pain. Not death.

That what you knew could be taken and replaced.

Swann made a small gesture toward the guard. "We are done for now," he said.

The guard turned toward the door, book held close. Hale did not move with him immediately. He stayed a heartbeat longer, looking at Eliza as if he wanted to say something else and feared whatever he said would be stolen and used.

"Pray," Hale whispered, and the word sounded desperate, not commanding. "Even if the words feel thick. Pray anyway."

Eliza's mouth trembled. She did not know if she could pray. Prayer had become another test in Salem, another place where failure could be recorded.

Swann opened the door. Corridor light cut into the cell, and with it came the smell of lye and damp wool. The guard stepped out, the black book vanishing into the narrow slice of brightness as if it had never been there at all.

But the air it had brought remained.

Hale followed, and just before he crossed the threshold, he glanced back once, quick and haunted.

Then the door swung shut.

The bolt slid home.

Eliza stood alone in the cell with her name still burning behind her eyes and the faint warmth under her ribs listening.

She waited for the sound of footsteps to fade.

When the corridor finally went quiet, she realized something that made her knees threaten to give.

The book had left the room.

But the feeling of being read had not.

And in the deeper hush, beneath the damp and the straw and her own breath, she heard, as clearly as if someone stood beside the cot turning pages, that dry, reverent sound again.

Paper moving.

Not in the corridor.

Not in the hearing room.

Here.

Inside the cell with her.

Eliza backed away from the cot until her shoulders pressed the wall, and she stood there trembling, not daring to sit, not daring to lie down, because she understood now what the oldest fear truly was.

It was not that the Devil might take your soul.

It was that something might take your life and write it down, line by line, until even you began to believe the writing more than your own remembering.

And somewhere, in a book without hands, a page waited for the night to do what it always did best.

Chapter 13

The Dreams That Stay

Eliza did not sleep.

She stood until her legs shook and then sank to the floor again, back against the wall, knees drawn up so tightly her joints ached. The cot remained across from her like a second door inside the cell, a place that remembered weight. She kept her eyes off it as much as she could, but every time she blinked the same shapes returned: the black leather cover, the pale page, her name dried into the fibers as if the parchment had grown around it.

Eliza Harrow.

The sound of paper moving would not leave.

At first she tried to tell herself it was only memory, her mind replaying the guard's hands opening the book, the way the pages had whispered like dry leaves. But the longer she sat in the dark, the more the sound seemed to find different places in the room. It came from the cot, then from the corner where the bucket sat, then from behind her own shoulders, as if the cell itself had learned how to imitate it.

She pressed her palm against her bodice, over the mark. Not hard enough to invite the voice again, only enough to feel her own warmth under cloth. The spot answered with a faint heat that was not pain, not comfort, but presence. An acknowledgment. The coal under ash.

Hale's last instruction returned, thin and desperate: Pray anyway.

Eliza tried. She formed the first words of the Lord's Prayer in her mind, the way she had been taught as a child, but the phrases would not hold their shape. They slid, broke apart, recombined with other words that were not prayer. Names. Ink. Record.

When she finally closed her eyes, it was not as a choice. It was because her body betrayed her. Her head sagged forward and her jaw went slack, and the cell's damp dark pressed in until it seemed gentler than keeping her eyes open.

She had the sensation of falling without moving.

The paper sound became clearer.

Not louder, exactly. Closer. Like someone turning pages in the same room but taking care not to be seen.

Eliza's eyes flew open.

For a heartbeat she thought she saw movement by the cot, a shift in the air the way heat shifts above a candle. Then the darkness smoothed itself again. The cot was only the cot. The blanket lay flat, though she could still make out the stubborn unevenness beneath it.

Her breathing came quick. She forced it slower. She fixed her gaze on the door, on the line of wood and iron where the bolt held. She counted her breaths. One. Two. Three.

Sleep returned anyway, creeping back like water seeping into seams.

This time she did not fall. She slid.

The cell's damp smell thinned. The air changed, becoming sharper, colder, as if she had opened a door and stepped into night. She felt it on her cheek first, then on her hands. Her fingers, still haunted by that clean cold since the touch test, seemed to welcome it.

Eliza was standing.

She did not remember rising. She did not remember putting her feet beneath her. But her legs held her weight, and the soles of her boots pressed against boards that did not feel like the cell's boards. These were smoother. Less swollen with damp. They creaked with a different voice.

She turned her head.

She was in a corridor, lit by a thin wash of moonlight coming through a high window. The lye smell was there, faint, and the wool smell, but under it lay something else, dry and old, like paper shut in a chest.

Eliza's mouth opened. Her breath came out as a small white ghost, and the sight of it startled her. The cell had been too warm for that.

Her heart thudded.

How am I here?

The thought should have brought panic, should have snapped her fully awake, but the fear felt dulled at the edges. Her mind moved as if under a heavy blanket. She knew she should run back to the cell, should press herself against the locked door and demand to be let in, because the corridor meant guards, and guards meant hands, and hands meant being moved like an object.

Yet her feet did not turn back.

They turned forward.

Eliza walked. Each step landed with quiet certainty, as if she had been doing this for a long time. She did not pass anyone. No constable. No watchman. The building's hush felt unnatural, like a church after the last candle is blown out, when you can still sense where the prayers had been.

At the end of the corridor the door to the hearing room stood shut. It should have been barred, but the latch was lifted. Eliza reached for it without thinking.

Her fingers touched the iron.

A brief pulse of warmth flared under her left ribs, quick as a blink.

The door swung inward.

The hearing room was empty. Benches sat in orderly rows like teeth. The magistrates' table waited at the front, its surface pale in the moonlight. The place smelled of old breath and sweat that had soaked into wood, and of ink that had been spilled and never fully scrubbed away.

Eliza stepped inside.

Her boots sounded too loud on the boards, though she did not feel she was walking heavily. She moved down the aisle where townspeople had leaned forward to watch her touch a girl's shoulder and turn relief into proof. She could still hear their uproar in her memory, but in the empty room there was only her own breathing and that other sound, faint and persistent.

Paper moving.

It did not come from behind her now. It came from the table.

Eliza's gaze lifted.

On the magistrates' table, where the constable had written with his eager quill, sat the black book.

Closed.

The leather drank the moonlight, making it seem like a darker void cut into the room. Eliza stopped walking. Her skin prickled. She waited for the book to be gone when she blinked.

It remained.

She swallowed, but her throat felt too open, too exposed. She could taste iron anyway, faint as a memory.

She should not go closer, she knew that with a cold certainty. But the knowledge did not control her limbs. Her body moved as if the floor itself guided her.

She approached the table.

The book's spine was cracked in the same places. The corners were blunted by handling that did not belong to any single person. Eliza could see, in the thin light, that the leather had small scars, slight abrasions like the surface had been scraped by something sharp and then healed.

Her name, she thought, and the thought made her mark answer with a slow, steady warmth.

Eliza reached out.

Her fingers hovered above the cover, trembling.

She did not touch it.

The book opened anyway.

Not with a dramatic snap. With careful slowness, as if a polite hand had lifted the cover from within. Eliza watched, frozen, as pale parchment showed, thick and slightly yellow at the edges.

The first page lay blank for a heartbeat.

Then faint writing began to surface, like bruises appearing under skin. Letters forming where the page had been empty.

Eliza's mouth went dry. She leaned in, unable not to.

Not names she recognized. Not at first. They shimmered at the edge of sense, like half-heard words. But one line, near the lower portion of the page, darkened more quickly, as if that ink had been waiting nearer the surface.

A name took shape.

Mercy Harrow.

Eliza's breath left her in a broken sound.

"No," she whispered, and the word felt thick, as if the room had stuffed cotton in her mouth. Her mother's name sat there with the same settled confidence as Eliza's had, the strokes clean and inevitable.

Her mind struggled to grasp what she was seeing. Mercy was at home. Mercy's hands smelled of bread dough and soap. Mercy had not come to Salem to sit in this room and sign anything.

But the book did not care where Mercy was.

The book only cared that Mercy could be written.

Eliza's hands flew to her chest. The warmth beneath her ribs pulsed, and for an instant she felt the sensation she had felt when she touched the afflicted girl: a shift, a thread pulling free. She had not moved, but something inside her did, turning toward the page as if her body were the ink that could be pressed into it.

The paper sound changed, becoming more like a soft, pleased rustle.

A presence gathered at Eliza's shoulder, not seen but felt, the way the afflicted girl had stared at empty air and whispered, It's looking. The room seemed to tilt toward that presence, as if all the boards had been built to hold it.

The voice came, close and gentle, not from the mark now but from the air beside her ear.

"You walk easily," it said.

Eliza's stomach lurched. She tried to turn, but her body moved too slowly, as if the air had thickened.

"I'm dreaming," she managed, though she did not believe it.

"Dreaming is only another corridor," the voice replied, patient as paper. "Another way in."

Eliza's gaze snapped back to the page. Mercy's name remained. Beneath it, faint as breath on glass, another line began to show, as if the book had heard her fear and decided to feed it.

Samuel Harrow.

Eliza made a sound that might have been a sob or a gasp. Her brother's name rose like a bruise, darkening into legibility.

"No," she said again, louder, and this time the word scraped her throat raw. She reached for the page with both hands as if she could smear the ink away, as if she could wipe the names back into blankness.

Her fingers did not touch parchment.

Her fingertips met cold air first, that familiar clean cold like reaching into water left out overnight. Then heat bloomed beneath her skin, not in the room but inside her palms, as if her hands were being warmed from within.

A pressure settled over her shoulders, gentle as someone placing a shawl, heavy as someone sitting.

It wants to sit, the afflicted girl had said.

Her.

On her.

Eliza's knees threatened to buckle, and she realized with sudden clarity that she was not standing alone at the table. Something stood with her, through her, using her nearness to the book the way it had used her touch to make a girl go quiet.

The voice spoke, almost fond.

"Do you see," it asked, "how quickly names come when the page is ready?"

Eliza's vision swam. She tried to force herself to look away, to shut her eyes, to wake, to run back into the cell and press her back against the damp boards and feel only the honest misery of straw and stone.

But the hearing room held her.

The book held her.

The presence held her, seated in her bones.

Eliza's mouth opened to scream, and no sound came out.

The room's moonlight flickered.

For a heartbeat, she saw the benches filled, not with people but with pale shapes, headless and still, as if the court itself had become a place where bodies waited to be named. The magistrates' table stretched longer than it should, reaching into shadow like the fog-table from her mind, and the black book sat at its center like an anchor.

The page turned by itself.

Eliza's heart hammered. She felt it in her throat. The paper sound was loud now, no longer hiding.

On the next page, writing rose in faint lines, not names this time but marks like the beginning of a record, as if the book were preparing columns.

Eliza's stomach heaved.

"Stop," she tried to say.

The voice, gentle, answered as if she had asked a foolish question.

"Why?" it asked. "They want it written. You felt their want. You gave relief, and they praised you. You gave quiet, and they called it proof."

Eliza's hands clenched into fists, nails biting skin. She needed pain. She needed something that belonged to her.

The presence on her shoulders leaned closer. She smelled it then, unmistakable: that dry, cold note of paper kept too long in a box, threaded with the damp leather scent of the book.

"It is easier," the voice murmured, "to walk at night than to sit in a cell and pretend you are not already mine."

Mine.

The word struck like a slap.

Eliza's eyes flew open.

She was on the floor of the cell again, cheek pressed to her knee, breath harsh in her throat. The darkness was the cell's true darkness, damp and close. The cot sat across from her, its blanket still.

For a moment she thought she had not moved at all.

Then she felt it.

A gritty cold at the bottoms of her boots.

She shifted, trembling, and scraped one boot against the board. Something fell away in a small shower.

Dirt.

Not straw dust. Not the gray powder of old wood. Real earth, dark and damp, as if she had walked outside.

Eliza stared at it, unable to breathe properly.

The paper sound came once, faint and reverent, from somewhere near the cot.

Eliza pressed her palm to her bodice over the mark and felt the coal-warmth answer, steady and awake.

In the stale dark of the cell, with dirt on her boots and names still ringing in her mind like a bell that would not stop, Eliza understood the shape of the new horror.

The dream had not ended when she woke.

It had followed her back.

Eliza kept her eyes on the dirt as if looking away would let it crawl back into her boots.

It lay in a small scatter on the boards, darker than the wood, damp enough to cling in tiny clots.

Not the dry rot-dust of the cell. Not straw chaff. This was soil the way she had known it all her life: heavy with water, smelling faintly of leaf mold and something living underneath.

Her breath came in short pulls that made her ribs ache.

"No," she whispered, because there was nothing else to say to it.

She lifted one foot a fraction and held it in the dim, trying to see the sole. The cell's light was wrong for it, a gray that never decided if it was night or day. But she could feel the grit under the leather, packed into the seams, lodged where the sole met the upper. When she scraped her boot again, more fell.

It made a soft sound on the boards, a quiet patter like rain beginning.

Eliza's stomach rolled. She pressed her forehead to her knee and forced herself to breathe through her nose so she would not retch and make noise that would bring the guard.

Outside the door, nothing moved. No footsteps. No key. The building seemed to hold itself still, as if it, too, were listening for the page-turning that had sounded near the cot.

She lifted her head slowly.

The cot sat in the same place it always did, the thin blanket smoothed as if smoothing could erase what lay beneath it. The unevenness in the straw still suggested a shallow hollow, not the clear oval of a seated body, but a stubbornness that would not settle into flatness. The suggestion made her skin prickle. Matter remembers, the voice had implied in a hundred quiet ways, even before it spoke from her ribs. Straw remembers. Wood remembers.

Eliza forced her eyes away and looked down at herself instead, because she needed something she could count and name that belonged to her.

Her skirt hem was darker in places.

At first she tried to tell herself it was only shadow. Then she pinched the cloth between finger and thumb and rubbed it. The fabric felt stiff, as if it had dried after being wet. When she lifted the edge closer to her face, she caught the smell again: earth, and something sharper beneath, like crushed green stem.

Her throat tightened so hard it hurt.

She did not remember walking. She did not remember leaving the cell. She did not remember any door opening for her. But her boots held soil, and her hem held the trace of damp ground.

A slow dread crept up behind her eyes, heavy and patient. The dream in the hearing room had been too clear, too detailed. She had felt moon-cold air on her cheek. She had seen the book on the magistrates' table. She had watched her mother's name rise as if the page had a bruise that could be coaxed to the surface.

Mercy Harrow.

Samuel Harrow.

Eliza's chest tightened at the names. She pressed her palm hard against her bodice over the mark as if she could press those letters back down into her skin, seal the way in. The warmth beneath her ribs answered, slow and steady, like a creature acknowledging a hand on its back.

She flinched and snatched her palm away.

"No," she breathed, and the word was not aimed at the dirt anymore. It was aimed at the quiet warmth, at the listening presence that did not need to speak to make itself known.

The cell did not answer. But the silence felt attentive, the way a room feels when someone stands just out of sight and waits for you to turn your head.

Eliza pushed herself up on trembling legs. Her knees cracked softly from sitting too long on the boards. She stood there swaying, listening for any sound beyond the door. Nothing.

She began to search, because terror demanded action even when action was useless.

The bucket sat in its corner, unchanged. The straw beneath the cot was not accessible without pulling the blanket aside, and she could not bring herself to do that yet. She looked instead at the door. At the iron bolt. At the line where wood met frame.

There were scratches.

They were small, shallow, and she might have missed them if she had not been staring so hard her eyes watered. Near the bottom edge, close to where her boot might scuff if she braced herself, the wood bore a fresh pale mark, as if something had scraped it recently and exposed lighter grain beneath.

Eliza crouched, slow, and ran one finger along the scratch.

A splinter rose under her nail. She jerked her hand back, sucking in breath.

Fresh.

Not the old scarring of a door that had been locked and unlocked for years. This felt new enough to bite.

Her heart thudded so loudly she was sure it would carry through the boards and bring someone down with a lantern and questions.

She stared at the scratch and tried to imagine her own body doing it. Bracing, pushing, pulling. Trying to force the door. But she did not remember trying. She did not remember waking and throwing herself against iron. She remembered only the hearing room dream, the book opening without hands, the voice at her ear, the pressure settling on her shoulders as if something had found a seat in her bones and leaned into her.

It is easier to walk at night than to sit in a cell and pretend you are not already mine.

Mine.

Eliza swallowed hard and tasted iron as if the word had cut her mouth.

She rose and stepped back from the door, forced her gaze to travel the boards near the threshold. There were smudges there too, faint darker streaks like damp rubbed into dust. Footprints, almost. Not clear enough to prove anything to anyone else, but to Eliza they looked like a trail half erased. The building's dirt had been disturbed. Something had passed through here.

She had passed through here.

The thought made her dizzy. She reached out and steadied herself against the wall, palm flat on the damp wood. The wall felt cold. It had always been cold, but now it seemed colder, as if she had brought night in with her and it had not yet left.

Eliza lifted her fingers and looked at them. For a moment she expected to see ink, as she had in the hearing room after touching the afflicted girl, as she had feared when she stared at her own fingertips in court. There was no ink. Only a faint gray smudge where she had touched the floor.

She wiped her hand on her skirt and the smudge disappeared into cloth.

That was the worst part. How easily it could be hidden. How easily it could leave nothing but doubt behind. A girl could be filthy in a cell. A skirt hem could be damp from spilled water. Boots could hold dirt from the day she was seized, from the common, from the road into Salem. Any sign could be explained away by someone who wanted it to be ordinary.

Swann would want it explained. Not because he believed her innocence, but because mystery was useful only in certain shapes. He would not allow a shape he did not control.

Hale would look at the dirt and call it delirium, or temptation, or a test. He had told her not to answer voices she could not place, as if the problem was politeness. As if refusing to speak could keep something from using her.

Eliza shut her eyes and tried to hold onto one clear memory, one honest thing that did not shift when she reached for it.

Her mother's hands. Flour dust on the knuckles. The heat of the hearth. Mercy's voice saying Eliza, not as a name to be recorded, but as a call across a room.

The memory trembled, wavered at the edges like a reflection on water.

Her eyes snapped open. She could not let herself sink into remembering too deeply. The visitor had offered her unnatural clarity before, sharpening Mercy's face in her mind as if offering it. A kindness that was not kindness. A gift that meant, Look what I can reach in you. Look what I can touch.

Eliza wrapped her arms around herself, then dropped them immediately, because even her own embrace felt like pressure on her shoulders.

She looked again at the dirt on the floor.

If she left it there, it would be seen when the guard brought food or water. It would become a question. And questions in Salem were never neutral. A question could be turned into a statement the moment it was written down.

She crouched and began to gather it with her fingertips, scraping damp soil into her palm. The act was absurdly intimate, like gathering evidence against herself. It clung to her skin, cold and gritty. She carried it to the bucket and dropped it in. The dirt made a soft, heavy sound as it hit the bottom.

Eliza stared at the bucket for a long moment. The water inside was murky already, barely fit to drink. Now it held something from outside the cell. A little piece of night smuggled into captivity.

She rubbed her hands together until they were dry, then wiped them on her skirt again. Her fingertips still tingled faintly with that clean cold she had felt since touching the afflicted girl. She could not tell where the cold ended and the dirt began. Everything in her body felt like a signal now, every sensation a possible message.

She sat back on her heels and looked at her boots. The soles still held grit no matter how she scraped them. It had worked into the stitching, stubborn as the cot's hollow, as if the leather had taken the night and would not give it back easily.

A soft sound came from near the cot.

Eliza froze.

Not a footstep. Not straw shifting under weight. A dry whisper, almost too faint to be real, like a page being turned slowly.

Eliza did not look at the cot. She could not. Her eyes stayed fixed on her boots, on the dirt that had no right to be here, and her breath slowed into something careful and quiet.

In that careful quiet, she became aware of another sensation.

Not the warmth at her ribs. Not the cold in her fingers.

Her muscles ached in places they should not.

Her calves felt tight, as if she had walked a long distance. Her hips carried a dull soreness like a bruise forming. Even her shoulders, beneath the thin fabric, had the heavy fatigue of bearing something that had leaned there for hours.

It wants to sit.

Eliza's stomach clenched. She rose slowly, as if sudden movement might invite something to press down harder. She took one step toward the wall opposite the cot and pressed her back against it, keeping as much space between herself and that remembered hollow as the cell allowed.

She stood there, listening.

No voice spoke. The mark under her ribs remained warm, banked and watchful. The page-turning sound came once more, so faint she almost convinced herself it was only straw settling, only her own blood moving in her ears.

Almost.

Then, from the corridor beyond the door, a distant sound: the drag of a boot, the soft clink of iron.

Morning, perhaps. Or only a guard making rounds.

Eliza's heart leapt with a panic that was half relief and half terror. Someone would come. Someone would open the bolt and see her standing, rigid, dirt scraped into the bucket, scratches on the door, and they would interpret it however suited them.

Or they would not see anything at all. They would see a girl in a cell, pale and shaking, and they would call it fits. Agitation. Guilt.

Eliza swallowed and forced her breathing steady. Whatever had happened, whatever her body had done in the night while her mind floated elsewhere, had left signs. Not proof for Salem, perhaps. Salem did not need proof.

But signs for her.

She stared at the scratches on the door, at her boots, at the faint stains on her hem, and she understood with a sinking clarity that the dream had been only part of it. The dream was the story her mind could bear. The rest had been done with her legs and hands while she was not fully inside herself to stop it.

Something had walked wearing her.

And it had brought the outside back in, not as escape, but as a promise that the cell's walls were not the limit.

They were only where she woke.

The clink of iron came again, closer this time, followed by the soft drag of a boot that did not bother to hide its weight.

Eliza pressed her spine harder into the wall. The boards were cold and damp against her shoulders, but she welcomed the sting of it. Pain was honest. Pain was proof of where she was. Her eyes fixed on the door as if staring could keep it shut.

The footsteps stopped just outside.

For a moment there was only breathing on the other side of the wood, a man's slow exhale that fogged nothing because the corridor was warmer than the dream had been. Then the bolt scraped.

Eliza's stomach clenched so hard she thought she might fold in half.

The door opened, and lantern light spilled in, staining the cell yellow. The guard stepped in with a tin bowl and a heel of bread. His face was half-shadowed by the lantern's hood, but his expression was the same as always: not cruel, not kind, simply emptied of anything that could be argued with.

He looked at Eliza once, quick and assessing. His eyes dropped to the floorboards, to the bucket, to the cot. He did not pause long enough for Eliza to know what he saw.

"You'll eat," he said, like an instruction for an object that required maintenance.

Eliza nodded because her throat had closed around every other answer. The nod felt like betrayal anyway.

He set the bowl on the floor near the door, far enough that she would have to cross the cell to reach it. The bread landed beside it with a dull sound. Then he lifted the lantern slightly and glanced at the bolt, checking it as if he mistrusted his own hands more than he mistrusted her.

As he turned to leave, his gaze snagged on the bottom edge of the door where the fresh scratches were. Eliza saw the smallest hesitation in his eyes, a pause too brief to be called thought. His jaw tightened.

He looked back at her.

Eliza held still. She forced her face blank, as if the lines in the wood meant nothing to her. As if she had not crouched there gathering dirt into her palm like a thief.

The guard's mouth moved, as if he might speak. Then it shut again. He stepped out and pulled the door closed. The bolt slid home with that final click that made Eliza's teeth hurt.

Eliza stayed against the wall until her legs began to tremble. Only then did she cross the cell, careful, as if the boards might betray her. She knelt by the bowl and stared down at the thin porridge. A skin had formed on top. It reflected the lantern light in a dull, oily sheen.

Her stomach growled, furious and simple.

She lifted the bowl with both hands. The tin was cold. She ate because hunger was another kind of weakness Salem could interpret. She chewed the bread slowly, as though moving her jaw might keep her from moving her feet.

When she finished, she set the bowl back down and sat with her knees drawn up. She kept her boots planted flat on the boards, as if lifting them might invite the dirt back into the seams, might invite the memory of walking.

Her muscles still ached in that unsettling way, as if her body had been used for distance her mind had not traveled. She flexed her calves and felt the dull pull. She rolled her shoulders and felt soreness bloom beneath the skin, the heavy fatigue of carrying something that leaned.

It wants to sit.

Her fingers went, without permission, toward her bodice. She stopped them inches short. She could not bear to press the mark again and feel that answering warmth, that steady acknowledgment like a creature being stroked. She sat on her hands instead, trapping them under her thighs.

The cell held the quiet of morning, if morning was what it was. Light leaked in through the crack under the door, a thin gray that did not brighten enough to be called day. Somewhere above, boards creaked. A voice murmured and cut off. Salem moved through its routines while Eliza sat at the bottom of the world.

She tried to pray again, not with the full words, which had become slippery, but with shapes: her mother's hands, Samuel's laugh, the road before Salem's gates closed. She pictured the road hard, tried to set it in her mind like a line she could follow back out.

But the image refused to stay still. It wavered, and in the wavering she saw something else: the hearing room aisle lit by moon, her boots sounding too loud as she walked toward the magistrates' table as if pulled.

The horror was not the dream.

The horror was that she could not say, with certainty, that it had been only a dream.

Eliza closed her eyes and tried to reconstruct the night as if it were a story she could lay out on the floor and examine. She had been on the boards. Her head against her knee. The paper sound. The falling sensation. Then corridor air and moonlight. Then the black book opening without hands, and Mercy's name rising like a bruise.

When she opened her eyes again, the cell was the same. The cot. The bucket. The walls. Yet she felt, under her skin, that sense of a path being used. As if her body had been a hallway.

Swann's words returned, calm and terrible: The oldest fear is that your life can be written without you.

Eliza had thought, yesterday, that he meant ink on parchment. That her name could appear in a book without her hand.

Now she understood the deeper cut of it.

Her steps could be taken without her choosing.

She stared at her boots as if they were not hers. They had always been simple things: leather and stitching, worn from work, shaped by her feet. Now they felt like evidence waiting to be interpreted. Now they felt like tools that could carry her anywhere while her mind floated above, thin as smoke.

She shifted her right foot slightly and the sole made a faint squeak against the boards. The sound was harmless. It still made her flinch.

Eliza forced herself to stand.

Her knees complained. Blood rushed to her feet with pins-and-needles sting. She stood in the center of the cell and looked down at the floorboards, at the narrow lines between them. She tried to imagine them as a map.

If she walked in the night, where did she place her feet? Did she step on the same boards? Did she avoid the squeaky one by the cot? Did she move like herself, careful and hesitant, or like something that had learned her body and found it useful?

She took one slow step forward.

The board creaked softly.

Eliza froze. Her breath stalled in her throat.

The creak was ordinary, only wood complaining under weight, but her skin crawled as if the sound itself could summon the other presence. She pictured the empty hearing room again, the benches like teeth, and in her mind she saw pale, headless shapes sitting where people should be, waiting to be named.

She swallowed hard. The iron taste rose faintly anyway.

Another step.

Another creak.

Eliza's heart hammered.

This was madness, she thought. This was how the afflicted girls spoke, how they jerked and cried out at empty air. This was how Salem made a story: a person flinching at ordinary things until the flinching became proof.

But Eliza could not stop. She needed to know if her own feet belonged to her in daylight.

She walked toward the door and placed her palm flat against it. The wood was rough under her skin. The bolt was cold through the grain. She leaned in and listened. She heard nothing but distant movement in the building.

Then, very faintly, as if from inside her own skull, she heard it: paper moving. A soft, reverent rustle.

Eliza jerked her hand away from the door. Her pulse surged. She backed up until her calves hit the cot, and the contact with the mattress made her stomach pitch.

She turned sharply and stared down at the blanket, at the unevenness beneath it. The straw did not shift. The hollow did not deepen. The cot did not betray a presence.

And yet she felt, with the certainty that had become her newest curse, that something was there in the room with her that did not require weight to make itself known.

Not a figure in the corner.

Not a shadow.

A readiness. A listening.

She backed away from the cot and pressed herself into the opposite wall again, putting distance between her body and the place that remembered being sat upon.

Her mind began to do what it had started doing since Salem: counting, measuring, trying to trap fear in numbers.

How many steps from the door to the cot? How many boards? If she woke and found herself at the hearing room again, could she remember the route? Could she leave a trail for herself that could not be explained away?

She looked around the cell for anything loose. There was only the blanket, the bucket, her own clothing.

Eliza's gaze fell on the hem of her skirt where it had dried stiff. She pinched the fabric and pulled. It did not tear easily. The cloth was too sturdy. The stubbornness of it made her want to weep with frustration.

Her fingers went to her hair. It hung loose still from the women's search, heavy against her shoulders. She had no pins, no ribbon. But she could pull strands free.

The thought came sharp and desperate: tie yourself down.

Eliza's hands trembled. She imagined wrapping hair around her wrists, around her ankles, braiding it into knots that would hurt if she moved, that would wake her if she tried to walk. Pain as an anchor. Pain as a bell.

She sat down hard on the boards and grabbed a handful of hair. The strands slid through her fingers like water. She twisted them, tried to bind them around her wrist. The hair tightened, bit into skin slightly. It was not enough. It would snap or slip. It would not hold against whatever could open doors in her sleep.

The hopelessness of it washed over her, hot and humiliating.

Eliza dropped the hair and pressed her palms to her eyes. She tried to breathe through the rising panic. She tried to tell herself she was only tired, only frightened, only trapped in a cell with too much silence.

But when she lowered her hands, she saw her boots again. She saw the faint grit still lodged in the seams. She saw her own footprints in her mind, walking a corridor without her permission.

And she understood the shape of what had changed.

Salem could accuse her in court. It could search her body. It could put a book in front of her and call ink proof. Those were horrors she could name. Those were hands she could see.

This was different.

This was her own body becoming a witness against her, moving through the night and returning with dirt in its teeth. This was her own legs carrying her toward a book, toward names she loved, toward a table where the page waited ready.

Eliza wrapped her arms around herself again, then stopped, remembering the pressure on her shoulders in the dream, the weight settling like a shawl that was not cloth.

She held herself anyway, because there was nothing else to hold.

In the dim gray that passed for day, Eliza sat very still and listened to the cell's hush. She waited for the paper sound to come again, and when it did, faint as a breath, she did not look toward the cot.

She looked down at her feet.

Because the thing that frightened her most now was not what Salem might do to her in public, under God and law and witness.

It was what she might do when no one watched.

It was the fear of waking to find she had gone somewhere again, leaving a trail of her own steps behind her like a confession she could not remember making.

And the deeper fear beneath even that, quiet and cold as old paper, was that she would begin to recognize those steps as familiar. Not because she chose them.

Because they had been practiced.

Chapter 14

The Second Voice

Eliza measured the day in sounds.

A bucket set down somewhere above. A board that complained under a familiar step. The rattle of iron, a door opened and shut, a voice that rose and then folded itself away. Each noise arrived as proof that the world still moved in ordinary ways, even if she no longer trusted what ordinary meant.

She stayed near the wall opposite the cot, knees drawn up, boots planted as if her soles might remember the cell better if she forced them to. Hunger returned in dull waves, but she had eaten, and eating had not made her feel more real. It had only reminded her that her mouth still worked when she asked it to do simple things. It was the other things it betrayed.

The paper sound returned twice, faint and reverent, never quite from the same place. Once it seemed to come from the cot, as if pages were being turned inside the straw. Once it came from the door, as if the wood itself had learned to read.

Eliza kept her eyes open until they burned and watered, and when she could no longer keep them open, she fought the closing like a condemned woman fighting the hood.

Sleep was not rest here. Sleep was a corridor.

She did not know when the light at the crack beneath the door thinned from gray to darker gray, or if it did at all. The cell's dimness only shifted the way breath shifts in cold air, nearly invisible but undeniable if you watched long enough.

Her head sagged, heavy with its own weight. She jerked it back up, hard enough to make her neck ache.

"I will not," she whispered, and did not finish the sentence because finishing it would give it shape. I will not go. I will not walk. I will not stand at that table again and watch names rise like bruises.

The warmth under her left ribs stirred, the coal under ash responding to the sound of her voice as if voice were invitation. Eliza pressed her lips together until her teeth hurt.

Silence.

Then, in that silence, something spoke.

Not the voice that had thanked her. Not the one that had leaned close in her dream and called her mine with gentle certainty. This sound did not come with that dry paper smell, that sense of something pleased with its own patience.

This was quieter in a different way.

It did not bloom from her ribs like heat. It came as if it had always been present and she had only just moved her attention far enough to hear it.

"Lie down."

Eliza's whole body locked.

The words were not loud. They were barely more than thought. But they were not her thought, and she knew the difference the way she knew the difference between hunger and nausea. This voice did not press on her shoulders. It did not carry that soft amusement she had begun to hate. It sounded almost like her own voice would sound if it had been steadier, older.

Eliza did not move. Her eyes darted, stupidly, to the corners, as if a mouth might be hiding there.

"I won't," she said.

The warmth under her ribs answered with a slow pulse. Eliza clenched her hands into fists to keep them from flying to the mark again.

The voice came back, not offended, not impatient.

“Not for it,” it said.

Eliza’s breath caught. Her throat tightened.

“What?” she whispered.

“Lie down,” the voice repeated, and in the repetition there was something that unsettled her more than command ever could: it sounded like advice.

Not a magistrate’s order. Not Swann’s careful instruction. Not the visitor’s coaxing, sweet as rot.

Advice, offered as though she still had the privilege of choice.

Eliza swallowed. Her tongue felt too big. “Who are you?”

No answer.

She waited for the familiar satisfaction of the other voice, the one that praised her for enduring, the one that spoke as though her fear were a gift freely handed over. She waited for the paper sound.

Instead she heard only her own breathing and, far away, a cough in the building that might have belonged to anyone.

"Lie down," the voice said again, and this time it added, very softly, "With your feet toward the door."

Eliza stared at the door. Then at the cot.

A cold sweat broke along her spine. Her mind leapt at once to the idea of waking in the corridor, to the hearing room's moonlight, to the black book opening without hands. She tasted iron as if the thought had cut her.

"No," she said, too fast. "No. I'm not going to make it easier."

The voice did not argue.

"That is not easier," it said. "It is harder."

Eliza blinked hard. Her eyes stung.

Harder how? She wanted to ask, and hated herself for wanting. Wanting to understand was how Salem caught you. Wanting to understand was how Swann slipped questions into you until you answered him without noticing you'd given him anything.

But she could not help it. "Harder for who?"

The voice paused, not for drama, but as if it was choosing its words with care.

"For whatever uses your feet."

Eliza's stomach pitched. She pressed her back harder against the wall as if she could press herself through it and disappear.

"You know," she whispered, and the words were not accusation so much as horror. "You know it's doing it."

"I know you are tired," the voice said. "And tired is when it happens."

Eliza closed her eyes briefly. In the dark behind her lids, her mother's face wavered like a reflection on water. She opened her eyes again at once, afraid that even that memory might be offered back to her in a sharpened, unnatural clarity, a gift meant to show her how easily her mind could be handled.

The voice, still quiet, said, "Do you want to wake with dirt on your boots again?"

Eliza's breath shuddered out. The question landed in her like a stone.

"No."

"Then lie down where you can see the door when you wake," the voice said. "If you wake."

Eliza stared at the cot's thin blanket, at the stubborn unevenness beneath it. She had refused to sleep there for a reason. The cot remembered a seat. The cot remembered weight.

The voice did not tell her to lie on the cot.

It had not said, Go to the cot. It had not said, Sleep, and I will keep watch. It had not offered relief with that gentle predatory tone.

It had given her a position. Feet to the door. Eyes to the bolt. As if it understood she was afraid of waking somewhere else and wanted to give her a way to measure herself against the room.

Eliza's skin crawled anyway.

"Is this another trick?" she asked, and her voice broke on the last word, anger and fear twisted together.

The voice did not soothe her. It did not praise her. It did not thank her.

"I cannot pull your hand," it said. "Only speak."

Eliza's heartbeat thudded in her ears. The phrase struck her as strangely specific, as if it were correcting something she had assumed without meaning to. The visitor had always felt like pressure, like a weight leaning. This voice announced a limitation.

"I don't believe you," Eliza whispered.

"That is sensible," the voice replied.

Eliza went still.

No one in Salem told her she was sensible. Not Swann, who made everything sound inevitable. Not the matrons, who had touched her like a page being inspected for flaws. Not Hale, whose caution had turned to strained devotion.

Sensible. The word sounded like her father might have said it when she was small and wary of storms, when he wanted her to listen without frightening her further.

Her chest tightened at the thought of him. She tried to hold his face, but it slid away into fog.

The warmth under her ribs pulsed, faint but insistent, and Eliza flinched as if something had tapped from inside.

"Don't," she whispered, not sure which presence she meant.

"Not that," the voice said, sharp enough to startle her, and then softened again immediately. "Not to it. Not with fear. Fear is a door."

Eliza's hands trembled in her lap. She stared at them as if they belonged to another girl.

A door. A corridor. A table without edges. Her mind was full of passages now, and she was trapped at the center of them.

"What do you want?" she asked, because the question was all she had left. Everyone wanted something from her. Swann wanted a record. The town wanted certainty. The visitor wanted her life written in a hand that wasn't hers.

This voice hesitated.

Then it said, "I want you awake."

The words were so simple they made her dizzy.

Eliza let out a breath she hadn't realized she'd been holding. Awake. She had not been awake, not fully, not since the road into Salem began to feel watched. Awake was what she thought she had been fighting for when she refused the cot and kept her eyes open until they burned.

But awake was not only eyes open. Awake was inside her own skin, inside her own choices, inside the minutes she could account for.

"How?" she whispered.

"Lie down," the voice said, and there was no command in it now, only insistence born of necessity. "Not on the cot. On the boards. Feet to the door. Your boots off."

Eliza's throat tightened.

Boots off meant vulnerability. Boots off meant she could not stand fast and ready. Boots off meant she would be slow if the door opened, slow if the guard came, slow if Swann returned with his mild questions and his book kept just out of sight.

But boots off also meant she would know.

She would know, if she woke with her boots on again. She would know, if she woke with grit in her soles. She would know, if the leather moved without her hands.

A small tremor ran through her, not with cold but with the first thin strip of something like strategy. Something like resistance that was not only refusal.

The voice did not rush her. It waited, patient in a way that did not feel pleased with itself.

Eliza bent slowly, fingers clumsy, and reached for the laces. Her hands shook so badly she fumbled them twice.

The warmth under her ribs stirred, as if watching.

"Not for it," the voice said, and the firmness returned. "For you."

Eliza swallowed, and blinked back sudden hot tears that had nothing to do with grief and everything to do with the shock of being addressed as though she still existed as a person separate from the record being built around her.

She pulled her boots off.

The air touched her stockinged feet, cool and strange. She set the boots beside her, soles up, and stared at them for a long moment as if they might leap of their own accord.

Then she lowered herself onto the boards with care, placing her body as instructed, feet toward the door. She lay on her side, knees slightly drawn, hands folded tight at her chest without touching the mark.

Her cheek pressed against the floor. The wood smelled of damp and old sweat. It was not comforting, but it was real. It did not smell like paper.

Eliza kept her eyes on the door's lower crack, on the thin line of dim light. She listened for the paper sound. She listened for breath that was not her own. She listened for the cot to shift under weight.

The voice said nothing more.

It did not offer comfort. It did not promise safety. It did not thank her.

It had suggested, and the suggestion had moved her body more effectively than any threat.

As her eyelids began to droop despite her will, Eliza felt the coal-warmth under her ribs pulse once, slow and deliberate, like a reminder that the other presence was still there, listening.

And beneath that, steadier than fear, the new voice remained like a thin thread pulled taut in the dark.

Awake, it had said.

Eliza clung to the word as sleep approached, not like surrender this time, but like a trap she had set with her own hands.

If she woke with her boots on, she would know.

If she woke with dirt in the seams, she would know.

And if she woke somewhere she did not remember walking to, she would know that even suggestions had limits, and that whatever wore her at night had begun to notice she was trying to notice back.

Eliza did not know when sleep took her, only that her eyes were open one moment, fixed on the thin line of light beneath the door, and then the line seemed to stretch and soften as if the floor itself had turned to water.

Her cheek stayed pressed to the boards. The damp smell stayed true. That, more than anything, kept her from panic. The cell did not fall away into moonlit corridors. No cold air touched her face. No benches like teeth waited for her. She remained where she had placed herself, as if the act of choosing a position had anchored more than her limbs.

Still, something moved in the dark behind her eyes.

Not a dream, not yet. A hovering, a pressure like the moment before a door opens. She felt the coal-warmth under her left ribs stir, the mark responding to the simple fact of her slipping.

Her body tensed.

The second voice, thin as a thread but present, spoke without raising itself above her own thoughts.

"Count."

Eliza's lips did not move. Her mouth had learned caution. But inside, she answered, "What?"

"Count what you know," the voice said. "Not what they say. Not what the book writes."

Eliza's breath hitched, then steadied again. She kept her eyes closed now, because keeping them open had not kept her awake before. She understood, suddenly, that wakefulness was not a matter of eyelids. It was a matter of holding her own mind the way a person held a candle in wind.

"One," she thought, and listened to her own pulse. "My name is Eliza Harrow."

The words felt dangerous, as if speaking her name might summon Swann's mild attention. But the voice did not correct her. It did not warn her away from it. It only waited, as if it had asked her to pick up something she had dropped and was letting her find it with her fingers.

"Two," she thought. "My mother is Mercy."

Mercy's face rose at once, too quickly, too sharp. The memory flashed like a polished plate catching sun. Eliza flinched inside herself, because she had learned that unnatural clarity was another kind of trap.

The coal-warmth pulsed, pleased.

Eliza's teeth clenched. She forced the image to slow, to dull into something more honest. She searched for imperfection, for the soft blur of real remembering.

Mercy's hands, she told herself. Not the face.

Her mother's hands were what Eliza truly held. Knuckles reddened by soap. Flour caught in the fine lines near the thumb. A small scar on the right hand from a burned pan years ago. Eliza focused on that scar, on the way Mercy's fingers moved when she tied a ribbon, quick and sure.

The too-sharp brightness of the memory faded into something that felt like it belonged to her.

The coal-warmth under her ribs sulked into quiet heat, still there, still listening.

"Good," the second voice said, and the word struck Eliza oddly. Not as praise, not like the visitor's gentle approval. More like a confirmation. As if the voice had been waiting for her to choose the correct door.

Eliza swallowed. Her mouth tasted of stale air and yesterday's porridge skin. "Three," she thought, and had to pause, because she felt how easily numbers could become a list a magistrate would love. Names. Connections. A record.

She pushed through it anyway.

"Samuel is my brother," she thought, and the thought clenched her stomach. Samuel's name had risen from the page in her night-walking dream like a bruise. She expected the coal-warmth to flare in satisfaction.

It did not.

Instead, in the dark of her closed eyes, Samuel did not appear on parchment. He appeared in a yard, chasing a hoop with a stick, laughing too hard, tripping and scraping his shin. The memory came with a sound: the sharp bark of her father's laugh, half scolding, half pride, when Samuel insisted he was not hurt even with blood on his leg.

Eliza held to that. Blood on a shin was honest. It was not ink. It was not a page deciding to show what it wanted.

For a moment, Eliza's body loosened. Her shoulders sank a fraction. The boards beneath her cheek felt cool and solid.

Then the other voice, the one that thanked her, brushed the edge of her thoughts like a page turned by an unseen hand.

You carried it well.

The coal-warmth pulsed, and with it came a faint scent she could not truly smell in the cell but could somehow sense anyway: old paper, shut too long in a chest.

Eliza's fingers twitched against the boards. Fear rose, quick and automatic, like a hand reaching for a latch.

"Do not," the second voice said at once, sharper now. "Not at it."

Eliza's breath caught. She tried to obey, but the moment she noticed fear, fear became larger.

"How do I stop?" she thought, the question frantic and childish in her own mind.

"You do not stop it," the voice replied. "You stop feeding it."

Eliza's heart hammered. The coal-warmth beat its slow, deliberate pulse beneath her ribs, out of time with her own. It felt like having another heart inside her, one that did not care if she ran or prayed or begged.

The visitor's tone slid into her mind again, soft as damp leather.

They want it written.

Eliza's throat tightened. The sentence landed with Swann's calm cruelty in it, and for a sick moment she could not tell which voice she was hearing. Swann and the visitor sounded too similar in the dark. Both knew how to make inevitability sound like sense.

Eliza clenched her jaw until her teeth ached.

"I want—" she began in thought, and stopped, because she did not know what she wanted anymore besides escape, and escape had already proven itself treacherous.

The second voice answered anyway, as if it had heard the shape of her need without the words.

"You want yourself," it said.

Eliza lay very still.

The phrase struck her harder than any threat. Want yourself. As if she had misplaced her. As if she had been set down somewhere and forgotten in the rush of Salem's hands, Salem's questions, Salem's certainty.

Her eyes stung suddenly. Tears pooled and slid sideways along her nose into the wood. She hated the weakness of it. The cell would not care. The court would not care. Swann would note it as agitation. Hale would call it a trial. The visitor would call it a gift.

But the tears felt like hers. Salt, simple, human.

Eliza took a careful breath and tried again, quieter inside.

"My father is Thomas," she thought, and the name brought a heaviness to her chest. She had seen him beaten when they seized her, his face turning into something shocked and helpless as hands pulled her away. That memory was sharp in the wrong way too, sharpened by terror.

She forced it back. Not the seizure, not the blood.

Her father's coat, she told herself. The smell of smoke and wet wool. The way he whistled when he worked, off-key and unbothered. The way he took a nail between his teeth when his hands were full. Ordinary things. Things that did not perform.

The coal-warmth pulsed once, slower, as if listening more carefully.

“You are doing it,” the second voice said.

“What?” Eliza thought.

“Remembering without begging,” it replied. “Without asking it to show you.”

Eliza understood then, with a small, sick clarity: the visitor had been offering memories like a host offers food, and she had almost taken them because hunger for home was stronger than sense. The visitor could sharpen Mercy’s face, could bring Samuel’s laugh close enough to touch, and the price would be simple.

Gratitude. Permission. A door opened.

Eliza let out a slow breath through her nose, forced her mind away from the temptation of brightness. She held to dull, imperfect recollection like a plank in water.

The cell around her remained quiet. No moonlight corridor intruded. No hearing room opened its mouth.

She felt the boards beneath her cheek, the cold seeping into her skin. She felt the itch at her scalp where her hair lay loose. She felt her stockinged feet, bare of boots, and that detail became a kind of prayer.

Boots off, she reminded herself. Boots off means you will know.

A small sound came from beyond the door. A distant cough, a board creaking above. Ordinary.

Eliza's eyelids fluttered. Sleep pressed again, heavier now, a tide returning. She feared it, because fear was habit, but she also felt the thin thread of the second voice holding steady.

"Listen," the voice murmured.

Eliza strained her attention, expecting the dry rustle of paper.

Instead she heard her own breathing.

In. Out.

And beneath that, faint but real, the slow scrape of straw settling in the cot. Not a weight sitting down. Not the visitor's deliberate presence. Just straw shifting the way straw always shifted in damp air, in old mattresses, under the small changes of a building.

Relief hit Eliza so sharply she almost laughed, and the near-laughter frightened her. She had become a creature who could not trust relief. Relief was how traps closed.

"Is it gone?" she thought.

"No," the second voice answered, and it did not lie kindly. "But you are here."

Eliza's chest tightened around the words.

Here. In her own skin. On the boards she chose. With her boots beside her, soles up, a small witness waiting.

The coal-warmth under her ribs pulsed once, as if annoyed to be ignored.

Eliza did not press it. She did not address it. She did not offer it fear, or denial, or pleading. She did what the second voice had told her to do from the beginning.

She counted what she knew.

"My name," she thought, slower now, more careful. "My mother's hands. My brother's laugh. My father's coat."

The list was not complete. It was not proof against Salem. It would not open the door or stop Swann's quill.

But as she held those ordinary pieces, she felt something in her mind settle into place, not like a miracle, not like salvation, but like a tool returned to its rightful peg.

The door remained shut. The bolt remained in place. The cot sat in its corner, stubborn and remembering.

Eliza lay on the boards with her feet toward the exit, and for the first time in days, the fear that had been chewing through her thoughts paused long enough for her to hear something else beneath it.

Not a command. Not a promise.

A quiet fact.

She was still herself, somewhere inside all the writing.

And if she could remember that much without being offered it, without taking it like a bribe from the dark, then perhaps the life being written over her had not yet reached the final line.

Eliza woke with her cheek still pressed to the boards and the taste of salt at the corner of her mouth where tears had dried.

For a moment she did not move. She lay perfectly still and listened, because listening had become the only way to tell whether she was alone. The cell held its damp hush. No moon-cold air. No corridor. No benches like teeth. Only the faintest seep of gray light under the door and the slow, stubborn breath of the building settling around her.

Her boots sat where she had placed them, soles up, like two dark, empty mouths.

Eliza swallowed and forced herself to look at them properly, to take account as the second voice had taught her. The leather was scuffed and ordinary. The seams still held a little grit, but no fresh soil had fallen in the night. Her skirt hem was stiff where it had dried, but it was not newly darkened.

She had not walked.

A tremor ran through her that was half relief and half grief, because it should not have felt like victory to simply remain in her own body through a night.

She pushed herself up to sitting, slow and careful, as if sudden movement might startle something that preferred her unsteady. Her neck ached. Her knees complained. She drew her hair forward and gathered it in her hands, twisting it once to keep it from falling into her face. Without pins it would not hold long, but she needed the small sense of order.

Her fingers drifted, without permission, toward her bodice.

She stopped them again.

The mark under her left ribs did not hurt. It never hurt. That was part of the horror: the place that should have been hers by right of sensation lay quiet like a listening ear. Even now, sitting upright, she could feel its warmth banked beneath the cloth, a coal that did not burn but did not cool.

The other voice, the one that thanked her, did not speak.

But it noticed her noticing. The warmth pulsed once, slow and deliberate, out of time with her heartbeat, as if reminding her it had not gone anywhere simply because it had been ignored.

Eliza pressed her palms flat on the floorboards instead and breathed through her nose until the iron taste faded from the back of her tongue.

"You're here," she whispered, not sure if she meant herself or the thing under her ribs.

The second voice answered, so close to thought it almost sounded like her own steadiness returning. "Yes."

Eliza's throat tightened. "What are you?"

No answer came at once. The voice had never rushed to name itself. It had never tried to win her. It had only suggested, and then watched whether she took the suggestion.

Eliza glanced at the door. The bolt had not moved. The scratch marks at the bottom edge were still there, pale against dark wood. She wondered if the guard had told anyone. She wondered if Swann already knew and was simply choosing when to use it.

Salem did not waste a detail. It let details ripen.

"What do you want from me?" she asked again, because it was the only question she understood anymore. Everyone asked something of her, even when they pretended they were saving her. Even Hale, with his strained prayers and warnings, wanted her to become a certain kind of girl in his mind: repentant, rescued, obedient to God's story.

The second voice did not soften its answer. "I want you to stop giving yourself away."

Eliza let out a breath that shook. "I'm not giving anything. They're taking it."

The warmth under her ribs pulsed again, almost in response, and with it came the faintest impression of dry paper, not truly smelled but sensed, like remembering a scent without meaning to.

The second voice cut in before Eliza's fear could swell around it. "You give it when you answer it."

"I haven't answered," Eliza whispered, and hated how defensive she sounded, as if she were being scolded for a sin she did not understand.

"You answer with fear," the voice said. "With pleading. With bargaining. With the part of you that wants relief so badly you would take it from anything that offers."

Eliza stared at the boards. A small splinter near her knee curled up like a fingernail. She picked at it until it snapped off, the tiny sting in her fingertip making her flinch. Pain was honest. Pain was hers.

"I can't help being afraid," she said.

"I know," the voice replied, and for the first time it sounded less like instruction and more like something that remembered fear from the inside. "But fear is not the only thing in you."

Eliza's eyes stung again. She blinked hard, because tears felt dangerous now, too close to gratitude, too close to that soft trap the other voice laid with manners.

"What else is there?" she asked, and the question came out bitter. "They've written my name without me. They've found a mark I don't remember. They bring a book into my cell and tell me it's mine even when I say it isn't. What else is there?"

The second voice waited a beat. In that beat Eliza felt the cell's damp cold, the ache in her back, the hunger beginning again like a low animal at the edge of her belly. She felt herself as a body that persisted in small, stubborn ways.

Then the voice said, "Tell the truth."

Eliza went still.

The phrase struck her like Swann's questions did, a lever under a loose board. Tell the truth. Salem's truth was not hers. Salem's truth was what the town believed, what the court wrote, what people swore they saw in dreams.

She swallowed. "I have," she whispered. "I've denied them every time."

"That is not all the truth," the voice said.

Eliza's mouth went dry. She thought of the hearing room dream, of her mother's name surfacing like a bruise. She thought of the touch test, the afflicted girl going quiet under her hand and the sensation that passed between them, clean and cold and real enough to frighten her more than the shouting did.

She thought of the moment in the scrubbed room when the mark had pulsed like a blinking eye and the voice had said, Thank you.

Her stomach tightened. "You mean… that."

"I mean what you know and keep trying not to know," the second voice replied. "Because you think knowing is the same as wanting."

Eliza stared at her boots. The leather looked cracked in the dim, like the spine of the black book. The comparison made her stomach lurch, and she nearly turned away from the thought, but the voice held her there without force.

"You felt something pass," the voice continued. "You felt the door inside you open when you touched her. You felt the mark wake when they pressed it. You feel it now."

Eliza's hands curled into fists. "If I admit that, they'll kill me."

The second voice answered without pity. "They may kill you anyway."

The bluntness stole Eliza's breath for a moment. That was what no one in Salem would say plainly, not even Hale with his warnings. Hale still held out prayer like a bargain: do this and perhaps God will spare you. Swann held out confession like mercy: do this and perhaps the court will.

This voice offered no bargain at all.

Eliza's throat burned. "Then why should I tell any truth? What good is it?"

"So you stop being surprised by your own skin," the voice said. "So you stop waking and wondering where your feet have been. So you stop believing the book knows you better than you do."

Eliza's heart hammered. The coal-warmth under her ribs pulsed once, as if in irritation at being discussed. The sensation made her want to press her palm against it, to test it, to prove to herself it was real and then hate herself for proving it.

She held her hands on her knees instead and forced the words out like a confession made to herself, not to Salem.

"I feel it," Eliza whispered. "I feel something. Sometimes."

The second voice did not react with satisfaction. It did not say good girl, the way the other voice might have. It simply waited, as if the truth was a door that opened on its own hinges if you stopped holding it shut.

Eliza took a careful breath. The damp air scraped her throat. "When they brought the book," she said, voice low, "my name was already there. And it… it wasn't like seeing ink. It was like seeing… something that had been waiting."

Her mouth trembled. She hated that part most. Waiting implied intention. Waiting implied she had been expected.

The coal-warmth pulsed, and for an instant Eliza's mind flashed with a table stretching into fog, leather under her palms damp as skin.

She clenched her jaw and kept speaking before the image could sharpen into something offered.

"And the dreams," she continued. "They don't feel like dreams. They feel like corridors. Like I'm being taken through somewhere inside myself." She swallowed hard. "And when I wake, I have dirt on my boots. Or my muscles ache like I've walked. Or I hear paper moving like someone's turning pages in my skull."

The cell's silence seemed to deepen, not with menace but with attention. Even the building felt as if it leaned closer to listen, as Salem always did.

The second voice said, "And what do you feel beneath all that?"

Eliza almost laughed, sharp and humorless. "Fear."

"Beneath it," the voice insisted.

Eliza's breath shook. Beneath fear there was usually only more fear. But the voice was not letting her off with the easiest answer.

She closed her eyes, briefly, and tried to sense herself without reaching for memory the way she had learned not to beg for it. She felt her heartbeat. She felt her lungs. She felt, like a hidden ember, the banked warmth under her ribs that was not quite hers and not quite separate anymore.

And beneath even that, she felt something else, faint but undeniable: a pull.

Not a desire, not in the way Salem would name it. Not a longing for evil. A pull like recognition, like a muscle remembering how it moves.

Eliza opened her eyes, horrified by her own honesty. "It feels… familiar," she whispered. "Like I've done it before."

The coal-warmth pulsed, pleased at last, and the faint paper-sense brushed the edge of her mind.

Eliza flinched but did not speak to it. She did not thank it. She did not bargain. She kept her attention on the second voice like holding a thread in the dark.

The second voice said quietly, "That is the truth within. Not that you are wicked. Not that you are innocent. That what is happening is not only being done to you. It is being remembered through you."

Eliza's stomach twisted. "Remembered by who?"

The voice hesitated, then answered as plainly as it could. "By the part of you that the book can read."

Eliza's hands went numb. She stared at the door again as if she expected it to open and reveal Swann's mild face, the guard's broad shoulders,

Hale's tight prayers. She expected, suddenly, to be punished for hearing this. For naming it.

But the bolt did not move.

Only the cell remained, and her own breathing.

"Eliza," the second voice said, and hearing her name spoken without hunger for proof made her throat tighten. "If you keep trying to be only what you were before Salem, it will take that shape and use it. It will wear your longing like a dress."

Eliza swallowed hard. The image landed sickeningly true. The visitor offering sharpened memories. Mercy's face made too clear. Samuel's name rising in the book the moment Eliza's fear reached for him.

"What am I supposed to be, then?" she whispered.

The second voice answered, quiet but unwavering. "What you are now. Awake to what lives under your skin. Awake to what your hands can do. Awake enough to choose what you will not do, even if it pushes from inside."

Eliza's chest hurt as if a band had been tightened around it. "I don't know if I can," she said, and the admission felt like stepping onto a board that might break.

"You can," the voice replied. "Not because you are strong. Because you are still here. And it does not like you being here."

The coal-warmth pulsed again, slower, as if listening and disliking being named.

Eliza looked down at her boots, at the soles turned upward like witnesses waiting to be called.

She took a careful breath and did not let it turn into prayer or pleading. She did not call out to God as a bargain, and she did not call out to the visitor as temptation. She simply held herself inside her own skin and spoke the smallest truth she could bear.

"I don't want to hurt anyone," she whispered.

The second voice answered at once. "Then do not let it teach you that relief is the same as harm."

Eliza frowned, confused despite herself.

"It will use your mercy," the voice said, and the word mercy landed like a blade because it carried her mother's name inside it. "You touched a girl and she went quiet. That was real. They turned it into proof of wickedness. It will turn it into proof of ownership. Do you see the trap?"

Eliza's mouth went dry. She saw it. She saw it too clearly. Every good impulse could be twisted into a record against her. Every refusal could become guilt. Every kindness could become the opening of a path.

“What do I do?” she asked, and the question came out raw, stripped of pride.

The second voice replied, steady as the boards beneath her. “When it speaks, do not answer. When it shows you names, do not reach. When it offers you relief, do not thank it. And when you feel it move toward your feet, toward your hands, toward your mouth, remember the truth within you.”

Eliza’s throat tightened. “Which truth?”

The voice held her there with a calm that did not pretend the danger wasn’t real.

“That you are frightened,” it said. “And that you are not only frightened. That you are capable. That you can be used. That you can choose not to be.”

Eliza stared at the cell, at the cot that remembered, at the door that held. She listened for paper moving and heard nothing but the soft shift of her own breath.

For a moment, in the dim gray light that might have been morning, she felt something settle inside her that was not comfort and not victory, but a shape of understanding hard enough to lean against.

Salem could write her name without her hand. It could find marks and call them proof. It could bring a book into a cell and make the air feel like an open page.

But there was a truth within her that Salem could not write unless she gave it the ink.

Eliza reached for her boots and pulled them closer, not to put them on yet, but to keep them where she could see them, where they could not become someone else's feet in the night.

She sat upright, back against the wall, and waited for whatever came next, holding the second voice's last words like a small, stubborn light.

Not to win.

To remain.

Chapter 15

The Names

The bolt scraped back before Eliza had finished deciding whether she was grateful for the sound or afraid of it.

Light fell through the opening door in a long, pale blade. The guard stood there with his lantern lowered, as if even flame ought to keep its distance from whatever lived in her cell. His eyes traveled over her quickly: her bare hands, her boots pulled close, her posture too upright to be called resting. He saw the same girl, but not in the same arrangement as before.

"Up," he said.

Eliza's mouth went dry. She slid her feet into her boots with shaking hands. The leather felt colder than it should have, as if it remembered night better than day. She laced them quickly, fingers clumsy, and stood.

The guard's gaze flicked to the cot, then back to her. Something in his jaw tightened, the smallest sign that he, too, had begun to register that the room did not behave the way rooms should. He did not speak of it. He only took her elbow with that practiced grip and turned her toward the corridor.

As they walked, the building's smells rushed at her in layers: lye, damp wool, smoke from somewhere far off. Under it all, threaded thin and sharp, came that dry, old note of paper shut too long in a chest.

Eliza swallowed and tasted iron.

Not a taste, she told herself. A habit. Fear making a familiar shape.

"Count what you know," the second voice murmured, so close to thought that it could have been her own steadiness returning. "Count it now."

Eliza fixed her eyes on the boards in front of her and counted without moving her lips.

My name is Eliza Harrow.

My boots are on my feet.

My hands are my hands.

The guard's grip is real.

The corridor bends left.

Each fact landed like a nail, pinning her to the moment.

They brought her into the hearing room the way they always did: through the side door so she could not enter like a person, only arrive like an object delivered. The benches were already crowded. Faces turned as one face, hungry for shape and meaning. Eliza felt their attention brush her skin like fingertips.

At the front, the magistrates sat stiff behind their table. The constable's quill moved over paper in quick, eager scratches. Reverend Hale stood off to one side, his posture careful, as though he were trying to keep his body from becoming part of the machinery. Ezekiel Swann was there too, of course, placed slightly forward as if the room arranged itself around him without admitting it had done so.

Eliza was set on the stool.

The room's murmur rose and fell like a single breath. Someone coughed. Someone whispered a prayer. A child began to fuss and was hushed hard. Above it all, Eliza became aware of a quieter sound that made her skin prickle.

Not paper turning.

A more delicate thing. Like the beginning of a word forming behind someone's teeth.

Swann's gaze rested on her, mild and attentive. His voice carried easily without shouting.

"Today," he said, "we will hear further testimony regarding Eliza Harrow's nighttime visits, and the inducements offered to godly people."

Inducements. The word made the crowd shift, as if it had been plucked like a string.

Eliza kept her eyes on Swann, because looking away was how panic found corners to grow in. Hale's eyes met hers briefly, tight with something that might have been warning.

Swann gestured, and the first witness was brought forward: a woman Eliza did not recognize at first, thin-faced and hollow-eyed, her hands twisting her apron into knots. The woman took the oath as if the words were stones in her mouth.

"State your name for the record," Swann said gently.

The woman's lips moved. A sound came out, and before Eliza could even shape it in her mind, something in her chest tightened, not at the mark, but deeper, closer to breath.

Not that one, the second voice whispered.

The woman said, "Abigail Pope."

The name struck Eliza with a strange sense of arrival, as if it had been walking toward her for days and had finally entered the room.

She saw it, suddenly, without seeing it.

Ink on pale parchment.

Abigail Pope.

The letters were not in front of her. The black book was nowhere on the table, not openly. And yet the name appeared in her mind with the same settled confidence her own had had: strokes pressed into something that would not forget.

Eliza's fingers curled hard around the edge of the stool until wood bit into her skin.

The second voice tightened, a thread pulled taut. "Do not reach," it murmured.

Eliza realized, with a sick jolt, that she had been reaching. Not with her hands. With that part of her that leaned toward what was being written.

Abigail Pope began to speak.

She told the court of a dream in which Eliza stood at the foot of her bed, her face lit like a candle from below. She described a book held open, the page pale as skin. She described a quill offered, and a voice that was not Eliza's urging her to make a mark.

As the woman spoke, the room leaned forward. People loved detail the way starving people loved bread. Every description fed the certainty they craved.

Eliza listened, and with every word the woman said, the image in Eliza's mind sharpened, not like memory returning, but like something being traced over.

Abigail Pope.

A name written before it was spoken.

The second voice pressed in, low and urgent. "Count what you know."

Eliza forced herself to count again.

I am sitting on a stool.

My boots are on.

The benches are filled with living people.

That name is only a name.

Swann thanked the witness with the politeness of a man receiving a gift he had requested. He asked a few careful questions that guided the woman into repeating the most useful phrases, the ones that would be easiest for the constable to catch with his quill. Then he dismissed her.

Another witness stepped forward, then another. Each one spoke a different version of the same story: Eliza in the night, Eliza at the bedside, Eliza with a book.

And the names. God, the names.

Swann called for the next person.

"State your name."

Before the witness spoke, Eliza felt it again: that tightening, that inward tug, like a hook set gently behind her ribs.

The second voice hissed, "Do not answer."

As if Eliza had been about to answer a question no one had asked aloud.

The witness said, "Josiah Rook."

Eliza's vision blurred at the edges. She saw the name in her mind as clearly as if the page were held under her nose.

Josiah Rook.

She had never met a Josiah Rook. The name meant nothing to her life. That should have made it harmless.

Instead it felt worse.

Because it was proof that the thing inside her did not need love to work with. It needed only a page ready to receive.

The witness spoke of waking with his hand cramped, ink under his fingernails though he kept no ink. He spoke of hearing pages turn in the dark of his own room, though he owned only a Bible. The crowd murmured at that, the sound of fear delighted to hear itself confirmed.

Hale shifted where he stood. His mouth moved as though he were praying, but his eyes stayed fixed on Eliza, and in them she saw something new: not only dread for her soul, but dread for the method they were all using to save it.

Swann's eyes flicked to Hale briefly, then returned to Eliza.

"Do you hear," Swann asked her, as if they were speaking privately, "how consistent the testimonies are?"

Eliza stared at him. She tasted iron again, sharp as a coin on her tongue.

"I hear them lying," she said, and her voice came out hoarse.

Swann nodded as if that, too, was expected. "Or dreaming," he corrected. "And dreams are not chosen."

The phrase slid under her skin like a blade.

Not chosen.

That was what terrified her. That Salem had built a world where choice did not matter, only what could be said aloud and written down afterward.

Swann turned back to the room. "We will proceed."

A girl was brought forward next, younger than Eliza, her eyes wide and unfocused with fear. Her hair was unbraided. Her hands shook. She looked like a person already half out of her body.

Eliza felt the room's mood shift. The afflicted always changed the air, made it denser, as if everyone's belief gathered closer to watch itself perform.

The girl began to sob before Swann even spoke to her. A murmur rose from the benches: pity, excitement, hunger.

Swann lowered his voice. "Tell the court what you saw," he said.

The girl lifted her face, wet and shining. Her gaze slid past the magistrates, past Hale, past Swann, and fixed on empty air above Eliza's shoulder.

Eliza's skin crawled.

It wants to sit, the afflicted girl from before had whispered.

The new girl's lips trembled. "She showed me," she said, and the words came out in a rush. "She showed me the names."

Swann's head tilted a fraction. "What names?"

The girl swallowed and squeezed her eyes shut as if the names were bright enough to hurt.

Eliza's chest tightened. The mark under her ribs pulsed once, slow and deliberate, as if waking at the word.

The second voice cut in sharply. "Do not reach."

Eliza realized she was holding her breath.

The girl whispered, "Abigail Pope."

The room erupted in murmurs, because the name had already been spoken today. It was a link. Salem loved links.

The girl's voice rose, gaining frantic certainty. "Josiah Rook. Martha Sibley. Daniel Price."

With each name, Eliza saw the ink in her mind, line after line, as if the page were being revealed under heat. Her hands went numb. It was happening too fast. The names stacked, and the sensation that came with them was not only fear.

Familiarity.

Not of the people. Of the process.

As if she had sat somewhere else, somewhere without walls, and watched names rise the same way, over and over, until the act of it became as natural as breathing.

Eliza's mouth opened.

The second voice snapped, "No."

Eliza closed her mouth hard enough her teeth clicked.

Swann's gaze slid to her face, watchful as a hand hovering over a quill. "Do you wish to respond?" he asked.

The room held its breath with him.

Eliza's throat worked. She could feel something behind her teeth, a pressure like words waiting to be pushed out. A list. A column. A record trying to use her mouth as the place it entered the world.

She clutched the stool again, grounding herself in splinters and pain.

"My name is Eliza Harrow," she thought fiercely. "My mouth is mine."

Out loud, she said only, "I don't know those people."

It was true, and it sounded weak against the girl's sobbing certainty.

Swann nodded as if he were being patient with a child. "Yet their names come," he said softly, to the room as much as to her. "Yet they come readily into the air around her."

Hale stepped forward suddenly, unable to keep still. "Swann," he said, and his voice carried sharper than Eliza had heard it in days. "This is contagion. You speak names, and they catch. You cannot call it proof because it repeats."

Swann looked at him with mild surprise, like a man interrupted during a careful reading. "Reverend," he said, "if it repeats, it is because it is true."

Hale's jaw tightened. His hands clenched and unclenched at his sides, a man trying to keep prayer in fingers that wanted to grab. "Or because you have taught them what to see," Hale said.

A ripple ran through the benches at that, part outrage, part fear. It was dangerous to accuse the procedure itself.

Swann let the room's reaction settle. Then he turned his attention back to Eliza.

"Eliza Harrow," he said, and the way he spoke her name made it feel less like a person and more like an entry, "you have heard names spoken today that you claim mean nothing to you."

Eliza's heartbeat thudded hard.

Swann continued, calm as ink. "And yet you have reacted to them. Your body does not remain neutral."

Eliza wanted to scream that bodies were not neutral in terror, that fear was not confession. But she had learned, painfully, that every protest became another line in the ledger.

The mark under her ribs warmed, banked and listening.

The second voice spoke, low and steady, as if placing a hand on the back of her neck and turning her away from a cliff.

"Count what you know."

Eliza forced herself to breathe. She counted.

I am here.

My boots are on my feet.

The floor is wood.

The room is full of eyes.

The names are only sounds.

But as she tried to hold to that, another truth slid under it, quiet and cold as old paper.

The names did not feel like only sounds.

They felt like recognition.

And the worst part was not that Salem might accuse those people next. Not that Swann would take the girl's list and turn it into tomorrow's arrests.

The worst part was the sense, deep in Eliza's bones, that the list could have kept going.

That if she had opened her mouth at the wrong moment, if she had let fear push words out, she could have given the court names they had not yet thought to ask for.

Names before the court.

Names before accusation.

Names that rose in her mind like ink surfacing on a page that had been waiting all along to be warmed.

The girl's list ended the way a candle ends when it is pinched out: not with a clean stop, but with a last thin thread of smoke that made the air smell different.

Abigail Pope. Josiah Rook. Martha Sibley. Daniel Price.

The names hung in the hearing room like damp laundry, each syllable heavy with the promise of what would happen next. Eliza sat rigid on the stool, hands locked around the wood. Her fingertips hurt where the edge bit in, and she welcomed the pain because it was simple. It did not ask her to believe anything.

Swann let the murmurs swell. He did not quiet the room. He let the town hear itself, let fear make a choir out of ordinary throats. Eliza watched his face and saw the same mild attention he always wore, the expression of a man watching a mechanism work as designed.

The afflicted girl's sobbing turned into hiccupping breaths. A matron took her by the shoulders and guided her back, stroking her hair as if smoothing it could smooth the story she had just told.

Swann lifted his hand at last, palm down. The room's sound obeyed, settling into a tense hush that still quivered with excitement.

"Eliza Harrow," he said again, and the words carried no anger, no triumph. Only procedure.

Eliza's name made something in her chest tighten. Not the mark exactly. Something nearer her throat, as if the sound of her name opened a passage upward.

"I have told you," she said, voice raw, "I do not know those people."

"You need not," Swann replied. "A key does not know the lock it opens."

Hale shifted, and Eliza saw him press his lips together as if holding back an argument that would only feed the spectacle. His eyes looked tired in a way she had not noticed before, as if the strain of keeping his faith from cracking had begun to show at the seams.

Swann turned slightly toward the constable. "Record the names spoken," he instructed, and the quill scratched faster, hungry.

Eliza's stomach rolled. Names became ink so easily here. Sound became evidence. Breath became a line you could point to later and claim it had always existed.

"Do you deny that you have the ability to bring names to the afflicted?" Swann asked, his tone almost gentle.

Eliza's mouth went dry. Ability. The word struck different from guilt. It held an implication of talent, of instrument, of something in her that could be used.

"I deny—" she began, then stopped because she did not know what to deny without lying.

She could deny that she went to bedsides at night, and it would not matter. She could deny that she urged anyone to sign the book, and it would not matter. She could deny the dreams and the corridor moonlight and the hearing room that had felt too real.

But she could not deny what she had felt when the girl spoke. She had felt the names arrive before they left the girl's mouth, each one tightening in Eliza's mind like a knot being pulled.

The second voice, thin and steady, moved under her thoughts. "Do not answer the question he wants."

Eliza swallowed. She could feel Swann waiting with the patience of a man who already had what he needed. The room leaned forward. Even the air seemed to lean.

"I deny that I have harmed anyone," Eliza said at last.

Swann nodded as if he had expected her to choose that line. "Harm," he repeated, tasting the word. "And what is harm, Eliza Harrow? Is it a bruise? Is it a cut? Or is it something quieter that spreads?"

A ripple moved through the benches at that. People shifted, eyes bright. They loved harm when it could be made invisible. Invisible harm meant anyone could be a victim, and anyone could be righteous.

Eliza heard herself breathe and hated how loud it seemed. Her muscles were tight with the effort of staying still. She could feel sweat cooling at the base of her spine.

Swann's gaze never left her face. "You touched one afflicted girl and she calmed," he said. "You sat in this room and names came into the air around you. Do you wish the court to believe these are coincidences?"

"No," Eliza whispered before she could stop herself.

The word fell into the hush like a stone.

Swann's eyebrows rose a fraction. Not surprise. Interest.

Eliza's heart pounded so hard she felt it in her teeth. She had not meant no as agreement. She had meant no as refusal of his framing, refusal of the neat little box he was building to place her in.

But Salem did not care what you meant. Salem cared what it could keep.

Swann turned his head slightly so the room could see his attention sharpen. "Then you admit what you are."

Eliza's throat closed. Heat pulsed under her left ribs, slow and deliberate, like a thing stirring at the sound of being acknowledged. The mark did not hurt. It only warmed, banked and listening.

The second voice cut through the rush of fear. "Count."

Eliza clung to the word like a rope.

I am on a stool.

My hands are on wood.

My boots are on my feet.

I have not spoken any name.

But beneath the counting, another awareness pressed in, dark as ink under parchment: she could.

The thought made her nauseous. She could feel it the way she could feel the weight of her own tongue in her mouth. She could speak, and if she spoke the wrong thing, it would not be only sound. It would be a key turned.

Eliza's gaze slid across the room without permission, skimming faces the way water skims stones. Some she recognized from the general store, from the road that had watched. Some were strangers. All of them looked at her as if her shape explained their own fear.

A man sat near the back, older, cheeks pocked from childhood illness, his hat clutched in his hands. He stared at her with a kind of blank devotion, as if he had come to church and found the sermon already written. Beside him a woman held a child close, the child's fingers in her mouth, eyes round and solemn.

Eliza did not know their names.

And yet, as her gaze passed them, she felt it: the faint inward tug, the hint of a list waiting just behind her teeth. Her mouth filled with saliva as if preparing to speak.

Eliza jerked her eyes back to Swann, horrified. The fear came sharp and immediate, a flare that made her mark pulse warmer, answering like a hand tapping from inside.

Fear is a door, the second voice had warned.

Eliza tried to pull the fear back down, tried to swallow it. Her breath caught, and the room mistook her struggle for something else. She heard it in the shifting, in the tiny exhalations of people pleased to see her falter.

Swann's voice lowered. "You feel it, do you not? The way the names come."

Eliza forced her lips apart. "They come to you," she said, hoarse. "You call them. You put them in the air and then you say it is my doing."

Swann did not bristle. He did not defend himself. He only looked at her as though she had finally said something useful.

"And if it were true," he asked, "would that make you less dangerous? A flame is no less a flame because another man struck the match."

Eliza's hands trembled on the stool. She pressed harder, digging into the wood until her fingers ached. She needed her hands to hurt so they would remember themselves, so they would not become instruments for anything else.

Hale spoke, voice tight. "Swann, you twist her words."

Swann glanced at him with mild patience. "I translate them for the court."

Eliza watched Hale's face and saw the conflict there, the strain of a man who had come to Salem to hunt wickedness and had found, instead, a hunger that wore righteousness like a coat. Hale's eyes returned to Eliza briefly, and in them she saw warning and something else: a plea not to let them pull her apart in front of him.

Eliza took a careful breath. The second voice steadied. "Stay in your body."

Eliza focused on sensation.

The stool's edge under her palms.

The rough weave of her skirt against her knees.

The weight of her boots on her feet.

Her tongue in her mouth, heavy and obedient if she made it so.

She had feared the visitor's power, the way it could wear her at night and bring dirt back into her cell. She had feared the book, the way her name sat on its page like it had been waiting for her birth.

But this was different.

This was not something done to her while she slept.

This was something that might come through her while she was awake.

The realization made her dizzy. If names could rise in her mind without her choosing, then what did it mean that she could keep her mouth shut? Was that restraint, or was it only delay until her body betrayed her again?

Swann leaned forward slightly. "Eliza Harrow," he said, softer now, as if offering a kindness. "You are weary. Your denials have not served you. Consider what mercy might look like if you cease resisting what is plain."

Mercy. The word struck Eliza like a blow to the chest, not because Swann said it, but because her mother's name had sat in the book with that same settled confidence.

Mercy Harrow.

The name flashed behind Eliza's eyes, too bright, too sharp. It came with the faint sense of paper, the dry reverent whisper of a page turning.

Eliza's stomach clenched.

Swann watched her flinch, and Eliza saw him note it as carefully as the constable noted ink.

He thinks I will say it, Eliza realized, panic rising. He thinks I will say her name.

The second voice spoke quickly. “Do not protect them with your mouth. Protect them with your silence.”

Eliza swallowed hard. Her lips trembled. She could feel the pressure of words gathering, not shaped yet, only wanting shape. It was the same feeling she’d had when she almost answered the list in the girl’s mouth, the sense of a column ready to be filled.

Eliza fixed her gaze on the table. On the constable’s paper, on the quill moving. Not the black book. She did not see it here, but she felt its absence like a space reserved.

“I want you to understand,” Swann said, and his tone made the room quiet itself again, leaning in. “The court does not require you to invent wickedness. It requires only that you acknowledge what you are. That you accept the names that come. That you stop pretending you are separate from what has been written.”

Eliza’s breath shuddered. Accept the names. Stop pretending.

The temptation was sick in its simplicity. If she accepted it, perhaps the struggle would end. Perhaps the pressure behind her teeth would stop.

Perhaps the visitor would sit fully and the aching vigilance would be replaced by a quiet that did not require effort.

And in that temptation, Eliza understood with sudden clarity why it was so dangerous.

Because it felt like relief.

She thought of the afflicted girl going calm under her touch, the sensation that passed between them. Relief had come so easily then. Relief had made the room erupt. Relief had been taken as proof.

If she let relief guide her now, if she let herself sink into it because she could not bear the strain of staying herself, she would become exactly what they wanted: not merely accused, but useful.

Eliza looked at Swann. Her voice came out low and shaking, but it was her own.

"I am afraid," she said.

The room murmured. Confession, they heard. Admission.

Swann's expression softened a fraction, ready to receive it.

Eliza forced herself to continue before fear could turn her into their instrument. "I am afraid," she repeated, "because I think you are right about one thing."

Swann's eyes sharpened.

Eliza swallowed, tasted iron, and held her mouth steady. "I think names can come," she said. "I think something in me hears them. But I do not know why. And I do not know who wants them."

The room shifted, uneasy now, because uncertainty was less satisfying than wickedness. Wickedness was clean. It allowed you to point and be done.

Swann's gaze remained on her, calm as ever. "And yet you admit the capacity."

Capacity. Again that word, like talent.

Eliza felt the mark pulse warm, and the paper-whisper brushed the edge of her mind as if pleased.

The second voice tightened like a thread pulled taut. "Now stop."

Eliza closed her mouth. She did not add another word. She did not explain. She did not try to defend herself further.

Silence, deliberate and chosen, settled around her like a garment.

Swann waited, perhaps expecting the next thing to spill. When it did not, his eyes narrowed slightly, not in anger but in calculation. He had found a new shape in her resistance, and he would consider how to use it.

The magistrates murmured to one another. The constable's quill slowed, uncertain what to capture when a girl refused to keep speaking.

Eliza kept her gaze on the table and held her tongue still. She felt the pressure of names behind her teeth, the list that wanted to form, and she let it sit there without release, like holding a mouthful of bitter herbs and refusing to swallow.

The fear in her was still there, sharp and living. But beneath it, another fear had taken its place at the center: not fear of what Salem would do to her, but fear of what might come out of her if she let herself become the open door they all assumed she was.

She sat on the stool, silent, and for the first time understood that the most dangerous thing in the room might not be Swann's questions or the town's belief.

It might be her own mouth.

And the names waiting, patient as ink under parchment, for warmth enough to rise.

Silence did not end the hearing. It only changed what the room fed on.

Eliza kept her mouth closed until her jaw ached, until the muscles beneath her tongue trembled with the effort. The benches rustled with disappointment, then with a different kind of appetite. If she would not speak, they would speak around her. They would speak over her. They would make a record anyway.

Swann let the pause linger just long enough for everyone to feel it as choice, then turned as though her quiet had been entered into the day's proceedings and settled.

"We will continue," he said, and his voice held that same mild steadiness that made cruelty sound like careful stewardship.

The magistrate nearest the center leaned forward. "Let the afflicted be brought again," he murmured, as if ordering a tool returned to the table.

The girl who had spoken the names was guided back, her eyes glassy, her breathing still hitching. She clutched the matron's sleeve as if the cloth were the only thing tethering her to her own body.

Swann asked her a question Eliza could not quite follow, something about the manner of the visions, the hour they came. The girl answered in fragments, and each fragment made the room murmur in recognition of its own fear.

Eliza listened with her gaze fixed on the magistrates' table. The constable's quill scratched. Hale stood rigid, his hands clasped so tightly the knuckles showed pale. The guard remained near the side door, a silent shape built for holding.

And beneath all the sound, Eliza became aware of something that had not been there a moment before.

That dry, reverent whisper.

Paper handled slowly.

Not the constable's brisk scratch. Not the shuffling of townspeople's feet. This sound was softer, as if the room had exhaled and the exhale had turned into pages turning in the dark.

Eliza's scalp tightened. She did not turn her head. She did not want to look toward the side door and find the black leather waiting there like a mouth.

The second voice, thin but steady, moved under her fear. "Do not reach."

"I'm not," Eliza told it in her mind, but even thinking the words felt like moving toward a ledge.

Swann's questions slowed. The afflicted girl's answers thinned into sobs again. The matron stroked her hair. The room's attention drifted, restless, seeking the next thing to latch onto.

Swann's gaze slid, briefly, to the side.

The guard stepped forward.

He carried the black book close against his chest, both hands around it as if it might shift. The leather drank the room's light and gave back nothing. Even across the distance, Eliza felt the air change, tightening as it had in her cell. The smell came with it, faint but unmistakable: old paper kept too long in a chest, and something damp beneath like leather held against skin.

Eliza's mouth filled with saliva as if preparing to speak. She clamped her teeth.

Swann did not announce the book with ceremony. He did not need to. The room recognized it the way a body recognizes a fever coming on.

"The record," Swann said, gently, and the word record made Eliza's stomach roll.

The guard placed the book on the table. The sound was quiet, but it landed in Eliza's bones like a weight set down on a floor above her. For an instant, she had a sick flash of the cot's straw deepening as if welcoming the book, the way matter remembered.

Hale's head lifted. His eyes fixed on the cover with open strain, like a man watching a knife laid beside bread.

Swann rested his fingertips on the black leather, not quite touching, hovering as though he, too, respected the boundary between object and appetite. “We have heard much today,” he said to the magistrates, to the room, to the hungry benches. “And we have been given names.”

At the word names, Eliza felt the tug behind her ribs, not in the mark itself but close to it, like a hook set in her breath.

The second voice whispered, urgent now. “Stay in your body.”

Eliza focused hard on the stool’s edge under her palms. The wood bit. She welcomed it.

Swann looked up, and his mild gaze swept the room. “It is not enough,” he said, as though disappointing a congregation. “Names must be fixed. Spoken air is too easily denied.”

The magistrate nodded, as if this were merely sensible. The constable leaned forward, eager.

Swann gestured. The guard opened the black book.

The leather creaked with that small, intimate sound that raised Eliza’s skin in gooseflesh. Pages shifted, thick and pale. The guard held it open on the table, angled toward the magistrates.

Eliza could not see the writing from where she sat, not clearly. Only dark strokes on light. But she did not need to see. Her body recognized the presence the way it had in the cell, the way it had in the dream hearing room when the cover lifted without hands.

Swann spoke without looking at Eliza. “Read what is written.”

The constable’s quill paused mid-scratch. One of the magistrates leaned closer, peering down. Hale’s lips moved in silent prayer that looked more like desperation than devotion.

Then the magistrate said, voice low, “Abigail Pope.”

A murmur ran through the benches. The name had already been spoken today, and hearing it now carried a different force, like a nail driven into wood.

The magistrate’s finger traced down the page, slow and careful, as if he feared the ink might smear onto him. “Josiah Rook,” he read next.

Another murmur, sharper.

Eliza’s hands clenched on the stool, and she felt the pressure behind her teeth shift, wanting to match the list, wanting to add to it, wanting to become part of the mechanism that turned breath into ink.

The second voice tightened like a thread. “Do not.”

The magistrate continued. "Martha Sibley. Daniel Price."

The afflicted girl, still clutched by the matron, made a small sound of triumph and terror. "Yes," she whispered, as if the book had proven she had not invented anything, as if proof mattered now that belief was already fed.

Swann let the room react. He let the murmurs swell into a kind of reverent fear.

Then, very softly, he said, "And the rest."

The magistrate's finger moved again.

Eliza expected more names. She braced herself for the hook, for the tug, for the list behind her teeth to surge forward and break loose.

But what happened next was worse, because it did not come from her.

The magistrate hesitated. "These," he said, and his voice shifted, uncertainty creeping in. He looked up at Swann. "These names have not been brought before the court."

Swann's mild face did not change. "Read them."

Hale's head snapped toward Swann. "No," he said, sharp enough that several heads in the benches turned. "You cannot—"

Swann did not acknowledge the protest. He kept his gaze on the magistrate.

The magistrate swallowed. Then, as if compelled by the weight of procedure, he read the next name on the page.

"Ruth Putnam."

The room stilled. Not because the name was unknown. Because it was too known.

A woman in the benches made a small, strangled noise, half laugh and half choking. A few heads turned toward her at once.

Eliza's heart hammered. Ruth Putnam sat somewhere in that room; Eliza had seen the Putnams' faces in passing, had heard their voices in the crowd. The name hit the air like a thrown stone.

"That cannot be," Hale said, and his voice cracked. "Swann, this is madness. You will set the town on itself."

Swann's expression remained careful, almost saddened. "The town is already set," he replied. "We only witness where it lands."

Eliza's skin crawled. Witness. Record. Names fixed.

The magistrate read again, slower now, as if each syllable cost him. "Isaac Fenner."

A man near the back stood up abruptly, face flushed. “I have done nothing,” he said, voice high with panic. His wife grabbed his sleeve, dragging him back down, hissing in his ear. The benches rippled with whispers.

Eliza’s mouth went numb. She knew, with an awful clarity, what would happen next. Not today, perhaps. Salem let details ripen. But soon. Soon those names would be spoken in accusation, and the people would remember they had heard them here first, read from the black book as if the book were God’s own register.

And if the book had written those names before any mouth asked for them, then the order of things had changed.

The book did not follow the court.

The court followed the book.

Eliza swallowed, and the iron taste rose sharp as a coin. The hook behind her ribs tugged, not with the satisfaction of power, but with the horror of recognition. In her mind she saw pale parchment and dark strokes, not because she wanted to, but because the book’s presence made her mind behave like a page warming under a hand.

She tried to look away from the table. Her eyes betrayed her, drawn back as if by thread.

And then, for an instant, she saw it.

Not the page itself, not clearly enough to read at distance. But a darkening at the lower portion, where the magistrate's finger had not yet reached. Ink that looked older than fresh writing, settled into the parchment in a way that made Eliza's stomach turn, because she had seen that quality before.

Her own name had looked like that.

This darkened line, too, looked already dried.

Already decided.

The second voice whispered, so low it almost vanished beneath Eliza's heartbeat. "Do not take it in."

Eliza's throat tightened. "I'm not," she tried to think, but her mind had already caught the shape, the way a person catches a word they wish they had not heard.

A name formed at the edge of her awareness, not spoken aloud in the room, not yet. It rose in her mind with the slow certainty of ink surfacing on a page.

Not because she chose it.

Because the book was near, and the page was ready, and something in her had learned how to read what was being made.

Eliza's breath hitched.

Hale stepped forward, closer to the table, his face white with contained panic. "Close it," he said, and this time he was speaking to the magistrates, to the guard, to anyone who still believed in stopping a thing once it began. "For God's sake, close it. You do not know what you invite."

Swann's eyes flicked to Hale, and for the first time there was something faintly sharp in his mildness, like the edge of a blade seen through cloth. "We invite what has already arrived," he said.

He turned then, finally, and looked at Eliza.

His gaze held her the way the page had held her in the cell.

"Do you see?" he asked softly. "It is not only that names come when they are spoken. They are written before they are needed."

Eliza's lips parted against her will. The pressure behind her teeth surged, the list straining to become sound. She tasted iron, and her mark pulsed warm as if answering a call.

The second voice snapped, hard and sudden. "Close your mouth."

Eliza clamped her jaw shut so tightly pain flared at her temples.

Swann watched the movement with quiet satisfaction, as if he had just seen the exact mechanism he'd hoped to reveal. He did not need her to speak the name her mind had caught. He only needed the room to watch her struggle not to.

He leaned slightly toward the magistrates' table, as if confiding in a record.

"The book predicts," Swann said, and there was no triumph in it. Only certainty. "It always has."

And in the hush that followed, Eliza understood the trap's final shape.

If the names were already there, then nothing she did could prevent them from being called. If she spoke, she would be blamed for bringing them. If she stayed silent, she would be blamed for withholding them. Either way, the ink would win, because the town preferred a written fate to the terror of not knowing.

Eliza sat on the stool with her hands bleeding small, unnoticed pain into the wood, and held her mouth closed around the name that had risen unasked in her mind.

She did not know whose life it belonged to yet.

She only knew, with a cold clarity that made her bones feel hollow, that soon the court would ask for it.

And when they did, they would call it prophecy.

They would call it proof.

They would not call it what it truly was.

A page turning, patient and reverent, toward the next line.

Chapter 16

The Breaking Logic

For a moment after Swann's last words, no one moved.

The black book lay open on the table like a wound that refused to close. The magistrate's hand hovered above the page as though he feared the ink might climb into his skin. The constable had stopped writing, quill poised and dripping a tiny dark bead that trembled with his breath.

Eliza sat with her jaw clenched so hard she could feel the tendons in her neck stand out. The name in her mind pressed against the back of her teeth, wanting air. Not a sentence, not a thought of her own, only a shape that wanted to become sound.

Swann watched her as if he could see the shape behind her lips. His mildness did not falter. If anything, it sharpened, becoming more precise, the way a man's hands become precise when he is tying a knot.

The magistrate cleared his throat, the sound small and human in the face of so much certainty. "Enough," he murmured, but it did not sound like authority. It sounded like a man trying to convince himself he could still stop something.

Hale stepped forward again, too close to the table now, his eyes fixed not on Eliza but on the book. "Close it," he said, and his voice carried a desperate edge. "You have done enough harm with it."

Swann did not argue. He did not need to. He only placed his fingertips on the page's edge, not turning it, not touching ink, but making a gesture that looked like reverence to those who wanted reverence. Then, with a calm that felt rehearsed by years, he nodded once.

The guard shut the book.

The cover closed with a soft, final sound that was worse than the pages turning had been. It sounded like a door latching.

The room let out a breath it had been holding. The benches rustled, not with relief, but with the uneasy hunger of people denied the last bite. Whispers spread immediately, quick and thin, racing each other toward conclusions. Eliza heard her own name pass from mouth to mouth as if it were a coin being tested for weight.

Swann turned slightly to address the magistrates, but his eyes did not leave Eliza for long. “The court has heard,” he said. “And the court has seen.”

One of the magistrates, an older man with heavy eyelids, leaned forward. “We have seen enough to know the danger,” he said, and the word danger seemed to settle on Eliza’s shoulders like a cloak. “The question now is what we do with it.”

Swann’s gaze returned to Eliza with careful gentleness. “We do what we have always done,” he replied. “We ask for the only thing that breaks the hold. Confession.”

Confession. The word moved through the room like a drafted wind. It was a word Salem loved because it sounded holy while functioning like a lock.

Eliza’s stomach tightened. Her palms ached where the stool’s edge had cut them. She looked down and saw thin lines of red along her skin, bright against the brown of her hands. The sight steadied her for half a heartbeat. Blood was not ink. Blood belonged to bodies.

Then her mind betrayed her with the faintest brush of that other sensation, dry and cold, like paper remembered. The coal-warmth under her left ribs pulsed once, slow and deliberate, as if something inside her had lifted its head at the word confession.

The second voice came tight and low beneath her thoughts. "Do not speak to it."

"I'm not," Eliza answered silently, and then hated that she had answered anything at all, even to the voice that had tried to keep her awake.

The magistrate with heavy eyelids continued, as though Eliza were not a person but a question being debated. "She has denied," he said. "Stubbornly."

"Not stubbornly," Hale cut in, and his voice broke on the edge of anger. "Faithfully. She has denied because she does not know what you are asking her to affirm."

Swann's head turned toward Hale, mild patience returning. "We are asking her to affirm what is plain," he said.

Hale's hands trembled at his sides. "Plain," he repeated, and it sounded like a curse. "Dreams are not plain. Hysteria is not plain. A book that writes without hands is not plain."

A ripple of unease passed through the benches at Hale's words. Some faces tightened as if he had spoken blasphemy. Others looked relieved to hear doubt named by a minister, even if they would never admit it aloud.

Swann did not raise his voice. He did not need to. "Reverend," he said, "plain does not mean ordinary. It means consistent. It means the same pattern appears again and again, regardless of who touches it."

Eliza felt Swann's logic slide into the room like oil. The pattern. The repetition. The way names came. The way the afflicted performed the same terror and called it revelation.

The magistrate nearest the center, younger than the others, shifted uncomfortably. "We cannot keep this woman in limbo," he said. "The town will tear itself apart."

Swann inclined his head. "Then we offer her the mercy of ending it."

Mercy again. The word struck Eliza so hard she tasted iron. The name in her mind surged, not her mother's this time, but the unnamed one that had formed at the edge of her awareness when she saw the lower portion of the page darkening.

Her lips parted without her permission.

The second voice snapped, sharp as pain. "Shut your mouth."

Eliza clenched her jaw again and felt her molars grind.

Swann noticed. Of course he did. His gaze flicked to her mouth, then back to her eyes, as if cataloging the small betrayals of her body. "Eliza Harrow," he said softly, and the way he spoke her name made it sound like an entry being read aloud. "We are not without compassion."

The benches murmured, approving. Compassion was another word Salem liked because it made cruelty feel like rescue.

Swann continued. "You have been tried. You have been tested. You have been made to answer to testimony you cannot disprove, because it takes place in the night where no law can stand as witness."

Eliza's throat tightened. The night. The corridor. The hearing room in moonlight. Dirt in her boots. A door that might open while she slept, her feet used like borrowed tools.

Swann's voice remained calm. "But there is one thing that ends the matter. Confession."

Hale took a step forward. "Swann," he began, but Swann lifted a hand, not to silence him with force, but to signal that he would not be interrupted.

“If you confess,” Swann said to Eliza, “you may live.”

The room stilled again, not from fear this time, but from attention sharpened into a point. Even the afflicted girl, being held at the side, seemed to quiet, her sobbing swallowed by expectation.

Eliza’s stomach turned. Live. The word was so simple it almost did not fit in the hearing room’s air. She had not heard it offered plainly yet. Not without conditions. Not without the sneer of, only if you cooperate.

“If you deny,” Swann went on, “you will perish.”

There it was, the other half spoken as calmly as the first, as if he were describing the weather.

Eliza’s breath caught. Her vision narrowed at the edges. Perish did not sound like a sentence handed down by a court; it sounded like a natural consequence, like falling when you step off a roof. Swann had moved the gallows into the realm of inevitability.

Hale’s face went white. “You cannot promise her life,” he said, hoarse. “Not in this town. Not with this crowd. They do not forgive even those who confess. They use confession as kindling.”

Swann's mild eyes slid to Hale. "Reverend, I promise what the court can grant," he replied. "If she confesses, she enters the path of mercy. If she denies, she chooses the path of judgment."

Eliza felt the logic being built around her like walls. Confess and the court becomes merciful. Deny and the court becomes righteous. Either way, the court remains pure in its own story.

One of the magistrates nodded. "We cannot allow a witch to stand unconfessed," he said, as if speaking of sanitation.

Another added, "Nor can we hang a repentant soul without offering her the chance to save herself."

Save herself. Eliza almost laughed, but no sound came out. How could she save herself by lying? How could she save herself by feeding the very thing that wanted names, that wanted ink, that wanted her mouth to become an instrument?

And yet the word live hung in the air and touched something in her that was not philosophy. It touched her body's animal will.

Her father's face flashed in her mind, then her mother's hands, Samuel's scraped shin, the smell of hearth smoke in wet wool. The second voice had taught her to remember without begging. But now memory came unbidden, not sharpened like the visitor's bribe, but raw and aching, because Swann had offered a future in which those memories might be seen again.

The coal-warmth under her ribs pulsed, slow and pleased.

Eliza's fingers twitched toward the mark, desperate to press it, to check whether warmth was real or imagined, to find some boundary. She stopped herself, hands curling into fists in her lap until her nails bit skin.

The second voice moved beneath her thoughts, tense but steady. "This is the breaking. They want your choice to look like theirs."

Eliza swallowed hard. Her mouth was dry. She looked at Swann and saw no hatred there, only certainty. Conviction's face, like the faces that had seized her in the road. The same expression that had frightened her more than anger ever could.

Swann leaned forward slightly, as if confiding something kindly. "Eliza," he said, and the crowd quieted further at the sound of her name spoken with such intimate calm. "Think carefully. A confession spares you. It spares your soul. It spares the town further suffering."

It spares your family, something inside Eliza wanted to add, though Swann did not say it. The thought arrived anyway, sharp and dangerous.

Mercy's name in the book. Samuel's name. The book did not care where they were. The court would not care either, if fear needed new fuel.

Hale's voice cut in, strained. "Do not let him make you believe confession is mercy," he said to Eliza, and this time he spoke directly to her, his eyes pleading. "Confession is a net. Once you speak, it will not stop at you."

Swann's gaze remained on Eliza. "A net," he repeated softly, as if amused by the metaphor. "Or a rescue line."

Eliza felt the room waiting for her answer the way a page waited for ink. Her throat tightened. The name behind her teeth pressed again, eager for air, and now it felt like part of the bargain itself. Confess. Speak. Let the words out. Let the record take you.

She drew a breath, slow and shaking, and tried to count what she knew, as the second voice had taught her.

My name is Eliza Harrow.

My mouth is mine.

They will kill me if I deny.

They will use me if I confess.

The last two facts sat beside each other in her mind like twin doors, both opening into dark.

Swann watched her breathe, watched the tremor in her jaw, watched the way her silence strained.

"Confess," he said again, not louder, not harsher. Simply closer, as if bringing the word nearer might make it easier to take.

Eliza's lips parted.

And in the fraction of a moment before sound could form, she felt it: the faintest suggestion of pages turning somewhere that was not the room. Not the constable's paper. Not the black book closed on the table.

Something in her.

A readiness, patient and reverent, waiting for her to choose the simplest path.

Confess or perish.

Swann had offered it as if it were logic.

Eliza understood, with a cold clarity that made her stomach drop, that it was not logic at all.

It was the shape of a trap that only worked if she believed she had been given a choice.

Eliza kept her lips parted and did not let sound out.

The room waited with her, a collective stillness so complete she could hear the tiny creak of the magistrate's bench as a man shifted his weight.

The silence was not mercy. It was a hand hovering above her, deciding where to press.

Swann did not fill the pause with anger. He let it lengthen until it began to feel like her failure, not his tactic. His voice, when it came, was almost tender.

"You understand," he said, "that the court cannot remain in uncertainty."

Uncertainty. As if uncertainty were the sin. As if the only evil in Salem was not knowing.

Eliza stared at his mouth to keep from staring at the black book. The book was closed now, but she felt it as if it were open anyway, as if the page had turned inside her and was waiting in the dark behind her teeth. The name she had caught earlier still hovered at the edge of her awareness, a shape without permission, pressing softly as breath against glass.

The second voice was there, thin and steady beneath her racing thoughts. It did not tell her what to say. It only reminded her of the only boundary she could still hold.

"Do not answer their hunger," it murmured.

Eliza's throat tightened. Hunger. That was the right word for what filled the benches. People leaned forward not like witnesses but like mouths.

One of the magistrates cleared his throat again, impatient now that Swann had offered mercy and Eliza had not taken it quickly enough to make the room feel righteous. "Girl," he said, and his voice carried the irritation of a man whose time was valuable. "Will you confess?"

Confess. Will you.

As if will remained uncomplicated. As if she had not been stripped of ordinary choice the moment her name appeared in a book before anyone spoke it.

Eliza tried to imagine what confession meant in this place. She had seen it already in fragments, heard the stories through the cracks in the building. Confession was not one sentence. It was a door opened to let the town walk through.

If she said yes, they would ask how. With whom. When. What names. They would ask until her mouth became a passage and her fear did the walking.

But if she said no, they would not stop either. They would call denial stubbornness, and stubbornness would become proof of a hardened soul. They would hang her as an example. The town would clap itself on the back for having removed uncertainty from its midst.

Eliza's mind reached, without her permission, for the cleanest truth: I did not do this. I did not go to their beds. I did not offer a book. I did not sign anything.

The truth rose in her chest like a prayer. It should have steadied her.

Instead it cracked under the weight of other truths, smaller and uglier, that had collected since the road into Salem.

I calmed a girl with my touch, and I felt something pass.

I woke with dirt in my boots.

I heard paper moving where no paper should be.

I recognized names before I knew the people.

I feel something warm under my ribs that is not only blood.

Her stomach turned. Salem had taken those details and built a story. She had resisted the story so hard she had begun to resist the details themselves, as if denying sensation could keep it from being used. But sensation did not care what she claimed. It stayed in her body anyway.

Swann's voice returned, very soft. "Your silence is also a choice, Eliza Harrow."

She flinched at her name. It always sounded in his mouth like ink.

Hale made a small sound, a protest swallowed almost immediately. Eliza did not look at him, but she felt his presence like a person standing too close to a cliff edge, unsure whether to reach out or step back. His faith had brought him here. Now faith was being used as a tool, and he was watching a girl be ground into something that fit.

The magistrate leaned forward. "Confess," he said again, harsher. "And you will have time to repent."

Repent. The word tasted wrong in Eliza's mind, because repentance assumed a sin she could name and own. She could not repent of what she did not understand. She could only submit.

But submission had its own shape of temptation, the same sick shape Swann called mercy. It offered relief. It offered an end to the constant counting, the vigilance, the fear of waking with her feet stolen.

A thought slipped in, quiet and treacherous: If I confess, perhaps the walking will stop.

Her mark pulsed warm at that, slow as a satisfied breath.

Eliza's fingers curled into her palms until her nails cut crescent moons. The pain was small but it helped. It reminded her that relief was not always salvation. Relief could be a hook. Relief could be the moment you let go of yourself because holding on hurt too much.

The second voice tightened. "Hear your own thought. Do not let it dress itself as goodness."

Eliza swallowed hard. Her mouth was dry enough to sting. She forced herself to consider the thing that made her want to confess, beyond fear of death.

It was not only fear of dying.

It was fear of being used.

The town's logic had been constructed so carefully that it began to feel like an altar. Confess and you live. Deny and you die. It sounded simple enough for a child to understand. It sounded like justice to a room that wanted justice to be easy.

But underneath, Eliza felt the machinery. Confession meant she would become a witness against herself, and then against others. Denial meant she would become a warning.

Either way, Salem would be fed.

The magistrate's patience broke into something sharper. "We have seen the names in the book," he said, and the mention made Eliza's mouth fill with saliva again, betraying her body's readiness to speak. "We have heard consistent testimony. We have observed your fits and your silence. What more do you think you can accomplish with denial?"

Fits. Silence. Observed, like a specimen pinned to a board.

Eliza's chest tightened until breathing hurt. She tried to summon anger, because anger at least had teeth. But anger dissolved into something thinner, something that frightened her more.

Calculation.

Her mind began to move in small, practical steps, as if survival were a ledger too.

If I deny, they hang me.

If I confess, they may spare me, at least for a time.

If I live, I might find a way to warn my family.

If I die, my mother's name might still rise in that book, and I will not be there to stop it.

Stop it. The thought was absurd and desperate. She could not stop ink from appearing. She could not stop Swann from reading. She could not stop a town from wanting a list.

But the thought came anyway, and with it came a terrible shift: her moral certainty, which had once been a straight line, began to bend under the weight of imagined consequences.

Eliza had always believed lying was wrong. Her mother had raised her with that quiet, stubborn insistence, the kind that did not need scripture to justify it. You did not lie because lying made a person split inside.

Now Eliza felt herself splitting anyway, not from lies but from the pressure of a truth no one would accept.

What is a lie, her mind asked, if everyone has already agreed on the story?

The question made her nauseous. It was Swann's logic, sliding into her. It was the town's certainty, crawling under her skin.

Hale spoke suddenly, as if he could sense the moment her thinking began to warp. "Eliza," he said, and his voice cracked. "Do not make yourself their instrument."

Swann did not turn his head. He only smiled faintly, as though Hale had just underlined the point. "Instrument," Swann murmured. "Or penitent."

Eliza looked at Hale then, finally. His eyes were bright with strain, his face drawn. He looked older than he had when she first saw him, as if Salem had been chewing on him too. He was afraid for her soul, yes, but he was also afraid of what this place did to meaning.

Because meaning was what was unraveling.

Not only the meaning of innocence and guilt, but the meaning of good.

If confessing saved her family, was it good?

If confessing damned others, was it evil?

If denying kept her mouth from becoming a passage, but led to her death and perhaps still did not protect anyone, was that righteousness or stubborn pride?

The questions made her head swim. Eliza had always thought morality was a thing you carried with you like a Bible: weighty, clear, meant to be opened and read the same way each time.

In Salem, morality was a tool used by whoever held it. Mercy became a lure. Confession became a rope that tightened. Truth became whatever could be recorded.

Swann leaned closer, lowering his voice so the room had to strain to hear, which made them lean in as if he were offering intimacy instead of coercion. "Eliza Harrow," he said, "you are not required to understand the full breadth of the thing that has touched you. Only to admit it has."

Touched. The word slid into her and caught on the memory of her hand on the afflicted girl's shoulder. The clean cold. The sudden quiet. The relief that had moved through the room like a miracle and been named wickedness within seconds.

Eliza's lips trembled. If she admitted it had touched her, would that be a lie?

No, her mind answered, horrified. It would be true.

And that was the most dangerous part: they did not need her to lie completely. They only needed her to hand them a true piece they could build the rest around. One honest thread, and they would weave the noose themselves.

The second voice was very quiet now, as if it knew she was teetering. "They will take whatever you give and call it the whole."

Eliza closed her eyes for a heartbeat, too long to be called a blink. In the dark, she saw her mother's hands again, imperfect this time, dulled by real remembering. She saw her father's coat. Samuel running in the yard. Ordinary things, not offered by the visitor, not sharpened into a bribe.

She opened her eyes.

Her mouth belonged to her, for now. Her silence belonged to her, for now. But the logic of Salem was doing something worse than threatening her body.

It was teaching her to treat her own conscience like a bargain.

Eliza heard herself inhale. The sound was too loud in the room's hush, and heads tilted, hungry for the moment she would break.

Swann's gaze held her steady, patient as ink. "Confess," he said once more, and the word landed not as a command now, but as the supposed reasonable answer to a question he had constructed so carefully she could feel her mind reaching for it like a hand reaching for a railing.

Eliza's jaw unclenched a fraction.

And in that small loosening, she felt the truth of her situation with sudden, bleak clarity: the choice was not between confession and death.

It was between one kind of unraveling and another.

If she held to a purity of truth, she would die with her mouth closed and her conscience intact, but leave the living to be named without her.

If she bent, even slightly, even with the intention of survival, the bending itself would become a new shape inside her. A new habit. A new corridor.

The room waited.

Eliza's throat worked. She tasted iron.

And somewhere beneath the taste, beneath the fear, beneath the terrible calculating questions, she felt the first thread of something in her give way with a soft, internal snap.

Not her resolve.

Her certainty that good and evil still meant what they had meant before Salem.

She looked at Swann and understood that whatever she said next, the words would not land in the world as she intended. They would be taken, turned, written down, and fed back to her as fate.

Her lips parted again, and this time she did not know whether she was about to speak truth or surrender, because the line between them had begun to blur under the weight of survival.

The magistrate leaned forward, ready.

The constable lifted his quill.

And Eliza realized, with a coldness that spread through her like damp, that in Salem the worst corruption was not being made to lie.

It was being made to believe that lying was the only moral thing left.

The constable's quill hovered, a black insect poised above paper. The magistrate's gaze fixed on Eliza's mouth as if the next sound would decide whether she was human or evidence.

Eliza stared back at them and felt, with an odd detachment, how much of the room depended on her making their story tidy. Confess and they could call themselves merciful. Deny and they could call themselves just. Either way, the record would read clean.

She tried to find the simple center of truth the way she used to find a straight pin dropped on a floor: by lowering herself to it, by feeling along the boards until the sharp point made itself known. But there was no pin. Only splinters, and each splinter could be called the point if you pressed hard enough.

Swann waited, his face composed into patient reason. Hale stood rigid, as if his own bones were the last thing keeping him from stepping between Eliza and the table like a man trying to block an axe with prayer.

Eliza's tongue felt too large for her mouth. The air tasted of old breath and ink and that faint, dry suggestion of paper that no one else seemed to notice, as if something in the room was being handled delicately just out of sight.

The second voice moved under her thoughts like a steady hand at her back. "They are not asking for truth," it murmured. "They are asking for words that can be used."

Eliza's throat tightened. Used. That was the right word for everything in Salem. Hands used her. Eyes used her. Belief used her. Even her own fear had been conscripted, turned into a witness that would testify against her without ever taking an oath.

Swann leaned forward slightly, softening his voice as though this were a private mercy offered in public. "If you confess, Eliza Harrow, you will be given time. Bread. Sleep. The ministrations of the Reverend. You will be spared the harsher measures that must be applied to those who harden themselves."

Harsher measures. He did not name them, because naming made cruelty too visible. But Eliza had heard enough in the corridor, in the guard's muttered jokes to another man, in the way the afflicted girls flinched at footsteps as though expecting hands.

She imagined herself back in the cell, not allowed to lie on the boards with her boots off, not allowed to count what she knew, kept awake until the boundary between dream and corridor dissolved completely. The thought made her mark pulse, a slow warmth under her ribs, like something stirring in anticipation.

Eliza clenched her fists, nails biting into her palms. Pain. Stay in your body.

The magistrate spoke, impatience slipping into his tone. “The offer stands. Confess and live. Deny and perish. We will not sit here all day.”

All day. As if her life were an appointment that had run long.

Eliza looked down at her hands, at the thin crescents her nails had pressed into skin. There were faint red lines from where she had gripped the stool earlier, small wounds that would heal and leave no record. The constable’s paper would outlast her flesh. That was the point of it. That was the hunger: to make something permanent out of something living and uncertain.

Her mind returned, unbidden, to the black book on the table. Closed now, but not gone. Names waiting under leather. Names that rose like bruises when warmed by attention. Mercy Harrow. Samuel Harrow. Those letters had not been spoken in this room today, not aloud, but they sat inside her like a swallowed stone.

If she confessed, Swann would ask for names. He would call it necessary, call it repentance, call it cleansing the town. And Salem would lean in to hear her mouth become a corridor the way her sleep had become one.

If she denied, she would be hanged, and the book would continue without her. The court would read names, the afflicted would chant them, and her family's names might still rise as easily as her own had.

Truth, the second voice had told her. Tell the truth. But truth here did not behave like truth. It behaved like a coin in a crowded market: anyone could grab it, bite it, declare it counterfeit or pure depending on what they needed to buy.

Eliza lifted her eyes to Swann. "If I say I did it," she heard herself ask, and her voice sounded far away, "will you believe me?"

A ripple went through the benches. The question was not what they wanted. They wanted a statement, not a challenge.

Swann's expression did not change. "We will accept your confession," he said. "We will praise God for your repentance."

"That isn't what I asked," Eliza said, and the words came more steady than she felt. Her heartbeat thundered in her ears, but she held his gaze. "Will you believe me?"

Swann's mild eyes remained on hers, and for a moment Eliza saw something cold behind the gentleness, something that did not care about belief at all.

"We will record it," Swann said, as if that answered every question worth asking.

Record it. Not believe it. Not weigh it. Not hold it up to the light of any honest uncertainty. Ink was better than belief because ink did not argue back.

Eliza's mouth went dry. She felt, suddenly, as if she were looking at the whole mechanism from above: the bench full of hungry faces; the magistrates with their weary authority; the constable's quill that would capture anything shaped like certainty; the minister whose faith had become a lever used against him.

Truth was not the thing they sought. Truth was the thing they manufactured, and confession was merely the raw material.

Hale spoke again, voice strained. "Eliza," he said, and there was a pleading in it that made her chest ache. "Do not let them make your words into a weapon."

Eliza wanted to tell him that the weapon was already made. It sat under leather on the table. It lived warm beneath her ribs. It waited patiently behind her teeth with names.

The second voice whispered, "Say nothing that gives them more doors."

Eliza swallowed. Silence had been her refuge earlier, chosen and deliberate. But now silence felt like another thing Salem could own. They would call it stubbornness, call it hardness, call it proof. They would break her with it the way they broke others: not with a whip, but with an interpretation.

She realized with a sick clarity that this was what it meant for truth to lose meaning. Not that lies became acceptable in the way she had feared, but that words stopped belonging to the person who spoke them. A sentence could be true and still serve falsehood. A denial could be honest and still be written down as evidence of guilt. A confession could be a lie and still be treated as salvation.

Even her fear, spoken aloud, had been received as admission. Even her careful statement, "I think names can come," had been taken as capacity. The court did not hear her. It heard only what it could use.

Swann watched her think, and Eliza hated him for it. Not because he could read her mind, but because he did not need to. He only needed her to exist in a room that had already decided what her existence meant.

"Eliza Harrow," Swann said softly, "this is your last opportunity to set your soul in order."

Soul. Order. Clean words, meant to tidy her into a shape that could be filed away.

Eliza's lips parted. The pressure behind her teeth surged again, urgent now, as if the name she had caught earlier, the one not yet spoken in court, sensed that the air was being prepared for it. It wanted to come out. It wanted to be written. It wanted to make itself real.

Her mark pulsed warm, and with it came that faint sensation of paper handled reverently. Not outside. Inside. A page turning somewhere in her.

Eliza pressed her tongue hard against the back of her teeth, trapping sound. The effort made her jaw shake.

The second voice held steady. "You are still here," it murmured, as if reminding her of the one fact she could cling to when every other fact became property.

Eliza stared at the constable's quill. The ink bead at its tip trembled, then fell, leaving a small blot on the page.

A blot could become a letter if you drew a line from it. A blot could be interpreted into meaning. Even accident could be made into intention if someone needed it.

The magistrate leaned forward. "Answer," he said, and the word had lost patience and gained threat.

Eliza drew in a breath through her nose. She tried to count what she knew, but the numbers slipped. My name. My mother's hands. My brother's laugh. Her father's coat. The list had steadied her in the cell. Here, surrounded by eyes and ink, even the list felt like something that could be taken and turned into evidence. If she spoke those names aloud, would the book answer? Would Salem seize them like offerings?

She kept them inside.

She looked at Swann one last time, and the strangest thing happened: she understood that he did not require her to be sincere. He required her to be usable. A confession was not a bridge to mercy. It was a bridge to more names.

Her lips moved.

The room leaned forward as one body.

Eliza felt the name behind her teeth press hard, a living shape demanding air, and for a terrifying instant she could not tell whether the name was hers to choose or the book's to claim.

Then she heard, faint but steady beneath everything, the second voice: "Do not make your mouth into their page."

Eliza's jaw trembled. Her tongue burned with the effort of restraint.

Out loud, she said, very carefully, "What you call truth, you will call truth no matter what I say."

The room went still in a different way, as if it had not expected her to speak a sentence that did not fit either door.

Swann's eyes narrowed a fraction. "You evade."

"I name it," Eliza whispered, and the words scraped her throat raw. "If I deny, you will write that I harden myself. If I confess, you will write that I am guilty. Either way, the ink is already decided."

A murmur ran through the benches, uneasy and angry. People did not like being shown their hunger. They wanted to believe it was righteousness.

Swann's mildness returned like a mask set back in place. "The ink follows the facts," he said.

Eliza almost laughed at that, because the lie was so cleanly spoken it could pass for scripture.

She shook her head once, small. "No," she said. "The facts follow what you can write."

For a heartbeat, she thought the magistrate might shout, might order her struck. But Salem's cruelty preferred to remain composed. Composure made it feel holy.

The older magistrate with heavy eyelids spoke, voice flat. "She refuses."

Swann did not argue. He only nodded, as if this, too, had been predicted.

"Then we will proceed as we must," the magistrate said, and in his tone Eliza heard the final transformation: her words, whether spoken or withheld, had ceased to matter. They had been swallowed by procedure.

The guard stepped forward. Hands took her arms.

As Eliza was pulled from the stool, she felt the warm pulse under her ribs answer, as if pleased by the room's decision. The page inside her turned again, patient and reverent.

And Eliza understood, stumbling toward the side door while the benches watched with satisfaction, that truth had not been defeated by lies.

It had been defeated by a town that no longer needed meaning, only a record.

Her feet moved because hands moved her. Her mouth stayed shut, aching around the unsaid name.

Behind her, the constable began to write again, and the scratch of the quill sounded, for the first time, exactly like pages turning.

Chapter 17

The Night Without Sleep

They did not take her back the way they had brought her out.

The first days had been a pattern: cell to corridor to hearing room and back again, as if they wanted her to learn the route so thoroughly her feet would keep walking it even when her mind refused. But after she told Swann that ink decided the facts, the guard's grip changed. It was the same hand on her arm, the same practiced control, yet now it carried a message.

Not anger. Ownership.

They moved her through a narrower passage, where the air smelled of old smoke and wet stone. No windows. No voices. The building seemed to hold its breath. At the end of the passage a door waited, iron-banded, its boards swollen with damp.

The guard did not speak. He opened it, pushed her inside, and shut it again with a weighty finality that sat in Eliza's spine like a second bolt.

Darkness settled immediately, thick enough to feel.

Eliza stood still, listening, because that was what she had become: a creature made of listening. For the scratch of a key. For the shift of a boot outside. For the faint paper-sense that meant a page had turned somewhere it should not.

Nothing came at first. Only her own breath.

Then a thin line of light appeared at the bottom of the door as someone passed with a lantern outside, and for a moment the cell was not entirely without shape. A cot in the corner. A bucket. Straw scattered as if it had been kicked. The same room, or one close enough to it that Salem could call it mercy and expect her to believe.

Her boots scraped the boards as she took a step and stopped, because the sound was too loud in the dark. She remembered, sharply, the soles turned up like witnesses. She remembered dirt that had not belonged to the floor.

Eliza bent and unlaced her boots with fingers that shook. Not because she wanted comfort. Because she wanted proof. She set them where she could see their outlines when the light came again, soles angled upward as if they watched her back.

The mark under her left ribs pulsed warm, slow as a patient eye opening.

Eliza pressed her palms to the boards and breathed through her nose until the iron taste thinned. "I am here," she whispered, and then felt foolish for making sound in a place that turned sound into record.

The second voice was present like it had been since she learned to count instead of beg. It did not answer at once. It was quieter than the building.

When it finally came, it was not comfort. "Do not sleep."

Eliza's throat tightened. "I have to."

"You will," the voice said. "But not now."

She leaned her head back against the wall. The boards were cold and the cold seemed to climb into her bones. She wrapped her arms around herself and tried to make her breathing steady, tried to keep her mind inside her skin.

A sound came outside the door.

Footsteps. One man, then another. They passed without stopping. Then the footsteps returned and halted directly on the other side, close enough that Eliza could hear the soft shift of weight, the leather creak of someone settling into a stance that meant waiting.

A guard stationed.

The message was clear. They did not intend to let her disappear into her own dark and come back with missing hours. They intended to watch, or at least to make her believe she was watched.

Eliza swallowed. "They'll keep me awake," she thought, not sure if she meant it as fear or as statement.

The second voice answered, thin and controlled. "They will try."

Time began to move in pieces instead of hours.

A lantern slid past the door, the light under the crack brightening and fading. Then again. Then again, as if someone had been told to walk the corridor at a steady pace, to make sure she could never settle into the deep part of dark.

At first Eliza tried to stand. She paced three steps and back, careful not to step on her boots, careful to keep her mind attentive to the boards under her feet, to the way the air cooled when the lantern moved away. She counted what she knew, again and again, because repetition was the only defense Salem had not yet stolen.

My name is Eliza Harrow.

My boots are beside me.

The door is shut.

The light comes and goes.

The mark is warm.

On one pass of the lantern, the paper-sense brushed the edge of her mind. Not a smell exactly. A memory of texture. Dryness. Pages kept too long, waiting.

Eliza's stomach tightened. She held her breath and listened for the cot to shift, for the straw to deepen as if taking weight.

Nothing.

But the warmth under her ribs pulsed, answering the faint paper-whisper the way an eye answers movement.

Eliza forced her exhale to be slow. "Not to it," she reminded herself, repeating what the second voice had warned her in the cell. Fear is a door. Do not feed it. Do not answer.

She did not know when her legs began to tremble. She only noticed when her knees buckled slightly and she had to put a hand on the wall to keep upright. The wood was damp. It left a faint chill in her palm.

A voice outside the door spoke to the guard. Low. Indistinct. Eliza caught only one word clearly, because Salem loved to make certain words sharp.

"Swann."

The guard murmured something back.

Eliza pressed her forehead against the wall and closed her eyes, just for a breath, and immediately the dark behind her lids softened, inviting.

Not sleep, yet. A corridor beginning.

Her own thoughts drifted like loose hair.

The hearing room. The quill. The blot of ink that had fallen and become meaning because someone wanted it to.

She opened her eyes again at once. The cell was still there, but her balance had shifted. The world felt slightly farther away, as if she stood behind a thin sheet of glass.

The second voice spoke, urgent. "Stay in your body."

Eliza curled her fingers into a fist until pain bit her. "I am," she whispered, but her whisper sounded wrong, stretched thin.

A key scraped in the lock.

Eliza's head snapped toward the door. The crack of light widened as the door opened, and for a moment the lantern's brightness stabbed into her eyes, making tears spring up from the suddenness of it. Two men stood there. One was the same guard who took her to the hearings. The other held a lantern high enough to fill the cell with wavering light.

"Stand," the guard said.

Eliza was already standing. The fact that he told her to do it anyway felt like cruelty made casual.

The lantern-holder's gaze moved over the room, pausing on her boots on the floor, soles up. His mouth tightened. He said nothing, but his attention lingered as if the boots were an accusation of their own.

Then the door shut again.

Darkness returned, but it did not return cleanly. After the lantern's glare, the shadows seemed alive, full of movement that might have been only her eyes trying to recover.

Her eyelids felt heavy, as if someone had laid small weights on them. She began to sway without realizing it. She caught herself by pressing her shoulder against the wall.

The lantern passed again. And again. A steady, deliberate rhythm.

It took her a long time to understand the rhythm was not meant to measure time. It was meant to ruin it.

At some point she slid down the wall to sit on the floor. Her cheek touched her knee. Her breath warmed the fabric of her skirt. She tried to keep her eyes open, but the effort became a physical ache, like holding a door against a crowd.

"Eliza," the second voice said, and hearing her name spoken without hunger made her throat tighten. "If you sleep now, you will not wake where you fell."

Eliza's mouth opened. Her tongue felt thick. "I can't—" she began, but the words did not finish. They drifted away before they reached the air.

A different voice arrived, soft as a hand smoothing hair.

"You are doing so well."

Eliza went rigid.

The visitor's voice. The one that thanked her, that coaxed, that offered relief with the gentleness of rot.

It was clearer than it had ever been, as if the sleep they denied her had thinned the wall between thought and sound. It did not come from a corner. It did not come from the cot. It came from everywhere her exhaustion had made hollow.

Eliza forced her eyes open wider. The room swam, then steadied.

The lantern's light passed under the door again, and in that thin wash of gray she saw the cot's outline more sharply than she should have. She saw the straw dip.

Not much. Just enough to suggest weight.

Eliza's heart slammed against her ribs. The mark warmed, eager, answering.

"Look at you," the visitor murmured. "Still counting. Still trying to keep yourself. They will take it anyway."

Eliza tried to speak. Her voice came out as breath. "Go," she rasped.

The visitor's tone did not change. "You are tired."

A small sound came from the cot. Not straw settling. Something else. A soft, deliberate shift, like a person crossing one ankle over the other.

Eliza stared, eyes burning.

The lantern passed again, and this time the light under the door caught the cot at the right angle.

A shape sat there.

Not a shadow in the ordinary way. The darkness around it seemed thicker, as if it drank the thin light and kept it. The figure's outline was human, seated at the cot's edge, shoulders slightly bowed as if in thought, hands resting in its lap.

It was not fully formed the way a living person was. Its edges wavered, as if it were drawn in ink that had not dried. But it had weight. The straw under it compressed. The cot's boards creaked once, faintly, with the complaint of wood bearing a body.

Eliza's mouth went dry and then flooded with saliva. She tasted iron and paper at once, a mingled sensation that made her gag.

She could not see a face. Where a face should have been, the darkness was smoother, like leather. She felt, with sudden certainty, that if it lifted its head she would see her own features arranged wrong, like a mirror that had learned to lie.

The visitor spoke again, and now the voice matched the shape. "You have been alone so long you have forgotten what kindness looks like."

Eliza's hands shook. She pressed her palms flat on the boards to keep them from rising toward the mark, to keep them from reaching for the cot like a child reaching for a parent.

The second voice cut in, sharp with alarm. "Do not listen."

Eliza swallowed, throat clicking. "I see you," she whispered, and the words sounded like defeat even though she meant them as fact.

The visitor's soft amusement brushed her skin. "Yes," it said. "Now you do."

It leaned forward slightly, and the cot creaked again. The movement was small, intimate. A person preparing to speak close, so their breath could be felt.

Eliza could not feel breath. She could only feel the warmth under her ribs answer, pulsing slow and pleased, as if recognizing a companion.

"They do not let you sleep," the visitor murmured. "They do not let you eat in peace. They do not let you be a girl with a name. But I can."

Eliza's vision blurred. The room tilted. She fought it, blinking hard, because she understood suddenly what the visitor was doing.

It was offering relief.

The same relief Swann had called mercy. The same relief that would turn her into a door.

The visitor's hand moved.

Eliza saw it clearly now, because the lantern's thin light slid under the crack again at the exact moment, as if the corridor itself wanted her to witness. The hand was shaped like a hand, pale where it should not have been pale, fingers long and still. Not flesh. Not bone. More like parchment pulled into form.

It reached toward her, slow, patient, not threatening.

Eliza's body reacted before her mind could. She leaned back, spine scraping the wall, heart hammering so hard her teeth clicked. Her mouth opened on a breath that wanted to become a name.

The second voice snapped, fierce. "Close your mouth. Stay."

Eliza clamped her jaw shut and bit the inside of her cheek hard enough to taste blood, real and metallic, cutting through paper-sense for a moment like a bell.

The visitor's hand paused in the air between cot and floor, as if surprised by resistance that hurt itself to remain resistance.

Then it smiled, though Eliza still could not see a face. She felt the smile anyway, the way she felt ink settle into a page.

"Clever," the visitor murmured. "You hurt yourself to prove you are yours."

Eliza breathed through her nose, trembling. Blood warmed her mouth, a small anchor.

The visitor's hand lowered slightly, still extended, and the lantern's light under the door faded as the corridor-walker moved away, plunging the cell into deeper dark.

In that dark, the visitor remained.

Not imagined. Not hinted. Fully there, sitting on the cot as if it had always belonged there, as if the cot had been waiting to remember its weight.

Eliza stared until her eyes watered, until the blackness of the figure and the blackness of the cell blended, and only one thing stayed certain.

She was not alone.

And whatever had been content to whisper from the edge of sleep had finally decided she was too tired to keep pretending it was not real.

The visitor did not withdraw its hand.

It held it there in the dark as if the gesture itself were proof of patience, as if the space between them were something it could own simply by occupying it. Eliza kept her back against the wall, knees drawn up, boots still turned like witnesses near her hip. Blood gathered at the cut inside her cheek, warm and coppery. She let it sit on her tongue. She did not spit. She did not swallow quickly. She used it the way she had used splinters and nail-marks, a small sharp fact that belonged to her body and not to the book.

The figure on the cot shifted, and the straw spoke softly under its weight. The sound was intimate, domestic, the sound of someone settling in as though they meant to stay the night beside a hearth.

"You hurt," it said. Its voice was not loud, but it filled the space in a way the guard's orders never had. The guard's voice had edges; this voice had depth. It sounded like it could hold anything you handed it.

Eliza breathed through her nose, slow as she could manage. Her jaw ached from clenching. She forced it to loosen without opening, without giving the visitor the smallest invitation of parted lips.

The second voice did not speak. It hovered beneath her thoughts, taut and watchful, like a hand held up to stop her from stepping forward.

The visitor's hand moved a fraction closer, not touching her, not forcing. Offering. Always offering.

"I can take it away," it murmured. "The ache. The trembling. The fear that keeps you counting until your mind breaks from the work of it."

Eliza's eyelids fluttered. The temptation was not in the words alone. It was in the promise of stillness. The guard's lantern had passed so many times that the changing light felt like a physical shove. Every time darkness thickened, her body prepared for something to move inside it. Every time the crack brightened, her eyes burned with the effort of staying present.

Now, with the visitor fully seated and watching her, the lantern's rhythm seemed far away, almost irrelevant. The visitor made its own time.

"How?" Eliza managed, and hated herself for speaking at all. The word scraped out of her, raw, because she needed to know the shape of the trap.

The visitor's hand paused, as if pleased by the sound of her voice. "Like this," it said gently. "Do you remember the girl? The one who quieted under you?"

Eliza's stomach tightened. The touch test. The afflicted girl's sudden calm and the sensation that had passed, clean and cold and undeniable. Eliza had been horrified then because it had not been imagination. It had been movement.

"I did not mean to," Eliza whispered.

"I know," the visitor said, with such easy sympathy it made her throat burn. "That is why you are sweet. That is why you are useful. You do not think of yourself as a hand that can do things. You think of yourself as a girl who is being done to."

The words slid into her, searching for the place where exhaustion made her most vulnerable. Eliza pressed her fingers hard against the boards to keep them from drifting to the mark, to keep them from seeking warmth as if warmth were comfort.

The second voice stirred at last, thin and urgent. "Do not argue with it. Do not explain yourself."

Eliza shut her eyes for half a heartbeat, a blink longer than she trusted, then opened them again. The visitor was still there, a darker darkness. She could not see its face, but she felt its attention like breath against her skin.

"You do not have to suffer this way," the visitor continued. "You are not required to be brave for them. Swann speaks of mercy as if it is his to grant. The magistrates speak of repentance as if it is a door they built. They did not make the door."

Eliza's mouth went dry. She swallowed and tasted paper in the act, as if the air itself had become old parchment. "Stop saying his name," she rasped.

The visitor's tone softened further, almost tender. "It hurts you to hear it. That is why I say it. So you learn what hurts, and then learn what can soothe."

Eliza's heart hammered. The visitor's hand remained extended, hovering. In the faintest under-light from the corridor crack, the fingers looked too smooth, too pale, as though the skin had been made from something that had never been alive.

"I am not alone," Eliza said, surprising herself with the statement. She did not say the second voice aloud. She did not know if giving it shape in the air would make it vulnerable.

The visitor tilted its head slightly. The cot creaked. "Yes," it said. "I have heard the other one."

Eliza's stomach dropped.

The second voice tightened beneath her thoughts, a thread pulled so taut it hurt. "Do not be afraid of that. It hears everything you hear. It is not the same as owning."

Eliza licked blood from her teeth, a small act of defiance. "What are you?" she asked the visitor, because naming had power, and because she could not bear the facelessness of it.

The visitor gave a sound that might have been a laugh if it had come from a human throat, but it held no joy. It held knowing.

"I am what comes when the page is opened," it said. "I am what sits beside the hand that writes. I am what you have been feeling as warmth, because warmth is kinder than truth. Would you prefer I be cold?"

Eliza shivered despite herself. The mark under her ribs pulsed, slow and pleased, as if recognizing its own description.

The visitor's hand lowered, not withdrawing, only changing its angle, palm up now as if asking for hers.

"You are tired," it said again. "So tired you cannot keep your own thoughts from turning into corridors. You count names. You count boots. You count boards. You will count until numbers lose meaning and then you will have nothing left but hunger. That is when they will take you apart and call it saving."

Eliza's eyes stung. The visitor's words were too close to what she had already begun to fear. Salem's logic breaking her. Her own morality unraveling. The feeling that truth had become a tool.

The visitor continued, voice warm as a blanket laid over a feverish body. "I can give you sleep without walking. I can give you quiet without the lantern's knife. I can give you relief that does not depend on the court."

"Nothing is free," Eliza whispered. She kept her mouth barely moving, afraid that fuller speech would become a door.

The visitor's hand rose a fraction, patient. "Of course," it said. "Nothing in you is free either. Your fear costs you breath. Your resistance costs you blood. Even your memories cost you. You have been paying since you stepped onto the road that watched."

Eliza flinched at the phrase. The road that watches. The visitor spoke as if it had been there. As if it had been watching with the town's eyes.

The second voice spoke, steady despite strain. "It wants you to believe it has always been with you. Do not accept its history."

Eliza forced herself to look at her boots again, to anchor. The soles were dark. They did not move. The cell remained a cell. The wall pressed cold against her spine.

"What do you want?" she asked the visitor, and her voice cracked on the last word.

The visitor's head dipped, almost reverent. "I want you to stop fighting what you are," it said. "The fighting makes you bleed in places you cannot see. The fighting makes you break apart and then they will put the broken pieces into their ledger and call it confession."

It paused, and Eliza felt the pause as pressure, like the moment before a quill touches paper.

"I want you whole," the visitor finished.

The lie was perfect because it wore the shape of compassion. Eliza felt something in her soften in spite of herself, some exhausted animal part that wanted to believe there was a hand offered that did not mean harm. She hated that part. She needed it to survive, and it would get her killed.

The second voice cut in, sharper than it had been. "It does not want you whole. It wants you smooth. A page without wrinkles."

Eliza swallowed, blood and spit and stale air. "If you want me whole," she said, forcing each word through clenched teeth, "then leave."

The visitor did not move. It did not withdraw its hand. It did not show anger. It did not even show disappointment.

Instead it leaned forward slightly, and the cot creaked like a sigh.

"You think leaving is what would make you safe," it murmured. "But you already carry the door."

Eliza's ribs felt too tight around her lungs. The mark pulsed, almost affectionate. It felt, horribly, like agreement.

The visitor's voice grew softer still, and that softness was the most dangerous thing in the room.

"Do you know why they cannot sleep you into submission anymore?" it asked. "Because you learned to count. Because you learned to keep your boots off. Because you learned to look at the bolt and call it a fact. Clever girl."

Eliza's stomach rolled. Praise. The visitor was praising her the way it had praised her endurance before. Making her resistance into another thing it could claim to admire.

"I can be clever too," it continued. "I can use what you learned. I can help you. Not to escape Salem. There is no escaping a town that has already written you. But to endure it."

Eliza's eyelids drooped. Her body wanted sleep so badly her bones ached with it. She imagined laying her head down and letting darkness finally become just darkness. No corridor. No hearing room. No table. No names pressing behind her teeth.

She nearly let herself imagine it fully, and in that moment she understood: the visitor did not need to threaten her with pain. Salem had already done that. The visitor only needed to offer the opposite.

"What do I have to do?" she heard herself ask, and the question horrified her as soon as it formed, because it was the question that opened every trap in the world.

The visitor's hand drifted closer, almost touching now. The air between them felt charged, like the moment before a storm breaks.

"Nothing you have not already done," it said. "Stop clenching. Stop biting. Stop making your own mouth a jail. Let your body rest. Let me hold the watch."

The phrase made Eliza's throat close. Let me hold the watch. As if the visitor could take her vigilance like a burden from her shoulders.

The second voice whispered, urgent and fierce beneath her exhaustion. "It cannot hold watch. It is the thing that walks. If you give it your rest, it will take your feet."

Eliza jerked her gaze back to her boots, to the soles that had stayed clean when she slept on the boards. Proof. She needed proof more than she needed comfort.

Her breath came in a shaky rush. She turned her face slightly and spit blood onto the boards, dark in the faintest light. It was a crude act, but it steadied her. Marking the cell with something that was not ink.

The visitor's hand froze.

For the first time its voice lost a fraction of its warmth. “You are stubborn.”

Eliza pressed her tongue against her sore cheek, tasting the injury she had chosen. “I am awake,” she whispered, and the word felt like a weapon even though it shook.

The visitor’s hand lowered slowly, back toward its lap, and the cot creaked as it settled again. The warmth under Eliza’s ribs pulsed, slower now, as if considering.

In the corridor outside, the lantern passed again, and the thin strip of light under the door returned like a metronome. The guard’s boots shifted. Salem’s watching resumed its rhythm.

The visitor sat in the cot’s corner of darkness as if it belonged there, as if it had always belonged there, and spoke with renewed gentleness, as though the brief edge had never shown.

“Awake,” it repeated. “Yes. Awake is good. Awake is when you can choose.”

Eliza’s throat tightened at the word choose. Choice was the lie Swann had offered. Confess or perish. A trap shaped like logic.

The visitor’s voice lowered further, intimate as a confession offered in a pew. “Choose relief,” it whispered. “Choose to stop hurting. Choose to stop pretending you can keep your mouth closed forever. You will speak eventually. Everyone speaks eventually. Better to speak with kindness beside you than to speak with their hands on your throat."

Eliza's jaw trembled. Her eyelids drooped again, heavy as stones. She fought them. She counted boards. She counted breaths. She counted the distance from her knee to her boots.

The visitor did not rush. It waited, patient as ink drying, certain that time would do what persuasion could not.

And as Eliza's body began to sway with exhaustion, as the line between waking and falling thinned, she realized the visitor's greatest cruelty was not in what it offered.

It was in how gently it offered it, as if kindness were a lamp in the dark and not the first light of a fire meant to spread.

The cot creaked once more, a small sound like someone preparing to stand.

Eliza's heart lurched.

But the visitor did not rise. It only leaned closer, as if settling into the space between one breath and the next.

“I will be here,” it murmured. “When you cannot be.”

Eliza’s head tipped forward and she caught herself only because her chin struck her knee hard enough to sting.

The sting helped for a breath. Then the heaviness returned, thicker, as if the air had turned to wool and she was breathing through it. The corridor lantern slid past again, its thin line of light under the door brightening and dimming with steady cruelty. Each pass felt like a finger tapping her eyelids.

The visitor sat where it had chosen to sit, a darker shape inside the dark, and did not move. It did not need to. It had time. It had the kind of patience that belonged to things that were not measured in hours.

“I will be here,” it had said. “When you cannot be.”

Eliza kept her eyes on her boots, on the soles turned upward. She tried to count the boards between her heel and the wall. The numbers slipped. Her mind began to slide over them as if the facts were greased.

My name is Eliza Harrow, she told herself, and the sentence felt like something spoken underwater.

The second voice did not speak. It was there, she thought. It had to be. But the second voice was a thread and she was losing her grip on it. Exhaustion was not merely tiredness; it was a hand on the back of her neck, easing her forward whether she agreed or not.

The visitor's voice returned, gentle enough to make her ashamed of her own fear. "You do not need to keep proving you can suffer," it said. "That is not holiness. That is not strength. That is only hunger with manners."

Eliza swallowed. Her throat clicked dryly. The bite she had taken out of her cheek throbbed, a small, chosen pain that had been her anchor. Now even that felt far away, a sensation happening to someone else.

"Stop," she whispered, but the word had no weight.

The visitor shifted. The cot creaked like a slow exhale. Eliza's spine pressed harder into the wall.

"I am not asking you to give them anything," the visitor murmured. "Not a confession. Not names. Not breath shaped into their kind of truth. I am asking you to stop fighting your own body as if it is the enemy."

The lantern passed again. The light under the door made a pale stripe across the floor, briefly outlining the visitor's long, pale hand where it rested on its lap. Not flesh, Eliza thought. Not skin. The hand looked like it had been made from something smooth and dry, something meant for writing.

Her stomach turned.

"You cannot keep your eyes open forever," the visitor said, and it sounded almost kind. "They know that. That is why they walk the lantern. That is why they wake you, why they open the door just to tell you to stand when you are already standing. They want you to fall apart so you will mistake surrender for mercy."

Mercy. Her mother's name flashed, but not as the visitor's sharpened bribe; it came as a dull ache. Hands red with soap. Flour in lines by the thumb. A scar. Real remembering, imperfect and heavy.

Eliza's eyes stung. She blinked and, for a moment too long, did not open them again.

Darkness folded over her lids and it was not a corridor yet. It was only dark. Relief ran through her so quickly it frightened her. She opened her eyes with a gasp as if she had nearly drowned.

The visitor's voice came at once, soothing, ready. "There," it said. "Do you feel it? How close you are to rest?"

Eliza's breath shook. "I can't," she whispered. "If I sleep—"

"If you sleep, you will be taken," the visitor finished for her, and there was no mockery in it, only calm certainty. "Yes. That is what you fear."

Eliza stared at the cot, at the shape that made the straw remember weight. She tried to reach for the second voice and could not find the exact place in her mind where it lived. She felt it like a distant pull, a thread stretched thin and far away.

"What are you doing to me?" she asked, and the question came out ragged.

"I am offering what you have been begging for without admitting it," the visitor said. "An end to vigilance. An end to the constant counting that makes your mind bleed."

Eliza swallowed again and tasted the copper of her own blood. It had dried in the cut, turning the taste small and faint, easily overwritten by the visitor's damp paper-sense that seemed to hover at the edge of every breath.

"No," she whispered, but the word sounded like a child refusing bedtime while already swaying on her feet.

The visitor's voice softened further. "You think acceptance is the same as defeat," it said. "But you accept many things already. You accept the bolt on the door. You accept the guard's boots outside. You accept that the magistrates will not hear you. Why is it only your own nature you refuse to accept?"

Eliza's heart hammered at the phrase. Her own nature. She felt the coal-warmth under her ribs pulse, slow as a blink.

The second voice, faint but present, rose at last like a hand from deep water. "It is making a door with that word," it murmured. "Do not step through."

Eliza clung to the sound with a kind of desperate gratitude that she did not dare speak aloud. "I hear you," she thought, and even that thought felt like it might be overheard.

The visitor tilted its head, as if listening to something Eliza could not quite hide. "Yes," it said, and the word was so knowing Eliza's skin tightened. "You do."

The lantern passed again. The light under the door thinned, then brightened, then thinned. Eliza's eyes burned. Her body shivered, not from cold but from the strain of staying upright against the wall, knees drawn up so tightly her joints ached.

"You cannot win this with pain," the visitor whispered. "Pain is only another kind of attention. Another way of pressing your will into flesh until flesh fails."

Eliza's eyes drifted, without permission, to the visitor's hand. It looked capable of holding. It looked capable of lifting something off her the way her mother used to lift a heavy pot from the hearth with practiced ease.

She hated that her mind made that comparison. She hated that exhaustion made everything in her reach toward anything shaped like comfort.

The visitor's hand rose again, slow, patient, palm up. The gesture was the same as before, but now it did not feel like a demand. It felt like the obvious end of a long struggle.

"Let me," the visitor said. "Not to give them names. Not to make your mouth into their page. Only to let you rest without being stolen. I can hold the watch."

The second voice tightened, thin and urgent. "It cannot. It is the thing that moves. It is the hand behind the page."

Eliza tried to breathe. In. Out. The air rasped. She thought of her boots, soles up, the small witness waiting.

What did she actually know?

She knew she could not keep her eyes open forever.

She knew Salem could force her body into breaking, and breaking would feel like consent to everyone watching.

She knew the visitor was real enough to compress straw, to make the cot complain, to reach a hand toward her that looked like parchment shaped into fingers.

She knew she was beginning to forget the edges of herself from sheer fatigue.

And she knew, with a cold, practical clarity that made her nauseous, that she might accept anything if it promised to stop the shaking.

Eliza heard herself speak before she could stop it. "If I let you—" Her voice cracked, and she swallowed, forcing the words into shape. "If I let you hold watch, what do you take?"

The visitor's hand did not move. Its stillness felt like restraint, like virtue. "Nothing you do not surrender," it said. "Nothing I cannot already reach when you fall asleep on your own."

"That is not an answer," Eliza whispered.

"It is the only honest one," the visitor replied.

The second voice rose, strained. “It is honest like Swann is honest. It tells a piece and calls it the whole.”

Eliza pressed her head back against the wall and shut her eyes for a heartbeat, then opened them again. The visitor’s shape wavered at the edges as if it were drawn in ink that never fully dried. The lantern light under the door stroked the floor, pale and indifferent.

“I don’t want to hurt anyone,” Eliza whispered.

The visitor’s voice warmed as if she had offered it a gift. “Then stop hurting yourself,” it said. “Stop treating rest as a sin. Acceptance is not harm.”

Acceptance. The word landed in her body like a stone dropped into water, sending ripples through everything already unsteady.

Eliza tried to imagine what acceptance would even look like. Not confession. Not Swann’s quill. Not naming others.

Only this: letting her muscles loosen. Letting her eyes close without fighting. Letting the dark come without turning into a corridor.

It sounded like salvation, and that was how she knew it was dangerous.

But her body did not care about danger the way her mind did. Her body cared about sleep. Her body cared about stopping the tremor in her limbs, the ache in her jaw, the burn in her eyes.

The visitor's hand hovered, patient.

Eliza's own hand lifted from the floorboards before she knew she'd decided. Her fingers trembled in the air, moving toward the pale, too-smooth palm. She did not feel like she was reaching for a monster. She felt like she was reaching for a railing.

The second voice cut in sharply, almost panicked. "Eliza. Stay."

Eliza froze. Her hand shook midair.

The visitor's voice slid between the second voice and Eliza's exhaustion with practiced ease. "You have stayed," it murmured. "You have stayed until staying has become a knife you hold to your own throat. Let go."

Let go.

Eliza's breath hitched. The guard outside shifted his boots. The lantern passed again. The metronome of punishment continued, indifferent.

Her hand moved the last inch.

Her fingertips met the visitor's palm.

The contact was not cold.

It was warm, as if the warmth under her ribs had climbed out through her arm and met itself halfway. For a moment Eliza could not tell where her skin ended and the visitor's began. The sensation was smooth, too smooth, like touching a page that had been rubbed until it shone.

Relief rushed through her so fast it made her dizzy.

The shaking in her legs eased. The tight band around her chest loosened. The ache behind her eyes softened as if someone had laid a cool cloth over her brow. The lantern's passing light became less like a blade and more like a distant tide.

Eliza made a small sound she could not stop, not a word, only the raw exhale of a body that had been braced too long.

"There," the visitor whispered, close now, intimate as breath. "Do you feel how easy it can be when you stop fighting what you carry?"

Eliza's eyelids drooped. The boards beneath her, the wall at her back, the boots beside her, all remained present, but their edges blurred in a way that did not feel like a corridor. It felt like sinking into a bed after days on hard ground.

The visitor's hand held hers with a gentle firmness. Not gripping. Simply keeping contact, as if contact were enough.

Eliza's mind reached for the second voice and found it still there, but distant, muffled, as if heard through a closed door.

"Do not," the second voice tried to say, but the words came thin, fraying at the ends.

Eliza swallowed, and the last taste of blood in her mouth faded under that dry paper-sense, now softer, almost pleasant, like books in a quiet room.

Her eyes closed.

For the first time since Salem, closing her eyes did not immediately open a corridor. Darkness came like a blanket instead of a passage. Her muscles unclenched without pain. The constant counting stopped, not because she had won, but because she had set the numbers down.

The relief was so complete it felt holy.

In the dark, the visitor's voice murmured, satisfied and gentle. "Sleep," it said. "And when they come with their questions, you will not be alone in your mouth."

Eliza's last clear thought flickered, small and frightened, like a candle trying not to go out: Boots. Remember the boots.

But even that thought loosened in her grasp, sliding away on the same tide that carried her down.

Her hand remained in the visitor's palm.

And as sleep finally took her without struggle, the warmth under her ribs pulsed once, slow and pleased, like ink settling into a line that had been waiting all along to be written.

Chapter 18

The Mirror of Self

Eliza did not know when she began to dream, because there had been no doorway into sleep. One moment she had been pressed into the wall with her fingers in the visitor's palm, her eyes burning, her body shaking with the effort of staying. The next, the shaking was gone, and the dark had softened around her like cloth.

She opened her eyes and the cell was not the cell.

It had the same dimensions, the same stink of damp wood and old straw, but the corners were too clean. The air lay still. No lantern slid beneath the door. No boots shifted in the corridor. Even her own breathing sounded distant, as if it belonged to someone lying further away.

Her hand was no longer touching anything.

She looked down. Her fingers rested on her lap, empty and obedient. The relief remained in her muscles, a heavy warmth that made movement feel unnecessary.

"Eliza," the second voice murmured, and it sounded as though it came through boards and earth, a voice calling up from under a pond. "Wake."

"I am awake," she whispered, and heard at once how wrong it was. The words carried no edge of effort. They were too smooth.

A small sound came from the cot, as intimate as a person shifting to make room.

Eliza did not want to look. She looked anyway.

The visitor sat at the cot's edge as it had before, a darker darkness, shoulders bowed with the imitation of patience. But now, beside it, something else waited: a basin set on the floor, a common thing, the kind a jail kept for washing, its rim dulled by use.

The basin had not been there when she fell asleep.

Water lay inside it, still as glass.

The visitor's hand lifted, palm open toward the basin, like a host offering a seat at a table. "They will come for you soon," it said softly. "Before they do, I thought you should see what they see."

Eliza's mouth went dry. The familiar iron taste tried to rise, but even that seemed muted, held at a distance by the warmth that still sat in her limbs.

"What is that?" she asked. Her voice sounded too calm, and the calm frightened her more than panic ever had.

"A mirror," the visitor said.

Eliza stared at the basin. Water in a cell. It should have been harmless. It should have been a tool for cleanliness. But in Salem even harmless things turned, became evidence, became ritual.

"I don't want it," she said, and tried to shift backward on the floor. The boards did not scrape under her as they should have. She moved as if the room had been waxed.

The visitor's head tilted, an approximation of sympathy. "You already have it," it murmured. "Everyone does. The only question is whether you look before they hold it up to your face."

The second voice, faint and strained, whispered, "Do not."

Eliza swallowed. The act felt distant, like watching a girl swallow rather than being inside the throat that did it. She pressed her palms to her thighs, searching for sensation sharp enough to cut through the smoothness.

She found only warmth.

"How?" she managed. "How is there water?"

The visitor did not answer the question she asked. It never did when an answer might give her footing. "Come closer," it said instead. "You have spent so long refusing to look at yourself that you have forgotten what you are fighting for."

Eliza's chest tightened at the word fighting. The last thing she remembered clearly was the exhaustion, the lantern, her hand reaching like a drowning hand. Then relief, and the visitor's voice saying she would not be alone in her mouth.

She licked her teeth and tasted nothing but stale dryness, the blood from her bitten cheek gone as if it had never been there.

"I need my boots," she said suddenly, and the words came out with a child's urgency. Boots. Remember the boots.

She turned her head.

Her boots were not beside her.

Panic should have flared. Instead it arrived slow, muffled, like pain felt through cloth. She pushed herself up with clumsy haste, but her body did not protest. It moved as if it had been spared.

Her boots stood near the door, neatly set together, soles down. Not turned upward. Not watching. Like a servant had come in and arranged them to look decent.

Eliza's throat closed.

"They want you orderly," the visitor said, as if reading her thoughts. "Even here. Even in the dark. Especially in the dark."

Eliza's gaze snapped back to the basin. The water waited, perfectly still, reflecting nothing yet because she was not leaning over it.

"No," she whispered, but the word came out tired, as if she were refusing a second helping rather than refusing a knife.

The visitor's hand drifted toward her, not touching, only shepherding the air. "Just look," it said. "It will help. You think knowing is danger, but not knowing is how they steer you."

The second voice tried again, stronger for a moment, like a hand tightening on her wrist. "Eliza, you do not have to—"

The visitor spoke over it with gentle ease. "That voice has kept you raw," it murmured. "Raw girls bleed ink. Let me give you a cleaner way."

Eliza felt something in her recoil, a thin remaining thread of herself that still recognized the shape of manipulation. But the relief in her muscles held her like a weight. Resistance required effort, and effort felt far away.

She took one step toward the basin.

Then another.

The room did not change with her movement. No creaks, no drafts. The door stayed shut, and yet it did not feel like a barrier. It felt like the idea of a door.

Eliza knelt.

The rim of the basin was worn smooth, familiar as any kitchen tool. She reached out and touched it. The metal was neither cold nor warm, simply present, like an object in a memory.

She leaned forward.

At first she saw only darkness in the water, a black that held the faint pale oval of her face like a moon in a night sky. She expected her own eyes, her own mouth. She expected the small changes fear had carved into her these past weeks.

What looked back at her was her face, yes, but arranged the way Salem arranged it.

Her cheeks were paler than they should have been, not from hunger but from purity. Her eyes were too wide, too shining, like the afflicted girls' eyes when they looked at empty air. Her mouth hung slightly open, as if always about to speak a name. Her hair fell loose around her shoulders in a way that made her look touched, disordered, inviting interpretation.

She drew back with a small gasp. The image did not ripple. The water did not behave like water. It held the reflection steady, unblinking, like ink set on a page.

"That is not me," she whispered.

"It is you," the visitor said softly from behind her, close enough that the words seemed to come from the nape of her neck. "It is you as they have written you."

Eliza leaned forward again, heart knocking.

The reflection changed.

Now she saw herself in the hearing room on the stool, hands bleeding into wood, jaw clenched. Behind her, benches full of faces leaned forward like a single animal. Swann stood near the magistrates' table, his mouth moving with calm certainty. The constable's quill scratched, relentless.

But Eliza's face in the water was not angry, not desperate. It was blank. Accepting. A girl already resigned to being an entry.

In the reflection, her lips moved.

Eliza held her breath, because she knew without knowing how that if the reflected mouth formed a name, it would not remain contained in water.

The reflected Eliza spoke, and the sound did not come from the basin. It came from inside Eliza's own skull, as if her mind were being used as the room where the voice echoed.

"Yes," the reflection said. "Yes, I did it."

Eliza jerked back, hand flying to her mouth as if to hold her own words in. Her palm pressed hard against her lips, and in that pressure she felt, with sudden cold clarity, that her mouth did not fully belong to her at this moment. It was a door held shut only by her hand.

"No," she tried to say behind her palm. It came out muffled, broken.

The visitor's voice was calm, almost pleased. "Do you hear how easy it sounds? How reasonable? They will love you for it. They will call it repentance."

Eliza's eyes burned. She looked down again, unable to stop herself.

The reflection shifted once more.

Now she saw herself standing at a bedside, candlelight flickering. A man lay sweating, eyes rolling, and Eliza's reflected hand held a quill. The black book lay open on his chest like a second ribcage. The scene was exactly what the witnesses had described, so exact it made her stomach lurch.

But the face on the reflected Eliza was not cruel. It was tender.

The reflected Eliza leaned closer to the man, and her expression was full of pity, almost love, as if she were offering him relief rather than harm.

Eliza's throat tightened. That was the worst version. Not a monster. A savior.

In the water, the reflected Eliza whispered, "It will end if you sign."

Eliza made a sound that was half sob, half choke. "I didn't," she said, and her voice shook as if the words were trying to climb out of her without her permission. "I didn't. I didn't."

"You do not remember everything you do," the visitor murmured. "That is what makes it simple. They tell you the story, and you begin to feel it as memory. You have already started. You saw dirt on your feet and did not know how it came. You heard pages and could not find the book."

Eliza's mind flashed to her boots arranged neatly by the door, soles down, the witness turned into decoration. She felt suddenly sick, because she understood what the basin was doing.

It was not showing her truth.

It was giving her practice.

Practice at seeing herself as Salem saw her. Practice at accepting the image until the image felt like her own skin.

The second voice surged, suddenly clearer, sharp as a slap. "Look away."

Eliza squeezed her eyes shut.

For a moment she saw the reflection anyway, printed on the inside of her lids: her pale face, her open mouth, her tender savior's smile. Her own features used as a mask to make evil feel like mercy.

She opened her eyes and stared at the floorboards instead, at the knot in the wood, at the fine splinters near her knee.

The visitor's tone remained gentle, but a thin impatience threaded through it, like a quill pressed harder. "You cannot look away forever," it said. "They will hold it up to you again and again until you nod."

Eliza's breath came fast. She pressed her fingertips into the boards, seeking pain, seeking the small honest bite of the world. She found it, faintly, and clung.

“I am Eliza Harrow,” she whispered, forcing the sentence into the air as if sound could anchor her. “I am here.”

The visitor chuckled softly. “You can say your name as many times as you like,” it murmured. “But you have seen the mirror now. You know what they will ask you to become.”

Eliza’s eyes flicked, despite herself, back toward the basin.

The water sat perfectly still, waiting to give her another version. Another arrangement. Another future she could be coaxed into wearing.

And in the silence around that waiting, Eliza understood with a dread that spread slow through her bones: the visitor did not have to drag her through corridors at night anymore.

It could bring the trial into her, image by image, until her own mind became the place where testimony was staged.

The door in the cell had not opened.

But something in her had.

The visitor leaned closer, and its voice slid into the space behind her ear like breath. “Again,” it said, soft as prayer. “Just once more. See what I can spare you from.”

Eliza stared at the basin's rim, at the stillness of the water that behaved like ink.

Her hand trembled.

And somewhere, deep beneath the relief that still coated her muscles, the coal-warmth under her ribs pulsed in slow agreement, as if the mirror's surface were not water at all, but a page ready to receive whatever version of Eliza the town needed next.

Eliza kept her eyes on the floorboards until the knot of wood began to look like an eye.

It was an old knot, dark at the center, rings tightening outward as if the plank had been trying to swallow something for years. If she stared long enough, the rings seemed to shift. Not moving, not truly, but offering the suggestion of movement the way the afflicted girls offered the suggestion of truth.

Behind her, the visitor waited without impatience, and that waiting itself pressed on her. It had said again, like a priest asking for one more prayer.

Eliza did not answer. She tried to gather her thoughts and found them slipping through her fingers like grain.

The relief still coated her limbs, heavy and false. It made the simple act of lifting her head feel unnecessary, like a thing someone else might do for her. That frightened her more than the basin, more than the reflection, because fear at least belonged to her body. This smoothness felt borrowed.

"Wake," the second voice murmured again, faint but insistent, as if it had been speaking for some time and only now reached her.

Eliza swallowed. The swallow felt delayed, like a message traveling through a long corridor before arriving. "I am," she whispered, though she was no longer certain what awake meant. Her eyes were open. Her knees pressed into the boards. She could feel the basin's presence like a cold circle near her hands. But her mind kept drifting up and away, hovering above the scene as if it could observe without being inside.

The visitor's voice threaded into the silence with practiced gentleness. "You see what happens when you fight," it said. "You split yourself into pieces. One that suffers, one that watches, one that counts, one that begs for sleep."

Eliza's mouth went dry. The words made a sick kind of sense, and she hated that. She hated how easily it could describe her, as if she were a simple mechanism. As if her soul could be taken apart and named.

“I didn’t ask you to explain me,” she said, and even her own voice sounded distant, like it came from another girl kneeling in another cell.

“You did,” the visitor replied softly. “When you put your hand in mine. When you asked for relief.”

Eliza flinched, remembering the warmth of that touch, the way it had seemed to settle her bones into place. She could still feel it in her muscles, a faint echo of being held. She tried to remember the sting of biting her cheek, the taste of blood, the crude proof of being in her body.

That memory was already thinning.

She reached up and pressed a finger inside her mouth, probing the tender place along her cheek. The skin was smooth. No bite. No swelling. Not even the rough edge of healing.

Her stomach turned.

The visitor’s voice came closer, as if it had leaned without making the cot creak. “Dreams do not keep your wounds,” it murmured. “They keep your needs.”

Eliza stared at her fingertip. It was clean. No blood. No copper taste. She rubbed the pad of her thumb against it as if friction could bring sensation back.

"This is not my cell," she whispered, and immediately felt foolish. The cell looked like her cell. The cot. The bucket. The door. The boots by the door set neatly, wrong in their neatness. The basin full of still water that behaved like a page.

But the air was too still. Her breath did not seem to disturb it. Even the smell was muted, as if the world had been wrapped in cloth.

"It is yours," the visitor said. "Because you are here. Your body is here."

The second voice tightened, a small snap of warning. "It is lying with true words."

Eliza looked toward the door. The crack at the bottom did not brighten and dim with the lantern anymore. No shadow passed. No boot shifted outside. The silence was so complete it pressed against her ears until she heard something else beneath it: not sound, but the sense of sound waiting.

Paper held between fingers.

A page about to turn.

Eliza's gaze slid, unwilling, back toward the basin. The water was perfectly still, reflecting the ceiling's darkness and nothing else, because she was not leaning over it. It waited with the patience of an object that knew it would be used.

"Again," the visitor breathed behind her ear, and the intimacy of the placement made Eliza's skin crawl. "Just once. You will understand. Understanding is a kind of safety."

Eliza tried to stand. Her legs unfolded without protest, too easily, as if someone had taken the ache out of her joints. She rose to her feet and for a moment the world wavered. Not a dizzy sway, but a brief uncertainty about where she was located inside herself.

She had the odd sensation of being above her own head, watching her body straighten.

Her hands hung at her sides, loose, obedient. Her boots stood by the door like a reminder that she had once been careful. She took a step back from the basin, and the boards did not creak.

"No," she said again, louder, and the word felt like it landed on nothing.

The visitor did not answer the refusal. It never did. It spoke as if the refusal were only a pause in an inevitable process. "You have already begun to practice," it said. "You looked once. You heard your own mouth say yes. Do you think the court will be satisfied with your silence when your own reflection confesses?"

Eliza's throat tightened. She wanted to reach for the second voice, wanted it to tell her what was real. But the second voice felt far away, muffled as if behind a closed door. She could still hear it, faintly, but she could not reach it with the same clarity she had in the hearing room, when counting had been a rope in her hands.

"I am Eliza Harrow," she said again, testing the sentence like a rung on a ladder. "My boots are by the door."

The visitor made a small sound of approval, as if she had recited a lesson. "Yes," it murmured. "You know the facts. But facts are not the self. You have learned to hold yourself by your edges, Eliza. Name. Boots. Boards. But what happens when the edges are rearranged?"

Eliza stared at the basin as if it might leap up at her. The phrase rearranged struck her with a cold understanding: that was what Salem did. It took pieces of a person and placed them in a new order until the person became unrecognizable even to herself, while still wearing her own face.

Her stomach rolled. She turned away sharply, intending to move toward the cot, toward any corner that was not the basin's rim.

The room shifted.

Not a change of light, not a corridor opening, but something subtler and worse: a relocation that happened without movement. Eliza blinked and found herself closer to the basin than she had been, her knees already beginning to bend as if her body had continued doing what her mind refused.

She froze mid-motion, horror blooming slow because it did not come with adrenaline. It came with numb recognition.

"I didn't move," she whispered.

"You did," the visitor said, calm as ink. "You simply were not present for it."

The second voice surged, sharper for a moment, like a hand catching her by the wrist. "This is what it wants. To make you doubt your own steps."

Eliza tried to obey that hand. She straightened abruptly, jerking her body upright, and the motion felt delayed, like she was pulling herself through thick water. Her own muscles did not feel fully connected to the decision.

She looked down at her hands. They seemed like hands, but wrong in the way a familiar word looks wrong if you stare at it too long. Fingers. Nails. Knuckles. Yet the idea of them was louder than the sensation. She could see them better than she could feel them.

She dug a nail into the pad of her thumb, hard. She expected pain. Instead she felt pressure first, then a distant, late-arriving sting that might have belonged to someone else.

"Eliza," the second voice said, and there was strain in it now, as if speaking cost it. "Do not look."

"I'm not looking," Eliza whispered, but even as she said it, her eyes lowered of their own accord toward the basin's dark glass. The motion felt inevitable, not forced by muscle but pulled by attention, like a needle drawn to a lodestone.

Her reflection appeared at the edge of the water, pale oval emerging as she leaned despite herself.

She tried to pull back, and the pullback happened half a moment too late.

In the basin, her own face looked up at her.

This version was different. Not the afflicted, wide-eyed purity. Not the resigned blankness on the stool. This Eliza looked calm, almost serene, her hair neatly smoothed back, her mouth closed in a small, knowing line.

A woman who had made peace.

Eliza's heart hammered, and even that hammering felt slightly distant, like she heard it through boards.

The reflected Eliza lifted her chin, and the movement was too deliberate to be a reflection. It was a performance using her features as costume.

The reflected Eliza's lips parted.

Eliza clapped a hand over her own mouth. The gesture was frantic, but it felt slow. Her palm pressed her lips closed, and for a moment she felt nothing at all, as if she were touching a door that did not belong to her.

In the water, the reflected Eliza spoke anyway.

The words did not come through Eliza's covered mouth. They came inside her skull, as if her mind were the room where the voice was permitted.

"I will help you," the reflection said, and the tone was gentle, reasonable. "I will tell them what they want, so they stop hurting us."

Eliza shook her head violently. Her hair did not shift against her shoulders the way it should have. The world remained too clean, too still. "That isn't me," she tried to say behind her hand, but the sound came out as a muffled whimper.

The visitor's voice slid in like a hand smoothing her hair. "It is you," it murmured. "It is you who wants to survive."

Eliza's eyes burned. She stared at the basin and felt herself slipping, the edges of her attention fraying. She was watching, and she was being watched, and she could not tell which was the true position. She had the terrible sense that the room contained two Elizas: one kneeling over a basin, trembling, and another sitting back inside her head with the visitor's hand on her shoulder, being told what she was.

The second voice fought to be heard, thin but fierce. "Survival is not surrender. Do not let it wear your face."

Eliza squeezed her eyes shut again, but the reflected face remained printed on the inside of her lids, calm and willing. She opened her eyes and looked away from the basin, forcing her gaze onto her boots by the door.

They were still neatly arranged, soles down, as if to prove the world could be ordered by someone else's hand.

A sob rose in her chest, but it did not feel like it originated there. It felt like a sound that belonged to the role of her, the way the afflicted girls' sobs belonged to the role of affliction.

She swallowed it. She could not afford to perform in front of the visitor, even if the visitor was the only audience.

"What are you doing?" she asked hoarsely, and the question seemed to come from a distance. "Why are you showing me this?"

The visitor answered without hesitation, as if it had been waiting for the question like a quill waiting for ink. "Because soon the magistrates will bring you a mirror that is not water," it said. "They will bring you words and demand you see yourself in them. If you learn to recognize the shapes now, you will stop fighting the inevitable and start choosing the easier path."

The easier path.

Confess and live. Deny and perish.

Let go. Let me hold watch.

The phrases stacked inside Eliza, not as thoughts but as lines in a ledger, orderly and inevitable.

Eliza pressed her back against the wall again, needing contact with something solid, something that could bruise her if she leaned too hard. The wall was cool, but even that coolness arrived muted, translated.

She realized, with slow horror, that the relief the visitor had offered was not simply rest.

It was distance.

A way to move her away from her own sensations so she could be guided without the rude interruption of pain.

Her mouth was still under her palm. She lowered her hand carefully and found her lips slightly numb.

The visitor spoke, soft as prayer. "You are not breaking," it murmured. "You are becoming bearable to live in. You are becoming smooth."

Smooth, the second voice had said. A page without wrinkles.

Eliza's stomach turned. She looked at the basin without leaning this time, holding her body rigid, as if rigidity could keep her from sliding.

The water's surface remained still.

Waiting.

Eliza understood then that dissociation was not a rescue. It was another corridor, one that did not require sleep. A corridor that led inward, where the visitor could stage any scene, speak with any mouth, and teach her, patiently, to accept it.

Her breath came shallow. She tried to count what she knew and found the list breaking apart.

My name is Eliza Harrow.

My boots are by the door.

This is my cell.

This is not my cell.

The contradiction sat in her mind like a stone that would not settle. She could not decide which sentence belonged to her and which belonged to the visitor's shaping.

The second voice, strained but present, whispered one last clear instruction, as if it had gathered its strength for a single thread of truth.

"Do not agree."

Eliza stared at the basin and whispered back, barely moving her lips, "I won't."

The visitor's warmth pressed close behind her, pleased by the intimacy of the struggle, pleased by how much of her attention it now owned.

In the basin, the still water held its dark shine like ink waiting for the next word.

And Eliza, standing in her too-clean cell with her boots made tidy and her mouth gone slightly numb, felt herself hovering just above her own body, watching a girl who looked like her try to remember how it felt to be entirely inside her own skin.

Eliza held her breath and waited for the visitor to punish her for saying no.

Nothing happened.

No slap of cold. No tightening around her ribs. No sudden corridor opening under her feet. The air remained too still, the boards too quiet, the basin too patient.

The visitor stayed behind her like a presence that did not need to move to be felt. Its silence was not withdrawal. It was appraisal, the way Swann listened when a witness spoke, letting the pauses do the work.

Eliza kept her eyes on her boots by the door, on their careful neatness. She tried to make that image mean something simple. Boots. Leather. Dirt. The world. But even as she stared, the boots felt like an illustration of boots rather than weight and smell and stiffness.

She pressed the heel of her hand hard into her thigh, grinding bone against muscle until discomfort arrived. It was faint, late, but it arrived. The fact of it steadied her more than any sentence.

"Again," the visitor murmured, and the word was mild, almost conversational, but it threaded through her like a hook.

Eliza did not turn around. If she turned, she would be looking at it directly, and she did not trust her mind to keep its edges when confronted with a thing that could look human without being human.

"No," she said, and the sound came out thin. She cleared her throat, tried again. "No."

The visitor gave a soft sound that might have been approval if it had come from anyone else. "You think resistance is purity," it said. "But you are already inside."

Inside what, Eliza wanted to ask. Inside the dream. Inside the bargain. Inside the door that lived beneath her ribs.

She did not ask. Questions opened space. Space became a place for the visitor to step.

The second voice hovered close to her thoughts, strained but present. "You can resist without speaking," it murmured. "Do not give it a conversation."

Eliza swallowed. Her mouth was still numb at the edges, as if her lips had been held shut too long and forgotten how to belong. She forced herself to breathe slowly through her nose. In. Out. In. Out. The breath felt real enough to count.

The visitor moved, and though the boards did not creak, Eliza felt a shift in pressure behind her, like someone stepping into her shadow. Its voice came nearer her ear, intimate in the way a confession was intimate.

"You are afraid of the mirror," it whispered. "Afraid you will see what you are."

"I am afraid you will make me see what you want," Eliza said before she could stop herself.

The words hung in the still air. She waited for the visitor to pounce on them, to twist them into a lesson.

Instead it answered with a gentleness that made her stomach clench. "What I want," it said, "is for you to stop bleeding yourself into shapes that cannot hold."

Eliza's jaw tightened. Bleeding. Her bitten cheek had been gone. Even the small proof of her own blood was taken in this place. She remembered spitting onto the boards, the crude mark meant to be hers.

She looked down.

The boards were clean. No dark spot. No stain. Not even the suggestion of where it should have been.

A coldness spread through her, slow and nauseating. Not fear exactly. The recognition of how thoroughly this place could be arranged.

"If this is a dream," she whispered, and her voice cracked because the word dream felt too small, "then where is my body?"

The visitor did not hesitate. "On the floor where you left it," it said, as if describing a basket left by a door. "In the cell you know. Breathing. Warm. Alive."

Alive. The word should have comforted her. It did not. Alive did not mean present. Alive did not mean hers.

The second voice tightened. "It is trying to make you accept distance as safety."

Eliza's gaze drifted toward the basin again despite herself. Not into it, not yet. Just toward it. The basin sat where it had been placed, and it looked so ordinary she almost hated it for that. A common thing. A household object. A tool for washing hands before prayer.

A tool for seeing yourself the way someone else wanted.

Eliza took one careful step away from it, toward the wall, toward the corner nearest the cot. Her foot did not scrape. The silence swallowed movement as if sound itself had been removed from the world.

She reached back and touched the wall. Cool boards. No damp. No grit. No uneven nailheads. It felt like a remembered wall, simplified.

The visitor spoke softly, as if in pity. "You keep searching for pain," it said. "As if pain proves you exist."

Eliza's throat tightened. "It does," she said.

For a moment the visitor did not answer, and in that pause Eliza felt something shift inside her, a small flare of anger. Real anger, hot and sharp, cutting through the smooth relief the visitor had layered over her.

They had taken her pain and used it. They had taken her fear and called it confession. They had taken her silence and called it stubbornness. Now this thing wanted to take even her resistance and make it into a lesson about her nature.

Eliza set her teeth. She forced herself to speak with care, each word placed like a foot on uneven ground. "If you can make me see myself confess, then you can make me see myself deny. You can make me see anything."

The visitor's voice remained calm. "Yes."

The simplicity of the answer hit her harder than argument would have. Yes. Of course. Of course it could. That was what it was.

"And you still think understanding is safety?" Eliza asked. "Understanding that I can be made into anything?"

The visitor's hand, unseen, seemed to brush the air near her. Not touching, but close enough to feel as a change in warmth. "Understanding is power," it murmured. "Not for them. For you. If you know what you are, you can choose how to be it."

Choose. The word made Eliza's stomach knot. Swann's trap had been shaped exactly like that. Confess or perish. A choice that was not a choice.

The second voice whispered, low and urgent, "It keeps saying choose because it wants you to think you are steering. Do not let it put its hands on your will."

Eliza closed her eyes for a heartbeat. In the darkness behind her lids, she saw the basin's surface anyway, black and still, waiting. She opened her eyes and looked at the door instead. The crack beneath it did not change. No lantern. No guard. No footsteps. The absence was loud.

"Wake," the second voice murmured again, and this time it sounded less like an instruction and more like a plea.

"I don't know how," Eliza whispered.

The visitor's voice curled around that admission immediately. "You do," it said. "You only fear what you will feel when you do. You will feel the bruises. The thirst. The ache in your eyes. You will feel the mark under your ribs answering when the book comes near. You will feel what you have been carrying."

Eliza's breath shuddered. The mark. Even here, in this too-clean version of her cell, she felt a warmth beneath her left ribs, slow and present. When she focused on it, it seemed to brighten, as if attention fed it.

She pulled her focus away with an effort that made her temples throb. "I will not agree," she said, out loud now, and the sentence was not meant for the visitor only. It was meant for herself. It was meant for the smooth, drifting part of her that wanted relief more than truth.

The visitor chuckled softly. "You already did," it murmured. "When you touched my hand."

Eliza swallowed hard. Her palm tingled as if remembering. The relief had been so complete it had felt like holiness. That was what scared her most: not that the visitor could force her, but that it could offer something that felt like mercy.

She looked down at her hands. They were trembling now, and the tremble was more real than any calm.

"Then show me," Eliza said suddenly, and the words surprised her with their steadiness. "If you want me to look, if you want me to practice, then show me something true. Not what Salem says. Not what you want me to become."

The second voice snapped, alarmed. "Eliza."

But Eliza could not stop. The anger had given her a kind of footing. "Show me my family," she said, and her throat tightened on the last word. "Show me my mother. Show me my father. Show me Samuel."

The visitor was quiet for a long moment.

Eliza's heart pounded. She had opened a door with those names. She knew it as soon as she spoke them. The names felt like bare skin in cold air, exposed. She cursed herself, but too late.

The visitor answered at last, gentle as ever. "You think seeing them will anchor you," it said. "But seeing is not the same as holding."

"Show me," Eliza repeated, and her voice shook now, because fear had flooded back in the wake of her boldness.

The basin's surface rippled.

It was the first time the water had behaved like water.

The sound was soft, but it landed in Eliza's bones as if something had cracked. She stared despite herself as the black surface shivered and began to brighten from within, not reflecting light, but producing it, like a page warming under a hidden hand.

In the basin, an image formed.

Not the hearing room. Not Eliza's face arranged into Salem's version of her. Something else: a narrow stretch of road bordered by bare trees, the kind of thin-limbed woods that looked like they were made of scratches. A wagon track. Mud. A figure walking.

Eliza leaned forward a fraction before she could stop herself, and the visitor's satisfaction pressed close behind her like breath.

The figure in the water turned its head.

It was Eliza.

Not as the town saw her. Not pale and holy or serene and willing. It was Eliza with her hair pinned back the way she wore it before Salem, cheeks flushed from cold, eyes narrowed against wind.

She was walking fast, boots sinking into mud, and Eliza watching felt a jolt of recognition so sharp it was almost pain.

The Eliza in the basin looked over her shoulder once, then again, and her mouth moved as if speaking to someone just out of view. Then the basin-image shifted slightly, and Eliza saw the edge of another presence beside her. Not a person fully shown. Just a dark shape keeping pace, close enough that Eliza's reflected elbow brushed it now and then as she walked.

Eliza's stomach dropped.

In the image, her own hand lifted, and she touched her left ribs, as if checking the mark.

The warmth under Eliza's ribs in the waking-not-waking room pulsed in answer, slow and pleased, and she knew with a sick certainty that the basin was not showing her an invented confession.

It was showing her something she had done.

Or something done with her.

"No," Eliza whispered, and the word came out broken, because it was not refusal now. It was grief.

The Eliza in the basin stopped walking. She turned fully toward the dark shape beside her. Her posture softened, just slightly, the way a person's posture softened when they stopped bracing.

She held out her hand.

The dark shape's hand met it.

Eliza's own palm tingled violently, remembering.

The visitor's voice slid into her ear, warm and careful, like someone teaching a child to read. "You asked whether you are resisting or revealing," it murmured. "This is what happens when you stop fighting. You reveal what you already are."

The second voice surged, strained but fierce, pushing against the smoothness coating Eliza's mind. "It is not revelation if it is arranged. It is training. It is rehearsal."

Eliza tried to pull back from the basin, and for the first time in this too-clean room, her movement had weight. Her knee scraped the boards. The scrape was small, but the sound felt like a miracle.

She jerked her gaze away from the water and clapped both hands over her eyes, pressing hard enough to see sparks.

"I will not learn myself from you," she whispered into her palms. "I will not."

Behind her, the visitor did not sound angry.

It sounded patient.

"Then learn yourself from them," it murmured, and in that sentence Eliza heard the shape of the next trap waiting: the magistrates' words. Swann's gentle logic. The black book opened like a wound and called a record.

Eliza lowered her hands. The room tilted slightly, as if she were being returned to her body inch by inch. Her palms felt gritty where they touched her face, though she could not see grit. Her breath came faster. Her heart felt closer.

The basin sat still again, surface black and quiet, as if it had never rippled at all.

Eliza backed away from it until her shoulders hit the wall. The wall felt colder now. More real.

She found the second voice like a hand in the dark and clung to it with her mind.

"I won't agree," Eliza whispered.

The second voice answered, low and steady, as if gathering itself for what came next. "Then when they show you the mirror, you must decide what kind of refusal you can afford."

Eliza's throat tightened. The hearing room flashed in her mind. The quill hovering. The blot of ink turning into meaning because someone wanted it.

Somewhere beyond this arranged stillness, her real body lay on the boards, and time was moving without her.

The visitor's presence remained by the cot, close enough to feel like warmth at her back. Its voice came one last time, soft as a page turning.

"They will ask you to reveal yourself," it whispered. "And if you resist, they will call the resistance proof."

Eliza closed her eyes for a heartbeat and forced herself to breathe into the coldness of the wall. She tried to remember boots turned upward like witnesses. She tried to remember blood in her mouth. She tried to remember the weight of her own name when it belonged to her and not to the book.

When she opened her eyes again, the basin was still there.

Waiting.

And Eliza understood that the mirror did not only show her what others believed.

It showed her what she might become, if exhaustion and kindness and fear could be made to wear her face long enough that she stopped knowing which mouth was hers.

www.ingramcontent.com/pod-product-compliance
Lightning Source LLC
La Vergne TN
LVHW050908080826
845145LV00001B/15

* 9 7 8 1 9 6 9 7 7 0 2 7 2 *